SWEET SALT

SWEET SALT

by

FELIX E. GOODSON

CHARLES E. TUTTLE COMPANY
Rutland, Vermont

REPRESENTATIVES

For Continental Europe:
BOXERBOOKS, INC., *Zurich*

For the British Isles:
PRENTICE-HALL INTERNATIONAL, INC., *London*

For Canada:
HURTIG PUBLISHERS, *Edmonton*

For Australasia:
BOOK WISE (AUSTRALIA) PTY., LTD.
104 Sussex Street, Sydney

Published by the Charles E. Tuttle Company, Inc.
of Rutland, Vermont, U.S.A.

© 1976 by Charles E. Tuttle Co., Inc.
All Rights Reserved

Library of Congress Catalog Card No.: 75-40585
International Standard Book No.: 0-8048-1173-3

First printing, 1976

Printed in U.S.A.

To Elvira J. MacLean
and her daughters

SWEET SALT

CHAPTER ONE

"Do you think we'd better go in?" Lonnie was looking out toward the center of the compound where a few stragglers were ambling in the direction of the stairway. "Don't you think we'd better go in?" he repeated. "Hell fire, the gong sounded at least ten minutes ago."

Ross didn't say anything. He adjusted himself more comfortably, leaning back against the hard stones of the wall.

"What the shit," said Lonnie. He leaned back too, feeling the warmth of the stone against his bare back, watching the last guy go up the stairway. "Hey, look at the sun," he finally remarked. "You can look right at it. By God, I can even see some specks in it. Look at that, like it was just perched up there taking it easy, right there on the wall. What in hell are those lines running through it? Must be the barbed wire. Yeah, it's the barbed wire. That damned Jap in the tower could reach out and give it a push. First time I ever noticed spots in the sun just from looking at it. Wonder how come we can look at the sun so easy, it doesn't even hurt your eyes."

"Haze," said Ross, looking up for a moment. "You're right, you can see spots. Some big explosion out there. An explosion maybe bigger than ten earths."

"You're full of shit," said Lonnie. "Couldn't be that big."

"Some of them are bigger than that," answered Ross. "Lots bigger. Maybe a hundred earths."

"Well it's all gone now," observed Lonnie, as he watched the last orange slice disappear behind the west wall. Almost immediately it was dusk, and he could barely see the small cook shed on the opposite side of the compound, could clearly make out the dim light that always stayed on just above the stairway unless planes came over. "Goddamnit, we'd better go in," he said again as he relocated his bare feet in the cement drain trench. "Some Japs are gonna come along and beat the shit out of us for being out here after curfew. What the hell are we sitting here for anyway, leaning against this damn wall? This damn cement hurts my ass bones. What are we sitting here for anyway?"

"Why not?" asked Ross. "You got some place to go?"

They both listened for a moment. Beyond the wall, the clatter of metal wheels against the cobblestones and the clopping sound of a trotting horse.

"Somebody's still alive out there somewhere!"

"Sure sounds like it," said Ross. "How would you like to have a big plate of fried chicken?" he added after a pause. "All dark meat, thighs and legs. I like backs too."

"I don't like fried chicken," said Lonnie. "But I guess I'd eat it now, since I'm starving to death. But I don't really like fried chicken." For a moment he could almost hear his mother's voice calling him in to dinner. "Orlando Ray, Orlando Ray," she would always yell, and he would come running. He wished to hell she wouldn't call him that when other guys were around, like Jimmy Wiggins and Jack Matt; they were always mocking her, screaming, "Orlando Ray, Orlando Ray," in high-pitched voices, "Orlando Ray." They'd had fried chicken that night. There they were all around the table, his brother Sam, his sister Edna with the fat legs, his daddy, Old Fred Claflin, and his Mama.

"Pass the chicken," his brother Sam had said, and Lonnie could tell from the smirk on his face and the shitty tone in his voice that something was wrong. And suddenly he knew.

"I can't understand what happened to this poor chicken," his Mama had said in her whiney voice. "I found it out next to the barn, lying in a heap, all torn up, bleeding inside."

Lonnie didn't look at anybody. He just kept looking at the

piece of chicken on his plate, thinking about how he and Jack Matt had performed the operation. He had jammed the fire cracker up its ass, a two-incher, a block buster, but old Jack Matt had lit it, and as he looked at the piece of chicken on his plate, he could see again the frenzied flight, the flapping wings, just for a moment could hear again the soft *blam*, and could see the chicken rocket skywards.

"Jesus Christ!"

"Eat your chicken. Eat your chicken, Lonnie," his mother had said. His father was looking at him too now, with that crazy questioning look in his eyes, he always seemed to have when he was looking at Lonnie.

"Yeah, eat your chicken, Lonnie," said his brother Sam with that goddamn smirk.

He could see that smirk right now, there in the twilight of the compound, that son-of-a-bitch.

"I like pork chops a hell of a lot better than I do fried chicken," he finally offered. Glancing at Ross, "I sure would like to have a whole plate of pork chops. Man, that's something. Or my name isn't Orlando Ray!"

Ross was suddenly interested. "Is your name really Orlando Ray?"

"Did I say that?" asked Lonnie.

"You know damn well you said that," said Ross. "You said your name was Orlando Ray. If your name is Orlando, how come people don't call you Lannie instead of Lonnie?"

"How in the hell should I know?" said Lonnie. "They call me Lonnie. Anyway, since you're so damn nosy, my father named me Lonnie. My mother tried to call me Lannie, but my father wouldn't have anything to do with it."

"What the hell difference did it make to him?" said Ross. "Lonnie, Lannie, sounds about the same. But Orlando, that's some name."

Lonnie didn't say anything. He was thinking about the letter, the one his brother Sam had found in his mother's cedar chest, from somewhere in Florida. Lonnie didn't read the letter, but every time his brother Sam got mad at him after that, he would call him a bastard and have that shitty look on his face like he knew something special. Lonnie had asked his mother about it once. She was just putting some pies into the oven when he asked her. She stopped, stricken, crouching there holding the oven door half-open.

"Did you ever go to Florida, Mama?"

She was silent for a moment, then placed the pies carefully on the second shelf, and shut the door. Turning to Lonnie, she said softly, "Yes, I went to Florida once, when your Aunt Salina died. I went to Florida and stayed three whole weeks, right in the middle of the winter, and down there it was as warm as summer time." She smiled a little and Lonnie thought she looked beautiful then, standing there before the stove, her face flushed with the heat. "I stayed three whole weeks," she continued. "They have the most interesting kind of trees. Some with fruit on them, oranges and grapefruit." And after a short pause, she went on, "And I met s-some most interesting people."

"When did all that happen?" Lonnie had asked.

"Oh, before you were born."

"How long before I was born?" His voice sounded a little funny in his own ears.

His mother looked quickly at him then, and said, "Go on now, go on out and do the chores. Your father will be coming in soon, hungry. Get the chores done, and then come in here and get ready for supper."

Jesus Christ, that was a long time ago, that time he had asked Mama about Florida. He couldn't have been more than ten years old, or maybe twelve.

He turned to Ross then. "Hey, you won't tell anybody, will you?" he asked, his voice plaintive.

"Tell anybody what?" said Ross.

"That my name is Orlando Ray."

"Why should I tell anybody? Even if it made any difference, why should I tell anybody? But why don't you like the name?"

Lonnie didn't answer for a moment. He was staring out across the compound, toward the small light above the stairway. "My father didn't like the name," he finally answered. "My mother named me that."

The guard seemed to appear out of the cook shed, a moving blob of grey suddenly outlined against the darkness of the west wall. They crouched down, trying to hide behind the stone buttress, peering intently toward the blob which had stopped moving for a moment. A match flared, the short bill cap, the face under it suddenly distinct, a puff of smoke visible for a moment. He was moving again, diagonally across the compound, toward the gate which separated the two sections of the prison, their part from the larger area where the permanent and sick prisoners were kept. He was just opposite them, a silhouette against the light above the stairway and for a moment Lonnie thought he would pass without seeing them, he seemed to be going on by. But suddenly he turned and walked straight in their direction, his hob-nailed boots scuffing the gravel as he came.

"Jesus Christ!" Lonnie muttered as he and Ross hunched down and flattened themselves even more firmly against the wall. He kept hearing the crunching sounds getting louder and louder, then he couldn't hear anything but the frenzied shouting of the guard. Loud and nasty sounds. Sounds Japs make when they're madder than hell. Mostly Japanese, but a few English phrases thrown in.

"You try to escape, *bakayro*! son-of-a-bitch! You want to die?"

They both stood up with their hands over their heads, still holding their mess gear.

"Son-of-a-bitch!" the guard said again, then made a bunch of deep-throated froggy noises. He knocked the empty mess gear from their hands, and it went clattering against the wall. Shoving with his rifle, he pushed them toward the center of the compound. They stood there at attention, back to back, with the guard walking around and around them, shouting, mostly in Japanese, but maybe in nothing.

"He wants you to lay down," somebody yelled from the doorway. It sounded like Gentry.

"You'd better lay down before that son-of-a-bitch kills you," another voice said. Big-mouthed bastard, old R. T. Barton.

Lonnie could see faces in the doorway, outlined by the dim light. The sons-of-bitches were enjoying this, the dirty bastards.

He lay down flat on his belly with Ross beside him, on his

[13]

hands and knees. He could see him outlined against the light striking the far wall, ass in the air like a praying mantis. Lonnie grinned a little. Jesus Christ, what a fucking mess. As from a distance now, he heard the high-pitched shouts of the enraged guard, once or twice felt blows from the butt of a rifle, occasional kicks. But they didn't hurt much. Thought he heard laughter coming from the doorway. Those dirty cunt-heads, they'd like to see us get our God damned brains kicked out.

The blows ceased and the guard started talking in English. "You tried to escape. Tomorrow you die. Maybe you die now!"

Nothing happened for a long time. No sound. Nothing! Lonnie looked up and the guard was just standing there, staring down. He kept waiting for another kick in the ass, but nothing happened. For just a moment it seemed that he could hear his mother's voice calling to him.

"Orlando Ray! Orlando Ray!" What a fucking name.

"You stand up now," the guard said in a calm voice. And Lonnie did, feeling over his body to see if there were any skinned places, any blood.

It was almost completely dark, but he could see the guard plainly enough, and Ross there beside him, his face pale in the light from the doorway, looking scared as hell.

"You come tomorrow eight o'clock, you see me eight o'clock tomorrow at the gate. You die tomorrow." The guard's voice was almost conversational. "You come to the gate tomorrow, eight o'clock." He turned away then and disappeared into the darkness of the compound. Lonnie and Ross listened to the sounds of his hobnailed boots crunching on the gravel until they were lost in the other sounds of the evening.

"You meatballs better get in here while you got the chance," a voice said out of the doorway. R. T. Barton again.

They both started running towards the doorway. Then Lonnie stopped.

"Come on, damn it," said Ross. "That guard might come back."

"I lost one of my clogs," said Lonnie. "I can't go in without my clog. I'm going back and look for it."

"What a piss brain," said Ross mildly. "Come on, we'll get it in the morning."

"Come on, you piss brains," voices echoed from the doorway.

Up the steps, toward the sea of faces, a lot of floating grins. The dirty bastards.

"You guys would be glad if that son-of-a-bitch had beaten our brains out, wouldn't you?"

"Yeah, anything for laughs," somebody said.

"What the hell were you guys doing out there anyway?" It was R. T. Barton. He was grinning, but Lonnie could see that there was a bit of concern on his face.

"We were trying to get away from you, you shithead," said Lonnie as he passed him.

Ross didn't say anything. As they walked among the individuals who crowded around them, Lonnie felt like an actor in a crazy picture show. Some show. They made it to the stairway, then on up to the second floor.

"What the hell happened down there?" somebody asked them. "What's all the noise about?"

"Beats the hell outa me," answered Lonnie.

They finally reached their blankets, over next to the north corner near the stairwell. Lonnie lit a candle, melted some wax, and fixed the candle to the corner of the orange crate they used as a table. Ross sat down, leaning against the wall, his arms folded over his knees, gazing at the small flame. He looked up at Lonnie framed by the candle's glow, sitting with his legs crossed, hunched over, the small light flickering in his brown eyes. Funny looking kid, reddish stringy hair scraggly over almost pointed ears, face spiked with freckles except for the nose where the sun had scorched them off leaving it red and peeling. White teeth which were always flashing, impudent grins suddenly flowering the visage to leave it curiously transformed as if he knew a joke about you but wasn't telling. The eyes, brown flecked, wide set in a forehead somehow too massive for the rest of him, eyes which were always restless, moving as if searching for something. Eyes that seemed to belong to someone else, every now and then to someone older and much wiser but usually to a little child, too open and

[15]

innocent even for a crazy skinny kid who was always asking dumb questions or trying to talk like Gentry. Eyes which were suddenly gazing directly at Ross, examining him with total comprehension.

"What in the hell are you doing setting there looking at me like I was a turd in a flour sack?"

Ross smiled. "Actually that's not a bad comparison."

"Fuck you," said Lonnie mildly. He looked away from the candle into the vagueness of the huge room, a room filled with sound and motion, people always fiddling around, doing things, talking. Some of them were looking in their direction, a few comments and grins. The news had spread. He glanced back at Ross, slumped down against the wall, totally relaxed, staring at the candle's flame, as if he didn't have a worry in the world.

"Jesus Christ! We can't show up at that fucking gate tomorrow. That crazy bastard will have us shot for trying to escape. Of all the nit brained shit we've pulled, this is the stupidest. I say we don't show up. It was so dark he couldn't recognize us anyway."

"Maybe so," said Ross, taking his eyes from the flame, "but we can't be sure. Why don't we move in close to the gate and wait for him? We'll let him pick us out. If he can't, we'll be in good shape; but if he can, it will mean that he could pick us out if he decided to search for us. We'd be in real trouble then. Actually I don't think he'll show up. He was just trying to scare us."

They kept talking about their problem, on into the night, even after the lights were turned out except for the small one above the stairway. Fear was not dominant in their conversation. Here was something of interest, a break in the monotony of the endless hours. Other men gathered silently around them, in some faces a flicker of envy and a new respect. For a few hours the story was the central topic throughout the building. Men who normally would long have been asleep discussed the various elements of the case, and Corso, eager for an easy buck, was offering two-to-one odds that the guard would show up at the gate.

As night progressed the noise level diminished. Most of the

two thousand men housed in the three story building were asleep. Lonnie still lay awake thinking about the gate and the guard. He hardly noticed the sounds of the hundreds who lay around him, the coughing, turning and snoring, the occasional farts. He felt his friend move and whispered.

"You still awake, Ross?"

"Yeah, after three years I still can't get used to sleeping on nothing but a blanket. Why don't you go to sleep?"

"Do you think the planes will come again tomorrow?" Lonnie whispered.

"Christ, I hope so. Maybe that bastard will forget all about us if they do. I hope they get here before eight o'clock."

Somebody near them whispered, "Cut it out you guys," and they stopped talking.

After awhile Lonnie heard his friend's breathing become deep and regular. He got up and found his clog, the one for the right foot, then slowly made his way barefoot over and around sleeping men, down the stairs, to the main door. In the shadows leaning against a tree, one of the three within the compound, he saw the privy guard, another grey blob standing there not moving. There was a bright moon now but the guard stood in the tree's shadow. Maybe he was the same one. The son-of-a-bitch. The small light from the privy let Lonnie make out the figure, but he couldn't see the face.

Lonnie sat on the steps leading down from the building and put on his clog. Then, making more noise than necessary, he followed the board sidewalk toward the latrine, clumping along with his one wooden shoe. When he came to a point near the guard, he turned directly toward him and bowed from the waist. The guard returned the salute and Lonnie saw his face clearly for a moment. It wasn't the same one.

"Jesus Christ, these things stink," he muttered, half aloud. "As little as they feed us you wouldn't think there could be so much shit." He sat there for a while thinking about it. About how his belly was a factory, gurgling away turning rice and greens to shit. He thought idly for a moment. Why isn't shit striped? Why is it always brown?

On the return trip he bowed once again to the guard, hesitated for a moment after the guard returned the salute, then walked deliberately to the center of the enclosure where he found his other shoe. The guard didn't say anything but Lonnie could feel him watching. He held the shoe up and waved it but the guard still didn't say anything. Ross didn't move when he lay down beside him. He was sleeping like he had just eaten a good dinner. Like that guard wasn't going to beat the shit out of him in the morning. Lonnie thought about it but not for long. After a few grunts, a dozen or so eye blinks and a "what the hell" half mumbled, he slept.

Lonnie awoke suddenly, too soon it seemed. Ross was shaking him. All around there was clatter, men getting dressed, folding blankets, rattling mess kits. He saw Corso arranging his belongings into a neat pile, saw him carefully pat a bulging spot at his groin. Everyone knew that Corso had a lot of money. Some said three or four thousand dollars. They kidded him about it and where he kept it. Lonnie had seen him count it once when he thought no one was watching. He kept it in a small leather pouch attached to a thong about his waist. Suddenly Lonnie shouted, "Hey, Corso, what you doing, checking to see if your nuts are still in place?"

Corso jerked his head up, astonished for a moment, his dark face perpetually needing a shave vaguely showed alarm, then broke into a smirky grin when he recognized Lonnie. "You check yours after that guard gets through with you. Two-to-one you won't have them."

"Hurry it up," said Ross. "We've only got three minutes."

Lonnie rolled up his blanket and placed his mess gear on it. On the way out for the count he seemed nervous.

"Jesus Christ, I wish we had a cigarette. You know that stinking Wop must have at least five thousand dollars in the ball sack. How in the hell do you think he's managed to collect that much in three years? You'd think the Japs would have gotten it off him before now."

"Beats me," said Ross. "He's a pretty bright guy—pretty clever, pretty clever. And he has a talent!"

"Yeah, some talent," replied Lonnie vaguely. He was thinking about the guard, the gate, his balls, no balls and Christ! Striped shit!

The men lined up twelve deep and the column stretched all

the way across the compound. A Japanese corporal gave the command *"bango!,"* and the men in the front row counted off in Japanese. Ross and Lonnie were there. They waited, ready as the numbers came toward them. The man on the right of Ross shouted out a number and Ross responded. Lonnie had been thinking of numbers that might come up and for some unaccountable reason had settled on *"hachi."* Now he shouted it at the top of his voice.

"Shichi, dammit, *shichi,"* whispered Ross.

Lonnie's guts tightened. Panic stricken, he began to shout, *"Shichi."* The entire column became completely silent. The counting had stopped, except for Lonnie who kept muttering *shichi* under his breath.

It seemed to Lonnie that the Japanese corporal took a long time walking toward him from the end of the column. His hobnailed boots made crunching sounds growing louder and louder as he approached. Lonnie stood at attention, rigid, waiting. The corporal was finally there, standing in front of him, small and heavy set, thick rimmed glasses and slightly protruding teeth, the God damned Jap bastard. Lonnie kept thinking how yellow his teeth were. He hardly heard him shouting, *"Bakayro,* son-of-a-bitch," and he hardly felt the blow.

The corporal returned to the head of the column and again shouted, *"Bango."* At the command the counting began again and when it reached Lonnie, he shouted, *"Shichi,"* lustily.

A small platform stood in front of the column almost directly against the wall of the compound. The men waited, and finally Major Imada, with briefcase and swinging sword, entered the compound. He stopped for a moment surveying the silent columns of men, his face a blank. He turned and approached the platform. Just as the first rays began to strike the upper portions of the building, a bugler played the Japanese version of reveille and everyone bowed toward the rising sun. When the bugler finished, ending with a slightly sour note, Major Imada took a scroll from his briefcase and in perfect English read the declaration of the Emperor. This was Imperial Rescript Day, December 8, three years following the outbreak of the war. It seemed funny now, Lonnie thought, all this shit and ceremony. The Americans were coming. They had been bombing Manila for weeks, and rumor had it that the Japs were getting their asses kicked all over the Pacific.

When Major Imada finished reading from the scroll he moved immediately down the steps of the platform and without a glance toward the men, walked through the gate into the adjoining compound. Everybody watched him, his swinging sword, his broad back, his shoulders straight and strong. Lieutenant Iwahara gave the command for dismissal and there was a general rush back into the building for mess gear. Lonnie and Ross grabbed their own and got into the rapidly forming line. After they were in place, somewhere toward the rear, Lonnie brought up the topic they had both been thinking about.

"I didn't see that guard in the formation. Maybe he's down with amoebic dysentery or something worse. Jesus Christ, I thought that damn Jap corporal was going to knock my head off. I guess I'll never learn Japanese."

Ross was sullen. "I'd think that after three years of this crap you'd have learned to count to ten. Sometimes I wonder why I've taken up with a piss brain like you."

"I may not be bright, but I have an excellent sense of humor. Maybe that's why, or maybe it's because you have a penchant for piss," said Lonnie grinning. "I'd still like to know what that bastard is going to do with us."

"Why do you keep trying to talk like Gentry?" asked Ross but he was smiling now. "I predict that he'll beat our brains out with the butt of his rifle, and right now I for one feel that you deserve it."

The line had started to move when Gentry came out of the building. He didn't go to the end of the line. He never did. He could crash anywhere and they always let him in.

"If I tried that," R. T. Barton once complained, "somebody would kick the shit out of me."

"No they wouldn't," Lonnie had replied, "they wouldn't want you to disappear."

This morning, perhaps because of their recent fame, Gentry chose to crash the line in front of Lonnie and Ross. He greeted them cheerfully.

[20]

"Well it's certainly unfortunate that we can't offer you anything better than our usual fare of watery rice and pigweed for your last meal. I can hardly wait until eight o'clock for the impending clash. In days to come it shall be called the *gate encounter* and shall no doubt rival in historical import such classic episodes as *Horatio at the Bridge* or *Leonidas at the Pass.*" He paused for a moment observing the stricken look on both faces. "Actually," he lapsed into an intimate and confidential tone, "it's my prediction that your friend won't show at all. But if he does and can't recognize you among the multitude who will be there watching, I shall feel it my duty to our kind hosts to point you out; even as did another in like circumstances some years ago. However, I doubt seriously that I shall begin a movement that will last two thousand years." Shame on you for trying to escape and thus putting the rest of us in jeopardy."

"Fuck you," said Lonnie, but he was grinning.

Gentry was an educated man, a fact one could hardly forget. According to R. T. Barton who checked up on him, Gentry had graduated *magna cum laude* from Princeton, had gone to Harvard Business School, and then had received a law degree from Columbia. In 1941 he had been drafted into the Army. Just before the American Forces in the Philippines had surrendered, he was promoted to Pfc. Everyone kidded Gentry about his high rank but privately it was agreed that he should have been in command of the Far Eastern Operations. He was such a grand bullshitter, always picking on people, but no one seemed to mind. He had a little gleam of humor in his eyes, a touch of kindness that took the sting away. He was the unofficial president of a literary circle consisting largely of officers, who gathered every now and then to discuss what Lonnie called "big round bullshitty issues."

During such discussions Gentry, with scarcely hidden sarcasm, always prefaced his statements with, "I must admit that I represent an enlisted man's point of view, but . . . ," and then would make his points with such cogency that many an opponent had been reduced to the eyeball meanderings typical of individuals at the end of their intellectual tethers. He was, he often stated, an atheist, not an agnostic mind you

[21]

but a true believer in no God. This to the great discomfort of what R. T. Barton called the "no guts" group of shit intellectuals who insisted that atheism was as dogmatic, or maybe more so, than being a Southern Baptist. The enlisted men loved Gentry. He was their champion.

Now both Lonnie and Ross grinned at his bleak pronouncements. "As a matter of fact," said Ross, "we have already decided to tell them that we were but innocent pawns in a much bigger crime, a vast plot for a general escape, master minded by one Gentry, A.B., M.A., LL.D."

"You compliment me," said Gentry.

The long line moved rapidly. From one barrel each man received a salmon can of watery rice and from another a smaller can of pigweed greens. The three took their food and retreated into the shadows at the edge of the compound and sat down with their backs against the wall.

"Well, Gentry, you were right about one thing anyway," said Lonnie. "Watery rice and pigweed it is."

"Fifteen minutes till the old zero hour," said Gentry. "Are you guys going to show up at the gate?"

"What would you do?" asked Ross. He was quite serious, as was Gentry when he responded.

"I think you had better put in an appearance. There will be a hundred guys close to the gate. Just stand fairly close. If he doesn't come, you lose nothing. If he comes, just stand and let him pick you out. Chances are he won't be able to, but if he can he could do the same thing during assembly. You might get off easy if you show up. If you don't go and he is able to recognize you, it would probably mean the box."

"Jesus Christ, you don't think we'll get the box, do you?" said Lonnie, looking at him quickly.

"Well, you spend at least half your time thinking along this line. Maybe you will get your reward," said Gentry. "Anyway it's almost time now. I hope you don't mind if I tag along. I can't resist the sight of blood."

"Shit on you," said Lonnie.

They stationed themselves about ten feet from the gate. Gentry was right. At least two hundred other men were loitering in the general vicinity. A hush fell over the compound. As Lonnie glanced about him, sly looks were cast in their direction, some shitty grins. Several of his friends winked, and a few made crude gestures. The sons-of-bitches.

"You'll be singing soprano when this is over," said R. T. Barton, making a scissors gesture with two fingers.

"Fuck you," replied Lonnie, a little weakly.

"Jesus Christ," said Ross, "there sure are a lot of vultures hanging around. Anything for laughs."

"I just wish there were more of them," said Lonnie. "It would be harder for him to pick us out."

At that moment the eight o'clock bell sounded. Some men near the gate began to move away, perhaps frightened by the prospect of being mistaken for the real culprits.

Lonnie and Ross waited a few moments more and were just beginning to feel relief when they saw the guard coming toward them through the gate from the other compound. He didn't hesitate. He walked directly up to them! It wasn't hard, they had both been standing at attention from the moment they first saw him. Then the guard made his speech. Apparently he had spent some time practicing it because it was quite clear and to the point.

"This time I forget. You be good. We have rules, you follow rules, next time you die!" This accomplished, he became more convivial. He poked Lonnie in the belly with his finger and said, "You too young to die, you be good boy," then he turned and walked across the compound toward one of the guard towers.

"Well I'll be damned!" said Ross.

"Jesus Christ!" exclaimed Lonnie.

"Of all the crap," said Gentry. "I come with you, freely offering all the expert legal advice you might need, and I find an obvious and gross miscarriage of justice. The criminals are released without a trial. This is the ultimate in the fine art of anti-climax." He was about to say something more when they heard the sirens.

They started far away, low, and moved toward them, getting louder as factories and fire stations all over the city began sounding off. In a few moments the air was filled with their sounds, undulating and piercing like the screams of a hundred frightened animals. The compound was immediately alive with shouting guards, herding the men back into the building. The Japanese didn't want their prisoners to witness air raids. Nobody knew why. The American planes had appeared daily now for almost a week. They came early and usually they stayed all day.

Ross and Lonnie were among the first back into the building. They hurried up the stairs to one of the windows. They had been boarded up when the air raids started but a bit of whittling had opened cracks big enough for limited observation. Lonnie watched, hoping to catch sight of an American plane, but nothing happened. Just the sound of sirens and the small patch of blue in front of his right eye. He got tired of seeing nothing and was almost ready to leave when something moving caught his eye. A small bug right in front of him, next to his nose. Funny looking little bastard, with a grey crusty back and two small hairs which wiggled around coming out the front. The sounds of battle came in then, muffled heavy thuds, dull monotonous reports, the bright staccato sounds of machine guns firing.

Now Lonnie could see smoke rising from the area where the dock was supposed to be; a plane no bigger than the crusty bug flitted across his field of vision, and disappeared. Finally when nothing could be seen except more smoke, rapidly increasing toward the north, he left the window and strolled casually around the large room, looking, listening. Things were as usual, a poker game was in progress over against the wall, here and there small clusters of men discussed the latest visit by the Americans. They were all in high spirits. Lonnie could hear familiar sounds, the voice of R. T. Barton loud and clear against the noisy background. "One of these days old Mac will walk right in here. You know what he said about the skies being dark with American planes—just look outside; man, just look outside! Just listen! I say to you that he shall return. One of these fine days he'll walk right in here and say, 'you men have been brave and true Americans,' and frankly," said R. T., "confidentially, I expect to get a medal for heroism above and beyond the call of duty."

"You do deserve a medal," said Gentry, "for outstanding contribution to the War Effort. By managing to get yourself captured, you probably shortened the war by at least six months."

"Are you kidding?" said R. T. Barton in his raspy monotone. "Hell, if I hadn't been captured I would probably be a major general by now." He was leaning back on his right arm, wearing nothing but a G-string. Now he sat up and glanced around the small group, nodding his head as his glance caught each individual with such vigor that his hair swept back and forth. Lonnie grinned, old R. T. looked like somebody shaking a dust mop, and a dirty one at that. "A God damn major general!" R. T. gave his hair an extra shake for emphasis and threw his head back and rolled his eyes, just like F.D.R.

"That's what I mean," replied Gentry. "Even the remote possibility boggles the imagination and strikes terror in the heart."

Then Gentry took on the retrospective air which usually prefaced one of his pronouncements on the state of things. Lonnie moved over and sat down beside him. Everyone waited, even R. T. Barton seemed subdued for the moment.

Gentry brushed his well trimmed mustache with his forefinger, surveyed his audience, then announced, "Let's admit it, the best thing that could possibly have happened for the American War Effort was exactly what did happen. I mean the rapid and complete elimination of all of us from the war. Everybody who has an ounce of candor or a grain of honesty knows that for the past fifteen years the Philippines has been the recipient of all of the eight balls in the Army, a real garbage can. In our happy little islands we have had more drunken, inefficient, inept, and just plain stupid officers per square inch than any other place in the Army. For enlisted men we have had a combination of kids, bums, national guardsmen, and reluctant draftees such as myself. We were the cancer of the armed services. It's better for all concerned that we were extirpated early. The one unfortunate circumstance in our demise is that the core of the disease has escaped to spread the malignancy. For the less enlightened, I speak of super leader Douglas MacArthur." At this the men around him applauded.

Gentry smiled and then continued, "Actually I am prob-

ably wrong. MacArthur demonstrates practically every attribute I despise; yet, it is probable that such characteristics are
essential during wartime. Here is one of the basic paradoxes of
a democracy. The principles we are supposed to cherish such
as freedom, individuality, kindness, and the general list
commonly ascribed Christian virtues are totally nonfunctional
in war. During war we need the demagogue. If there is a touch
of megalomania, a bit of just plain ham with a fine overlay of
bullshit, so much the better. In order to fight a war the
individual must be brutalized, his individuality submerged.
He must be able to kill without compunction. He must be able
to rationalize mass murder, either in terms of expedience or
under the guise of heroism. War becomes, as Henry Adams
once said in relation to something else that I can't remember
now, 'an insanity of force.' And we, my little sheep, are caught
between two such forces—one as inhuman, insensate, and as
destructive as the other. Let us only hope that our leaders,
particularly the much maligned MacArthur, are more practiced in the art of mass extermination than our gentle hosts."
Here Gentry paused and looked about him. Most of his
listeners seemed disturbed and a number of them would not
look at him. Some were drifting away.

Finally R. T. Barton without his usual bullshit said, "You
scare me, Gentry. Seriously, how do you figure our chances?"

"Your guess is as good as mine," said Gentry. "But this is
the way it looks from here. The Japs are determined to get us
out of the Philippines. Hell, you know their peculiar philosophy about prisoners as well as I do. To lose us back to the
Americans would constitute, in their thinking, some kind of
cosmic insult. They will do their best to get us out. Thus far,
the constant bombings by the Americans have kept us here at
Bilibid. If the bombings let up, we—my dear colleagues in
agony—are going to take a trip. The question is, how long a
trip. From here it looks like the Americans are bombing
everything that moves in or out of the Philippines. Let me put
it simply. If the Americans quit bombing Manila Bay, we are
going to start toward Japan. Frankly, I don't think we will get
very far."

He paused for a moment, rubbing his mustache with his

thumb, looking about him. Only Lonnie and R. T. Barton remained. Lonnie was disturbed that the others had left. "Those bastards have shit for brains. They can't stand a little intelligent conversation," he said.

Gentry laughed, "It's not the conversation that they are avoiding but the brutal echoes of a very inauspicious reality." As if to emphasize his statement, the sounds of battle, which had remained constant in the background of the conversation, broke forth with extreme clarity. There were three heavy explosions in succession which were felt through the building before the sounds were heard.

"It sounds like our buddies are busy," said Corso as he made his way over and among reclining figures on his way toward them. He sat down, filling in the small circle. He was smoking a tailor-made Japanese cigarette.

"How about butts, Corso?" asked Lonnie.

"Why not have a whole one?" said Corso. He removed a fresh pack of cigarettes and offered them around the circle. Both Lonnie and R. T. Barton helped themselves. Gentry smoked but he didn't take one.

"Jesus Christ, thanks, Corso," said Lonnie.

"I'm just helping you celebrate," Corso said, his voice deep, almost guttural. "Anyway I like good boys." He leaned over and gave Lonnie a playful dig in the belly.

"Oh, for Christ's sake, Corso, keep your damn hands to yourself." Corso's smile died and he sat for a few moments looking down at the smoke circling up from his cigarette, his face expressionless.

"What odds are you giving that we make a ship within five days?" asked Gentry.

"I'd say about fifty-fifty," answered Corso.

There was a long silence, everybody just sat there, not looking at each other. A few half-hearted attempts at conversation but nothing worked; the group soon drifted apart. Lonnie moved back to his place near the stairwell but Ross wasn't there. He stood for a moment looking at his friend's blanket, folded neatly with the corners tucked in, and then started ambling among the men looking for Ross' blond head.

It was a large building, big rooms which seemed to stretch

[27]

on endlessly, with high ceilings. It must have been under construction when the war started because there were no small rooms at all. Just three large barn-like enclosures—one for each floor—about one hundred feet long and sixty feet wide. The sixteen hundred nineteen men who made the building their home had grown accustomed to its darkness and dampness, when it was over a hundred degrees in the compound, it remained relatively cool inside.

Lonnie searched the top level and then made his way down the stairway to the next floor. Here, as on the level above, men were everywhere. Some of them were reading, most were lying down, sleeping or staring at the ceiling. A few were carving things out of ironwood, pipes and chess pieces. One guy had been working on the same pipe for over a year. Lonnie had tried making something out of the stuff once and gave it up. It was harder than a damn rock. A number of poker games were underway under the lights and here and there individuals gazed studiously at a chess board. Lonnie knew a few of them. They came from Davao Penal Colony in Mindanao where Lonnie had spent his first two and one half years as a prisoner of war. Half of them were enlisted men, the rest officers, from second lieutenant to lieutenant colonel; all of the full colonels and generals had been moved from the Philippines early, to somewhere in Formosa.

As Lonnie made his way along, stepping over and going around, a few of the men spoke. He saw Bessel, the bastard who had tried to fuck him up with the Captain, and Williams, another guy from his outfit, out of it in a game of chess. He watched for a few moments and then moved on. Neither of them had seen Ross.

On the way back to the stairway he heard his name called.

"Hey, Lonnie, you old pussy hound! How would you like some pussy?" It was Rutledge, a medical officer who had been in command of a quarters compound back at Davao. Lonnie had always liked him. They had a great secret. Lonnie had caught Major Imada's pet cat, when it sneaked through the fence from the Jap's quarters, and Rutledge had cooked it in the sterilizer. Jesus Christ it was good. Lonnie's mouth began to water just thinking about it.

[28]

"We have a very difficult question to decide," said Rutledge, "and we need your expert opinion."

"At your service, sir," said Lonnie. "I may not know a great deal about a lot of things, but on a few subjects my knowledge is profound and one of them is pussy." He winked at Rutledge.

"You are close to the question," said Rutledge, smiling. With his brown hair standing high, sticking out every which way, and his long hooked nose, he looked like a happy hawk. "If you had the choice between a large steak and sleeping with the girl of your choice for one night, which would you take?"

"Shit there's no choice," said Lonnie. "I'd take the girl. Wouldn't everyone?" He gave the group around Rutledge an appraising glance.

"As a matter of fact, I have just taken a vote on this momentous decision and you will be interested to know that we are the only people in this immediate group capable of rising above the purely sensual. How rapidly some people forget which values are truly basic. I wonder how long it will take before we become as demoralized as the rest of these people?"

"Me never," said Lonnie. "My last thought when I'm dying of starvation will be about pussy."

Everyone laughed and Lonnie felt good, almost happy as he made his way down to the bottom floor. There was security, a feeling of belonging and strength in being with all these guys, whatever happened. He kept thinking about Rutledge and how they had laughed as they ate the Major's cat. Old R. T. Barton was always talking about eating pussy. Well, he and Rutledge had actually done it, and man, it was tasty.

He found Ross playing poker with some of the officers from his outfit. He watched a while and then went back upstairs and lay down on his blanket. Outside the noise of battle had become sporadic and soon, as Lonnie dozed, the sounds died away completely.

Lonnie was awakened by the *all clear* and found Ross asleep beside him. He lifted himself on his elbow and watched his friend as he slept, saw how thin he was, how the ribs showed clearly all along his chest and how each muscle traced itself. The skin along the shin bones shiny and spongy, early signs of beriberi. The dullness of his light blond hair and the too red mouth, petulant now in sleep. All signs of slow starvation. The heritage shared by all, the universal bond of hunger.

As Lonnie watched, Ross awoke. He smiled as he observed the concerned look on Lonnie's face. "What you staring at me for? I was just catching a nap like you were when I came up. Boy you're sure a lazy bum. Your mouth was wide open, catching flies I guess. I heard you snoring from the stairway."

"Just my way of trying to do something about the protein free diet," said Lonnie. That was a good answer, he thought as good as Gentry could do. "How did you do in the poker game?"

"Well, let's put it this way," said Ross, "tonight I don't have to eat pigweed and watery rice—as a matter of fact at least for this evening I'm saved from indulging in the disgusting habit of eating entirely."

"Jesus Christ," said Lonnie, "you mean to say that you lost your chow again tonight? We don't even get enough to live on and you go and lose what little these yellow shitheads hand out. Sometimes I wonder why I ever took up with such an ignorant bastard."

"Thats not a very polite way to address an Officer in the United States Army, particularly since you are just a lowly enlisted man, and one that can't even count." Ross was grinning.

"Fuck you." Lonnie was grinning too now. "That rank shit went out years ago. I still say that anybody who loses his food in a poker game is an ignorant bastard, *and* a lousy poker player.

"Well, if you can't count, I guess it's my prerogative not to be able to play poker. Anyway, when the *all clear* sounds, let's go dig up some of our friends."

"It's sounded already," said Lonnie. "Get the shovel."

Ross pulled a triangular piece of tin from beneath his gear. They went down the stairs, to the northern corner of the compound directly beneath the guard tower. As one dug, the other collected. A Jap guard came by. He observed them for awhile, looked speculatively into the can, and then went away. A few of the other prisoners watched them but didn't say anything.

[30]

"Actually," Lonnie told Ross in a confidential voice after they had washed their worms and had them cooking at the edge of the large fire used by the compound cooks, "once you get used to them they aren't bad at all. At first I used to try to imagine I was eating red spaghetti, but now I don't need to."

"A worm is a worm is a worm," said Ross.

At the mid-afternoon meal Ross gave his food to one of the officers from the poker game. Then they split Lonnie's food and the worms between them. Lonnie was right. They weren't half bad.

The day dwindled into evening and just as the shadow from the west wall reached the middle of the compound, the "all inside" bell sounded. Slowly at first and then more rapidly the men gravitated toward the large door and began to stream inside. Two guards came from the outer compound and began to shout, *"Hayaku! Speedo!* hurry up!" But there was no urgency in their voices and the men moved methodically. This was ritual, nobody thought about it, the prisoners expressing resentment with a slow shuffle and the guards showing acceptance with shouts that lacked the ring of urgency.

The men moved into the building, climbed the stairs, and fanned out to assigned places . . . then the activities began, exercises to stave off boredom, frustration, or fear; chess games, the incredibly tedious whittling of a pipe from ironwood, rereading a worn out book, poker games for the next meal. But mostly it was conversation about nothing in particular, except maybe food. The need for something to eat lurked in the shadow of all conversation; there in the periphery, a companion of each statement, the hovering background of a double exposure.

When night came, everything but the talk stopped. There was a blackout throughout the city and in the building the darkness was complete except for a small light directly above each of the stairways; a concession born of expediency since many of the men had dysentery and there was perpetual movement to the outside latrines.

Lonnie didn't have dysentery but he made at least three trips to the latrine each night. Such trips broke the monotony of the long evening, but more important they gave him a feeling of power over his captors. Once he had sat undisturbed on one of the many seats for two hours waiting to see what the guard would do about it. The guard had watched him from a distance for almost the entire period and finally approached, sucking air through his teeth, and had told him to hurry up. Lonnie didn't hurry. He had discovered an interesting phenomenon. The Japanese had an extreme respect for somebody in the act of taking a crap. The privy was sanctuary, and sometimes he and Ross sat there side by side for hours talking about home and food and maybe women.

Tonight, however, Lonnie cut his trips to the essential one. Company had come calling and a discussion was under way. Perhaps it was more an argument. R. T. Barton, as he invariably did, was picking on the Japanese and Gentry, for some reason that Lonnie couldn't understand, was defending them. Ross and Corso occasionally made comments, but they were definitely on the edge of the conversation. Lonnie just listened.

"Didn't the bastards start the war, didn't they bomb Pearl Harbor with one of the sneakiest attacks conceivable while their Ambassador in Washington was talking about peace when he knew the attack was already in progress? It's as clear as the nose on your face which," here R. T. Barton assumed his F.D.R. stance and looked about the group for affirmation, "is pretty evident."

Gentry disregarded the personal reference. He sat silent for a moment squinting his eyes, smoothing his small mustache. When he spoke a little smile touched his features for a moment.

"You have a genius for emphasizing the obvious, R. T. I am going to tell you a small story, and then we will test your ability to generalize. Once there was a man . . ."

"For Christ's sake this isn't going to be another one of your 'once upon a time' stories, is it?" yelled R. T. Barton. A loud clamor for R. T. Barton to shut up and for Gentry to continue arose from the group, with Lonnie making his contribution to the uproar.

Gentry began again, looking benignly at R. T. Barton. "As I was saying, once upon a time there was a man (we shall call him our hero) who had a great many unfortunate attributes.

[32]

He was very poor and felt inferior to his rich neighbors and he compensated accordingly. He was obsequious to a fault in their presence, but when alone he maligned them and privately planned their downfall. But while waiting for his plans to hatch he had to feed his many children. So he poached on the land of a neighbor, a person as unfortunate as himself. Now another neighbor, a very wealthy and powerful individual who lived across the lake from him, resented our hero's blustering manners . . ." Gentry stopped for a moment, looked slyly around the circle, "as a matter of fact our hero was a bit reminiscent of someone here, somebody that we all know and love." There was general laughter throughout the group with all eyes on R. T. Barton.

"Fuck you," said R. T. Barton, but he was grinning.

"Anyway this big guy didn't like our hero's big mouth and sneaky ways. He wanted very much to come to blows with our hero, but inasmuch as he was a gentleman, and gentlemen do not strike the first blow, he designed a careful plan. Although our hero was poor he was proud, inordinately proud. So our wealthy friend decided he would do something to place the poor man's conception of himself in jeopardy—feeling sure that under such circumstances our hero would attack him and be beaten in the ensuing struggle. Systematically he began to stab our unfortunate friend in his various points of pride until under the lash of such devices a battle ensued. Our hero, driven to a soul-ravaging distraction, struck the first blow but finally succumbed to the greater power of the other man. After a struggle of some duration it turned out exactly as the wealthy man had planned."

"What a crap story," said R. T. "You said that you were going to test my power to generalize. Hell an idiot would make the inference you intended. The trouble with your little story is that your view of the world is all fucked up. You're a God damn Jap lover."

Here Ross broke in. "Hell, Gentry, you shouldn't be talking like this. One of the things that keeps the lot of us alive is the belief even if it is illogical that we have right on our side."

"And everybody knows that right always wins in the long run . . . is that it?" said Gentry.

[33]

"Yeah, maybe that's it," said Ross. He laughed but he seemed disturbed.

R. T. Barton didn't laugh. "As I was saying, Gentry, sometimes I think you are a dirty Jap loving son-of-a-bitch!" This new outbreak from R. T. was greeted by a chorus from the others for him to be quiet.

The atmosphere had become tense. R. T. Barton glanced around the group, but none of them looked at him. "Well for Christ's sake," he finally said, "what are you gettin' sore about? I was just kidding. You know I was only kidding, don't you Gentry?"

"Sure, I know that," replied Gentry and he said it in a way that convinced both R. T. Barton and the others present that R. T. actually had been kidding at the time.

At this moment Father Maloney, perceiving that a conversation was underway and that Gentry—as usual—was central to it, joined them. "Is this a joke telling contest? If so, I imagine that they're the type that a person in my august profession shouldn't hear. But perhaps I should. It's important that a priest be able to deal with and understand all kinds of people and situations . . . some of your stories should be quite broadening to a person such as myself who has been protected from the naughtier aspects of the human condition."

Everyone laughed. They liked Father Maloney and they understood and appreciated the friendship which existed between the Father and Gentry. They were hoping that they could get Gentry and Maloney into one of "the battles" as they were called.

Lonnie suddenly heard himself saying, "We were all trying to point out to Gentry the importance of religion, Father, but as usual he either can't or doesn't want to see the light."

"Ah, seeking blood as usual, Lonnie. Well, what say you, Gentry . . . how goes the light today?"

"Some brighter now that you have joined us," said Gentry half seriously. "We have just been having a discussion, with R. T. as the major protagonist, and you can well imagine to what intellectual depths we have plunged. It's certainly good that you interrupted us—for my sake that is. R. T., as usual, was getting the better of the argument."

"Somehow when I argue with you, Gentry, I always get screwed; even when I win, I get screwed," said R. T. doubtfully. He looked about at the others and they were all nodding in agreement.

"Nobody deserves it more," said Lonnie, grinning.

"But you can't screw the Padre," continued R. T. Barton without looking at Lonnie. "Maybe you would like to defend atheism, right here in the presence of the Padre."

This statement of R. T.'s was greeted with affirming comments from the others. Gentry looked pleased and Father Maloney suddenly appeared quite interested. The group spread out so he could sit down opposite Gentry and a few onlookers from nearby came to form an outer circle of listeners.

"Jesus Christ," said Lonnie under his breath, "this thing sounds like its going to be a real biggie."

"Sure does," said Ross. "Light against darkness . . . and all that kind of crap."

"Shut up, you guys," said R. T. "Let's get this debate on the road. As I understand it," he said in his raspy voice, "this is to be about the pros and cons of atheism. I suggest that first we have a pronouncement from the old pro." At this everybody laughed and Gentry smiled a little.

"Okay," he said, "I'll start the ball rolling. The question, it seems to me, is really quite simple. Why am I an avowed atheist? Why in the face of a broad-minded liberalism which pleads the rationality of suspended judgment in areas which science cannot touch, do I choose to state the negative of this case? I have a very simple answer. I do not believe in any God that I have ever heard defined. It is the typical approach of those happily ensconced in religion to look at me with awesome pity and a little fear and then to ask the big question." Gentry looked intently at Lonnie. "Do you believe in God?"

Lonnie was momentarily startled by the piercing eyes, the sudden question. He paused and then answered, "You can bet your cotton pickin' life I do. Others chuckled at his response. Lonnie felt good.

"Oh shut up!" said R. T. Barton. "Well master, what do

you say when somebody asks you this original and fundamental question?"

"I merely ask him to define the God he thinks I ought to believe in. A few of them, these true believers, fumble at a definition. Then I quite truthfully and sincerely say that I do not believe in any God so defined. Thus far in my delvings into the spiritual worlds of such people I haven't been able to find a God kicking around any place that I can believe in. Perhaps the Father has a better definition."

The priest paused a moment, as if thinking. He had been through this before. "I may not be able to give you a definition of God that you can believe in, Gentry, but I can truthfully say that you are as wrong as your demands are unfair. God, by definition, defies definition." He paused and looked around at the group. "Could the limited intellectual power of an ant give definition to our brilliant protagonist Gentry? Of course not! To the ant Gentry must exist as some incomprehensible and inscrutable entity whose powers and purposes cannot be understood. I am the ant . . . and you . . . and even Gentry, though it must be admitted that in his case," and here the Father's smile removed the edge from the sarcasm, "we are dealing with a relatively large one and one that can undoubtedly see better than most."

"I'm glad you made that last point," said Gentry, also smiling. "I am driven to concur heartily if your explanation is representative of what ants normally produce."

"You don't need to be so fucking impolite to the Father," said R. T. Barton.

"Well now for the mite's appraisal," said Gentry, ignoring R. T.'s mutterings.

"Father, a long time ago a very brilliant ant pointed out that he could find no justice in a God, admittedly incomprehensible, who castigates puny man merely because he finds God incomprehensible. If God's ways are inscrutable to man, as you imply, then indeed you have proved my point for me. How can any human being be expected to believe in that which is admittedly incomprehensible to human beings?"

"I am pleased to note," said the Father, "that we are now discussing God's incomprehensibility and not whether He exists." He smiled at Gentry. A gentle smile, touched with affection.

"It seems to me," said Gentry with acid in his voice, "that there is but a small step from an admission of the incomprehensibility of some entity to the honest admission that such an entity may only be supposed."

"Truthfully," said the Father, and he spoke slowly and for the moment seemed shy and vulnerable, "my own belief in God comes from an experience which defies denial." As he continued Lonnie thought he perceived a note of pleading in his voice. "A man who has risen early in order to see the sun rise cannot then at some later moment be convinced that he has not seen the sun. This thing lies beyond the works of reason. You cannot give a logical analysis of an intense pain nor can I give a logical analysis of my intense experience of God."

"You must realize, Father," said Gentry quietly, "that once you have based your argument upon the intensity of your own experience you have removed the entire issue from the realm of discussion. I can only say that I sincerely respect your experience, whatever it may have been, but you must admit that I have no way of knowing the nature of that experience myself. If you plead the existence of God upon the power of your own experience, you must in fairness allow me to question the existence of that which I have not had the experience of existing." Gentry hesitated and stopped, his eyes sought those of the Father but the priest seemed suddenly withdrawn and alien. A long silence followed. Some of the men lit cigarettes and made a great deal of noise clearing throats and relocating butts on the concrete.

Finally Gentry laughed, "Well this has turned out to be one hell of an argument, Father. We both wind up encapsulated in our own private worlds."

"Well there is certainly one thing we can say about this discussion," said Ross. "It's been friendly."

"And why not?" said the Father, smiling, his face suddenly warm. "After all I feel quite responsible for Gentry's transport to a higher plane of emotional insight. Gentry is, if you will pardon this parry, what I wish to call 'logic limited.' Nothing has any meaning for him unless it can be dissected and analyzed. If he were to see the face of God, he would measure it in millimeters and then render his experience in terms of syllogisms . . ."

"Logic limited!" exploded Gentry. "Since you have personalized the argument, what kind of limitation do you place on your validities? We have our asylums full of people who have had the ultimate experience in religion. If we can't use logic as an instrument of truth, if we have to throw out reason and summarily dismiss objective observations, we are left to the mercy of the most vocal individual's hallucination as a base for knowledge. You know as well as I do that Jesus Christ would be locked up and given shock treatments if he were to demonstrate the same grandiose delusions today that he did some time ago."

The Father's face had become red and his voice shook when he spoke. "When you become personal in your references, I wish you would direct them at me and not at our Lord and Savior. Someday you may have to beg forgiveness for that statement."

Gentry looked incredulous. "That, my dear Father, is a statement that I would never have expected from you. Suddenly I hear the iron jaws of the inquisition snapping shut and see eternal verities streaming from the flaming mouth of Hell. Look Father, as miserable as I am and as much as I may need to be better than others, I wouldn't get any particular enjoyment out of having them come and bow down to me! If I could help the miserable, I would do it without demanding their mortification. To make my point quite clear, I could not tolerate a God who would require me to bow down to him. Nor can I understand a religion which makes its God into such a petty egomanic!" As Gentry approached the end of this pronouncement his voice rose in pitch and trembled slightly.

Lonnie wasn't thinking about what was being said. With deep enjoyment he watched the faces, particularly the eyes of the protagonists. The flushed face of the Father with eyes downcast as if somehow ashamed for someone. The face of Gentry, thinner now it seemed, with mouth drawn and eyes brittle. Lonnie glanced around the circle at the men who listened and who watched; R. T. Barton, face suddenly immobile, caught in the aspect of being struck by a new idea remained momentarily fixed in small surprise; Ross, unusually thoughtful, pursing his lips while tenting out his cheek, in the manner characteristic of him when contemplating complicated notions; Corso, eyes shifting back and forth between Gentry and the Father, face expressionless, fingers unconsciously stroking the goody bag which bulged at his groin. What a crazy bunch of bastards—half starved, many suffering the pains of beriberi, all dirty and stinking, and here they were listening intently to an argument as old as intellect and about as futile. The Father's voice interrupted his ruminations and now he listened carefully.

"When I said that you would have to beg for forgiveness," explained the Father quietly, "I did not mean that some agent would extract such a plea under penalty of punishment. I meant that God, working in your life, would someday make you realize the empty, futile, and superficial nature of that gross philosophy which you apparently represent. And so realizing you will choose to beg forgiveness of Christ even as you would apologize to a friend whom you had unknowingly hurt. As for God requiring that we bow down to him: this observation demonstrates what I have long suspected, that your understanding of the relationship between God and man is indeed a peculiar one. Man does not rightly worship God because he feels that God desires such adulation or to propitiate in some fashion a higher power. Man's worship of God is a spontaneous and unsolicited act of adoration once man has been touched by God's grace."

"*Quel* horse offal," said Gentry, now back in good humor. "You know as well as I do that most people pray because they want to get something or because they want to get rid of something. And even if we were to assume that you are correct, even according to your ungross philosophy man has nothing to do with whether or not he receives grace. This is left up to the haphazard and apparently random machinations of your deity. In an interesting demonstration of justice your God hands out the grace which automatically *ipso facto* makes the recipient good. Then he beneficently rewards such good people and punishes the ungraced, ungood ones; some justice, some impartiality, some kind deity!"

The Father did not seem to be listening. When Gentry stopped speaking the priest looked around him at the various members of the group and then declared, "Christ came to this earth and suffered the bright agony of humankind so that we might be freed from sin and find eternal salvation. To you salvation can have very little meaning simply because you refuse to conceive of sin in any of its various forms. To me," and here he gazed directly at Gentry, "this seems a more fundamental deviation than any sin that might be committed, because in denying sin you deny the necessity of salvation and make Christ's life and death a hollow mockery." The Father paused and the group lapsed into silence. There was an uneasiness around the circle and when the strangely sad almost mystical sound of Japanese taps, muffled by the barred and covered windows, found its way into the clefts of quiet the men somehow felt relieved.

"I am sure of one thing," said Gentry. "If anybody gets some pie in the sky by and by, the Father is in for a large slice."

"You had better hope there is no Heaven," laughed R. T. Barton. "If there's a Heaven there will probably be another region also and we can figure where you'll wind up."

"In that case," agreed Gentry good-naturedly, "I'm sure I'll be blessed with your not-so-good company and of course Lonnie will be there to put a bit of uncertainty into the warmer scheme of things."

"And Corso still wearing his ball sack," giggled Lonnie, "except instead of money it will be filled with hot coconut oil."

This remark was greeted by shouts from the group and even the Father smiled. Corso tried to look angry but Lonnie could see that he was secretly pleased.

As the laughter trailed away the small light over the stairway suddenly went out and the darkness was complete. Unease gripped the men, conversations quieted, there was an air of listening. As if to confirm this expectancy a shout which rose into a guttural scream flared into the silence. There was a general intake of breath throughout the building, a collective

[40]

gasp and then silence as total as the darkness settled in again, but not for long. Almost immediately Japanese guards began to shout. Their voices came from different areas of the compound, calling and answering, and the sound of their hobnailed boots could be heard, running.

"Sure sounds like the fit hit the shan," observed R. T. Barton. "Maybe old Mac's boys are coming in right now, sneaking up to the fence and getting ready to come on over."

"Who's got a candle?" the Father asked.

"I have," shouted Lonnie, and started feeling around for his pack. "Just hold everything for a minute and I'll have one." He finally felt his mess gear and found the three candles he had been saving to eat in case things really got tough. "Who's got a light; I've got the candle."

At his elbow, a match flared. He bent the candle toward the little flickering fire and stared intensely at the wick as it let off drops of melted wax, smoked momentarily, finally developed a little pod of flame which grew in size and brightness. Then he looked up and saw that Corso was holding the match and saw the eyes of Corso strangely, so it seemed to him afterwards, fixed upon his own.

"Thanks a lot, Corso," Lonnie said, a bit too loudly.

"That's Okay," replied Corso. "If you've got the candle, I've always got the heat."

Lonnie didn't respond. Tilting the candle ahead he made his way back to the group. He placed it on a small box where it sputtered bravely and beat back the darkness for a little way. By this time the shouting of the guards had died down, and except for the murmuring of the men there was silence. No one in the aura of the light spoke, they stared at the candle and they saw it flicker in each other's eyes.

After a few minutes the men on the lower floor started making noise, loud voices and occasional bursts of laughter.

"My curiosity is killing me," said R. T. Barton. "I think I'll make a little safari downstairs and find out what happened. Can I use the candle?"

"Sure, go ahead," said Lonnie. "Just make it fast—we're burning up my last meal."

"You're better off than most of us," Gentry said as R. T.

[41]

took the candle and made his way toward the stairs. "I haven't had a good eating candle for ever so long—but I'll bet Corso can't say the same for himself, with all of his money and other talents."

As R. T. disappeared down the stairway the darkness was complete again. Lonnie kept waiting for Corso's voice to dispel the tenseness which suddenly filled the darkness. But it was Father Maloney who finally spoke.

"It may seem a small thing, but the night is filled with our lack of light and defined in terms of its absence. Without God, man's lot is not unlike ours here, a darkness and a waiting and hundreds of voices asking what's happening."

"Oh come now, Father," laughed Gentry, "the argument is over with the retreat of the Forces of Evil, and it's not very kind of you to use this situation to emphasize a point just because it's pertinent. But since you brought it up our situation seems to much better symbolize man's state when science was slumbering and religion was the source of truth. You know, the Dark Ages."

"Behold, the light returneth," continued Gentry. "Ah yes, how fitting that R. T. should be our Renaissance, the bearer of bright intelligence to light our darkling world."

"You'd never guess it in a million years—man, it's great—great!" R. T. Barton was laughing so hard Lonnie feared for his candle and took it from him.

"Well for Christ's sake, tell us what happened," said Ross. Many of the others had gathered around R. T. Barton, all waiting for the news.

"Quit the horseshit, R. T., and give us the dope," yelled Lonnie. "What happened—what happened?"

"Sit down everybody and I'll tell you," said R. T. Barton, arranging himself so that the light from the candle struck his face. "You know old Speedo? Well, he's deader'n a doornail and you couldn't guess in a million years how it happened. The lazy bastard, the lazy yellow son-of-a-bitch!" Here R. T. paused and gazed around the circle and seemed satisfied. "You know what happened? That bastard was too lazy to get down from the guard tower. He pissed on the high tension wire and got electrocuted through the cock!" Suddenly

[42]

pandemonium reigned in the group, a contagion of wild laughter moved through the building as the story spread.

"How's that for a way to get your rocks off?" yelled Corso.

"Yeah, the granddaddy of all blow jobs," howled Lonnie.

"I wonder what that son-of-a-bitch thought when it hit him," shouted R. T., "like having ground up razor blades jammed up the old ying yang, or pissing hot lead."

Suddenly all of the lights went on again and the men, no longer laughing, looked at each other in the glare. The Father searched the faces of those near him. He seemed disturbed. They, in turn, looked away and after a while drifted back to their blankets. Once again the lights were turned out and quiet settled over the building. Lonnie kept thinking about Speedo and ground up razor blades, and couldn't go to sleep for a long time.

CHAPTER TWO

"How can such little bastards have such big mouths?" Ross was yawning as he rolled up his blanket. "Show, boy, show. Come on, greet the dawn. Once again we rise bright and early to do absolutely nothing. If we could just sleep as long as we wanted to in the morning, the time would pass faster and pretty soon we would have miseried out the allotted days."

"Yeah," responded Lonnie, "and you know, you're not so hungry in the early morning, not until you get out there in line and start thinking about it."

On the way down the stairway Lonnie paused. "You know, I had almost forgotten about old Speedo. What a way to take off. Just too lazy to come down off that guard tower to take a leak. He wasn't such a bad Jap—hell, you remember, he gave us a cigarette butt a couple of days ago."

"Sure, he was a great guy," said Ross. "Your old buddy. It hasn't been a month since you were screaming that you were going to, and I quote you, 'kill that yellow son-of-a-bitch' if it was the last thing you ever did. And all he did to you was kick your ass for stealing cassava. Boy, I'll never forget it. There you were with the cassava sticking out from under your arms and him kicking your butt with you trying to keep from dropping your load. It was funnier than hell."

"What a sense of humor," grinned Lonnie. "A poor guy dead from having his balls fried off and you talk about ass kicking."

They were among the last to leave the building. Then they were in the line-up and facing the rising sun. Sixteen hundred and nineteen men ten deep waiting for the count-off, waiting while the guards checked for empty spaces, checked off the ones too sick to make the count, and added up the total. *Bango!* The number checked out as it always did, no one ever escaped from Bilibid, probably no one had ever tried. The line-up to get watery rice and brown sugar, and the line-up to wash the mess gear. Suddenly it was ten o'clock and the compound was hot, and there was nothing to do until the second and last meal of the day which came at four.

The day passed into early afternoon and the men hugged the shaded walls or moved into the relative darkness of the building. A strange silence rested over the city and over the prison, a quietness and a waiting. The momentary sputtering of a truck motor beyond the walls was enough to turn a thousand hopeful faces toward the sky. But the planes did not come. Lonnie and Ross were crouched down in their favorite spot against the west wall. From where they sat, absorbed in their own thoughts, the murmur of the compound rose and fell, punctuated occasionally by a curse or loud laughter.

Lonnie looked at Ross. "They're not coming today, they've never been this late before, it almost seems like they've never been here at all—that we're going to have another two years of waiting and looking. Jesus Christ, I'll never forget the first time we saw them. There we'd been waiting for two years not knowing if we'd ever get home—thinking, like they told us, that we were losing the war. You remember," he asked looking into Ross' face, and Ross smiled, remembering.

"You were cutting the cassava from that damn tree and I was loading it on the carrier," continued Lonnie. "And I looked up and suddenly there they were. Spread out all over the sky like a bunch of geese gone crazy. No formation, just a bunch moving in toward Manila. You know, it's funny the way they fly—not pretty formations like the Japs—but just in a bunch with bombers in the middle and the fighters weaving in and out, and sometimes when they're really high, so high they leave vapor trails—great big dollar signs. Hey, there's old Gentry, and the bastard's smoking a cigarette. Hey Gentry!"

Gentry turned his ambling steps in their direction. As he

approached, the sun glinted off his brown shoulders giving a
red tinge to his cheeks. Apparently he had just shaved because
his mustache was newly trimmed and he seemed to exude an
atmosphere of well being—almost of indestructibility. When
he sat down an optimism suddenly pervaded the afternoon.
He took a heavy drag and passed the cigarette to Ross. "And
one for the mathematical genius," he said, smiling at Lonnie.
Lonnie grinned back and waited for his turn on the cigarette.
When it was passed to him, he carefully knocked off the ashes
and let it cool for a moment. Then the inhalation, deep into
the lungs, a singing of blood, the ebb and flow of light and
grey. And now another until the lips parch, and hold till the
good lung hurt reaches a half-sickness.

"For Christ's sake," the far off voice of Ross complained,
"you might have at least left a last drag for Gentry."

"Jesus Christ," said Lonnie, "I'm sorry, Gentry, a damn big
hog, I guess. You know cigarettes are just like poontang.
Before you get 'em, you'd eat 'em, and after you get 'em you
wouldn't piss on them. Say, what's new Gentry? Have you
gotten over the trouncing Father Maloney gave you last
night?"

"Ah, the guilty one changing the subject, placing the
opposition on the defensive. I, of course, was not bested by the
good Father, nor was he bested by me. Both of us are so committed to our positions that nothing short of a self-confirming
revelation is going to change either of us."

"You make it sound like you and the Father are both pretty
rigid in your thinking," said Ross. "Now you wouldn't admit
that, would you?"

"No, not entirely," smiled Gentry. "Your statement is only
half true."

"You know what I think?" asked Lonnie affectionately. "I
think you're an old bullshitter. How many years of education
did it take to make you such an expert? I'll bet it was all of
that training in law that did it. Say, tell us about one of those
juicy cases you read up on in law school."

"Yeah, come on," said Ross. "We can use a little diversion."

"Well, I don't know," said Gentry doubtfully. "There was
one case that I remember being fairly unusual. Maybe I've

already told you about it—the case where a woman was declared legal father of her own daughter's child."

"You're kiddin'," said Lonnie.

"You're crazy," exclaimed Ross, but both he and Lonnie looked expectantly at Gentry, who gave each a quick glance.

"I'm hurt at your incredulity and shocked by your lack of respect for my broad experience in varied legal enterprises."

"That sounds like bullshit," said Ross, grinning.

"Well perhaps," agreed Gentry.

"Oh for Christ's sake, tell us," said Lonnie. "Tell us the damn story."

"Well, it happened in southern Illinois, not far from the town of Boskeydell, which is located approximately four miles northeast of Carbondale. This part of Illinois is farm country, rolling land with an occasional high hill, and one of the highest overlooked the small hamlet in question. Perched on this hill, almost seeming to be a part of the land and trees themselves, so rustic it was, stood a farmhouse, old and cumbersome, representing both solidity and a way of life outmoded. The inhabitants seemed to reflect the mood occasioned by the dour aspect of the house. The husband in his fiftieth year was as solid, reliable, responsible and seemingly as durable as the house itself. The wife complemented her husband in every respect. A virtuous, industrious, religious, homely woman: a good woman deeply concerned with the plight of those less fortunate and willing to succor the ill or comfort the aged at any time or place, day or night. But the prime interest, the major focus of our story, as was so with Dickens, is the daughter, Nell. She was a child late in coming, having been born when the good wife was in her thirty-sixth year. Little Nell immediately and continuously received all of the adoration, affection and solicitude the parents were capable of giving. And as if in response to this loving environment, Nell grew into a most beautiful and loving child—and thence into a most voluptuous and love-wanting woman."

Here Gentry stopped and seemed to become lost in inspecting an ant which was trying in vain to climb out of a small hole which it had apparently just fallen into. "Ah, look at this poor fellow," said Gentry. "He takes one step and slides back two. Not much progress there. Just like our situation—the farther we go, the deeper we seem to sink. And there is a terror in the bottom of the hole. An ant lion. I wonder what waits for us?"

"Jesus Christ," said Lonnie, "forget that fucking ant and get back to the story." He picked up a rock and brought it crashing down upon the struggling insect. Then he removed the rock and found the crushed body, legs still feebly moving, riven by the stone. A dead-live little machine moving automatically. Just like his own shit making guts.

"Well," continued Gentry, as if nothing had interrupted him, "the general tempo of our friend's condition moved with little variation. Love, happiness, security, these dominated their lives until there came a day, a terrible day when one of the horses which the father was leading to the wagon, for reasons known only to horses, reared on his hind legs and brought his hooves crashing down upon the head of his unsuspecting master—killing him quite dead.

Bewildered and overwhelmed by this upheaval in their world, Nell and her mother tried to keep the farm running. Life must continue. But there was too much heavy work. They needed help. After interviewing numerous candidates, the widow finally settled on one young man who by his composure and bearing during her rather direct questioning about personal habits, the Catholic Church and the Republican Party, seemed to demonstrate that he was bland enough for the job. Having passed the test, our unattractive young friend—a fact not completely unrelated to the fact that he got the job—was given a room, as is usual in such cases, in the attic.

Nature works in mysterious ways and so it did in this one. The subtle alchemy of loneliness made Nell a paragon of unsurpassing beauty in his eyes, and transformed him, as unkempt and disheveled as he was, into a composite of Billy Sunday and Clark Gable. One evening after the milking and the chicken feeding and the hog slopping, it so happened that the good widow was summoned to the bedside of an expectant mother who had been for twelve hours in painful though unproductive labor. Nell went to the barn just as Ned, for he was so named, was feeding the horses hay from the loft. Ah, the catalyst of a summer evening upon the chemistry of youth. As if in a trance, Nell climbed the ladder to the loft, her bosom heaving, her wide eyes black pools in the semi-darkness. Caught in an agony between hope and fear, Ned wildly threw hay onto the rapidly growing pile beneath. But to no avail. The die was cast! The impetus of love forced him to turn suddenly and face her as she waited fearful in a darkened corner. They stood facing one another, enthralled by what neither could admit was possible, with what the combined knowledge of all past generations signified was soon to come to pass. She with pallid face, eyes dilated, breasts outyearning toward the hands that groped for her. He with the groping hands and groin swollen to the bursting point. So it happened, there in the dusk in the hayloft, the usual place for such occasions, the consummation. No word spoken, none was needed, those vital processes which evolution had labored countless ages to effect were brought to fruition as smoothly and as completely as if our young friends were demonstrating the laws of reciprocal innervation."

"Jesus Christ," interrupted Lonnie, "you tell us a simple story about a little screwing in a haystack and it sounds like it came out of a fucking encyclopedia. Get to the point!"

"As a matter of fact, it does come from the encyclopedia of life," continued Gentry, undisturbed. "In the fulfillment of our young friends you find a knowledge more profound than any dissertation, an art more subtle than any masterpiece."

"Go on and tell the fucking story," howled Lonnie.

Ross was laughing but his face was tense. "Go on Gentry, and keep your prick under control, Lonnie, it's Gentry's story—let him tell it the way he wants to."

"Thanks, Ross, I can see that you perceive the underlying significance of this tragedy, for such it is. Well anyway, they were there in the hayloft, interacting when it suddenly occurred to Ned that this is the way babies happen. It occurred to him with such overwhelming clarity that at that last and most exciting moment—he, as they say in vulgar circles, withdrew and allowed himself to be spent in aimless consummation.

"Summer passed into winter and thence into spring and

many were the loving trysts in the hayloft, but on every occasion just at that most delirious but vitally dangerous moment, Ned practiced the basic separation. And thus the relationship continued to mature in its emotional and spiritual significance without the usual result—the inopportune intrusion of a child.

"But as time passed, the good widow began to suspect that something was amiss. A peripheral uneasiness grew into a doubt and flowered into gross suspicion. Finally, although Ned was an excellent worker, she summarily dismissed him with the instructions that if she caught him on the premises again she would have him locked up as a trespasser, vagrant, and chicken thief.

"Ned left the farm, heartbroken; but not so bereft as Nell. Life seemed to lose significance for her. She became pale of complexion, languid of manner, only picked at her food, and where she gazed despair pervaded space. Ned, however, was not without some ingenuity and certainly not without a yearning for Nell. One evening just after midnight, he returned to the farm and awakened Nell by throwing gravel against her window screen. Even as she heard it, she knew that it was he. How stealthily she stole past her mother's bedroom, down the hallway, down the stairs, and with what joy she saw him there in the barnyard in the moonlight. What had once been an all-consuming passion in both breasts erupted into a cataclysm of mutual need. Take a passion, season it with separation, esculate it with yearning and it may become, as it did in this case, irresistible.

"There in the barnyard, in the moonlight, just after midnight our young couple was united, and the eternal processes again were manifested. But by some prescience the mother wakened and called for Nell. As there was no answer she hurriedly put on her dressing gown and rushed to Nell's bedroom. Imagine her dismay when she discovered Nell's empty bed. Wildly she dashed out of the house, almost blindly she stumbled toward the barn. There to her horror and revulsion she observed our young friends in the throes of final consummation. Filled with insensate anger, the good woman reached for what might come to hand and found a huge rock

[50]

which had been used as a door stop. Rage giving strength to gentle hands, she hoisted the rock high above her head, and with a frenzy which would have delighted the great Sigmund, brought it down upon the posterior of young Ned who was just at that well practiced point of withdrawing coincidentally from the pool of ecstasy and the well of danger. Needless to say, he didn't make the grade."

Here Gentry was interrupted by unbelieving comments from Lonnie and Ross. Both seemed transfixed by the circumstances of the story.

"Jesus Christ," murmured Lonnie, his face filled with a diminishing lust and a growing admiration. "That's the damnedest story I've ever heard; that's the craziest most fouled up story I've ever listened to."

"Yeah, that's a corker even for you, Gentry," admitted Ross. "What finally happened?"

"Well, as you no doubt have anticipated, a number of things happened. Nell became pregnant, the mother brought the case to court, and all of the savory and unsavory details of the case were brought out. Since Ned had adequately demonstrated the art of withdrawal up until the untimely interference of the mother, the court declared that she was responsible for the birth of the child, and so—she was declared the legal father."

"Why in the hell didn't they just get married?" asked Lonnie.

"Well, it seems that the widow discovered that Ned was actually not a God-fearing young man as he had indicated. As a matter of fact, he was an atheist. Under those circumstances, she preferred to raise the child herself."

After this comment, all three men were silent, the sounds of the compound rushed in and disrupted their little island of interest.

"Things seemed to happen parallel in Boskeydell," said Ross.

They all laughed, but suddenly the aimless wandering men were there again, the walls with their growing shadows, and the shouts of the guards calling the prisoners to line up for the afternoon count.

"They won't come today," said Ross. There was a quietness and foreboding in his voice that made both Lonnie and Gentry look at him.

"Yeah, but they'll come tomorrow," said Lonnie. "Just wait and see—they'll come in bright and early, and noisy, real noisy—just wait and see."

"They'd better," said Gentry. And as they walked toward the rapidly forming lines of men, they searched the cloudless sky.

"There's one," thought Lonnie, but he knew even as he saw it that it was nothing more than a figment of the eye itself . . . a small floating substance designed to startle one when fearing or hoping for planes.

The day dragged on into late afternoon, and still the planes did not come. The men moved around the compound, went in and out of the building, played chess and poker for the evening meal, lay on their blankets and stared at the ceiling and thought about women and going home. But the planes did not come. Finally Ross and Lonnie heard the old Colonel sound the five o'clock bell.

"The old bastard is still beating that gong like his life depended on it," complained Lonnie. "And the Japs give him worker's rations for that. Some job, just banging that gong on the hour and half hour!"

"A bit demanding for a Lieutenant Colonel, I'll admit," said Ross. "Remember that crazy Jap guard who had to kill himself over the Colonel's watch?" And they both remembered and savored in unison the strange story.

It took place in Mindanao at Davao Penal Colony right after they had first met. They had only been prisoners a year then and everybody was still convinced that the war wouldn't last much longer. Life had assumed a ritual. Get up at six; eat at six-thirty. Into the rice fields by seven. Work till three. Back to the compound by three-thirty. Eat at four. To bed at nine. And always the miserable and unalterable tempo of their lives was punctuated by Colonel Nelson's gong. His position of responsibility and relative opulence was insured by the ownership of a magnificent 21 jeweled Waltham pocket watch. A treasure which he had somehow managed to hang onto during the early days when certain Japanese, almost indiscriminately it seemed, declared open season on the prisoners' possessions. As the months passed it became more than a way of telling time; it became the mechanism which gave rhythm and continuity to their lives. Lonnie had seen the watch on a number of occasions, and it had gleamed with extraordinary luster. The Colonel polished it every evening.

But one morning, just two days after the earthquake caused the flag pole to whip back and forth and the palm frond and bamboo building in which they lived to sway, the watch was missing. The Colonel awoke to find that someone had cut the leather thong, and had removed it from around his neck.

The news spread through the compound. THE WATCH IS GONE. SOMEBODY STOLE THE WATCH. The Japanese commander, Major Imada, was notified and all of the work details were delayed, as the Japanese and American MP's searched the buildings. But the watch wasn't found and everyone suffered from a sense of loss and timelessness, especially the Colonel. Days passed and the watch didn't reappear, and everybody speculated and hypothesized and looked for suspicious signs in other people's faces. Finally, almost by universal consensus, it was agreed that one of the Japanese guards had taken the watch. After all, didn't they make hourly trips through the barracks? A number of people even remembered one guard in particular who seemed unduly interested in the watch, who on one occasion had even asked to see it. So the American commander of the camp, Colonel Watson, was delegated to report to Major Imada that the Japanese guard had taken the watch.

Lonnie remembered how Colonel Watson had made his report at the evening count and could still hear the sharp smack Major Imada's hand made on the Colonel's cheek and could see again the growing red splotch. Then Major Imada gave a speech both impromptu and vehement to the effect that no member of the Japanese Imperial Army would ever stoop to stealing a stupid watch from an inferior American Colonel.

That seemed to end it. Another watch was found and old Colonel Nelson continued to strike the gong, but something was missing and everybody, especially the old Colonel, felt it.

THE WATCH WAS GONE. But that wasn't the end of it! One morning after all the men were lined up to march into the rice and vegetable fields, nothing happened. The order to march was not given. The Japanese guards seemed as mystified as the prisoners, and kept looking toward the Japanese officers' compound. Finally Major Imada came down the steps from his office and was joined there by Lieutenant Iwahara. They talked for a few moments, while the four thousand prisoners and two hundred guards watched in growing anticipation. Something unusual was about to take place. At last the two Japanese officers moved across the compound, their long swords bouncing off their legs. Lonnie always wondered how they kept from tripping over the damn things. The Major mounted one of the wooden platforms which the Japanese always had handy—R. T. Barton said that the "crummy little runts" used the platforms so they wouldn't have to look up to the Americans—and in a voice remarkable for its quietness and seeming humility, made the following announcement.

"As representative of his Imperial Majesty, the Emperor of Japan, it is my duty to report that one of the men in the 23rd Prisoner Guard Regiment was found guilty of taking the watch. Colonel Nelson will come forward and it will be returned to him."

Lonnie saw the old Colonel moving around the formation. He walked proudly with the sun glinting off his boney shoulders, his bare legs looking like they belonged to a skinny plucked chicken. He came to attention before the platform and Lieutenant Iwahara handed him back the watch. The Colonel bowed to the waist, did a sharp about face and returned to his place among the quarters patients who had come out of the barracks to be in on the activity.

Major Imada gave an extended speech in Japanese with all the guards standing immobile, like "lumps of yellow shit," as R. T. Barton said later. After the speech one of them, his face deathly pale beneath a heavy tan, moved slowly forward to stand at last before the platform. No word was spoken. A Japanese sergeant ran forward, his sword making smacking sounds against his leg. He stopped before the platform, saluted and handed the Major an ordinary rifle. The Major descended the platform, bowed before the pale faced guard and handed him the rifle. The soldier returned the bow, placed the rifle under his chin and shot himself. Lonnie could still see him lying there when he glanced back from the formation as it moved toward the rice fields. He was still there in the evening, slightly bloated by the sun, but the next morning he was gone.

The Colonel still had his watch and his job as gong sounder and he still received his worker's rations. The echoes of his efforts had hardly ceased bouncing off the walls of Bilibid when the main gate which separated their building from the hospital compound opened and three Japanese trucks lumbered single file into the enclosure. They finally stopped in front of the main building just as the call to general formation was given.

"Jesus Christ," said Lonnie, "maybe we are going to get Red Cross packages."

"Fat chance," said Ross. "More likely they are going to ship some of us out to the work gangs. Let's get the hell into the back rows!"

They ambled around until the formations were becoming well-established, then moved toward the back to become a part of row ten. Gentry was already there, true to his often announced dictum that his every action was designed to minimize the chance of his ever having to do anything. Lonnie and Ross were glad to see him.

"What do you think, Gent? What's with the goddamn trucks?"

"I know already," said Gentry. "A guy just came back from the hospital compound and gave us the dope. There are Japanese winter uniforms on those trucks as you will soon see when you get one issued to you. We, my dear friends, are going on a little trip!"

Lonnie felt the fear. Not the dull foreboding which always hung in the background, but a sudden flare that dried the mouth and tied knots in guts and made eyes look funny, like they were staring at something far away. He saw the same fear in the eyes of Ross, and saw him moisten his lips.

[55]

"You're not kiddin' are you Gent?" Ross' voice was shaking a little. "You're right about the trip if Japanese winter uniforms really are under those tarpaulins. It's hot here in the Philippines but it's the 12th of December. Must be colder than hell in Japan."

"We'll soon know," said Lonnie. "Here comes Imada and his platform. I still say it's Red Cross packages," but his voice drifted as if he wasn't listening.

All of a sudden Major Imada was on the platform, making the announcement which all of them dreaded most. He spoke with unusual urgency and his typically impeccable English seemed slurred.

"The son-of-a-bitch is scared," thought Lonnie. "At least that's something."

"Tonight," announced Major Imada, "you will be issued warm clothing. A gift of the Japanese Empire. Yesterday in retaliation for the inhuman bombing of Tokyo and Nagoya, the Japanese Imperial Air Force bombed New York City, Washington, D.C., and Chicago. These cities are now in ruins. Remember that the Japanese Empire is not Santa Claus. Tonight you will receive warm clothes and tonight every man will receive workers's rations. Early in the morning every man will march to the docks and be placed on a ship. If you try to escape you will be shot."

He descended the platform, walked diagonally across the field with two of his junior officers and disappeared through the gate. Mr. Noda, the interpreter, now took up position on the platform and announced, "If you are big, go to truck number one; if you are middle sized, go to truck number two; and if you are little like me," he said laughing at his own joke, "go to truck number three."

None of the prisoners laughed; they remained at attention, frozen into desperate immobility. Guards began to shout, and the columns finally dissolved and a line formed before each of the three trucks. As each prisoner approached, a guard threw down the traditional uniform of the Japanese army. No hats or belts or shirts or underwear or shoes, just the coat and peg-legged trousers.

Lonnie and Ross, following the lead of Gentry, kept edging

toward the rear, hoping the Japanese would run out of clothes, feeling somehow that if they did, they might not have to go. But their time came at last; three sets of "middle sized" which turned out to be "little" coats and trousers. As the guard threw his coat and trousers down, Lonnie shouted up that he wanted a sword if he was going to be in the Japanese army, but the guard either didn't understand or didn't want to mess around. He just kept throwing down coats and trousers, as another guard made marks on a piece of paper.

The afternoon meal came late that day, not until six o'clock. Lonnie could hardly wait for the long line to move up to the black cauldrons which contained the rice and the fifty gallon drum which contained the soup. As he and Ross inched forward, he kept hearing the rhythmic click of the salmon can which the man on the food detail used to put the rice into each mess kit. Lonnie closed his eyes and counted the clicks. He figured he would have his rice after one hundred clicks, but he accidentally stepped on Gentry's bare heel with his wooden clog. Gentry didn't say anything but he caught Lonnie with his eyes closed. Lonnie felt like telling Gentry that he was counting and not praying, but he didn't know which would sound stupider. At last Gentry got his food: a full salmon can of rice, a tomato can of soup, a piece of fish, and, Lonnie couldn't believe it, two tablespoons of sugar. He felt faint and could hardly control the saliva which suddenly filled his mouth.

"Looks like our last meal is going to be a good one," he said, glancing at Ross behind him. "Give me a head," he begged and the man handing out the pieces of dried fish obligingly placed a desiccated fish head into his mess kit, right on top of the sugar.

Later that night when all of the men were in the building, there were a number of fashion shows with lots of hysterical laughter. Everybody agreed that Corso was the outstanding model. He stood before them with his Japanese trousers failing to circumnavigate his ponderous belly by at least six inches. Lonnie could see the dark thick mass of his pubic hair at the bottom of the triangle surmounted by the huge gut which moved as if it were inhabited by jumping creatures as Corso did a little dance. The overhead lights went out just then, but

[57]

Lonnie could still see the pubic hair gleaming in the light from the bulb above the stairway. Everybody applauded and Corso pranced back and forth like a happy bear.

"You've got an overhang like the cliffs of Dover," Father Maloney observed, and everyone howled with laughter. Corso stuck his belly out farther to emphasize his achievement, as indeed it was, considering that practically everybody else was on the verge of starvation. Lonnie once asked Ross how Corso could stay so fat while everyone else was so skinny. Ross figured it was the protein that Corso got from all the cocks he sucked, "one orgasm is like two teaspoons of blood," he confided to Lonnie, "so you can figure that old Corso is doing pretty good."

"You mean to say that every time anybody has an orgasm they lose the equivalent of two teaspoons of blood?" asked Lonnie suddenly interested.

"That's right, at least that's what my uncle told me. He's a veterinarian in Spartanburg, South Carolina. You better quit beating your meat so much, the way I figure it, you only have about a hundred times worth left."

"Shit on you," said Lonnie.

He turned now to look at Corso and the layers of fat which caressed one another as he sat down. Lonnie felt it was all pretty ridiculous but thought maybe it could be true. He decided to ask Rutledge about it.

His thoughts were interrupted by somebody shouting at him. It was R. T. Barton. "Hey Lonnie, how about lighting up one of those candles of yours. Let's live it up. Be merry, for tomorrow we will probably die. I wouldn't mind it if there was a little eat and drink. But we just got the merry and the dying. I'd even settle for a little pussy to eat. You know me, I got a magic tongue." He stuck out his tongue and wagged it at Lonnie. "Shit you know what women really like; a good tongue job, that's what they like."

"Well if they liked a big mouth, you would certainly be popular," said Gentry as he moved into the group. "But do light up one of your candles, Lonnie. Let it burn at both ends and even though it may not last the night, it will warm us for a little while. Don't forget that it is better to light a candle than to curse the darkness. Isn't that so Father Maloney?"

Father Maloney looked up from where he was sitting on Lonnie's blanket and smiled at Gentry. "Still looking for an argument I see Gentry."

"I don't think so, Father," Gentry said as Lonnie placed his next to last candle in a pool of melted wax on the bare floor. "I may be looking for security. I have always wondered why so many of my friends, and particularly on this night I place you in this category, are ministers of this or that gospel. The terrors that I feel right now at having to face tomorrow give me knowledge. If perchance the darkness is not total on the other side but has within it some strange dream which hurts, I know that all of you good people will come to my defense. Even now I can hear your many voices pleading in unison from your happy places there on the right hand, 'Don't burn him so much; he's actually a good guy; he was only kidding.' "

Father Maloney laughed almost gaily and those around the candle glare marveled that he could, and admired his strong teeth and the way his eyes danced. He looked so young then, a boy of mischief.

"So now we know," he said looking at the others in the light. "I thought I was a friend and now I find that I'm just a fire insurance policy. But you can depend on me, Gentry, to say a few good words for you. As a matter of fact I have already said quite a number in your behalf and also for the rest of you." He glanced around the faces disembodied by the darkness, faces that shone in the candle glow. Faces with brave eyes, Lonnie thought, and suddenly he was proud to be with them sharing this strange thing. What a bunch of bastards.

"Oh bullshit, Father," said Gentry good naturedly. "Keep your prayers for the bad guys like Lonnie and Corso and R. T. Barton. Seriously, Father," and Gentry's pale face seemed even paler yet there in the flickering light, "what do you think of our chances?"

A complete silence settled over the group, with all eyes turned to the Father. Even R. T. Barton looked serious and Corso sat brooding over his large belly.

"We have fairly accurate information that the last prison ship which left Manila got only a hundred miles before the Americans sank it," the Father answered quietly. "Only sixty men survived. Since that time the frequency and magnitude of the bombings have increased. So I'm afraid we are in for a bad time. Now I want to offer a small prayer for our safety." He looked at Gentry, almost imploringly Lonnie thought. But Gentry nodded and seemed to bow his head. As the Father prayed some of the men looked down in semblance of piety while others looked away in quiet embarrassment.

"Oh, Dear Jesus, intercede with Thy Father, the Creator and Destroyer of universes and the reservoir of all power and love, help us in this our hour of great trial. Help us to understand that human tragedy and disappointment arise from our limited vision and that a broader view would transform even the most hideous predicament into a meaningful part of a larger plan. Use this circumstance of hazard as a condition for reinspiring in those who have lost direction a desire to reaffirm the truth of your life and sacrifice. Amen."

Lonnie repeated the amen and was astonished to hear a number of the others give like emphasis to the prayer. He even thought he saw Corso's lips moving in silent response. But Gentry did not join in this affirmation; he sat there in the circle of light, his face livid.

"Jesus Christ, Father, how can you use this situation, this crazy, fucked up, phony, meaningless situation as a platform from which to mouth your verities. There is a damn fine chance that all of us will be dead by tomorrow night and there you are, putting out the same old crap that has clouded the vision of men for two thousand years. I know I may die tomorrow but at least let me die without the indignity of a lot of bullshit. You don't really think that ignorant Jewish carpenter was the son of the creator and destroyer of universes. You can't really believe that there is a deity who gives a shit about us and who had the power who would let humans get into this stupid predicament. And surely you can't believe that your puny little prayer would make any difference if He did. And that crap about all the pain and terror and death becoming reasonable and bright if viewed in terms of the larger plan. I know of a three-year-old girl who died slowly and terribly at the bottom of an old well and of a mother who kept calling to her child for three days before they finally dug her out dead. How in the hell is the agony and terror and loneliness of that small being going to be shined up, justified and colored beautiful?

"And here is another thing. Don't you know that there isn't a human being alive who wouldn't be transformed and his entire life and energy dedicated to any god he could be sure existed and who needed him and cared about him? If this god of yours has all the power and knowledge and love which you people have been proclaiming, why doesn't he make himself known in a manner which he would know how to make convincing instead of indulging in all of this circumlocution and gobbledygook? As vulnerable, as weak, and as transitory as we are, don't you think we wouldn't all come running? You know damn well we would. But you people keep it up, trying to drive us into your idiotic preconceptions either with the carrot of a childish heaven or a whiplash of an equally infantile hell."

"For Christ's sake," broke in R. T. Barton, "what in the hell is wrong with you? All Father Maloney did was offer a little prayer for us and you start talking like a God damn maniac. You got anything better than some prayers to offer right now? You think that great big piss brain of yours is going to do you any good in a mess like this?"

"Yeah, think yourself out of this one, bright boy!" said Corso. His voice was low and angry. "Don't pay any attention to the son-of-a-bitch, Father. He's a mean bastard and if you say the word, I'll kick the shit out of him."

"That would be a fine way to emphasize that we feared the possibility that he might be correct," said Father Maloney. His voice was surprisingly strong and forceful. Lonnie looked directly at him now and instead of a face ashen with anger, he saw the fine features of the priest fixed in resolve, his eyes shifting from face to face as if spoiling for the battle.

"How can you take from these men the small security of a simple prayer? We may die tomorrow and it is in such times that man needs God rather than some cynical and pessimistic evaluation. You, Gentry, like so many men, are filled with high elocution and fine logic, some of which might work in an intellectualized world where there are never any problems. My position has arisen out of the universal condition of man's

[61]

suffering and death, out of his fear of annihilation, out of his
terror of becoming nothing. And though I hope such an
eventuality may not come to pass, I'll wager that in the throes
of death, Dear Gentry, you will find a new appreciation of
Christ and His sacrifice."

"Dammit Father, there you go again," Gentry spoke now in
a calm voice. The color had returned to his face, but there was
still a furious intensity about him. "The people of your
persuasion can't seem to realize that truth is not necessarily
tied to strength of belief, or that something is not necessarily
false simply because its contemplation is hideous. Hell, I know
we may die tomorrow. Am I afraid? I'm so yellow that I have
a perpetual case of diarrhea. Every time I think of these
fingers and arms and legs being shattered," and he looked at
these members in mock affection, "or immobile in the sweaty
posturings of death, the scream which I keep imprisoned in my
brain starts breaking through the bars. Do I ever have the
urge to call to SOMEBODY, EVERYBODY, ANYBODY for
help? Sure I do. Every time I think of Gentry NOTHING,
NULL, ZERO, I have to keep swallowing to keep all of those
prayerful platitudes which I mouthed so faithfully as a child
from leaping unbidden to my tongue. THOUGH I WALK
THROUGH THE VALLEY OF THE SHADOW OF
DEATH, PROTECT ME IN THE HOUR OF MY
DEATH, HUMPTY DUMPTY SAT ON A WALL. Yes, I
know that I may die tomorrow, and I *am* afraid. Under the
misery of a high fever, a shattered body, or a cataclysmic fear I
may cry out to those lost saints of mine; you see, I was a
Catholic once. But I say here now, and all of you in the light of
Lonnie's candle can be my witnesses, that if a demented brain
drives me to mouth such drivel, I abrogate it now before the
fact. I am more capable now of knowing what is truth for me
than I shall be when I am driven to the verge of death. There
may be no atheists in fox holes, but there are no sane men
either! But I'll take your wager, Father. I don't think illusion
is any more necessary in death than it is in life. So all of you
guys watch me: if you see my lips moving suspiciously or if you
detect little implicit crossing movements when things get
tough, then give me a kick in the ass. I'm sure I can depend on
a number of you to perform that office. Corso wouldn't mind

right now and R. T. Barton would help, and Ross too. Lonnie, in the vast wisdom of his simplicity, is too involved in being real for nonsense such as this."

"Like hell I am," laughed Lonnie, relieved that the tension had dissipated. "If I hear you say even one 'Hail Mary,' you are going to get one hell of an ass kicking." He looked around the circle for appreciation, but none of the others were smiling. Ross was fiddling with his clog strap, R. T. Barton straightened the candle and reset it in some newly melted wax, the somber eyes of Corso darted back and forth between Gentry and Father Maloney who was deadly serious as he spoke.

"Gentry, I sometimes wonder why I endure you. I despise your callous pessimism. I abhor the manner in which you run rough shod over the ideals and values of other people. Your faith in the truth of your own observations is boundless. You sir," and his voice held a passion which was all the more evident because of its quietness, "are true anti-Christ. You represent everything which every fiber in my being must reject. You are beyond redemption which in itself is bad enough, but your every word is designed to mislead, to corrupt and to betray. I have been trained to be tolerant and I have tried, but this is enough." And now his voice rose, and Lonnie could see that many others beyond the lighted circle had moved closer to listen. "I despise your ideas and now let me admit it, may God forgive me, I despise you as a person." His voice was shaking now. He stood up, his eyes dimming with tears, his voice ragged and hoarse. "And I think I despise you most because in making me despise you, you have made me less a Christian and more an animal like yourself."

With this comment, he turned out of the circle of light and disappeared into the darkness. Lonnie kept looking in that direction, hoping he would suddenly see his face again with the anger washed away, smiling. But he didn't come back, and the men sat there in their circle, silent and strangely afraid. Even Gentry seemed apprehensive. Lonnie coughed and Gentry's head jerked in his direction. R. T. Barton finally broke the silence with a half-cackling laugh which was meant to be humorous but failed.

"Well, you've lost one of your go-betweens, Gentry. You're

sure to go to hell now with the good Father urging the powers to send you in that direction. You deserve it, of course. I keep telling people that if you don't quit corrupting the morals of young people like me and Lonnie, you are going to really get yours. You should help the young solve their problems the way Corso does and then you'd get the pie rather than the fry, bye and bye."

"Shut up, you big mouthed cunteater," Corso's voice started quietly and then rose to a shout as he ended the sentence. "And as for you, you son-of-a-bitch," he turned his baleful glare on Gentry, "I've been waiting to punch that smirky mouth of yours for a long time and by God I'm going to do it!" He had risen on his haunches, and now he launched himself across the candle directly at Gentry. Gentry tried to dodge, but was too late; he was suddenly engulfed by the heavy sweaty body, borne violently over backwards until his head struck the cement floor. Then both Ross and Lonnie were on Corso's back, trying to pull him off, while R. T. Barton rescued the candle and held it high to illuminate the shattered remnants of the friendly circle. Three or four bystanders rushed in and pulled Corso, still cursing, into the darkness. Lonnie helped Gentry up and saw blood dripping down his chin from a cut in his upper lip. He was deathly pale and to Lonnie's horror, began to cry, heavy sobs which immediately turned to heaves as he started to vomit in his old denim hat.

Suddenly Lonnie was on his feet, screaming, "Get out of here, you sons-of-bitches, all of you, get the hell out of here." He turned and grabbed the candle out of R. T. Barton's hand and snuffed it out, and the darkness, except for the small light above the stairway, covered everything.

Lonnie and Ross sat for a long time without speaking. They watched the dim light over the stairway seem to get brighter and brighter. Finally Lonnie said, "Well, Gent, I guess we better hit the old blanket, big day tomorrow." There was no response, Gentry had gone back to his own place. Lonnie heard Ross arranging his blanket so he unrolled his own, then decided to make his evening pilgrimage. He enjoyed the sound of his clogs clacking against his heels as he made his way to the latrine. It was a sixteen-holer, but no one else was there. He chose the eighth hole, the one under the small bulb and sat there unmindful of the hideous stench which engulfed him.

Then he took THE PICTURE out of a blue denim pouch he had made for precious things. He unfolded it carefully, it was coming apart at a number of creases, a page from an old *Life* magazine showing a girl who had just fallen on the ice while skating. Her long graceful legs were wide apart and Lonnie could see the bulge of her vaginal mound through the scanty briefs. He could feel an erection growing, but looked up to see one of the guards observing him from the stairway. He hurriedly put the picture away, his erection dwindling. Another guy was coming toward the latrine now anyway. On the way back into the building the door guard gave him butts, almost half a cigarette. He took a short drag, cupped the rest of it in his hand and made his way up the two sets of stairs to the third floor. He knew about where Gentry's place was and finally found him, huddled under an old piece of straw matting, barely visible. Lonnie waited for a moment, suddenly afraid but reached out and touched Gentry on the shoulder.

"Have a drag, Gent, I just got it from the guard, it's one of their good ones." There was no sound, but Lonnie was gratified to feel Gentry's hand touch his arm. Lonnie took a drag and in the drag light saw Gentry's pale face. He handed him the cigarette, saw it flare up as Gentry took a heavy drag, then another.

"Thanks, Lonnie, goodnight," he handed Lonnie back the butt which was almost finished now.

"Goodnight, Gent."

Ross was asleep when he got back to his place. It was just as well because the butt was already gone. He lay down on his blanket, thought about Gentry and Father Maloney and about dying. Then he thought about THE PICTURE and could feel his erection growing again. His right hand found his penis, began to caress it. He could see THE PICTURE more clearly now, particularly the area of the bulge. It got clearer as the tempo increased and for a moment seemed etched in spangles, warm and accommodating. Then there was the wet hand and the smell of hot semen. He hoped Ross was still asleep. Then he began to think about losing two teaspoons of blood, just before he went to sleep.

CHAPTER THREE

As if no time had passed, Colonel Nelson's gong was sounding and the Japanese guards were shouting, *"Kisho, kisho"* at each of the stairways. Lonnie was having a fine dream, undulating through billowing, swirling, mists with his LIFE WOMAN when the noise started and now she went spinning away becoming smaller and vaguer to be replaced by clacking mess kits, the muffled curses of hundreds of men, and the fear. He looked up from the blanket to see Ross observing him, on his face a peculiar mixture of annoyance and anxiety. He already had his blanket rolled up and was standing above Lonnie fiddling with his mess gear.

"What the hell you still doing in the sack? We're going to get the 'outside' in about two minutes and there you are still nursing a hard on."

"Shit on you," said Lonnie. But he got up rapidly, put his Japanese uniform, which he had been using for a pillow, inside his blanket and rolled it up. The gong sounded "outside" just as he adjusted his G-string and slipped on his clogs. He and Ross joined the men now funneling into the stairway. Lonnie looked for Gentry and couldn't find him, but he saw Corso moving down the stairs ahead of them. He walked regally within the little cocoon of space the other men always made for him, regardless of the crowding. At the turn in the stairway he glanced up to catch Lonnie's eye. He grinned and waved his hand, but Lonnie quickly looked away.

"The son-of-a-bitch," Lonnie muttered.

"Who are you picking on now?" asked Ross.

"Nobody, why should I pick on anybody? Hey Ross, you know that rock in the northeast corner of the compound? You know, near where we usually sit to have our cigarette? It must weigh about fifty pounds. If somebody had a broken leg, the Japs wouldn't send him. How could they send a guy with a broken leg?"

"I guess you're right," said Ross. "I've been thinking about the same thing. One clonk by that rock and a guy would wind up in the hospital compound for the duration."

"Yes, but if the Japs caught you doing it, they would shoot your ass off. Right?"

"Right!"

Lonnie started to say something else, but was interrupted by a peculiar gasp from Ross. And then he saw them too, through the doorway the lights of the compound were burning brightly. It was still dark out.

"Jesus Christ, we are going on that trip today. Why else would we be getting up at this hour? It can't be more than four o'clock."

The men straggled down the main steps of the building, blinking at each other in the strange light. There was an unusual quietness, even the mess gear seemed muffled, and the clattering of clogs. The moon still hung big and yellow over the west wall and the faint rays of a beginning dawn turned the east wall into a dark outline against the paler sky.

As they made the innumerable starts and stops which always mark the pace of feeding armies, Lonnie could see THE ROCK become perceptible as the dawn leaned more heavily over the eastern wall. It seemed almost insignificant, hunched there next to a pile of rubble, a small lump of gray indiscriminant matter, becoming clearer and clearer as they inched along.

They were within a few yards of the cooking pots when one of the men ahead of them suddenly threw the food he had just received high into the air. Lonnie watched with astonishment as it went up and saw the spinning mess kit glint momentarily in the first rays of the new sun. He watched with more astonishment as Corso moving with startling agility—a synchrony of muscle and fat—neatly fielded a large blob of watery rice just before it reached the ground. He was immensely pleased with himself and stood there grinning for a moment, poised, his mess kit held immobile in his outstretched hand, as if expecting applause. But none came, everybody was looking at old Ledrosa, the one who had thrown the food in the first place. He was running and leaping and whirling and uttering strange guttural noises. R. T. Barton observed later that he sounded just like an Eskimo strangling on a piece of blubber.

Lonnie knew old Ledrosa. Everybody did and everybody agreed that he was crazy. Didn't he pick the cobra up by the tail? Who but a crazy man would do that? Lonnie could still see the pulling match which took place under that little bridge. It was a long time ago, before he had met Ross, when the Japanese used the Americans on road gangs. Anyway, there was old Ledrosa pulling and screaming bloody murder and there was the cobra trying to get into a hole among the rocks. Old Ledrosa won the match. The snake suddenly let go and old Ledrosa, with the cobra still held firmly in his grasp, fell over backwards in the muddy creek bed. He rose from the mud to display his prize which by this time was putting on a display of its own. Its hood was spread at least six inches and for a moment it charmed all observers with its darting tongue and undulating head which had risen on the arching body until it was as high as old Ledrosa's. As R. T. Barton said, "It looked like old Ledrosa was holding a large curved black stick with a devil's head on it." The charm lasted a few seconds, then prisoners and guards alike fell over each other getting out of the way. None too soon. Ledrosa began to whirl around and around, faster and faster. When he was almost a blur of motion, at least so it seemed to Lonnie who was watching from the bridge, he cast the cobra into the middle of the largest group. There was another panic stricken scramble, the snake escaped into a banana grove, and old Ledrosa got another beating from the Japanese corporal. But everybody could see that the corporal wasn't hitting him very hard.

There was that other time when old Ledrosa found the

heavy black frames for a pair of glasses; no lenses, just the frames. He started wearing them around and practicing sticking his front teeth out and making gibberish sounds which sounded exactly like Japanese. Some people thought old Ledrosa believed he was one. He looked just like Lieutenant Iwahara during one of his bad days. One morning at count, Ledrosa was in the front row as Lieutenant Iwahara went down the line checking the columns. Suddenly there was confrontation. Two sets of dark eyes peering through identical frames, except the Lieutenant's frames were filled by thick lenses, took scrutiny of one another. The Lieutenant stopped short. He placed his forefinger first through one and then the other of the holes in the frames and then after a gently muttered, "Ah, so," hit old Ledrosa so hard the frames went sailing over ten columns of men and surprised a guard at the rear of the formation.

And then there was the time that Lonnie himself was involved. He was on the same honey brigade with old Ledrosa, back at Cabanatuan. He recalled how two men had to carry a five gallon can slung on a pole between them, filled to the brim with its precious cargo. And how somebody had to pour a small can full of honey on each plant. There were three men to a detail, two carriers and one dipper. Lonnie preferred being dipper, it was less work and the carrying pole always hurt his shoulders. But the worst job of all was honey badger. Somebody had to get down into the old latrine hole and fill the five gallon cans as the details brought back the empties. The guard usually gave Ledrosa the job of honey badger and Lonnie could still see him standing there in the muck and flies and stench and hundred degree heat, laughing as he filled the empties and steadied them as the men on top pulled them up. After two rows of onions and one of okra had been finished, and it was getting close to noon, old Ledrosa started showing the effects of being honey badger. He leaned against the side of the latrine hole as Lonnie handed him down the bucket and didn't help with it when they pulled it out.

Then Lonnie couldn't stand it any more. He looked down at Ledrosa, up to his knees in the murky solution and said, "Hey Ledrosa, how about letting me be honey badger for a while?"

Ledrosa's shoulders suddenly straightened and he shouted up at Lonnie, "To hell with you, you fuckhead, do you think I'm going to take any shit from you?"

Within a day everyone knew the story, even the Japanese guards were laughing about it. Lonnie felt famous and was pleased when people he hardly knew kept asking him if he had taken any shit from anybody lately. Everybody admired old Ledrosa, but from afar, because he insisted on keeping his job as head honey badger right up until the day they left Cabanatuan. And here he was now screaming and whirling and making rattling sounds. A lot of people gathered around him, a circle of interested observers. As old Ledrosa would whirl toward the edge of the circle, it would bulge outwards and then give in again as he moved back toward the center. Finally, he gave one last leap in the air, released a maniacal scream and fell to the ground, writhing.

The circle suddenly parted and Lieutenant Iwahara walked up to the prostrate Ledrosa, his sword clacking. He gazed down at the stricken man whose body now was being racked by a series of jerks and twitches and made the following announcement: "This man goddamn goldbrick. He make a big game. I have test to see if he sick. I count ten. If he still on ground making like crazy man when I count ten, I cut off his head."

He took out his sword and held it poised in both hands above old Ledrosa and suddenly the circle around the drama widened perceptibly. The Lieutenant began to count in a loud, shrill voice, *"Ichi, ni, san, shi, go."* But the longer he counted, the slower he got as he watched the convulsions increase in magnitude. Lonnie could see flecks of blood on old Ledrosa's lips and in the corner of his mouth and his eyes were rolled back in his head so far only the whites showed. It was as eerie as hell.

"roku, . . . shichi,. . . . hachi..........kyu............" Lieutenant Iwahara hesitated and glanced around the group which by now had increased to three or four hundred interested spectators. A few enterprising individuals had climbed the only tree in the compound and a large number was congregated on the main stairway of the building in order to have a

better view. Some of the Japanese guards had climbed the cement posts which held the main gate between the two compounds and were watching in fascination. Suddenly Lieutenant Iwahara began to kick Ledrosa and to scream, "Get up, you crazy man, you want to die? You want to die? You crazy!"

Then he stopped the kicking and the screaming, and stood for a long moment looking down at the form of Ledrosa which now was strangely still. Finally he placed his sword back in its scabbard, turned both hands outward in a small gesture of appeal and walked through the circle of men into the hospital compound. Old Ledrosa kept lying there as quiet as a dead man. And he looked like one too when they brought a stretcher and took him through the gate, but Lonnie who had looked closely could see that he was breathing.

Everyone got a full salmon tin of rice, three tablespoons of brown sugar and a piece of smoked fish for breakfast that morning. Just after Lonnie and Ross had finished eating the Colonel's gong sounded again. This time for general formation.

Sixteen hundred and eighteen men lined up in columns ten deep. First the count and the check for empty spaces. Everyone was present except old Ledrosa. Then Major Imada's platform was brought to the center of the compound and four chairs were placed on it. The Major walked up the steps first, followed by Lieutenant Iwahara. Then Colonel Watson, looking like a scarecrow in his Filipino jacket and shorts, ascended the platform. Finally, to Lonnie's surprise, Father Maloney took the fourth chair. He seemed abstracted and his eyes kept searching, or at least so it seemed to Lonnie, through the columns of men.

"Father Maloney looks pretty good, doesn't he?" Ross whispered to Lonnie. They were about eight rows back and could see the four men on the platform clearly.

"Yeah, hardly shows the marks of the great battle," agreed Lonnie. "Wish we could say the same for old Gentry."

Colonel Watson made the first speech. His voice trembled like an old man's, and he looked like one even though he couldn't have been more than fifty.

"We are going to leave Bilibid this morning. I have been

[72]

told by Major Imada that we are to be taken by ship to Japan. I know that all of you are afraid of being bombed by the Americans so I have asked Major Imada to see if the Japanese authorities will allow us to place a large P.O.W. sign both on the aft and fore sections of the ship. . . ."

He was interrupted by a roar from the columns of men. A collective gasp of relief, an audible reduction in tension which quieted almost immediately as the Colonel continued.

"Major Imada has promised to give a response to this request this morning. I would like to say this to you. Whatever the decision of the Japanese authorities may be, I know that you are all brave men." His voice lost its quaver and a semblance of the authority and pride which he had once known as an American Army commander seemed to return. He did not appear ridiculous now in his frayed jacket and Filipino shorts, and even Lonnie could feel himself standing a little straighter, a little prouder.

"I know that you will behave as American soldiers and officers. Remember this, whether you are courageous or whether you are cowardly cannot possibly alter what will happen to us on this voyage, so," and now his voice rose, "since being a coward cannot possibly help, let us be brave men."

Lonnie thought the Colonel looked like a brave man standing there with the morning sun glinting in his grey hair, his eyes scanning the hundreds of hope-filled faces. And Lonnie felt braver too, and so did all the other men.

Major Imada rose to speak. Almost six feet tall, his black hair and dark eyes made his pale face seem paler yet.

"Jesus Christ," thought Lonnie, "that Jap sure is a handsome bastard."

"The exception which proves the stereotype," whispered Ross, as if reading Lonnie's thoughts.

The morning sun glanced off the ornaments in Major Imada's sword and cast light flashes into the dark corners of the east wall. He seemed pensive, almost disinterested as his gaze took in the ragged columns. When he spoke, his English flawless, there was an edge of tenseness in his voice which caused a surge of fear in Lonnie.

"Now we are going to begin our voyage. If we die, we die

[73]

together and we die with honor. I am an officer of the
Japanese Empire, a soldier of the Emperor. I may die but I
will not hide like a coward under a coward's banner. You, all
of you," his dark eyes swept the columns which seemed wilted
now, burdened by a doom, "have shown your cowardice by
becoming prisoners of war. I cannot believe that you can wish
to be cowards twice. There will be thousands of Japanese
women and children on our ship. Whatever happens you will
not hear the women moaning nor the children crying. Perhaps
you will not moan or cry." He paused now for a long moment,
his immobile face, the way he stood, his gently swinging sword
and his piercing eyes conjoining to signify the full measure of
his contempt. "And now," he continued, glancing toward
Father Maloney, "one of your priests will try to bring your
God to your defense. Do you think he can help you? We shall
see." With one last look over the defeated columns, he
descended the steps from the platform and walked toward the
gate. His every step could be heard, rhythmic crunching
sounds, and his sword clicked at his side.

Just as he was disappearing through the gate, somebody,
Lonnie was sure that it was Gentry, said in a voice which was
studied in its pathos, "Pardon me while I vomit."

The statement hung there in the silence, reverberating,
seeming not to end. There was a ripple of laughter through the
stunned columns. And suddenly there they were, sixteen
hundred and eighteen men laughing like crazy. Lonnie stood
with the tears running down his cheeks, and Ross beside him
was laughing like a maniac.

"Did you hear that goddamn Gentry?" howled Lonnie.
" 'Pardon me while I vomit,' Jesus Christ, did you hear that?"
His body was wracked with new gales of laughter, and he
leaned down and blew his nose on the flap of his G-string.

Then suddenly the columns were quiet again punctuated by
a few ripples of laughter which trickled away until the silence
was complete, even more complete than it had been. Lonnie
kept hoping somebody would say something so they could
laugh, but nobody did. Father Maloney stood up and
contemplated the men, his face was strangely joyful, his voice
clear and steady.

[74]

"Never have I been so proud to be a human being or to be God's man. In a moment of bleakness and despair, God has come to us in the guise of laughter. Truly He is with us though we walk through the valley and the shadow. With God's gift of laughter, we have washed the doom away. With God's gift of laughter we have cancelled the contempt of our captors and recaptured the courage to be the kind of American soldiers our people would be proud of." He paused momentarily to glance at Lieutenant Iwahara who was still looking at the men, his face fixed in astonishment. "By refusing the protection of the banners and thus placing not only us and themselves in jeopardy, but their women and children, our hosts demonstrate the callous and insensible character of their cause. By placing a dubious point of honor above the welfare of people they demonstrate the insanity of a position which can place a strange distorted pride above human concern. . . ."

At this moment, while Father Maloney's head turned slightly toward another section of the assembled prisoners, Lieutenant Iwahara sprang from his seat and struck the priest sharply across the face. Lonnie had noticed Lieutenant Iwahara leaning down to ask Mr. Noda something, and had seen him listening to Mr. Noda as Father Maloney spoke. The Lieutenant drew his hand back to hit Father Maloney again but it remained there outstretched, stricken into immobility by the volume of sound which suddenly struck him. An ominous roar from the men filled the compound and some of the columns suddenly moved towards the platform. At that moment a large number of Japanese guards came charging through the gate screaming *"kiotska, kiotska! Attention, attention!"* They ran between the columns of men and the platform and formed a circle around it, their bayonests ready. But Lieutenant Iwahara did not hit Father Maloney again. Instead, with fists clenched and pounding the air, he went into a kind of up and down tantrum dance and screeched.

"You priest, you supposed to pray! Priest no make crazy talk! Priest supposed to pray! Now you pray. Goddammit, everybody pray!"

"Very well," agreed Father Maloney. Slowly and with dignity he raised his hand and the men quieted and moved back to their places. Lieutenant Iwahara's blow had left a red splotchy area on his right cheek but when he smiled nobody noticed it.

"Let us repeat the Lord's Prayer," he said. And they did, as the Father kept his hand upraised and as the Japanese guards and Lieutenant Iwahara looked on with a mixture of bewilderment and contempt. Lonnie didn't pay attention to the words. He was listening to the peculiar rise and fall of the many voices and thinking about vomiting. Now he actually felt like it himself.

Then Mr. Noda was on the platform, grinning as usual.

"Okay you guys, no more fun today. You have thirty minutes before march. Go fill your canteens. Roll up your blanket. Don't forget your new uniforms. Good luck, you guys. I almost forgot," he said grinning even more broadly, "don't forget to go *benjo*, okay!, okay! You are dismissed now." He stepped down from the platform and walked with Lieutenant Iwahara, who was not grinning, toward the gate.

CHAPTER FOUR

On the morning of December 13, 1944, the gates of Bilibid prison were opened for the exodus. Lonnie and Ross were at the very end of the long column. They had waited behind the stairway in the large building hoping that something, anything, might happen, some miracle which would cut off the column and leave them stranded. But nothing happened. The guards who made a final check of the building found them with about thirty others with the same half crazy hope, and herded them out. After the count the column began to move, slowly at first as the front section stretched out like an accordion and then faster and faster as the men in the back almost ran to catch up, "to suck up the slack," as they always said.

As Lonnie went through the gate into the hospital compound, he turned to get a last look at THE ROCK still hunkered down next to the north wall. A flash of fear came then, like a flare going off in his chest, and a knowledge came that the path was fixed, the options gone; the fear welled bitter in his mouth and glistened on his forehead. He patted the blue denim bag with his LIFE WOMAN in it and turned to catch a glimpse of Ross walking directly behind him in the line. He noticed they were in the hospital compound and started looking for old Ledrosa among the prisoners who stared quietly at them from the doorways and windows. He thought he saw him looking from one of the windows in the lock-up section, but wasn't sure. Ahead of him he could see the column disappearing through the main gate, and then as if he were programmed into some crazy kind of moving belt, the great gate in the grey wall grew larger and larger until he passed through it, and Bilibid was gone.

Suddenly they were in the streets of Manila walking over damp cobblestones which glistened in the morning sun. The streets were almost deserted. But Lonnie observed one Filipino putting up posters. He had his back turned but every now and then he would glance at the column. Just as Lonnie went by him, he put his arm down between his legs and made the victory sign. Even though it was up-side-down, Lonnie got the message and was suddenly filled with optimism.

"See that Filipino?" he whispered over his shoulder to Ross. "He's an American spy."

"How in the hell do you know that?" queried Ross, his voice hopeful.

"I saw him make the victory sign. He's a spy all right. He'll tell the Americans. Shit, they probably know all about us and our trip, right now. We don't have to worry, they wouldn't bomb a ship with us on it, would they?"

"I hope you're right, but you know as well as I do that there isn't one Filipino in the Islands who doesn't want us to win the war. So I wouldn't put too much importance on that victory sign, if it was one. I saw it too, and he could just have been scratching his balls."

"Shit on you," said Lonnie.

Just ahead of them, a young American officer dropped out of the line and hurriedly began to remove a pair of shoes. To Lonnie's amazement, he was dressed in what appeared to be a new khaki uniform complete with a gleaming set of captain's bars. When Lonnie saw his shoes, he couldn't believe it. They were a rich golden brown, the product of fine leather and the outcome of much polishing. One of the Japanese guards waited patiently until the captain had removed the unaccustomed shoes and then put him back into the column only a few feet ahead of Lonnie and Ross. Lonnie couldn't take his eyes off the shoes. The captain had tied the strings together and carried them over his shoulder where they swung in cadence with his steps. Lonnie's eyes followed their rhythmic movement as he walked along.

The long column moved on, an army of skinny men, dressed in G-strings and the odds and ends of old uniforms, American and Filipino. The newly issued Japanese uniforms were carried in bundles or wrapped up in blankets. It was too hot for them. Some of the men whistled as they marched along and a few of them sang, but it was the song children sometimes sing on a dark night. Every now and then the men in a small segment of the column would unconsciously march in step for a few minutes, their bare feet striking the pavement making a curious rhythmic rasping sound. Clogs had either been discarded or were being carried; they were no good for marching.

On each side of the street numerous posters were pasted on the sides of buildings and on store windows. One in particular drew Lonnie's attention away from the shoes. It showed a Filipino woman holding a dead child in her arms, in the background a jumbled wreck of buildings. At the top of the poster was written: "Arise Fellow Asiatics and Repel the Bloody Invader." On other posters, Japanese and Filipinos were shown working in cooperation and apparent friendship. Many of the posters hung in shreds but Lonnie could make out the slogans as he marched along: "Asia for the Asiatics," "The Filipinos are an Integral Part of the Co-prosperity Sphre."

Another flare burst in Lonnie's chest! He saw where bullets had thrust harsh fingers into the pavement and into the sides of buildings. Here and there (and the flare burned more intensely) bomb holes had been crudely patched, but in a few places they were still raw, untreated wounds in the buildings and in the pavement.

They were nearing the waterfront now. Lennie could smell the musty odor of rotting wood, and the bloodlike odor of rusting iron. This part of the city seemed deserted; only the sound of padding bare feet and dull murmuring intermingled with an occasional shout from a guard. The men in front of Lonnie became very quiet and started throwing guarded glances toward their left. Suddenly there was a break between

[79]

the buildings and Lonnie could see the water for a moment, just before another building obscured his view. In that moment he saw ships starkly etched against the calm water of the bay. Some of them lay on their sides, others had completely overturned, and further out, nothing but a smokestack remained in sight.

"Jesus Christ, did you see that?" he said in an incredulous voice to Ross. "Did you see that?"

"Yeah, I saw it!" Ross answered, and Lonnie thought he heard a catch in his voice.

Then they had a prolonged view of the bay. As far as they could see, ships silent and unmoving, a tableau of jumbled iron set at odd angles, cluttered the water. Lonnie felt pride then and his voice choked.

"The yellow bastards are getting it. Look at that! Look at that! That'll teach the bastards what happens when they try to kick Uncle Sam around."

"Trouble is," said Ross, "we may get taught the same lesson!"

Lonnie didn't say anything. The flare had burst again even more brightly as he heard the sound of airplanes. The column began to move erratically as men searched the sky. Then they saw them, two antiquated Japanese sea planes flying at low altitude over the city.

"There goes our Air Force," whispered Ross.

"Yeah, some Air Force. They'll last about two seconds when the big boys come."

The planes moved away toward the southwest, getting smaller and smaller until they were lost among small hills. The column plodded on, each moment bringing new views of the harbor and destruction of ships and buildings. Lonnie could see the men toward the head of the long line entering a huge barn-like structure which stood on one of the many piers lining the Manila water front. It was a long low building which jutted out far enough to allow two or three ships to come in at the same time. As Lonnie entered through the broad door he saw that large sections of the roof had caved in where bombs had struck. Where the roof was relatively intact countless bullet holes let the light through, like stars shining.

Many of the holes had probably been made by the Japanese themselves when they invaded Manila in 1942 because rust had widened them a great deal. The building was almost empty, except for the entering prisoners. On one side two Japanese soldiers were guarding a small pile of bags; on the other a few fifty gallon drums lay on their sides against the wall, rusting. Bits of old machinery were strewn here and there. Down the length of the building the men were spreading and converging as they found places to lie down or to play cards. The Japanese guards had disappeared, probably no danger of anybody escaping, Lonnie thought, where in the hell could they go?

"Hurry up and wait," observed Ross. "I'll bet that principle applies to every army in the world or that ever existed."

"Suits me," said Lonnie. "The sooner we get on some ship the sooner we are going to get our asses bombed off." He kept looking for Gentry but couldn't see him any place. He thought he heard Corso's voice above the general drone of conversations which ebbed away to leave quiet pools of apprehension each time the sound of an engine seeped into the building from the outside. He listened carefully, but couldn't be sure, probably some other big-mouthed queer, the son-of-a-bitch!

Ross nudged him and he followed his glance to the large side door. Conversations died and all eyes followed the different sections of a large ship moving soundlessly before the opening. Even as they watched small reverberations could be felt through the building as the ship nudged the pier and finally came to rest. After a few minutes they saw three Japanese in sailor uniforms place a gangplank from the ship to the cement dock. Then in the distance a new sound could be heard, a rustling like the wings of insects, low murmuring, and a muted clattering. The sounds grew louder, and a straggling line of Japanese women and children came into view. To Lonnie's astonishment the women were dressed in gay clothing covered with embroidery work, flowers and birds and dragons and their black hair shone.

"Look at those crazy women," he said to Ross. "What in the hell are they all dressed up for? Where in the hell do they think they're going?" Ross didn't answer but there was

[81]

something in his expression which turned the look of curious amusement in Lonnie's face to one of cold terror.

"Don't say it," he finally said, his voice shaking. "I get the point."

Hours passed and the long line continued up the gangplank. Some of the children were old enough to walk but many were being carried. Sometimes Lonnie would see their black eyes peer intently into the gloom of the building, little boy-girl dolls riding there on their mothers' backs. Not once during the long wait did he hear a child cry.

"I wish one of the little bastards would snivel a bit," he observed to Ross. "It would make me feel better for being such a coward. That damned Major Imada was right. Jap kids don't cry. Jesus Christ, I'm thirsty." He started to take out his canteen. "I'll just have a. . . ."

"For Christ's sake," interrupted Ross, "don't start drinking your water already. Who knows when we are going to get more. You sure got a short memory. We damned near starved to death coming up on that ship from Davao and you start hogging your water already, you goddamn piss brain."

"Shit on you," Lonnie intoned. But he didn't drink any water.

Lonnie looked up to see a Japanese guard leaning against the door opening, smoking a cigarette.

"I'm going to get us a smoke," he told Ross. He made his way toward the door, stepping over people who were apparently asleep, looked into an occasional poker hand in passing, and finally approached the guard. Lonnie had never seen him before, he must have been a new transfer. When he glanced up Lonnie made like he was smoking an imaginary cigarette, pointed and said, *"buttu, buttu."*? Slowly the guard took the cigarette from his lips and ground it into the cement floor with his hobnailed shoe.

Lonnie glanced at the women then. The line moved only a few yards away. As he looked a pair of small, dark, almond-shaped eyes caught his own and continued to gaze at him askance as its mother moved down the line. When she turned to go up the gangplank the child's eyes, much to Lonnie's astonishment, remained fixed upon his own. All the way up

[82]

the gangplank and until the mother disappeared from sight the child's unblinking eyes stared into Lonnie's. It was eerie as hell. "The little bastard had to turn his head clear around," he told Ross later. "He looked just like a little crock-headed, slant-eyed owl."

"*Bakayro,* son-of-a-bitch!" shouted the guard at Lonnie. So he made his way back toward his place, across the bodies, past the poker games. "Where's the cigarette butt?" queried Ross. "I saw you trying to make a pass at one of those Jap women."

"Shit, they wouldn't even look at me," responded Lonnie, remembering the child. "That fucking guard is a mean bastard. But we can smoke anyway." He took a cigarette, made of brown paper filled with scroungings from between the latrine planks, from his pocket, but he didn't have a match. And Ross didn't. He handed the cigarette to a skinny looking kid who was eying it like a hungry dog and asked him to pass it down for a light. He could see somebody smoking about ten men away. When the cigarette got back there wasn't much left of it. Lonnie watched in frustration as everybody who handled it took a drag or two. Finally the skinny kid had it and was about to hand it over. "Hell, take a couple of drags," said Lonnie expansively. The skinny kid did, and his eyes grew distant as his lungs stretched the shiny skin taut over his ribs. He didn't say anything when he finally handed back the butt but he looked at Lonnie with his cocker spaniel eyes, and that was enough. Ross and Lonnie took two drags apiece, then Lonnie snuffed it out and saved the few grains of tobacco which were left.

The hours dragged on. The men became more restless and apprehensive. Sounds of engines would come into the building from the outside and there would be a moment of silence, of waiting, and of listening. Hundreds of faces tilted upward, expressions frozen, balanced for a few seconds, between hope and fear.

"Why don't they come now?" said Ross in a low voice, as if to himself. And then more loudly as he caught Lonnie staring at him. "If they hit us now we got a chance, but if they hit us after we get on that ship, we've had it."

[83]

Lonnie had another burst of fear in his chest and was about
to answer when he noticed many of the men looking toward
the back section of the pier, some of them were grinning. Then
Lonnie saw him swaggering along beside Lieutenant Iwahara
as if he had the world by the balls. Old Ledrosa, that
son-of-a-bitch, smoking a Jap cigarette too. He was chitchat-
ting with Lieutenant Iwahara as they walked along, just like
they were asshole buddies.

"Jesus Christ, look at that," said Lonnie, grabbing Ross'
elbow. "Look at that. Here comes that crazy son-of-a-bitch,
looking as good as new. Shit, I'll bet he was putting on about
having that fit. I'll bet he was putting on that whole deal, I'll
bet there wasn't a fucking thing wrong with him."

"I never thought there was," said Ross. He was smiling as
he watched Ledrosa approach.

As he walked along beside Lieutenant Iwahara, Ledrosa
picked up the bowlegged crow-hopping gallop which was
characteristic of the Lieutenant. They looked just like a pair of
bums doing a cripple dance in a burlesque, as R. T. Barton
observed later. That goddamned Ledrosa.

"Hey, Ledrosa, how's it going, man? How'd ya get out?"

"Where did you get those cigarettes?"

"Which twin is the yellowist?"

Voices greeted Ledrosa as he walked between the columns.
He kept grinning and swaggering and waving. Lieutenant
Iwahara didn't seem to mind. Lonnie was watching him and
thought he noted a grudging admiration in the way the
Lieutenant glanced at Ledrosa every now and then.

Finally Ledrosa stopped in the column next to Lonnie and
Ross.

"I'll stay here," he announced loudly. He waved jauntily as
he took his place in line. "Thanks for the escort," he said to
Lieutenant Iwahara.

Lieutenant Iwahara grinned and then made a little bow.
"Good-bye, you crazy man," he said, then walked away out
the open door where the Japanese women and children were
still moving quietly along.

"Why didn't you stay put?" Lonnie heard somebody ask
Ledrosa.

"Yeah, how come you're here?"

"You are nuts," somebody else said.

"What did old Iwahara do to get you to volunteer?"

"He didn't get me to volunteer," said Ledrosa with a proud smirk on his face. "The son-of-a-bitch bribed me. He came to the maximum security section where I was being held for my own protection and offered me five packs of cigarettes if I would volunteer to come along. Shit, who could resist five packs of Golden Bats? Not me," he said. "And anyway," he continued in a confiding tone, "I wouldn't have missed this trip. Hell, this is where the action is. Do you think I want to stay back there in that goddamned stinking hole with people running around acting like I'm crazy? Shit, you know what? I'm the sanest man here."

"How do you figure that?" somebody asked him.

"Well hell fire, it's easy," said old Ledrosa. "I got five packs of cigarettes. How many you got?"

That damned Ledrosa. Lonnie couldn't keep from grinning, that son-of-a-bitch, he was something else. He heard Mr. Noda's voice then shouting for them to move out. Lonnie noticed that the Japanese women and children weren't moving by the door any more and probably hadn't been for some time.

Suddenly everybody was scrabbling around, finding their bundles and canteens, and almost before he realized it Lonnie was walking up a steeply slanted gangplank with Ross right behind him. When they reached the deck, two lines of Japanese guards were directing traffic toward an open hatchway.

"Jesus Christ," said Ross, his voice shrill with terror, "they're going to put us down in the hold."

Lonnie was too overwhelmed to respond. He could see Japanese guards with long poles prodding men toward an open hatch where even as he watched they began disappearing down. He tried to hide between two steam winches on the deck but a guard pushed him back into line just in time to see Ross' blond head disappearing and then he too, as if caught in the terror of a slow motion dream, found himself climbing endlessly, it seemed, down a rope ladder. He looked up as he

[85]

went and saw the diminishing square of light and the skinny, disembodied legs of others moving on the ladders. Below him, nothing but darkness and the sound of men shouting for one another. Finally his feet struck the steel bottom of the ship where for a moment he staggered helplessly around before he saw Ross in the periphery of the dim area of light coming from the open hatchway and heard him shouting.

"Come on dammit, quit standing there like a virgin watching a screwing."

Lonnie made his way among men milling around under the hatchway, men with bewildered faces, whose eyes reflected light as they cast unbelieving glances at the square of sky far above them, and finally reached Ross who was waiting by a large steel pillar which extended from the ceiling to the floor of the hold. As Lonnie's eyes became accustomed to the semi-darkness he could see two layers of bays, one on top of the other, built of lumber, running clear around the hold. He followed Ross into one of the lower bays, and kept crawling back toward a small light which gleamed hopefully ahead. All around him men were making nesting movements, unwrapping blankets, sipping from canteens, lighting up cigarettes; and near the light, Lonnie felt strangely relieved, a poker game was already in progress. He couldn't help peeking at one of the hands as he crawled by: aces and eights. He felt a sudden chill.

Ross was waiting for him in a corner where the bulkhead met the outer skin of the ship. This was it, there was no place else to crawl. Lonnie felt the metal, it was cool and moist, they were probably below the water line.

"What in the hell are we doing way back here?" Lonnie complained. "If we get bombed we don't have a snowball's chance in hell of getting out. Why don't we stay close to the hatchway?"

Ross was busy unrolling his blanket, and didn't say anything for a moment. "I'll tell you why," he finally said. "If the Americans start bombing us there is going to be one hell of a stampede toward that hatchway. You want to have a couple of hundred of these dumb bastards trampling on you? We're better off here, at least it will be quick, if it comes."

Lonnie cursed under his breath and began to unroll his blanket. "I've got to take a drink of water," he said weakly, looking at Ross hopefully.

"Yeah, maybe we better take a sip," agreed Ross, "but just a sip, dammit."

Lonnie could hardly stop but after two gulps he put his canteen back in its carrier on his web belt. He watched Ross. He only took a sip from his canteen.

Other men were crowding in around them now. Lonnie could hear them moving in the bay directly above, cursing and clicking mess gear. And still they kept coming. Lonnie and Ross placed their backs against the bulkhead and defended a small territory with their extended legs. By pushing back against the encroaching bodies they managed to keep enough space to stretch out a bit, but not to lie down. To Lonnie's surprise he saw that one of the men directly between him and the light was Lieutenant Rutledge. No mistaking that hooked nose. Lonnie called and he came crawling towards them around and sometimes across other individuals who grunted tolerantly as he moved along. Ross and Lonnie shoved outward with their legs and made a space for him beside them.

"What the hell is happening, Rutledge?" queried Ross. "Are they trying to get all sixteen hundred of us down in this one hold, the crazy bastards?"

"Looks like it," replied Rutledge, his eyes peered intently into their faces, eyes like hawk's eyes in the semi-darkness accentuated as they were by his long nose. "Are you guys okay? Glad to see a fellow pussy hound, hey Lonnie?" he dug his elbow into Lonnie's ribs and emitted a great laugh which echoed through the bay and brought empathetic smiles from the men close to them.

Lonnie felt better. "You got my number, okay," he grinned. "Particularly if it's eatin' pussy, and it's been sterilized."

Rutledge's great laugh rolled again. Even Ross joined in, and Lonnie chortled, pleased with himself. The apprehension seemed to dissipate a little.

They heard them even as they felt the vibrations running through the steel and timbers of the ship; the propellers were turning. They were underway. A bell somewhere on the

[87]

topside began to ring. It had an urgent demanding sound, and
suddenly there was silence and an air of listening. But nothing
happened! The propellers increased in cadence and small
creaking sounds suggested the ship was moving in open water.
Lonnie took another sip from his canteen and replaced it in its
holder on the web belt. The air was hot, moist and oppressive
but the cool metal of the ship and a slight breeze from a
ventilator somewhere above them made the situation endura-
ble. Ross and Rutledge relaxed back against the bulkhead and
Lonnie, calmed by the presence of Rutledge and the throbbing
of the propellers dozed off for a few moments, his right hand
holding the pouch containing his LIFE WOMAN.

Ross was shaking him and he could smell food. He found
out later that buckets of rice and soup had been let down from
the deck on long ropes and that the men had been divided into
groups of twenty while he slept.

"Your number is R-17," Ross informed him. "I counted off
for you while you were sawing logs."

"Thanks," muttered Lonnie, still groggy. "How in the hell
did they get people organized in a mess like this?"

"I was wondering how they could do it myself," replied
Rutledge. "But those little yellow bastards are pretty good at
getting things straightened out in impossible situations. Old
Noda just said, 'Okay you guys, you are going to eat pretty
soon,'" and Rutledge screwed up his face and put on a crazy
grin until he looked a little bit like old Noda. Lonnie couldn't
help laughing at him, the nutty bastard with his long hooked
nose and Jappy accent. "'Okay you guys,'" Rutledge continued, "'the first man who counts is A-1, the next one is A-2.
Keep counting you guys until you get to A-20, then the next
man counts B-1, and so on, and so on. Get it? Get it?'"

Rutledge was interrupted by somebody shouting out
"Group R" from the direction of the open hatchway. Two
men made their way toward the sound and soon returned with
three mess kits filled with rice and four canteen cups of soup.
As everyone in Group R watched, the food was divided into
twenty portions and each man got his share. The rice was
excellent, light unpolished brown rice and the soup had meat
and potatoes in it. Lonnie ate his portion in huge gulps. He

[88]

would have enjoyed it more if he hadn't been so thirsty. He shook his canteen and was relieved to feel that it was still over half full. Someone came crawling back toward them then shouting for them to stop eating and to return part of the food. Apparently it had run out before all the men were fed, but none was returned. Lonnie kept waiting for the tea which somebody said was coming, but it never showed up.

Lonnie pressed himself against the bulkhead. The heat was intense but he could still feel the slight breeze drifting in from above him; it seemed to come from a small crack where the lumber of the upper bay failed to lay flush against the steel plates. He could see Ross and Rutledge, vague outlines in the semi-darkness, bodies hunched over, their heads down as if asleep. He looked out toward the hatchway, could see dozens of figures silhouetted against the light area. Many of the men were sleeping, leaning against one another, propped in grotesque positions, their skin glistening with sweat.

He figured it must be night. According to the sun he had glimpsed as he was being poled back into line, it must have been four o'clock before they got down into the hold. Yes, it was probably night now. He felt more secure. The Americans couldn't bomb the ship at night, at least he didn't think so. The creaks and groans of the timbers were more pronounced as if the ship had entered open sea. He leaned his head back against the metal of the bulkhead, the throbbing of the propellers and the rumble of the ship seemed to be transmitted to his brain. "I'm too young to die," he thought, just before he went to sleep. "Hell I've never even had a piece of ass."

Lonnie knew something was wrong as soon as he awoe. And then he heard it, the bell on the topside ringing again, in short frantic bursts. Suddenly there was a deafening explosion and the entire ship shuddered and rang. Immediately another explosion came from the aft section of the ship. A moment of silence, the men stricken into an immobility of total terror; then they started screaming and shouting and many began to pray aloud. Dimly through a haze of fear Lonnie saw them milling about, climbing over each other, or huddled down with their backs humped like cockroaches.

"What in the hell is happening?" he screamed.

As from far away he heard Rutledge's booming voice, "Cut it out you bastards, it's just anti-aircraft practice. It's just anti-aircraft practice," he said again to Lonnie, more softly. He reached out and touched Lonnie on the shoulder, and Lonnie wasn't afraid anymore. He had seen an anti-aircraft gun on the deck just before he went into the hold, and felt reassured.

"Those yellow bastards ought to give a guy a little warning," he said weakly. "That really scared the shit out of me."

"Me too," offered Ross, "and it still does!"

The two explosions came again. First in the fore and then in the aft sections of the ship. Lonnie could feel the smack of both repercussions through the steel of the bulkhead. Then there was a new sound, like a dozen old John Deere tractors banging away. The heavy, slow, monotonous reports of pom-poms and then as if some conductor of war had pointed his baton in their direction twenty millimeter guns opened up. For a few moments the entire ship was one great roaring, reverberating, totally terrifying drum, and they were inside of it. Suddenly all sounds ceased. There was a moment of silence and Lonnie both heard and felt four heavy explosions near the ship. They came in rapid succession and each made a sharp crackling sound against the steel plates before the actual explosion could be heard.

And then they knew; the waiting was over. Lonnie had moved beyond fear into a state of paralyzed acceptance. He looked up and caught the hawklike visage of Rutledge, grotesquely frozen into a grimace of terror. He turned his head and glanced at Ross, vaguely outlined beside him, his back humped, his head resting on his knees. He was looking directly at Lonnie but he didn't seem to see him.

Then Lonnie started laughing, a small whimpering sound that grew into a cackling scream, "What's the matter with you bastards? We been waiting three years for this." He cupped his hands around his mouth and shouted out to the screaming, praying men. "The Americans are coming! The Americans are coming!"

A voice came to him, out of the fear, out of the confusion,

Rutledge's voice, calm, sad, resigned, "You're wrong Lonnie, they're here!"

Eight times in as many hours the planes came and went. The beginning of each attack would be signaled by the deafening roar of the five inch guns, the "forty millimeters" would soon open up and then the "twenties" would be heard as the planes came within their range. Lonnie could always hear the explosion of bombs, sometimes near and sometimes at a distance from the ship. When the planes departed, the sounds of battle ceased completely; then Lonnie could hear the men shouting and praying in hoarse desperate voices. But as the hours passed the strange chorus of terror became muted, a dull diapason of woe that would have brought tears to the eye had there been tears to shed. During one of the attacks the ventilators had stopped working and the heat rose until it was unendurable. Lonnie pressed harder against the cool steel of the ship's side and was glad, for a moment, that they were below the water line. Little drops of moisture condensed on the metal. He tried licking them off but it didn't help, and it left a strange taste in his mouth, rusty and salty, like blood.

The eighth attack started like the others, the same two explosions, the "forties" and then the "twenties" could be heard. But there was a new and different sound, the roar of metal against metal as machine gun bullets from an airplane struck the steel deck. Lonnie thought he heard the high whining roar of an airplane engine, the ship lurched, then hunched down in the water as if struck by a giant hand. The steel bulkhead sprang out momentarily and Lonnie felt a sharp stinging pain across his shoulders where he had been leaning against the metal.

Lonnie prayed then, a slow mechanical utterance, "Jesus Christ, God don't let me die here in this stinking hole, Jesus Christ, Jesus Christ." He expected to hear the water rushing in, to feel himself suddenly borne up by the salty tide, he hoped toward the open hatchway but the ship righted and remained underway. Lonnie couldn't believe it. He took out his canteen and took three large gulps of water. It was still half full. He noticed then that all of the lights in the hold had gone out, they were in total darkness. A strange sound puzzled him for a moment, rhythmic and undulating, a low thunder of feet trampling, bodies striking each other, curses and cries and low moans; an army gone epileptic.

"Those bastards have gone crazy!" It was Ross at Lonnie's shoulder, his voice hoarse and ragged. "Are you okay Lonnie?"

"Why not, why shouldn't I be?" responded Lonnie. "I'm starving for water, we just got the shit bombed out of us, and pretty soon that bunch of cattle out there is going to smear us right into this steel deck, but other than that I'm pretty good."

"That's the old fight," somebody said out of the darkness. It was Rutledge, all traces of fear gone from his voice. "Listen to those guys!" Crazy sounds, the contortions of hundreds of wild beasts caught up in some primordial compulsion; trampling, heavy breathing and cries which seemed inhuman. "I'm damn glad we're here in this corner or they would probably get us before the bombs do!"

Lonnie felt a hand trying to get his canteen and shouted and kicked someone away with his foot. "The bastards are coming now," he screamed with fear and revulsion in his voice. "Watch your canteens!"

"What for?" said Ross weakly, "I don't have any water."

"You don't what?" shouted Lonnie in a frenzy. "Why you son-of-a-bitch, you hogged all your goddamned water."

"Cut it out, Lonnie. We've got enough trouble without you going crazier than you already are. Let's sit with our legs sticking out together so if somebody tries to get to us we can kick him away."

Lonnie didn't say anything but he arranged himself as Rutledge suggested. He was between Rutledge and Ross and in spite of the fear and heat and thirst he felt a little more secure. He took out his canteen and nudged Ross. "Have a sip," he whispered.

Lonnie kept waiting for the planes to come again but nothing happened. There was no sound except the panting, trampling, and crying of the men out there in the darkness. Suddenly the ship shuddered and groaned and it seemed to Lonnie that he could hear scraping sounds against the steel side. After a few moments the throbbing of the engines ceased; the ship was not moving.

Lonnie heard Rutledge shouting and began to kick. His foot struck somebody in the chest and he felt him go over backwards. Time passed, minutes fused into hours with no meaning, a haze of heat and thirst, of bodies moving, a mortal rhythm. Lonnie lost count of the times they kicked someone away. He awoke once to feel lips sucking at the skin of his leg and he beat down on a head with his fist, again and again until he was tired, and the head withdrew into the darkness. Once he thought he heard a voice above the turmoil, muffled and distant, then he was sure of it, Father Maloney reciting the Lord's Prayer. Lonnie moved his lips in unison with the distant words and felt better. He finished the water in his canteen, lay his head back against the bulkhead and went to sleep.

When he awoke he could see Rutledge staring dazedly at the faint light coming down into the hold from the hatchway. A large number of men lay under the opening, their bodies faintly outlined against the lighted area, some were moving but others remained fixed in strange postures. Lonnie was sure that they were dead. The turmoil and confusion of the night had ceased. The monster had spent itself.

The bell on the topside began to ring again. A few men lifted their heads to stare toward the distant light but many others didn't move at all. Yes they are dead, thought Lonnie, or maybe they just don't care any more. He was amazed to realize that he wasn't frightened, and even when he heard the throbbing of the machine guns, and the drumming of the bullets against the deck above, he felt no fear. "It's coming now," he thought; he reached out and grabbed Ross' hand and bowed his head, waiting for the blow. But the bombs missed the ship. Lonnie heard the familiar smacking sounds as the concussions struck the steel plates and then heavy booms, in rapid successions, muffled and dull.

"Hold my place," he told Ross and Rutledge, "I'm going to see what's happening." He made his way over and around prostrate figures, toward the area of light and finally could look up and see the blue sky, forty feet above. The scene under the hatchway struck him then, a curious tableau of twisted limbs etched in shadows and occasional blotches of bright red. Most of the men were dead, many had been struck by the machine gun bullets of the dive bombers, bullets and cannon, it must have been cannon, the wounds were so huge. Other bodies seemed unmarked: dead, peaceful, counterpoint to the violence which had been visited upon their companions. Three buckets, used as latrines, were overflowing. The excrement covered the floor and intermingled with the bodies of the men. At the periphery where the tiers began, Lonnie could see individuals like himself, staring hopefully toward the square of light far above.

Even as he looked he heard the whining roar of an airplane, the heavy hammer blows of the pom-poms, and the fear rushed in again. He scrambled wildly back under the tier toward Ross and Rutledge but had gone only a few feet when the bomb struck. The ship lurched downward for a long moment, shuddered, emitted peculiar banging sounds and then righted itself again. Lonnie could feel a slight list growing; an almost imperceptible slope in the floor and from somewhere aft he could hear water rushing in. He looked over his shoulder as he scrambled into the darkness toward Ross and Rutledge and to his surprise saw sand sifting down over the dead and wounded under the hatchway. "Sand, Jesus Christ, sand! Where in the hell could sand come from way out here?" He knew hope then, bright and joyful, life seemed possible again. In the darkness he bumped into the bulkhead and yelled for Ross. "Hey you guys, we're going to make it, we're going to make it. We're right next to land, that bomb blew a bunch of sand down in the hold!"

"Maybe not," volunteered Rutledge. "Maybe the Japs were using sandbags around their gun emplacements."

Lonnie didn't answer. Minutes passed and the ship listed more perceptibly. Strange cracking and popping sounds which grew in amplitude resounded through the metal, seeming to come from everywhere.

From far away up on topside Lonnie heard Mr. Noda's voice, faint, barely intelligible. "Okay you guys, you can come out now. Okay you guys, you can come out now. Hurry up! Hurry up!"

Lonnie moved in a frenzy of fear, careening over those lying in his path, clawing his way around those crouching in his way. He didn't look back into the darkness. He thought he heard Ross call his name but he didn't stop. Suddenly he was at the tier's edge looking up and sure enough there was Mr. Noda still shouting down. Four rope ladders, one on each side of the hatch, reached the floor of the hold. Even as he watched, the tiers erupted with screaming desperate men, slipping and sliding over the dead and wounded under the hatchway. Lonnie had almost stepped over a body in his path when he looked down and saw them, the same cocker spaniel eyes, pleading and desperate. He reached down and helped the skinny kid to his feet and began to shout.

"Help me you sons-of-bitches, help me get this wounded man out of here," but no one even looked his way. They continued to scramble over the bodies, to fight their way up the swinging ladders, their eyes staring at the square of light above them. Lonnie dropped the skinny kid and didn't look as he slumped down. He grabbed the rungs of the ladder closest to him and began to climb. Somebody grabbed his foot but he kicked him away, and continued up, rung by rung, dodging the bare feet of the individual just above him. When he was half way up someone above lost his grip and came plummeting down screaming as he fell. As he passed Lonnie his hand clutched out, a fiery claw which made a long scratch from Lonnie's shoulder to his hip, and in passing took Lonnie's denim shorts along leaving him holding the undulating ladder dressed in nothing but his G-string, web belt and empty canteen. Lonnie heard him smack against the bodies below, but he didn't look down, he was afraid to look down. Panic blocked out the pain and he began to scramble up the ladder again. Then as if bursting out of some hideous nightmare into the quiet of an ordinary morning he was over the edge of the hatchway, his feet on the deck of the ship. No one could be seen except the frenzied prisoners pouring out of the hold and disappearing over the side into the water.

Lonnie didn't feel any fear now, it was washed away by the glaring sunlight on the deck and by the sight of land a few hundred yards away. He looked at the riddled ship, the signs of battle. Thousands of holes speckled the walls of the cabins, some small and others large enough to put a hand through.

The ship itself lay at a peculiar angle, solid and unmoving. Smoke was rising in huge puffs beyond the bridge, and from somewhere deep within an occasional explosion rumbled and vibrated.

"Where did all the women and children go, and the Japanese guards?" Lonnie thought about the little crock-headed kid who had ridden on his mother's back up the gangplank. But there was no sight of anyone but the prisoners fleeing across the deck.

Then from over the water like the revisitation of an impossibility came the sounds of airplanes and Lonnie was seized again by the old terror. He ran to the side of the ship and was on the verge of jumping when he looked again and saw that he was high above the water and that land was almost a quarter of a mile away. He ran down the scarred deck as the sounds of aircraft moved from a murmur into a perceptible drone, looking, looking. He saw it then, there between two steam winches, and he didn't know what he was looking for until he saw it; a life jacket. With terror giving deftness to his fingers, he put it on, tied granny knots and ran again to the side of the ship. But it was still too high, he couldn't make the jump. "I'm going to die here, right here on this goddamn deck," he thought, "shot to pieces by some son-of-a-bitch from Terre Haute, Indiana." He fled down the deck again, looking, and suddenly there it was, almost at the very prow of the ship, dangling from the deck into the water, a rope somebody had left, just for him. He shoved himself through the rails, over the side, the rope intertwined about his hands and feet, down, down, taking the hide off the inside of his right hand, but he didn't notice. He was in the water, comforting and cool, buoyed up by his life preserver, swimming away from the ship, one among hundreds now fanning out toward the land.

The airplanes came in low, five of them, skipping playfully over the water like kids from Terre Haute High messing around with a basketball. They roared down over the ship and when they were directly overhead they waggled their wings and pulled up sharply so everyone could see the white star of the United States of America displayed beneath their wings and suddenly a mighty shout rose from the water and Lonnie was so damn proud and relieved that he cried as they zoomed up and away.

As he swam Lonnie looked back towards the ship. It lay at an odd angle, immobile, stuck almost directly in the center of a fairly large inlet. Smoke and flames were pouring from its rear hold, the entire upper deck had been crushed down by the force of the bombs. The last bomb had dropped directly above the hold in the aft section, the hold where most of the officers had been placed, Lonnie found out later. Even as he watched, men came scuttling like frightened ants out of the smoke and broken girders. Many of them leaped over the side but others were climbing down ropes and rope ladders extending from the deck into the water. They fanned out on three sides of the ship, some swimming strongly, others floating inertly in the water. A few had already reached shore. Finally his own feet touched bottom and he began to walk toward a small promontory which jutted out toward him. At last, crawling on his hands and knees, he moved up out of the water into dry land. He lay down and rested for a while, his head on the life preserver. Then he thought of Ross and guilt came and settled like a lump in the chest.

"I'm a real low son-of-a-bitch, to run off and leave my buddy, Jesus Christ, Jesus Christ, what a bastard," he said half aloud. He raised himself on his elbow and looked out over the water toward the ship. It seemed deserted now, with a great plume of black smoke rising from it. He could see dark red flames amid the smoke and could hear the staccato roar of ammunition going off, and every now and then heavy muffled explosions. Most of the men had reached shore and were spread out by the hundreds in a wide arc around the inlet. But some of them were having trouble, splashing around, getting nowhere. Others floated in the water, motionless, the nucleus for hundreds of dead fish which gravitated toward them, disturbed only by small waves, subdued by a thin sheen of oil which covered the water.

Then Lonnie saw Ross. Not more than thirty feet from shore, pushing a crazy contraption of boards and buckets which had been lashed together into a raft. Four men were holding to it and Ross was puffing away, his feet making a fine splash, his arms resting on one of the planks. He finally reached shallow water where the men deserted him without even a backward glance.

"Over here, Ross, over here!" screamed Lonnie, too loud since Ross was only a few feet from him. Ross stopped and stared at Lonnie, his face suddenly contorted by a momentary sob.

"Where you been you crazy son-of-a-bitch? I looked all over that damn ship for you. And here you are sitting smug and happy, already on shore. You son-of-a-bitch!"

"Shit on you," said Lonnie happily. "Come on up here and I'll let you sit on part of my life preserver." Then looking more closely at Ross he exclaimed, "What in the hell happened to you, you look like a damn scarecrow?"

"Try looking at yourself," responded Ross, and Lonnie gazed down at his legs and then at his arms. "Jesus Christ," he whispered in bewilderment. His legs looked like poles with knobby bulges where the joints hooked them together and his arms as if some giant leech had sucked all the blood away; they didn't seem to belong to him.

"What happened to us?" he asked weakly, looking at Ross.

"Two days in a hundred and twenty degree heat without water will do it every time," offered Ross as he moved back into the water toward the raft. "Come help me with this thing. There are some guys in trouble out there."

Lonnie just stared at him. "Do you mean to say that you're going back out there? Those planes will be back and bomb your ass off. Do you know what happens if you're close to a bomb when it hits the water?" Lonnie's voice rose and trembled. "The concussion breaks you open and spills your guts out all over the place. Shit, man," his voice took on a pleading note, "don't go back out there."

Ross didn't say anything for a moment, he kept looking toward a knot of men who were floundering in the water. Some of them kept screaming for help, their voices shrill and desperate. "There are men drowning out there," said Ross, firmly. He moved out toward the raft.

"I'd help you, Ross, but I burned the hell out of my hand

coming down that rope. See? See?" He held up his hand, but Ross didn't look at it, he didn't even look back.

Lonnie sat on his life preserver and waited. All around him men laughed and joked about the situation. "Look at that baby burn." The voice was familiar, unmistakable. "Those little yellow bastards will never get us off these islands now," said T. R. Barton. "Hell, we'll be back in the States in two weeks. And I'm going to get into that new Ford which old Henry has promised all of us for being such heroes. Actually I figure that I deserve a Cadillac," R. T. confided to those near him. "And I'm gonna get me a big T-bone steak and a good looking blonde."

"Which one will you eat first?" somebody asked.

"Shit, you know me," said R. T. Barton waggling his tongue. "The blonde, of course."

Lonnie laughed, everything seemed better with old R. T. there with his big crock of bullshit. He could see Ross pushing his crazy raft, getting closer to the men who were still out there screwing around in the water. With the fear gone, his thirst came back sharp and strong, he looked out at the ocean, all that water. He filled his cupped hand and rinsed his mouth but the salt burned his cracked lips and coated his swollen tongue. He picked up one of the dead fish and tried to bite into it, as others were doing along the shore line, but the scales hurt his mouth. Then he crushed the fish between two rocks and began sucking on the mulched flesh. He felt pretty good, his shoulder and back hurt where he had been scratched by the falling man and his hand burned because of its new immersion in the salt water, but hell, he was alive and the fish wasn't half bad. He found three more fish which had just floated into shore, and hid them under his life jacket.

At last he saw Ross, still waist deep in the water, about a hundred feet out; he had come in without his raft. Further out Lonnie could see it being pushed slowly and laboriously toward shore by four or five men. Lonnie started shouting and finally Ross saw him. Gasping for breath and staggering, he pulled himself up out of the water. His eyes were hollow and his bones and muscles seemed to be outlined just beneath the surface of his skin. Lonnie offered him a part of his life preserver and he sat down, hardly able to remain upright. Lonnie gave him some of the fish he had mulched up and he ate it greedily, then immediately wretched it up. Lonnie felt his own gorge rising in sympathy but managed to control himself as Ross buried the residue in the sand.

"Guess who's right over there?" said Lonnie, trying to change the subject.

"Yeah, I already know," responded Ross in little short gasps. "I could hear his big mouth yapping from clear out there in the water." He raised his head from between his knees and grinned, some of his color had returned. "Got any more of that fish?"

For the first time since they left the ship, Lonnie saw a Japanese guard. He was making his way among the prisoners picking up items that had been taken from the ship. Lonnie tried to hide his life jacket but the guard saw a corner of it sticking out and took it from him. It was placed in a pile which kept growing as various objects were added to it. A number of guards were involved in the same activity, up and down the shore line. Lonnie noticed then that many of the men were stark naked and that most of the rest were dressed only in G-strings. Some of them still had their blankets and a few had managed to hold on to the newly issued Japanese uniforms. To Lonnie's astonishment he saw the young Captain whose shoes he had admired. Though the salt water had dulled them a little THE SHOES still shone with the same rich luster. The Captain wore his khaki uniform, wrinkled now, but still resplendent with the shiny bars.

It was late morning and the sun was beginning to add more misery to their thirst and hunger when the Japanese guards shouted the order to assemble. Slowly at first and then more rapidly as the stragglers moved in from the edges the men gathered into a long looping formation around the inlet. Lonnie and Ross were on the water side and could see the entire column.

"Look at those crazy bastards," said R. T. Barton, who had moved in beside them. "Did you ever see such a skinny, crummy, thirsty bunch of shitheads in your life? Man, what an army!"

Lonnie interrupted him, "Did you see old Gentry any place?"

"No, I haven't seen him, but shit don't worry, nothing can kill that pretentious bastard, he's probably over there somewhere on the other side." R. T. Barton looked at Ross who was still shaky from his exertion in the water. "How you doing, Ross? You look like you had been shot at and missed and shit at and hit."

"I'm okay. Where do you think they're taking us now?"

"Probably back to Bilibid, or maybe back to Cabanatuan. One thing is sure, they'll never get us out of the Philippines now. Christ I'm thirsty, if they don't get us some water soon, we'll all be dead."

"You're right for a change," responded Ross grimly.

They heard the shouts of Japanese guards and the long column began to move. Up a rock embankment, which apparently served to keep the sea from eating away at the shore during storms, and on toward a grove of trees Lonnie could see in the distance. As they walked through a field of okra and onions Lonnie managed to pluck three onions and two okra as they moved past. He still carried his three fish, stuck in a row between his stomach and his canteen belt; the fins and scales kept gouging him as he walked along.

Finally the column stopped under the edge of huge trees that loomed up and up almost endlessly. Lonnie threw his head back to look, the branches tangled into greater profusion the higher they got, really high, maybe two hundred feet. It was cool under the trees, almost dark with bright splotches of sunlight dappling the leaves in the upper branches. The men ahead of Lonnie were moving forward in single file now, disappearing around a small clump of bushes. Finally it was his turn. He followed Ross through tall grass, sure that he could hear water running somewhere ahead. He could count every bone in Ross' spine and could see where the ribs were attached to each vertebra.

Lonnie was being subjected to a similar scrutiny. R. T. Barton's voice boomed out behind him, "Oh, the rib bone connected to the backbone, the ankle bone connected to the leg bone."

[101]

"Fuck you, you shithead," said Lonnie over his shoulder.

Finally Lonnie saw the water. A large pipe jutting up out of the ground was throwing off fresh water in a full stream, bright and sparkling in the sunshine. Men were filling their canteens and mess kits, anything; those who had lost their equipment drank from their cupped hands. Two Japanese guards kept prodding and shouting but progress was terribly slow. The men behind Lonnie started screaming for those at the pipe to hurry up, but still the line inched along. At last it was his turn. He and Ross and R. T. Barton all put their canteens under the stream at the same time and the water washed over their hands but some of it went inside.

Ross kept whispering, "Drink a little, drink a little," so Lonnie took his canteen when it was only half full and drank some of it. It was very cold so he took small sips. The guard started shouting so he filled his canteen and moved away from the pipe. He waited a few moments for Ross and R. T. Barton, then the three joined others who were straggling toward a fenced-in area a few hundred feet away, not far from the beach. It was a tennis court.

They walked together, side by side, through a green meadow. Lonnie could see a number of verandas with screened porches under the edges of the trees, real ritzy places. Here and there guards relaxed in the noonday sunshine. One fairly near them was smoking a cigarette, leaning on his rifle. It was the guard of the gate episode. "Jesus Christ," thought Lonnie, "it seems like that happened a million years ago." To Lonnie's surprise the guard grinned at him as they passed his position.

"Hey you good boy? You still good boy? You want cigarette?" and he held out the butt, at least half a cigarette toward Lonnie.

"Thanks, Tojo," Lonnie grinned in response as he retrieved the butt. "Americans come soon. Then I give you cigarette, okay?"

But the guard wasn't grinning now, he was looking out toward the ship which was still burning, spewing out great plumes of black smoke.

"Of all the crazy bastards," whispered Ross. "Let's get the hell out of here before he beats the shit out of us again."

"Yeah," agreed R. T. Barton as they hurriedly made their way toward the tennis court. "You sure are a diplomatic bastard, Lonnie. I'll bet you used to let loud farts in church."

"How in the hell was I supposed to know he didn't have a sense of humor," complained Lonnie as he took deep drags on the butt. "That's why they're going to lose the war, no sense of humor. You guys want a drag?"

They went through the gate into the tennis court. Mr. Noda and Lieutenant Iwahara were both there with a Japanese non-com taking count, keeping tallies on a piece of paper. Within the enclosure three different courts were separated by about ten feet of neatly cut lawn. To Lonnie's surprise he saw Gentry lying comfortably on the grass next to the fence beyond the third court.

"Hey, Gentry," he yelled across. Gentry raised a hand and casually waved for them to come over. They started directly toward him across the cement but changed their minds; it burned their bare feet, so they skirted the edge, walking in the green grass. The enclosure was still fairly empty, men lay in small groups on the grass, next to the fence or between the courts. Many of them were already asleep.

"Have a seat, Gentlemen," Gentry smiled up at them as they approached. "I was afraid you were all back there cooking in the rear hold of the ship, but it looks like your frying is destined to be postponed."

"Same old Gentry," Lonnie observed. Indeed he seemed completely unaffected by the experience. There was no mark on him except the small cut on the lip that Corso had given him. His mustache was well trimmed, as usual, and he looked like he had just given himself a shave. Gentry the indestructible. He had managed to bring his blanket and his Japanese uniform off the ship and he leaned against them as he chatted. He didn't even look like he had lost any weight.

"Dammit Gentry," Ross complained, "here we are damn near dead from hunger, dried out from two days in that sauna bath, still unable to accept the enormity of the thing that's happened to us, and there you sit acting like you owned the world. How in the hell do you do it?"

"The bastard doesn't have enough common sense to know what's happening to him," R. T. Barton observed, but he smiled at Gentry with affection. "He was probably thinking up another one of those bullshit arguments and didn't even notice we were having trouble."

"Hacking away, as usual, hey R. T.?" Then looking at the others he said, "Old R. T. is just jealous of my vast intellectual attainments and cosmic insights. But you do have one talent, R. T., that even I have some difficulty in surmounting, your grasp of the totally vulgar. You are a true fecal monist, everything you look at is pervaded by a mist of mustard. When you have time, R. T., I hope you will give me lessons in the fine art of the four letter word."

"I wouldn't piss in your ass if your guts were on fire," offered R. T. grinning.

"Unless he could piss gasoline," added Lonnie. "By God, Gentry, you've met your match in something. Nobody's got a dirtier mind than old R. T."

Gentry looked towards Lonnie for a moment, a little smile played momentarily on his lips, a glint of mischief in his eyes. Then he gazed directly at R. T. Barton and said, "I'm not so sure of that. I have depths as yet unplumbed, great cesspools of filth, legions of dirty words unmentionable. While old R. T. there has his limitations. As a matter of fact, R. T., if you had shit for brains, you couldn't think a fart."

There was a moment of silence and then they all burst out laughing and R. T. Barton laughed loudest of all.

"Dammit, Gentry, you're the greatest," gasped Lonnie. And Ross just sat making little convulsive strangled sounds as tears ran down his cheeks. For a moment the danger went away and even the hunger seemed diminished. There was just the green grass and the warm afternoon sun and old Gentry, grinning at his own commentary, indestructible and imperturbable. Others near them moved over to find out why they were laughing. R. T. told them and the laughter spread outward across the tennis courts and grew in volume.

At first they didn't hear the airplanes when they came again. They appeared suddenly over the water, low and fast; dark blunt shapes with white stars, not fiddling around this time. They zoomed up and up, leveled off for a few moments zigzagging among the puffs of smoke which magically appeared around them, then dived toward the ship, which by now was almost entirely engulfed in flames. The bombs made heavy booming sounds, a series of secondary explosions echoed for a moment then a great shock which caused the men to flatten themselves against the green turf spread out across the water. A huge gout of flame billowed upward, and pieces of the ship gyrated end over end in slow motion through the air. Most of them fell back into the water but one or two went over the tennis court and fell in the trees beyond. Ammunition in the rear section of the ship began to go off in a continuous deafening roar.

Suddenly an anti-aircraft gun located about two hundred yards from the tennis court opened up, the puffs of smoke coming dangerously close to one of the planes. For a long moment it just seemed to hang there in the sky with its engine screaming as it climbed away. It disappeared for a while and then five or six planes returned following the shore line, weaving in and out. They pulled up, circled for a few moments then dived directly at the tennis court.

Lonnie flattened himself against the ground burying his head under his arms, afraid to look. He could hear the machine guns and cannon of the airplanes, the low pitched whine of released bombs blending with the crescendo of accelerating engines. The bombs fell among the trees along the shore line. The planes were attacking batteries of artillery ranged among the trees up and down the beach. Usually they came in directly above the tennis court and released their bombs in series, so they fell one right behind the other describing a precise arc overhead, a trajectory which carried them among the trees, to explode there in great earth-shaking thuds. Once when one of the planes released its bombs directly above them, a small propeller which served as a fusing mechanism unscrewed itself and struck one of the men near Lonnie on the head. He could see a trickle of blood running down the man's forehead but he didn't seem to be hurt very much.

Toward nightfall the attacks dwindled, then ceased all together. The wind rose slightly and blew the smoke from the still burning ship across the water, a long black plume which blended with dark clouds low on the horizon. At last there was silence but it was a quiet filled with hunger and for some of them, pain. At the far end of the enclosure, near the gate, Lonnie could see thirty or forty wounded men lying on the grass between the court and the fence. Some were moaning and one in particular kept emitting an eerie scream about every three minutes, as regular as clock work.

Lonnie noticed activity then at the west side of the enclosure, just beyond the fence. The Japanese were setting up a small platform. After a few minutes he saw Major Imada coming toward them, across the meadow from one of the houses, walking slowly, head down, silhouetted against the lighter sky, a dark brooding figure, somehow larger than life. He climbed the steps of the platform and stood looking at them through the wire mesh of the fence, his face impassive, strangely pale there in the gathering dusk, his eyes dark shadows under the bill of his small military cap. At last he spoke, his voice quiet, restrained, and it seemed to Lonnie, infinitely sad.

"This has not been a good day for you. Four hundred of your comrades lie dead out there, burned with the ship, killed by your countrymen. Four hundred Japanese women and children also died there, killed by the machine guns of the airplanes and by the bombs. Hundreds more lie wounded, over there," he lifted his hand toward the darkness of the woods. He paused now, surveying them again in the semi-darkness and then his voice took on an intense demanding quality, "Did you know that you almost died twice this morning? You almost died from the bombs of your airplanes. You know this, but did you know that the Japanese soldiers who line this shore by thousands wanted to kill you too? They took the women and the children off the ship last night, the dead and the wounded. They wanted to kill you!" Now his voice rose, and Lonnie suddenly forgot his hunger and even the wounded men were quiet, "And I wanted to let them kill you!" He paused again, his form barely distinguishable in the almost total dark. When he continued, his voice was flat, emotionless, disinterested, "You are alive. The Japanese do not shoot animals helpless in the water. What will happen to

[106]

you now, I do not know. There is no food for you. Your food burned up out there on the ship. I do not know what will happen to you now. We will wait and we shall see."

The night was pervaded by an ominous, forbidding silence. Lonnie kept waiting for Major Imada to say something more, a word of cheer or encouragement, but the silence remained as total as the night was dark. Finally it was broken by Mr. Noda's high raspy voice, short choppy sentences which the prisoners normally ridiculed; but tonight nobody mocked him. They listened to his disembodied voice, familiar and strangely comforting, coming out of the darkness.

"Okay you guys. We all had a bad day today, but you guys are okay. Things are not so bad, we are alive, we are on dry land, we have water. There is no food tonight but maybe tomorrow. I know you are sad because some of your comrades are dead. The Japanese are sad too. Five of the guards are dead and Major Imada's wife and baby were killed on the ship. But maybe tomorrow will be better, maybe we will have some food for you tomorrow. You go to sleep now."

With the silence, the foreboding and the despair returned, and the hunger. Then they heard his voice, strong and resolute, Father Maloney reciting the Lord's Prayer. In the beginning only a few took up the prayer but as the Father's voice dominated the darkness other voices blended in until it became more than a prayer; a statement of togetherness, a shield against terror, a balm for hunger and pain, a unified and tangible expression of their hope.

Lonnie heard the voices of the men as from a great distance. Out of the darkness, sprinkled with star froth, spangled with life light, he saw eyes looking at him, those of the crock-headed Japanese baby and those of the skinny kid he had dropped there among the bodies under the hatchway. Eyes that blended and flared brightly for a moment before they dulled and went pinwheeling away and away until they were lost among the light flecks which showed where great stars burned. Lonnie began to cry, quiet muffled sobs. He was glad that it was dark so no one could see him sniveling there like some snotty nosed orphan kid weeping for his lost mother. He opened the small pouch which still dangled around his neck

[107]

and searched for his LIFE WOMAN but the paper had been
turned to mulch by the salt water and she came apart and
sifted through his fingers as he unfolded her.

Then he heard someone speaking his name. It was Gentry,
his voice steady and calm. "What did you do with those fish
you had when you came in here, Lonnie? I've got some salt.
Let's eat 'em up."

"Right," exclaimed Lonnie, "I've got them right here." He
found them where he had placed them under his web belt, and
to his gratification they were still fresh. "I've got some onions
and some okra, too," he announced.

"I've got two sweet potatoes," volunteered R. T. Barton.

"I've got an overwhelming appetite," said Ross cheerfully.

They gave everything to Gentry who divided it into four
piles. He still had his mess kit knife and he carefully scaled
and cleaned Lonnie's fish, without nicking himself. The others
gathered close around him. They couldn't see what he was
doing but the sounds and smells of his preparation, the
scraping and cutting of the fish, the pungent odor of the
chopped onions, brought concreteness and tangibility into the
amorphous darkness.

"And now for the salt," said Gentry with satisfaction. They
could hear the small scrufting sounds his fingers made as he
sprinkled a pinch of salt over each pile.

Lonnie thought it was the best food he ever tasted. He
didn't mind the dirt which still clung to the sweet potato and
onions or that the fish was spoiled a bit after all. He felt good.
He couldn't help laughing when he heard R. T. Barton say,
"Hey Gentry, I saw your lips moving when the Father was
praying. Man, you lost your bet. I saw you sneaking in a little
prayer, trying to up your odds. What will you give me not to
tell the Father?"

"Yeah," agreed Lonnie, "and don't forget you've got an ass
kicking coming from me."

Gentry laughed good naturedly, "You guys better be glad
that somebody around here has a pipeline to the Big Man.
Somebody with equal intellectual endowments. Someone he
listens to and respects. I had a little friendly conversation with
him just this morning. You know what I told him? I said God,

you and I been buddies for a long time and never once have I taken advantage of our friendship. Now I've got a small favor to ask. Take care of old Lonnie, he's still a virgin and a man shouldn't die before some Helen has made him immortal with a kiss. Look out for old R. T. Someday he is going to write the great American dirty book. And old Ross there, we need him to pull us out of the water when we're drowning. You know what God said? He said, 'Okay Gentry, I'll let them live a while. Just for you.' "

Gentry's rare laughter rang out across the tennis court, and Lonnie felt momentarily safe, secure. The fatigue came then, like warm lead oozing into the marrow of his bones, the legs first and then the arms. He put his head down on his canteen, still held securely in its holder on his web belt, and just before he went to sleep he saw that the moon had risen above the trees which crowned the mountains in the southeast and that small tufts of clouds in that direction were suffused with a warm glow.

CHAPTER FIVE

There was no food the next day or the next. The sun rose each day into a cloudless sky. The men gravitated toward the grassy areas surrounding the courts when the mid-morning heat became intense; with the coolness of the evening they returned to the cement to pick up the lingering warmth. Twice each day water details gathered canteens and filled them at the flowing pipe. Lonnie volunteered for one of these deatils, the one in the late afternoon of the second day, hoping to find something to eat along the path.

The metal chains dug into his arms and hands, and he wished he hadn't gone. Everything had been picked, not a single okra or onion anywhere, even the small flowers which had lined the path were gone, all of them. He dropped one of the canteens, the others slipped from his grasp as he tried to grab it. "Dirty son-of-a-bitch." He picked them up, one by one and started out again. A guard over by the fence was watching, he'd probably come over and beat the shit out of him in a minute. Hell there wasn't any food anywhere, nowhere. Two days now and not a fucking thing to eat. Nothing but water and the sun, hotter than hell in the day time, making the cement so hot nobody could stay on it. Nothing but cold at night except for the cement which stayed warm for a while and felt good on your bare back. That was all. The chains were biting into his arms again, but he was getting close to the gate, where another water detail was waiting, ready to take off, eight canteens to a man.

"I hope somebody kicks my ass off if I ever volunteer for anything again," he said to the American Major who was in charge of water distribution.

"They wouldn't have much trouble doing it," the Major said looking at Lonnie appraisingly. "You don't have much left."

"Fuck you," said Lonnie.

As he returned to his place he saw Rutledge lying on his back, looking up, staring like he wasn't seeing anything. He looked more like a hawk than ever, a skinny hawk. Rutledge didn't see him and Lonnie didn't speak.

"Where's the food?" Ross asked as soon as he had reseated himself.

"Yeah, where are the goodies?" intoned R. T. Barton.

"Shit on you bastards. There's nothing out there," he shouted almost crying. "Goddammit there's nothing any-where! Those yellow motherfuckers are going to keep us in this God damn pen until we die. We'd have been better off if the bombs had got us or if the Japs had shot our asses off when we were in the water." Then he began to shout at the top of his voice, "Hey, Noda, hey you, get us something to eat. Hey Noda, Noda!"

Other prisoners took up the cry until there was a deafening chorus of men screaming for food. The guards looked up from their stations around the court. They shouted a few words back and forth in Japanese but they didn't do anything, and Mr. Noda didn't appear. The screaming diminished by degrees and then died completely except for the wounded man who still punctually emitted his strangled cry, one about every two hundred heart beats; Lonnie had kept track.

Just after sunset, somebody, Lonnie thought it was Colonel Watson, asked for volunteers to bury the dead, but nobody came forward. Finally one of the guards came into the enclosure and selected ten individuals who looked fairly healthy. Bitching and cursing, they went out the gate single file toward the edge of the trees where they took turns digging; at dusk they came back into the enclosure, hardly able to stand. The Japanese selected other prisoners to carry out the bodies. Slowly the procession passed down the side of the tennis courts, four men to a body, one for each arm and leg. As Lonnie watched them angling out toward the pile of fresh dirt, he heard the sound of motors and saw a line of trucks draw up beneath the trees skirting the buildings a few hundred feet away. They remained there immobile for a little while, then one of them moved toward the tennis courts; its headlights gleaming through small holes made narrow bright streaks, parallel light slits on the crushed stone of the road. Lonnie could see sacks, piled one on top of another, fat and bulging. Something to eat.

Three distribution points, one for each court, and the men filed past; two tablespoons of uncooked rice and a piece of dried fish. Lonnie ate his rice grain by grain, enjoying each gritty crunch, and washed it down with water. He saved the dried fish for later; it fitted snugly in his LIFE WOMAN pouch. He felt a little more secure knowing that it was there, available, in case he really needed it. He lay back then, his head on his canteen holder, watching the moon rise to cast a silver sheen over the tennis courts, almost as bright as day.

"Let's go piss," he said aloud. But no one answered. Ross lay beside Gentry and R. T. Barton, three in a row, sleeping on the warm cement. "I'll go by myself then," he grumbled under his breath. "Lazy bastards."

On the way out the gate, one of the guards gave him a Japanese cigarette. How about that for luck? He held it cupped in his left hand as he went about his business fearing he might fall into the trench and ruin it. For a few moments he stood watching his stream describe a sparkling arc in the moonlight before it disappeared down into the darkness of the trench. When he went back the guard was still passing out cigarettes, one by one. He waited around for a moment hoping to get another but the package became empty leaving a number of individuals who had gathered in a small impromptu line stranded, smokeless. The guard tore the pack open and displayed its empty tinseled interior, and the men ambled away toward the latrine ditch without looking back or at each other. Just as Lonnie went back through the gate a cloud cast a dark moving shadow across the enclosure but he found Rutledge where he had first seen him, his hairy, thin body stretched out on the warm cement, his hawk-like visage stark in the shadow, his black eyes staring up at Lonnie as he approached.

"Hey Rutledge, you want a couple of drags on a cigarette? I got one if you can find us a light." Suddenly a match flared at his elbow; he turned his head to look directly into the eyes of Corso, grinning and as fat as ever.

"I've still got the heat, if you've got the meat," he intoned as Lonnie bent forward and lit the cigarette from the extended flame.

"Shit on you," responded Lonnie. And Rutledge's great laugh boomed out into the night.

"By God, Lonnie, you are a survivor," he observed. "Give me those two drags but be damn careful you don't let Corso here have any."

Lonnie handed Rutledge the cigarette and saw his face light up, once, twice in the drag light. Rutledge returned the cigarette to Lonnie without looking at Corso who had sat back on his haunches, a large shadowy hulk in the semi-darkness.

"I'm not worried about old Corso," Lonnie said quietly. "Here, Corso, have a drag." A puzzled look flickered over Corso's countenance, a fleeting glint of recognition and resignation almost hidden by the darkness and his thick matted beard. But he reached out for the cigarette and kept looking at Lonnie even as he took a heavy drag. Lonnie could still feel his eyes upon him as he moved among the reclining men toward his place with Ross and the others. On the way, he took two deep drags and suddenly felt elated and free and then dizzy.

"By God, Lonnie, you are the damnest scrounger I ever saw," observed R. T. Barton as Lonnie passed around the fast diminishing cigarette. "I'll bet you could find hair on a cue ball. The next time you go out bring me back a T-bone steak and some table grade pussy."

"An interchange with a healthy woman would kill you, R. T.," said Gentry, taking his turn at the cigarette. "Here Lonnie, you found it, you finish it," he handed Lonnie the short butt. Lonnie carefully snuffed it out and emptied the remaining tobacco into his LIFE WOMAN pouch, next to the piece of dried fish. He lay down trying not to think about the fish but finally couldn't stand it any more. He took it out of the pouch and smelled it. Christ it smelled good! What the shit. Just before he went to sleep he caught sight of the moon about three feet above the mountains far in the distance, and for a fleeting moment he thought of the crock-headed baby and of the kid with the cocker spaniel eyes. The cement was warm, comforting. The dried fish had left a spicy pungent taste in his mouth.

He felt someone shaking him, and could see Ross' face directly above, clearly outlined in the dawn light which was dim but getting brighter with each moment. Ross didn't say anything, he just kept beckoning with his right hand and pointing to Lonnie's canteen and web belt. Finally Lonnie understood. Slowly he followed Ross towards the gate, stepping over sleeping men. The light of the new morning showed a weird mosaic of naked bodies, entertwined, motionless; three-dimensional desperation silvered by dawn light. Little clusters gathered for warmth's sake, isolates coiled like fetuses, skinny arms wrapped around skinny chests, elbows and knees large and knobby, shining.

"What in the hell are we doing?" Lonnie asked when he finally caught up with Ross who was standing near the gate. "What in the hell are we doing sneaking around this pile of bones this time of night? Hell it must be four o'clock in the morning."

"Probably," responded Ross. "We're leaving here this morning, I'll bet on it. Anywhere is better than this. I want to be first in line. And since, by some trick of lousy fortune, I have been saddled with the job of looking after you, we are now involved in this early morning maneuver to get us up front."

"Shit on you," said Lonnie. "Where in the hell are we going to sit down? These bastards are laying all over the place. We can't just stand here with our thumbs up our asses. You really are a crazy bastard."

"Shut up and sit down," responded Ross in a disinterested

voice. He sat down on his haunches right next to the gate where an empty space had been left for the men going to and from the latrine.

"Those bastards will be walking on us all day," observed Lonnie, sullenly, but he sat down next to Ross. They pushed back against the circle of sleeping men, and little by little it gave way until a fair hole had opened up among the tangle of legs.

"And what about Gentry and R. T.? Are we just going to sneak out and leave them there? What about them?"

"Oh, for Christ's sake, quit mouthing. They need us like Richmond needed Grant. Anyway I told them about it and they both decided to stay there together. And a fine team they'll make," said Ross, in a better humor.

"Yeah," agreed Lonnie, grinning in spite of himself. "Old R. T. will run Gentry crazy in about two days."

They sat leaning against each other back to back, relaxed. The rays of the new sun tinted the clouds golden far in the east toward Manila. Ross' back felt warm, comforting. Something was missing, the wounded men wasn't screaming anymore. Poor son-of-a-bitch. No more worries there.

Lonnie must have dozed off because suddenly it was broad daylight and Japanese guards were shouting. A little platform had been placed before the gate and Mr. Noda was already there getting ready to make a speech. Little nondescript bastard in a baggy uniform without insignia or sword to dignify it. A perfect representative of the super-race, a true spark off the Godhead, the little shithead.

"Okay you guys, some of us are going to leave today. The rest will leave tomorrow. The sick and wounded will leave today. Okay you guys start moving out and line up in groups of forty."

Lonnie and Ross were first out the gate and first in line. After a Japanese corporal checked for holes, the formation moved out toward the trucks parked under the trees, with Lonnie and Ross leading the way. As they passed the first truck, a guard threw down some clothing. Lonnie got a pair of Filipino shorts and a small blue denim jumper. Ross received a jumper, he still had his shorts. At the second truck they were

[115]

given two tablespoons of uncooked rice each and a piece of dried fish. Then on down the line to the last truck. They climbed up, eating their rice and fish and moved back until they were leaning against the cab. It was nice there under the trees, warm now that the sun was up, and no airplanes.

"I'll bet we're going back to Cabanatuan," observed Lonnie as he took a swig from his canteen. "I sure wish I had some more of that fish. Shit, did you know that in New Mexico we don't even eat fish? My mother tried to get us to eat fish, like she tried to get me to learn to play the piano. She said we needed the iodine. She was always trying to get us to do something we didn't want to do, like trying to get my sister who was as big as a horse to learn tap dancing. I can still see her banging away with her feet, first one and then the other beating the floor, with her fat legs shaking like jelly. Do you have a sister?"

"No such luck," responded Ross.

"You'd like my sister," continued Lonnie. "Real black hair. I'll never forget when Mama caught me sticking matches in her pussy. I had them lined up like little soldiers, right down the line, when I looked up and saw Mama watching me. Funny thing, she didn't even touch me but she beat the shit out of Edna. You'd like Edna."

"You make her sound very attractive," said Ross agreeably, as he watched the men getting into the truck, "but I'm already married."

The truck filled up, crowding Ross and lonnie back against the cab but the guards kept shouting. Finally even the Japanese were satisfied; they were packed in like a bunch of vertical sardines, with no place to sit down, hardly able to breathe.

"Dammit Ross," said Lonnie with a note of admiration in his voice, "you were sure right about getting to the head of the line. Look at those poor bastards standing in the middle of the truck with nothing to hold on to."

"They're not so bad off," observed Ross. "They couldn't fall down if they wanted to. I just hope we don't have any sudden stops. How would you like to be shock absorber for about forty men?"

[116]

Lonnie didn't say anything.

"And if we get strafed," continued Ross, "The guys in the middle will have the rest of us to shield them from the bullets."

"Well you sure are an optimistic son-of-a-bitch," yelled Lonnie. "We got a good deal and you know it. What the hell you trying to scare me for? You shithead."

The truck started and moved slowly along a dirt road toward a large building. As they made a small turn Lonnie got a last look at the enclosure. It still seemed full of men, but all the trucks were in motion now; a long convoy moving over the narrow road, through the barrio and on toward the mountains. As they went up an incline which preceded their entry into a narrow canyon, Lonnie saw the small bay. To his astonishment the ship was still smoking, black and battered, listing at an odd angle. So much for that. He turned his head and looked up the road.

Japanese soldiers were everywhere, digging holes in the ground, building log fortifications, putting large artillery pieces and mortars into place, getting ready. The convoy passed numerous barricades, usually at small bridges. They didn't have to stop, soldiers waved them through and then looked intently at them as they passed.

"Probably trying to figure out what kind of enemy they are going to face," said Ross.

"They're going to be in for one hell of a big surprise," observed Lonnie with some satisfaction. "We're about as similar to the guys who are coming to get them as Rumpelstiltskin was to Hercules."

"That's a pretty apt comparison," agreed Ross, and Lonnie looked pleased.

The truck slowed, they were passing hundreds of Japanese troops which moved to the side of the road to let them by. Once again they were subjected to the silent scrutiny. No word spoken, no sound, just intent brown eyes set in impassive Japanese faces, searching. Toward the end of the column one of the soldiers threw a pack of cigarettes at them. Lonnie tried to catch it but missed and it landed in the middle of the truck. One man tried to keep the entire pack but after a small scuffle the cigarettes were passed around. Lonnie kept shouting,

"Over here, over here," but they ran out before the pack got that far.

"Some son-of-a-bitch took more than one," sniffed Lonnie. "The goddamn hog."

The road was smoothing and straightening, leaving the mountains. Large trees arching the road like protective umbrellas began thinning out to let them see patches of blue sky, occasional sprays of white clouds. Lonnie thought he heard airplane engines above the truck noises and felt the old familiar flare in his chest. Some of the others apparently heard them too, they were casting nervous glances toward the sky. Lonnie saw them then, like a flock of blackbirds in the distance, flying without formation as was the American way, moving toward the southwest away from them. The trucks waited beneath a grove of trees for a while, just in case, then they moved into open country, a plain almost completely devoid of trees where small farms and numerous barrios lined the road. Lonnie could see Filipinos loitering behind open windows and doors. A fleeting and ephemeral gesture flickered against the darkness of the interior of one of the nipa houses, the victory sign. Once he heard a small clear voice, distinct and emphatic above the truck noise, cry, "I shall return."

The barrios grew thicker and by degrees merged into the outskirts of a city. The streets were empty but Lonnie could see vague shadows moving in the semi-darkness within the buildings and could feel eyes watching. The trucks stopped at last under a grove of trees. They were in a public park. Flowers grew in well cultivated plots and benches edged small circuitous paths leading in and out among the trees. Bright water spurted in a continuous stream from the mouth of a hideous gargoyle into a large basin.

Mr. Noda's familiar voice sounded above the drone of conversations, "Okay you guys, out of the trucks, fill your canteens, drink some water."

"I'm dying to take a piss," said Ross. "What about pissing?"

"What about pissing?" Lonnie echoed at the top of his voice. "Hey, Noda, how about pissing?"

"No pissing," responded Mr. Noda. "Drink now, piss later."

"That figures," muttered Ross.

Lonnie and Ross were last out of the truck, they couldn't even see the fountain. It was surrounded by men three deep trying to get their canteens filled. Finally it was their turn. Lonnie immersed his canteen and listened to the "glug, glugs" change tone as it filled. He saw gold fish in the water and tried to grab one as it swam near but it was too fast for him. When his canteen was full he drank as much water as he could then filled it again. Others were pushing at him so he finally relinquished his place. He couldn't see Ross for a moment but soon found him waiting at the edge of the crowd, looking strained and uncomfortable. Lonnie moved up behind him, stuck his finger in his back and shouted, "Piss now, piss now!" And Ross did, just a little, before he could get control.

"You goddamn creep," shouted Ross. "You want me to piss my pants? How in the hell do you think I'd be able to wash them? You goddamn creep. I ought to kick the shit out of you!"

"Sorry Ross," said Lonnie, whose howls of laughter at his friend's discomfort ebbed to grins which kept breaking unwanted over his features. "But you looked so damn funny standing there with everything screwed up tighter than a cow's ass in fly time." The screams of laughter broke through again, and tears ran down his cheeks.

"You goddamn creep," said Ross halfheartedly. He was beginning to grin too, as they walked back toward the truck. The men were lining up so they moved into the third row almost in the middle of the formation.

"Go ahead and piss," said Lonnie. "The guard can't see you, he's clear over on the other side of the truck." And Ross did, unmindful of the startled glances turned in his direction from the men near him in the formation.

They didn't get back into the trucks. The guard shouted and the column moved out. Some of the men had to be helped along by other prisoners but Lonnie and Ross didn't get drafted for this extra duty. They enjoyed the walk, the novelty of being in a city again, even a city which was almost empty. Occasional trucks loaded with supplies or silent soldiers rattled down the streets. They passed one large building, apparently a barracks. A few soldiers who were policing the grounds cast

[119]

curious looks in their direction. Finally they came to their destination, ugly and squat, made of red brick.

Single file through a massive doorway, on through two rooms filled with desks and ancient typewriters, then into an open enclosure. They were in the city jail. A low wall surmounted by a high tension wire jutted into the building, providing an enclosed area of about an acre. Three small sheds with tin roofs and two trees seemed lost in the huge compound. In the center a small tank was kept filled by water running from an open pipe. Barred windows near the ground were spaced about every ten feet down the entire length of the building. As soon as they were released from formation Lonnie looked through one of the windows into an empty prison cell. Systematically he went down the line looking into the semi-darkness but all the cells were empty. He heard Ross calling him, from near one of the sheds, and found him puffing away on a cigarette.

"Where in the hell did you get that?" queried Lonnie. "You didn't tell me you had a whole cigarette. Where in the hell did you get it?"

"Have a drag and shut up," replied Ross. "What the hell do you care? Anyway I've got lots of things you don't know anything about."

"Like lice and amoebic dysentery?" said Lonnie as he inhaled deeply. "Do you hear airplanes?"

"Yes," responded Ross absently. Other men in the enclosure heard them too, they kept looking toward the northwest, listening. There was no doubt about it. The sounds grew from a distant rumble into a thunder which seemed to come from everywhere.

"Boy, the Japs are going to get their little red gonads fried today," shouted Lonnie above the roar. Then they saw them, flying high and moving fast. With a lurch in his chest Lonnie knew that something was wrong. The planes were flying in tight even formations, V upon V upon V like a vast armada of geese migrating toward Canada. They covered the sky in all directions, at many different altitudes and on the wings of those in a low formation Lonnie saw the terrible evidence of what he already knew, the rising sun. The planes were Japanese and they came on endlessly, wave after wave.

"Did you ever see so many red assholes in your life?" asked Lonnie with a catch in his voice.

"Shut up, dammit, I'm counting," responded Ross.

At last the planes were gone from sight. The sounds diminished from thunder to low rumbles which waxed and waned from almost silence to heavy reverberations which rattled the windows in the prison cells and produced eerie responsive resonances in the tin roofs of the sheds.

"How many did you count?" asked Lonnie.

"Over eight hundred, something over eight hundred," Ross responded, his voice shaking. "Where in the hell did they get that many airplanes?"

"Eight hundred airplanes," said Lonnie incredulously. "Something big's happening down south somewhere. Or maybe," He paused with sudden hope in his voice, "the invasion of the Philippines has started. Do you think so? Do you think the invasion has started?"

"I think our boys are in for a rough time, whatever's started," said Ross. "Eight hundred zeros!"

"I'm tired," said Lonnie, "and it's going to get cold tonight. Let's see if we can find a place in one of the sheds, that one nearest the north wall of the compound."

To their surprise it was almost empty. They appropriated a corner and leaned against the warm tin, their legs at right angles. Most of the men were ambling around the enclosure talking about the airplanes. Their conversations came through the tin side of the building as a steady drone of intermingled rattling sounds like a crowd of people talking in a foreign language at great distance.

"Do you think we're going to get back?" Lonnie heard Ross's question but he didn't answer for a few moments.

"Back where?"

"Back home, for Christ's sake, where else is there to go back to?"

"What a dumb question," shouted Lonnie. "Of course we're going to get home. Hell's fire we've made it now. We're off that damn ship and we didn't get killed. We didn't even get hurt. All we have to do is wait around for a little while and they'll be here. They're probably coming in right now. Sure we're going to get home."

[121]

"I'm not so sure," said Ross quietly. "I've felt for some time that I wouldn't get back. And when I saw all those Jap airplanes I was sure of it."

Lonnie just kept looking at him. Finally he said, "You know, you're crazy, you really are. Every bastard on this trip has felt at least a dozen times that he wasn't going to make it. I have! Everybody has! What's so God damn special about your feelings? I didn't think I was going to get off that damn ship but I'm sitting right here. I'm sitting right here talking to you, you dumb bastard."

Ross smiled, "All the same I want to make a pact with you, for what it's worth."

"Like what?" said lonnie looking at him suspiciously. "I don't trust you when you start talking like this. You're going to talk about dying aren't you? Shit I know I'm going to die but I don't want to talk about it. The way I figure it as long as you're living you ain't dead, and when you're dead you ain't anything. So dying simply isn't worth talking about. I'd rather talk about pussy. Now that's something worth talking about. And eatin' and shittin' and pissin'. That's life, that's what life is and life's worth talking about." He stopped, Ross was grinning at him.

"By God Lonnie that was quite a speech. Old R. T. Barton would envy your definition of life. Life is a warm pulsating pussy." He had raised his hand and arched his neck in a manner typical of R. T. Barton and his voice had the same nasal raspy quality.

Lonnie laughed, "Damned if you don't sound just like him, the dirty mouthed shithead. I'll bet he's running Old Gentry crazy right now. Anyway what kind of pact did you have in mind? Hell I'll do it, whatever you want, you know that."

"Well just in case I don't make it, I want you to go and see my wife and tell her about everything. It'll make her feel better." Ross's voice had become quiet and for a moment he seemed almost shy. "You see I'm worried that she might keep thinking I'm coming back when I'm not. I just can't stand the idea of her waiting and waiting, when I'm not coming back. If you go and talk to her and tell her about everything, she'll know."

He turned to look at Lonnie and saw that his head was down; his eyes were hidden by his hand, but tears were dripping off his nose.

Finally Lonnie responded in a strangled voice, "Cut it out you son-of-a-bitch, you goddamn bastard, sniveling about dying. Sure I'll go tell her. I'll tell her what a crazy bastard you are. I'll tell her about how you went back to get those creeps in the water. Then she'll know you're crazy. Anyway she's probably forgotten about you by now. She's probably shacked up with some dumb 4-F hoping you don't come back so she can get your insurance."

Ross was grinning at him again. "I didn't know you cared so much about me, Lonnie. I'll tell you what I'll do. In case I get back and you don't, I'll go see your mother and tell her what a noble character you were. I might even give her your definition of life."

"Shit on you," said Lonnie. "I'm going to make it. I'm going back. I don't care what happens, I'm going back." He looked intently at Ross, "And you're going back too, if it kills me."

They heard one of the Japanese guards shouting. The men were moving out of the shed into the open enclosure so Ross and Lonnie followed. When they got out, a line was already forming. It was just beginning to get dark, and Lonnie could see the remnants of a brilliant sunset over the west wall.

"Jesus Christ, I hope it's food," he said. "I'm so damn hungry I can't stand it any more."

"It's food, alright. Look there."

Four prisoners were carrying a sheet of tin covered with cooked rice, the steam still rising from it. They came into the enclosure from the red brick building and were soon followed by three other men carrying sacks of something. "Anything," thought Lonnie, "anything at all will do." The sight of the steaming rice made him weak and slightly nauseated. The line was slow, incredibly slow, like somebody had slowed time down. He tried counting his heart beats but kept losing count. Once he got up to thirty-five before he had to start over. Then he counted firefly flashes which could be clearly seen now in the growing darkness. He counted fifty-two above the building and thirty within the compound before he was finally there. One of the prisoners took his canteen cup and scooped it full of rice. He was also given three small sweet potatoes and a pinch of salt which he carried in his closed hand.

When they were back in their corner in the tin shed, Lonnie ate the salt first. Large crystals which melted on the tongue and burned the inside of his mouth.

"Jesus Christ, that salt's sweet, best damn stuff I ever tasted. Now this is what life's all about, when you need something real bad, and you got it. Like this salt." He made slavering noises as he licked off the palm of his hand. "You know there's a whole ocean of that stuff out there, and only about four days ago we were swimming in it, and I didn't even take time to drink any of it."

"It would have killed you deader than a doornail," said Ross thoughtfully. He had sprinkled the salt on his rice. "But I like your notion of life. It's the sweet taste of salt," and he also licked off the inside of his hand.

"Did you ever eat any pussy?" asked Lonnie as he washed his sweet potatoes with water from his canteen.

"Sure, lots of times. Well quite a few times."

Lonnie looked up with interest, his mouth full of rice, "What did it taste like? Kind of fishy?"

"Not at all," confided Ross. "More like salty mushrooms."

Lonnie was intense with interest now, "You're kiddin', salty mushrooms?"

"Salty mushrooms," Ross repeated positively.

"You're lying," said Lonnie, looking intently at Ross. He had even stopped eating for the moment.

Ross looked hurt. "Have I ever lied to you about eating pussy before?" he asked.

"Shit on you," said Lonnie.

They sat in silence for a few moments, enjoying their rice and potatoes.

"You know I've never had a piece of ass," volunteered Lonnie.

"So you've told me."

"But I thought I was going to get some once," he paused retrospectively. "Have you ever been in the Copper Inn on Arapahoe Street in Denver?"

[124]

"No such luck," replied Ross but he seemed interested. "What happened in the old Copper Inn on Arapahoe Street in Denver?"

"I'll tell you if you'll promise never to tell anybody." Lonnie looked plaintively at Ross. He seemed embarrassed.

"I promise, cross my heart," Ross was smiling. "What happened?"

"Well I was in there by myself one night, sitting at the bar. I always liked the Copper Inn, kind of dark and crummy. And they always served me drinks without asking a lot of dumb questions about how old I was and that shit."

"How old were you?" interrupted Ross.

"What the hell difference does that make, dammit, I was seventeen. Quit interrupting or I won't tell you what happened.

"Anyway I was in there that night sitting at the bar, drinking a sloe gin and soda (that's my favorite drink) when this girl, maybe about twenty-three or twenty-four, sat down beside me. She was real good looking with big boobs. She was kind of freckled with red hair, and she had on this black dress with some kind of red trim. You could see part of her boobs. Well, she sat down there beside me and asked me if I would buy her a drink. Well you know me, I can't stand to see anybody thirsty, so I bought her a drink. Then we started talking and I told her about being from New Mexico and about running off from home and joining the army. And she told me about how she was real religious and that the end of the world was going to happen soon. Well we kept talking and I kept buying us drinks and then she started rubbing my leg. I couldn't believe it, then she started playing with my cock with her hand. Jesus Christ! There we were sitting there with her telling me about going up on the top of Pike's Peak with a bunch of people so they could see the end of the world first, and all the time she was sipping her drink with her right hand and her left hand was playing with my cock. Can you believe it?"

"Hardly," admitted Ross, "but go on."

"Well finally she said real casually that she had something for me and suggested that we go to one of the booths. Man I could hardly walk, my cock was as hard as a rock."

[125]

"I can believe that," observed Ross. "But what did you think she could do over in that booth? Weren't there other people in there?"

"A few," admitted Lonnie. "Hell, I didn't know what she was going to do but I was past caring as long as it was something. Anyway she slid into the last booth, so far away from the bar that it was damn near dark and pulled me in beside her. We still had our drinks. There we were sipping our drinks and chatting while she was playing with my cock again. But this time she unbuttoned my pants and finally got it out. I wear tight shorts. Well she had it out and was stroking it and telling me about how it wouldn't be long until the end of the world would come."

"It sounds more like something else was about to come," Ross said, smiling at Lonnie.

Lonnie didn't notice, he cleared his throat and looked entreatingly at Ross, a vague indistinct figure there beside him. It was getting dark in the shed.

"Now you promise you won't tell if I tell you what happened?"

"Hell no, I won't tell. What in the hell happened? Damned if you're not worse than Gentry for stringing a story out. What in the hell happened?"

"Well I can remember it like it happened last night. I can remember exactly what she said. She whispered in a real low voice, 'Gee, you've got a nice big hot one there. Do you want me to take care of it?' "

Lonnie paused for a long moment and then continued, his voice tense.

"I told her to take care of it, and by God you wouldn't believe it. You just wouldn't believe it."

"Well for Christ's sake, what did she do?"

"She poured her drink on it," said Lonnie, his voice strained by embarrassment, "ice and all."

"Well I'll be goddamned," said Ross, unable to contain his laughter. "She cold cocked you!"

"Cold cocked. I thought that meant to get hit on the head," said Lonnie, relieved to change the subject.

It was almost pitch dark now. Lonnie could see the faint

[126]

outline of the open end of the shed as a lighter square against the deeper dark of its walls. The other men were becoming quiet, sporadic ripples of conversation and soft snores.

"I'm going to make it," said Lonnie to himself just before he went to sleep. "Before I die, I'm going to screw me a woman." The cement floor of the shed hurt his hip, the canteen holder under his head was hard and uncomfortable but he didn't notice long. He was in a vast ocean filled with icebergs searching for his LIFE WOMAN, an ocean which changed into a grey and endless plain filled with odd angles, angles which went on forever, sharp steel wedges, with ragged sides. He knew she was there somewhere, lost among the angles, but he couldn't see her. He thought he heard her calling to him but it was not a human voice, it was a sound he had heard once as a little child when he had held a rubber band stretched taut in the wind; a weird undulating sound which grew in volume until its oscillations filled the grey plain and caused his bones to ache.

After an endless time the sounds faded, the angles became vague and dawn turned the doorway of the shed into a faint rectangle. For just a moment suspended there between nothing and potentiality he was overwhelmed with the impossibility of it all, of himself, of a crazy war in a crazy world, of anything. The eerie humming sounds came again, grew louder and suddenly were transformed into the dull roar of airplane engines. Out of impossibility the actuality of sounds undulating and shifting from low drones to labored screams and in the background the hunger, steady as always. Shit it couldn't be true. He raised on his right arm and stared at Ross still sleeping next to him, his face clearly etched in the light of the new morning, every rib distinct under the shiny skin, the knob of his hip showing itself through the Filipino shorts, the muscles of his right leg drooping down, loose in the skin. It was true, the whole goddamn miserable mess.

"Wake up, you son-of-a-bitch," Lonnie heard himself saying, his voice so loud that others near them stirred in their sleep. Then more quietly as he shook him, "Hey Ross, there's something crazy going on outside." Just then the engine of an airplane, starting as a low drone moved up the register, higher

[127]

and higher, until it achieved an ear splitting crescendo almost directly above them. Everyone in the shed, including Ross, was awake now, staring vaguely around at one another. A few individuals near the open end of the shed had crawled out and were looking up.

"What's happening?" asked Ross.

"How in the hell should I know?" replied Lonnie. "You know as much as I do. I've been asleep right here in this shed just like you, and the Japs haven't called me in for a conference lately, you shithead."

"It sounds like an air battle," offered Ross, undisturbed. "Let's take a look."

Everyone in the shed seemed to get the same idea simultaneously. There was a general rush through the opening into the compound. Mouths open, jaws slack, the prisoners and a number of Japanese guards stared upwards. The sky was filled with airplanes, airplanes which produced weird light flashes, reflections of the new sun, as they turned and spiraled and dived. There were hundreds of them, at all altitudes, darting in and out and around. They moved as if caught up in some haphazard compulsion, an undulating distribution within which for a moment consistent patterns might appear only to dissolve into the development of some new configuration. Strange slow motion world of shifting light points, the hieroglyphics of contrails, "like Japanese writing," thought Lonnie, which drifted and expanded toward the southwest. There was thunder in the patterns, sometimes short bursts and sometimes long reverberating roars which masked all other sounds. Lonnie saw a number of the moving light points leave gentle arcs of smoke indelible against the sky, to show for a moment that some boy whose mother waits had passed that way. Parachutes sprang suddenly into sight like instant mushrooms in a sky blue field where all the clouds were made by men. At one time Lonnie counted six of them drifting down so slowly that they didn't seem to move at all unless one looked away and then looked back at them.

Suddenly a number of the Japanese guards started running around the enclosure shouting and making crazy gestures with their hands. One of them kept screaming, "No look! No look!"

and put his hands over his own eyes and held his head down toward the ground. The guards tried herding the prisoners into the sheds but there wasn't enough room for all of them. The remainder including Ross and Lonnie were forced to sit and hold their heads down between their knees. Lonnie couldn't resist sneaking a look and was rewarded with a smart crack on the top of his head with a stick.

"Of all the stupid things I've seen the Japs do, this is the dumbest," observed Ross in a loud whisper. "Did you get hurt?"

"Shit no, just a little clunk. I got a head like a rock. I wonder who's winning? Must be the Americans or they wouldn't be so upset about us watching."

"They don't know who's winning either. How could they? Old Iwahara is just in one of his lousy moods and this is just another one of his stupid orders. It must be Iwahara, Major Imada wouldn't give an order like this."

"You're right," agreed Lonnie. "It's that fucking Iwahara."

They sat in the center of the compound, back to back, leaning against each other listening to the sounds of battle shift in intensity, ebbing as the center of the conflict moved away or increasing as it moved back toward them again. Once they heard an eerie "fruf, fruf, fruf" like a huge boomerang whirling through the sky, getting closer and closer. They hunched down close to the ground waiting for the sound of an explosion which strangely never came.

"What in the hell was that?" gasped Lonnie. "I never heard anything so goddamn weird in my life and what the hell happened to it?"

"Probably the wing of an airplane which fell in the woods someplace," said Ross.

The battle went on, the sun rose until it was hot in the compound, almost noon Lonnie thought, before the sounds began to diminish, moving away toward the southwest. The men started moving around again, the Japanese guards didn't seem to care even though no order had been given.

"They probably thought it was as stupid as we did," said Lonnie. "Let's get some water." They filled their canteens at the pipe which was still flowing in the center of the compound next to the tall tree. It wasn't much of a tree any more. Most of the bark had been picked from it and all the leaves. Lonnie peeled off a bit of the bark which remained but it was bitter and too stringy to swallow.

"Whoever ate that stuff is in for a real gut ache," he observed, spitting the green fiber out on the dry ground. "You know," he said observing the sky, "we haven't had a drop of rain since we started on this trip. That's damn funny isn't it?"

"Not really. It's the dry season. Look at that."

Lonnie looked up and saw two airplanes, weaving in and out, so high and so far away that they seemed like small slivers of steel playing a harmless game in a world that had nothing to do with them. He saw the small white puff of a parachute and one of the planes fell like a tiny flaming arrow out of sight behind the wall.

He heard the noise of motors then, from beyond the red brick building, the sound of trucks stopping. After a few minutes he saw them coming through the inner door of the building into the compound, the seven hundred men who had been left in the tennis courts, a skeleton army dressed in denim shorts with web belts tight around skinny bellies, except for Corso who seemed as fat as ever as he greeted Lonnie.

"Hey Chicken Lickin', how's the candle?"

"Fuck you," said Lonnie absently. He was looking for Gentry and R. T. Barton and finally he saw them coming through the door, R. T. Barton in front talking and Gentry following, not listening.

"You're not being very nice to a sweet guy like me," said a voice at his elbow. It was Corso standing there with his arms resting on his huge belly. "I've got a present for you."

Lonnie turned to see a full pack of cigarettes held out toward him with two or three standing up straight, inviting. Gentry and R. T. Barton came up just then and Corso turned the cigarettes in their direction, his face impassive, his small dark eyes moving back and forth not quite looking at anyone.

"Thanks Corso," said Gentry. As he reached over and took a cigarette, Corso started to grin happily and to rock back and forth on his feet.

"I'm a mean son-of-a-bitch," he observed as he offered cigarettes to R. T. Barton and Lonnie.

[130]

"Yes you are," Gentry agreed. There was a small smile on his lips as he watched R. T. Barton take two cigarettes from the pack and Lonnie hesitate for a long moment before finally taking one. "But fish got to swim and birds got to fly."

"Gee thanks Corso," said Lonnie. "How in the hell do you get all these cigarettes? Damn good ones, too. Golden Bats. How in the hell do you do it?"

"I haven't had any complaints," replied Corso, still grinning. He placed the cigarette pack into one of the large bulging pockets of his blue denim jacket. He was wearing a pair of Filipino shorts which matched the jacket, probably large size for Filipinos thought Lonnie, but they failed to circumnavigate Corso's huge belly by at least six inches, just like when he tried on his Jap uniform back in Bilibid. They were fastened by a string running between the two front belt loops leaving a large V which showed the bulges of his white belly and finally terminated in a mass of black tangled pubic hair.

"I like your new style of clothes," said Gentry. "Décolleté."

"Yeah," agreed R. T. Barton. "You really got something going there Corso. You could probably sell it to Paris and start a new clothes trend."

"I'm sure Helen wouldn't mind," said Gentry mildly, as he watched Corso do a little stylistic dance. "Where's Ross?"

"He was right here a minute ago," said Lonnie. "He probably went to the crapper. Have they given you guys anything to eat? We got some rice and sweet potatoes. But dammit we haven't gotten anything to eat today and it's already afternoon. What did you think about that air battle?"

"We didn't see much of it," said R. T. Barton, as he looked around the compound. "The little yellow cuntheads always stopped under the trees when they got close. We couldn't see a damn thing. Is that a water pipe over there? I'm dying of thirst. I'm dying of hunger. I'm dying!"

They moved in among the men who were crowded around the water pipe and waited their turn. Lonnie was alone. He started looking for Ross but couldn't see him anywhere; the compound was crowded now that the others had come. Once or twice he thought he saw him and moved in that direction but it was just another skinny guy with blond hair. He began to walk faster, peering into strange faces, down the side of the red brick building, across to the first shed. He stood peering for a long moment into the semidarkness shouting Ross's name, but there was no answer. He went on to the next shed and the next and did the same, but still there was no answer. Finally he thought he saw him, huddled down next to the west wall, lonely among many others who had crowded in to take advantage of the shade. It was him, his face drawn and shriveled. He didn't seem to recognize Lonnie at first, but just kept looking up, his pupils so large he seemed to have black eyes rather than grey.

"What's the matter with you, you crazy bastard?" screamed Lonnie. "You're sitting over here feeling sorry for yourself, thinking about dying and all that shit. You crazy bastard! I ought to kick the shit out of you, right now." To his relief he saw that Ross was looking at him now, smiling a little, so he lowered his voice, "Guess who I was just talking to?"

"I saw them," said Ross weakly. "Old R. T. and Gentry and Corso."

"Well why in the hell didn't you come over and say something?" said Lonnie, furious again. "Do you know what you missed? A Golden Bat, that's what. Old Corso was feeling guilty and he was handing them out to all comers."

"That figures," said Ross, now grinning widely. "Let's light up and enjoy the fruits of that fruit's guilt. I've got some matches. I found a folder that still had three in it. Let's light up, that is if you're going to share your ill gotten gains with me."

"I ought to hog the whole thing myself," said Lonnie. But he was grinning too, happy to see that the pinched look had left Ross' face.

"You know," said Ross, as they were taking turns at the cigarette, "I've just figured out what you ought to be, if you get back to the States all in one piece."

"I'm going to get back," affirmed Lonnie, taking a deep drag. "I'm going to get back alright. And so are you, you crazy bastard."

"You ought to be a psychologist," continued Ross. "You've got a talent."

"I've got a cigarette," said Lonnie.

CHAPTER FIVE

When the shadow from the west wall reached the small tree which stood naked and forlorn near the closest shed, they heard the sounds of clicking mess kits. It was rice and sweet potatoes again, but not so much this time. When they had finished the small meal, Lonnie pursued each lingering grain of rice around the bottom of his canteen cup, and even licked out the interior as far down as his tongue would reach. He sat back then overwhelmed by a storm of hunger.

"Jesus Christ, I can't stand it," said Lonnie. "Let's dig."

Within two hours they collected twenty-seven long fat earthworms, in the shadow next to the west wall. Lonnie gagged in the beginning. It was the first time they had eaten them raw, but the more he ate the better they got. He didn't mind the grit and the dull pungent taste of earth.

"Hell fire," he grinned at Ross, "birds get up early to do this sort of thing."

That night they tried to get back into the shed but it was too crowded. They went back to the wall but their places had been taken. Finally they lay down next to the small naked tree and slept for awhile. Lonnie woke stiff with cold just as the moon was beginning to rise over the east wall. He shook Ross and they made their way into the shed stepping carefully over sleeping men until they came to their corner. They managed to make a place for themselves by gentle but persistent pushing. Lonnie kept shoving and taking up space until he was able to lie completely flat. Ross lay beside him, warm and comforting, and just before Lonnie went to sleep he heard him snoring softly.

As each day passed they dug more and more worms. Other men had taken up the practice now and by the fourth day the earth in the enclosure looked as if it had been plowed for spring planting. On the evening of the fifth day, just before twilight, they heard airplanes coming in low over the city: short, squat and ugly, ten of them flying in disarray, moving in and out like pointers covering a field looking for quail. As they flew over, Lonnie saw white stars clearly outlined on the dark wings.

"So much for eight hundred Jap airplanes," said Ross, a note of pride and awe in his voice. "Where are they now?"

"All gone, now," echoed Lonnie almost stupidly as he kept

[133]

staring up after the planes were gone. It seemed he could still see the white stars lingering in the darkening sky even after the engine sounds had been displaced by the cries of the "fuck you" lizards which always started their insults about this time of night. "Fuck yourself," said Lonnie. Then they heard Mr. Noda's voice, small and plaintive and alien, announce that they would all be leaving early in the morning.

"Where we going?" somebody in the darkness shouted. This cry was taken up, first by a few, then by hundreds until every man in the compound was screaming out the question. "Where we going? Where we going?"

Finally above the expression and reverberation Lonnie could hear Mr. Noda's voice pleading, "Okay you guys, quiet down, quiet down, and I'll tell you." There was quiet then, complete and sudden, in the almost total darkness.

"Maybe back to Cabanatuan," said Mr. Noda, his voice strangely loud and piercing against the silence. "Maybe back to Cabanatuan."

Lonnie heard himself screaming, "What the fuck does maybe mean?" Other prisoners took up the cry, but Mr. Noda didn't answer. He had left the compound, but he had also left hope with them and optimism. Far into the night there were little bursts of song.

"What the fuck does 'maybe' mean?"

That night Lonnie and Ross waited until the moon had risen above the east wall before they crept into the shed. They couldn't see a thing. Just kept easing along, feeling their way over the welter of intermingled limbs; finally to their corner, already occupied. Gentle pushing worked again, the sleepers made way and they lay down in relative warmth. Lonnie went to sleep almost immediately and had slept for just a moment so it seemed when he felt someone shaking him. It was Ross. They crept out of the shed as quietly as they had come, rewarded once or twice by curses for their trespass.

"Drink all you can hold," said Ross as Lonnie took his turn at the water pipe. Lonnie kept drinking until he felt on the verge of gagging, then filled his canteen again. They sat down then among individuals already waiting by the door leading out of the compound, just as a faint glow from the east was beginning to lighten the upper portions of the west wall. Lonnie tried to see the changes in the light as it moved from dimness into morning. But he couldn't. It's like getting old, he thought, but faster. You can't see it until after it's happened.

But he could see the men coming awake, stretching and slowly getting to their feet moving out of the clusters into which they had gathered for warmth, blinking in the morning light, then lining up. By the time the first glint of sun struck the northwest guard tower every man in the compound had found his place in the formation, waiting, looking towards the door. As if on cue, it opened and there stood Mr. Noda beckoning. Lonnie and Ross were first to go through into the sunshine where the guards and a little bit of food waited. Each man received a small salmon can of rice, no sweet potatoes this time, and then lined up for the count; twelve hundred and thirty-three men. It was the day before Christmas.

CHAPTER SIX

Lonnie and Ross were the leaders of the first column. Out ahead of him Lonnie could see Mr. Noda and a Japanese non-com, the one with the ratty face, pointing the way. The sun was warm on his naked chest and the grass, still wet with dew, felt good on his bare feet. Behind him he heard somebody, he was sure it was R. T. Barton, singing, "I'm goin to buy a paper doll that I can call my own." He was always singing that song. Lonnie had to grin to himself remembering Gentry's comment that old R. T. had gotten his tongue confused with his prick and wouldn't know what to do with a real woman. Lonnie looked back and sure enough it was R. T. Barton, leading the second column. Gentry was with him looking bored and to Lonnie's surprise Corso was walking at Gentry's right. The three musketeers, thought Lonnie, and laughed out loud.

After they had gone nearly half a mile Lonnie could see railroad tracks ahead and a small red brick station. Railroad engines and cars were laying around the yard, some damaged and a few totally demolished. The old familiar flare went off in Lonnie's chest. As they got closer he could see large holes left by bombs in the station yard. The northern section of the red brick building was missing completely and the rest of it had been gutted by flames.

They waited near a locomotive which had great holes in its

steam tank. It grew hot in the station yard and many of the men fell asleep in the warm sun, looking like long rows of skinny corpses. Finally Mr. Noda gave the order to move out again and the column angled across a series of tracks toward a grove of trees a few hundred yards away. As they approached Lonnie could see a train half visible in the gloom under the trees; an engine exuding hisses of steam and a number of box cars, crummy little bastards, about half the size of American railroad cars. Lonnie and Ross were the first men in the first box car. It was a fair climb but they both made it without help and were surprised by the intense gloom of the interior. More and more men kept pouring into the car, forcing Ross and Lonnie back until they were pressed against the rear wall, and still they could hear the Japanese shouting for the men to move back and to make room.

"There isn't any more room, you yellow cuntheads!" screamed Lonnie. All around him men were shouting and cursing and shoving. Lonnie was pressed against the rough boards of the back wall with such force that it took all his strength, shoving with both his arms and legs to get a little room for breathing. He heard Ross muttering right next to his left ear; he could just see the outline of his face in the dim light coming in from the door.

"See what you've done, you son-of-a-bitch," screamed Lonnie. "Get up and be first you said. Get up and be first for what? You son-of-a-bitch! To be sardines, that's what!"

"Ah, quit sniveling like a baby," said Ross. "You wanted to be first as much as I did and you know it. You're just a goddamned baby."

"Shit on you," said Lonnie. But he didn't say any more. He heard the sound of the door closing and suddenly it was pitch black in the box car. Almost immediately it began to get hot and the flare in Lonnie's chest changed into an ague of cold terror.

"We're going to suffocate in this fucking place," he screamed and others took up the cry and began to undulate back and forth with such frenzy that the entire car swayed. Lonnie heard somebody shouting for them to be quiet, that everything was going to be okay. It was Ross's voice, loud and firm, and pretty soon everybody did quiet down and the shoving became less extreme. Then Lonnie heard movement overhead, scuffing sounds and muffled voices and he started shouting again.

"Be first you said. Goddammit we should have been last. You know what's happening! Those lazy bastards which were last are going to get to ride on top of the cars, that's what! They're up there in the fresh air, enjoying the scenery while we're down here playing sardine, suffocating!"

"Shut up, you goddamn baby," said Ross.

As his eyes became used to the darkness Lonnie could see little cracks of light, one large one where the side of the car met the roof and another smaller one in the corner about a foot from the floor. He had managed to relax a little, his right shoulder and head resting against the side of the car, his back arched against those pressing in against him.

"Are you in the corner?" he asked Ross.

"Yes, I'm in the corner," responded Ross. "So what?"

"So don't let anybody root you out of there, that's what. There's a crack close to the floor and we may be down there sucking for air if it gets much worse in here."

The car made a sudden lurch forward and the men oscillated back and forth, alternately releasing and then applying so much pressure on Lonnie that he thought his ribs would break. But finally the car settled down to a smooth acceleration marked by the increasing cadence of wheels striking rail connections. The pressure ceased shifting and became a constant slippery contact of sweating bodies transfixed in vertical misery. Air was entering the car now. Lonnie could feel a considerable draft coming in from somewhere above him, probably through cracks, there didn't seem to be any ventilators. He stood there leaning against the side of the car listening to the ka-thunk, ka-thunk, ka-thunk. Hours passed and fatigue moved up his legs, spread out into his arms, settled like a burning coal in his back.

"Goddammit I can't stand it any more," he shouted. "I can't stand it! I got to sit down!"

"You can sit down under me," said Ross. "I've got a space under me. Scooch down and get under me if you can." Lonnie

[138]

let himself down, pushing back against the pressure of bodies until he reached the floor. He inched into the corner, humped up like a beetle with Ross leaning over him and the fatigue washed away, out of his arms and legs but it remained in his back like a knot. By lifting his head and turning it to a peculiar angle he could see out the crack. He remained in that odd position watching the trees and nipa huts flash by. A sudden clearing and he saw the mountains in the distance. He saw the mountains, saw them again a frozen image and the small pleasure he felt in seeing them suddenly flared into anxiety and then congealed into dull terror. He began to cry, no longer looking through the crack, his head down on his two hands.

From a distance he heard Ross's voice shouting, "What's the matter with you? What in the hell are you sniveling about now?"

"We're going north!" Lonnie heard himself screaming. "We're going north! They're going to try to get us out again. That goddamn lying Noda, that son-of-a-bitch. He knew it all the time."

Then he heard Ross's voice, desperate with fatigue, "Can you change places with me for a little while? I've just about had it."

"Sit down on me," said Lonnie. He could feel Ross turning above him, and then felt his weight and his sharp tail bones as he sat down shaking with fatigue. He heard the other men repeating the information and a numbed silence stretched out and emphasized the ka-thunk, ka-thunk, ka-thunk of the wheels.

"Move around a little bit," he said to Ross. "Your ass bones are killing me!"

Ross shifted a bit and then said in a conversational tone, "Well I guess we know what maybe means."

"Yes," responded Lonnie from below him. "It means we are probably going to get our asses blown off. You're getting heavier than hell. How about letting me ride for awhile? I'm tired of playing horse."

After much scrabbling around they changed places. Ross on his hands and knees and Lonnie sitting comfortably on his

[139]

back. "You know I read in some magazine about an African chief who kept a number of natives around just to sit on. He had one who was kind of bony that he used as a straight chair. There was another one with a big fat ass that he used when he wanted to lounge a bit. Man that would be a crummy job, being a chair."

"Yes it sure is," agreed Ross.

"Any time the chief wanted to sit down he would just look at one of those guys and they would get down and make like a chair. It didn't matter where it was, sharp rocks, mud, it didn't matter. Crummy job."

"It sure is," repeated Ross. "How about you being chair for awhile?"

Lonnie lost count of the times he and Ross changed places. Finally he couldn't see any light coming through the cracks and knew that it was night. Many of the men were lying on the floor beneath the feet of the others and a heavy stench of urine filled the car. At last Lonnie heard the train slowing, the ka-thunks came less often and less often until they ceased. After fifteen or twenty minutes Lonnie heard the door being opened, sliding back; an eerie flickering red light lit up the interior of the car.

"We are here," he said to Ross as they waited their turn to go through the open door.

"Yep, we're here," agreed Ross. He jumped down from the car and then turned to help Lonnie. It was a good four foot drop. On every side Japanese guards held red flares, so bright it hurt to look at them; flares which painted everything in red wavering light, an island of brightness within a darkness which pushed in from just beyond where the flares burned and sent spirals of smoke upward. Out of the door and down from the top of the cars, into formation, twelve deep. A Japanese guard came down the line holding his flare high while another guard checked the rear of the formation, keeping pace, looking for gaps. At least twenty prisoners didn't make the formation. Lonnie could see them lying quietly on the upward slope of the embankment, one moved now and then but most just lay there motionless and silent, the red light flickering over their bare legs.

The order came to move out up the embankment, past an old red brick station house, on into the deserted street of a fairly large town. Lonnie and Ross were in the first column at the front of the formation. The guards walked on both sides, their flares burning and smoking, brighter than hell. Once Lonnie thought he saw somebody watching from an open window but he wasn't sure. There was no sound but the rasping of naked feet on the cobblestones, the occasional shout of a guard and a subdued whispering among the marching men.

"Why is everybody whispering?" said Lonnie aloud. "It's like a goddamn funeral procession." His voice echoed back from the walls of the buildings, reverberated in his own ears.

"What's wrong with you bastards?" he said, his voice faltering. He turned and looked over his shoulder at the formation and he too became silent. An army of almost naked men, bare knobby joints and skinny chests where ribs showed and sunken bellies were holes of darkness, stretched back as far as he could see, walking in a kind of shuffling, rhythmic cadence. The red light from the flares wavered and cast overlapping shadows on the walls, a grotesque shadow army in quadruplicate, bigger than life. From behind him someone began to sing the hopeless dirge of the Volga Boatmen and others took up the song until it swelled through the streets and filled the night with its desperation. The guards looked nervously from side to side, their flares held high, but soon some of them began to grin. For a new song, a song which they had heard many times, could be heard; at first in the background of the other song, then rising above it, displacing it completely. Lonnie had started the singing and then Ross and hundreds up and down the columns joined him . . . "Fuck 'em all, fuck 'em all, the long and the short and the tall, there'll be no devotion this side of the ocean, fuck 'em all, my friends, fuck 'em all," Lonnie screamed at the top of his voice. It seemed now as if every man was singing, even the Japanese guards, and the people hidden away deep in the interior of the buildings; and the night itself.

Through another gate into another compound, a large building outlined by the torches, a few trees scattered about and a hedge which seemed to enclose about an acre. Lonnie didn't notice any more but lay down on the ground where they had stopped and went to sleep. Toward dawn he awoke, cold and wet from the dew which had come with the morning. He looked for Ross but couldn't see him in the dim light. He called his name softly but there was no response. On all sides of him men slept, scattered around the enclosure, gathered into small clumps to keep warm. He went to sleep again and this time when he awoke the sun was warm on his bare skin and Ross was shaking him.

"Are you okay? You were making the damndest noises, whimpering like a dog and gritting your teeth."

"Probably dreaming I was eating a big turkey dinner," said Lonnie raising on his elbow. "Where were you about dawn? I woke up and you weren't here," his voice had an accusing note.

"I was doing something important," responded Ross.

"Yeah, sure, like taking a piss."

"Right," said Ross. "Look at those trees."

Every tree in the compound had been stripped of its leaves and bark; a few individuals were still working on them, peeling them down to the wood. Others were trying to get to the hedge but the Japanese guards kept driving them back.

"I don't blame them," said Lonnie. "I'm so goddamn hungry I can't believe it. There must be something to eat some place." He looked around the compound, then up toward the eaves of the building and Ross's eyes followed his glance.

"I can damn near see bananas up there," said Lonnie looking toward the roof of the building. "Big bunches of long yellow bananas ready to pull and peel. You know, right now I think I'd rather have a bunch of bananas than a piece of ass."

"How about just one banana?" asked Ross.

"Yes, even one banana," said Lonnie absently. "Maybe there's something under that building, at least it will be out of the sun. Let's go under there. We might find something. I don't think those bastards are ever going to feed us. They're going to let us starve right here in this damn compound."

"Maybe not," said Ross. "But it's getting hot so let's move; there's sure nothing out here." Ross led the way toward the

[142]

building, an old school house, squat and square, showing dark places where the boards had been ripped away from the siding beneath the floor. They found an opening and crawled back into the semi-darkness; it was cool and peaceful. Lonnie could smell the dampness of the earth and hear movement on the floor above.

"Should be some worms under here," he said to Ross. "Want to do some digging?"

"I'm tired of digging worms," responded Ross. "I think I'll just lie down here and sleep awhile. You go ahead if you want to."

"Fuck the worms," said Lonnie. He lay beside Ross trying not to think about being hungry, listening to the sounds of scraping and muffled voices above him. Other prisoners were moving under the building now; it was getting crowded. Lonnie looked for Gentry and R. T. Barton and Corso but he didn't see anybody he knew. I'll find them later, he thought, and went to sleep. When he awoke it was warm and quiet under the building and Ross was still asleep there beside him. Maybe he's dead. In a fit of terror he began to shake Ross and to call his name.

"What's the matter with you?" he was relieved to hear Ross saying.

"I thought maybe you were dead," said Lonnie meekly. "I couldn't hear you breathing."

"No such luck. Let's see what's happening outside."

They crawled out and stood blinking for a few moments in the late afternoon sunshine. Hardly anyone was moving. The men lay in the shade of the building and in the shadow of the hedge, looking around, first at one thing and then another. Probably looking for bananas thought Lonnie.

They began to dig in the shade on the east side of the building with a triangular piece of tin Lonnie had found, but they didn't find any worms. There was too much gravel. They tried again in a grassy spot close to the water pipe but still no worms. Fuck it. They sat back to back leaning against each other, looking at men who wandered aimlessly about or used up time making the journey from the drinking pipe to the latrine trench and back again. A Japanese guard on the other side of the hedge was leaning against a cement post, smoking a cigarette. No use asking him for butts. It became dark in the compound; stars were beginning to show above the hedge. They lay down on the ground, still warm from the sun, and just before he went to sleep Lonnie had a funny thought.

"Merry Christmas," he said.

"Well, I'll be damned, you're right," said Ross. "It is Christmas!"

Lonnie raised himself on his elbow and shouted out, "Merry Christmas. Merry Christmas." His voice echoed back from the side of the building but no one said anything.

"Merry Christmas," Lonnie shouted again at the top of his voice. Then somebody out of the darkness answered.

"Shut up, you goddamn creep!"

"Fuck you," said Lonnie. He lay back down and looked into the night sky at the millions of light points. The impossibility of it all came over him again, of himself, of the stars, of anything. From somewhere far away, just on the edge of sound or thought he heard the whining sound, like a taut rubber band keening in the wind. It must be my hunger that I'm hearing, he thought, just before he went to sleep.

Dawn came and with it the damp cold. They moved under the building again and shoved gently against sleeping men until a space was made for them. They slept for a while, then moved back into the compound, looking for food, hoping for some change. The sun rose until it was directly above them and still no food, the day moved into afternoon and nothing happened. But just as the shadow from the hedge reached halfway to the school house Lonnie looked up to see Mr. Noda coming through the gate into the compound.

"Let's get to the head of the line," Lonnie said to Ross. "We're going to move again."

"Where we going?" Lonnie shouted at Mr. Noda as he came toward them but Mr. Noda didn't answer. He stood for a moment looking at the prisoners most of whom still lay on the ground staring, not seeing anything. Like a bunch of zombie skeletons thought Lonnie, following Mr. Noda's gaze.

"I thought you didn't want to be first," said Ross, cinching up his web belt, "and here we go again. I don't want any bitching out of you even if they shoot us."

"If they shoot us, I won't bitch a bit," said Lonnie, proud of his levity. "I figure that about a third of those bastards back there won't be able to walk very well and you know what that means, somebody is going to have to carry them. Do you want to carry somebody?"

"No," admitted Ross. "I can hardly carry myself."

The long column moved out through the gate and up a cobblestone street between empty nipa shacks. Lonnie was right. Almost immediately some of the men began to stagger and to fall out of formation. The guards picked other prisoners out of the line to help them along, and the column kept moving, getting more and more strung out as the weaker ones fell behind.

"What in the hell are those?" Lonnie asked Ross, pointing.

"Sand dunes. I'll bet your left testical we are going to get on another ship and soon."

"Jesus Christ," said Lonnie under his breath. Then he nudged Ross. "Isn't that old Colonel Nelson?"

"Yes," replied Ross. They both watched in amazement as the old man walked in a tangent away from the column. His head was held high, his shoulders back. He didn't even look around when the guards started shouting at him but kept walking away with funny jerky steps, looking toward a grove of trees which skirted the sand dunes. Suddenly he fell down and lay there quietly in the grass and weeds. One of the guards poked him with a stick and he moved a little. Another guard came over and selected two men, Lonnie and Ross were both looking the other way, from the column and made them pick the old man up. They half carried, half dragged him back. Lonnie remembered how tall and dignified he had been and how he took pride in ringing the bell and in his watch. But he wasn't dignified now. He had soiled his shorts and had removed them and now was only wearing a small Filipino jacket which was too short for him. As the men half carried him along he would lurch from side to side, at times almost tripping them. Below the knees his legs were like sticks, his joints like large knobs; bloody excreta flowed down his legs in a continual stream. Where buttocks had once been only loose skin remained and the bones of his pelvis could be clearly seen beneath the skin. The men who had been forced to help him complained about it and kept asking for help but nobody volunteered.

"I wonder what happened to his watch?" Lonnie whispered to Ross.

"For Christ's sake, what kind of goddamn ghoul are you?" replied Ross. "That poor old man is dying and you start worrying about his watch."

"Well somebody is going to get his watch," said Lonnie defensively.

"For Christ's sake," repeated Ross.

"I wish I had a cigarette," said Lonnie. "Look at that sunset." They gazed toward the west where banks of clouds flared by the sun showed bloody red and great fans of light sprayed out to tinge high wisps of clouds with rainbows.

"See that sundog?" asked Lonnie looking up. "Doesn't that mean good luck or something?"

"Yeah, it means something," responded Ross. Their bare feet sank into warm sand as they walked along, they had reached the sand dunes.

"Jesus Christ," said Lonnie, "I think I can smell the sea. Do you smell the sea?"

"I smell something to eat," said Ross.

When they came to the top of one of the dunes they saw a number of guards carrying large tubs filled with something round and white, like snowballs. Each man received a ball of rice a little bigger than a man's fist. Lonnie and Ross sat down in the sand near the top of one of the dunes and nibbled away, savoring each little compact bite, washing it down with water. The long line kept coming over the sand dunes, the weak being helped by the stronger. But as soon as they saw that others were being given food they dropped their burdens and quickened their pace toward the tubs. Lonnie remembered how cattle, tired and thirsty after a long day's drive, would alert and start moving fast when they came within smell and sight of a river.

"Let's get in line again," he said to Ross. "Nobody will know the difference."

"I will," replied Ross, but he followed Lonnie down the side of the dune where they mixed in with the stragglers just coming into the area. As a guard gave each of them another ball of rice Lonnie saw that there was only one tub left and that the line was still coming over the hill.

"I feel like a son-of-a-bitch taking more than my share. I can't eat it," said Ross. "I just can't eat it."

Lonnie, stuffing his down, could hardly be understood, "Eat it, goddammit." He looked at Ross accusingly. "What the hell is wrong with you? Have you gone crazy?"

Ross sat with the rice ball in his hand watching the stragglers move in toward the tubs. They were still coming when the rice ran out. They started shouting and cursing, but there wasn't any more. The guards took the empty tubs and disappeared into the increasing darkness. Ross got up and walked down the hill. Soon Lonnie saw him, barely visible in the dim light, making his way back up the sand dune. He didn't have the rice ball.

"Who did you give the rice ball to?" Lonnie asked.

"To Rutledge," said Ross.

They sat at the very peak of the sand dune and watched the night move in. Most of the red had gone from the clouds, they were black now with feeble glows around them. Somewhere over toward the line of trees a bird kept repeating the same shrill cry.

"I'm a no good bastard," said Lonnie finally, with a catch in his voice.

"No you're not. You're just a hungry bastard," said Ross gently. "Let's get some sleep. Something tells me we are going to have a big day tomorrow."

About two hundred feet away near the top of the largest sand dune flares were lit and they soon saw men digging. Later Lonnie heard Father Maloney's strong voice saying a prayer for the dead, and he felt better.

"Did you see Gentry, or R. T.," and then almost guiltily, "or old Corso?"

"No," said Ross quietly, still looking at the flares. "But I'm sure they're okay. You can be sure of one thing," he paused for a moment, "you can be sure that old Gentry will live as long as Father Maloney does. He made that bet, remember?"

"Yes, I remember," replied Lonnie. "Gee this sand is warm. I'll bet it will keep us warm all night."

They buried themselves in the warm sand and just before

they went to sleep Lonnie noticed that something was missing. For the first time in many days he wasn't hungry.

I ought to feel guilty, he thought. But he didn't. He went to sleep, snug and comfortable in the warm sand. Somehow in his sleep he heard the monstrous machinery of time passing, the mighty crashing thunder of suns colliding in the slow inexorable swirl of milky ways; the Colonel's watch dangling on its gold chain held by a hand which he knew was there but which he couldn't see. He could hear the ticking and feel the thrill of impulse from the main spring. Then he heard his own heart beating, magnified by the sand against which his ear was pressed. He raised up and saw Ross' face brightly visible in the light of a late moon, but his body was a pile of sand.

Lonnie woke to the sounds of Japanese guards shouting, "Kisho, Kisho." It was just beginning to lighten in the east; a crescent moon shone feebly above the far sand dunes, and somewhere to the northwest he could hear the sound of surf crashing. In the dim light he saw men climbing up out of the earth, sand spilling from them. Already a small line was forming.

"Hurry up damnit," he shouted at Ross. But Ross was already buckling on his canteen belt, looking down at him still buried in the sand.

"Hurry up, hell," Ross responded. "Get your lazy ass out of the sand pile."

Lonnie scrambled out feeling the cool wind on his bare chest. He stood for a moment pissing, watching it disappear into the sand. It was lighter now, almost day, and his urine made an interesting hieroglyphic in the sand. He tried to write his name but had only reached the first N when he ran out. He looked up to see Ross watching him, grinning.

"Ran out of ink," he said noncommittally as he buckled on his web belt. They started moving down the dune toward the growing column of men. Lonnie took a sip from his canteen and shook it. It was still nearly full.

"Save your water," he told Ross. "I've got a notion we're going to need it."

"Yeah, I know," said Ross. He was watching some of the guards checking the sand piles.

"I guess they think somebody is going to escape by staying buried," said Lonnie following his glance. The guards were probing into the piles of sand with long sticks, but as far as Lonnie could see they didn't find anybody. Up towards the top of the largest dune he could see men digging. Somebody else didn't make it.

"I'm gong to make it," he said aloud as they moved into the middle of the second formation. When the order finally came to move out, the sun had edged over the top of the far dunes. As they walked along, Lonnie pushed his bare feet deep into the sand. It felt good; on the surface it was cool but just underneath it was warm and squirted up between his toes like a heavy liquid.

They came to the top of a slight rise and below them, just where he knew it would be, Lonnie saw the ocean. Five transports lay at anchor in a small bay, and further out a Japanese destroyer sat motionless in the center of the outlet. Beyond the destroyer large waves crashed against jagged rocks, occasionally sending columns of spray high in the air. Most of the waves were dampened but some came on through the inlet, past the destroyer causing the transports to rock gently. Six different docks piled high with bags and boxes jutted out into the water. Trucks were being loaded by Japanese soldiers, chanting in unison, as they heaved large objects to others who seized them and put them carefully into place. Lonnie calculated that it only took four minutes for them to load a truck. Some fast work.

The prisoners moved out on the largest dock, past the piles of bags and boxes, to the very end of it. No place to go now, without swimming. Ross leaned against a huge piling which gave support to the structure and Lonnie sat with his feet hanging over looking down at the water, imagining that it was going to engulf him as it rose higher and higher. It would almost touch his feet before dropping away as each wave moved on past toward the shore. He looked up to see a number of small boats moving slowly toward the dock, single file, closer and closer until they disappeared from view beneath the wooden overhang at the very end. They weren't out of sight long, maybe five minutes, until they appeared again, filled with prisoners now, moving away towards the anchored transports. As the loading continued, Lonnie and Ross inched down the dock until they were near the end. Every now and then Lonnie thought he heard shouts and once there was a long drawn out scream of terror which caused a thrill of apprehension to run through the men.

"What in the hell is happening up there? It sounds like they are dehorning somebody." Lonnie was grinning but he looked nervous.

"We'll know soon," Ross responded as they moved even closer to the end of the dock, and Lonnie could see what was happening. When a wave came in the boat being loaded would rise until it was just below the level of the dock, but as the wave subsided the boat would drop rapidly until it was a good eight feet below the men who were trying to get into it.

"Watch that damn boat," Lonnie shouted to Ross. "Don't get in until it's just right." They waited together, arm in arm, as the boat lifted higher. Lonnie could see the Japanese pilot and two guards looking up fearfully as it rose towards the dock.

"Now," he said to Ross, and they both stepped easily into the boat just before it sank down. But a number of others didn't judge so carefully. Some of them stepped down as the boat sank away, and fell, one of them almost striking one of the Japanese guards. Another nearly missed the boat completely. He struck the edge and bounced over into the water, screaming as he went. A guard on the dock probed around for a while with a long stick but he didn't come up with anything.

"Jesus Christ," said Lonnie, his voice shaking. "Did you see that poor bastard hit the boat and fall over, and did you hear him? That poor bastard didn't have a chance even with that Jap guard trying to help him."

Ross didn't say anything for a few moments. He was watching the prisoners get into the boat each time it rose toward the level of the dock. Even as he watched another man slipped and fell screaming into the water.

"The Japs aren't trying to help those guys," Ross finally observed, looking back toward the dock as their small boat pulled away. "They are drowning them, holding them under water with those long sticks."

[150]

"You're full of shit," said Lonnie, looking back toward the dock. But he couldn't see anybody in the water. Another boat had pulled up and men were scrambling in on each rise of a wave. That's that, he thought and turned toward the bow of the boat. A Japanese guard stood right next to him; one he hadn't seen before, a kid about eighteen years old. The guard was crunched back into the corner of the boat by the prisoners pressed in against him, but he didn't seem to mind. He was smoking a cigarette and observing the prisoners. He had a quick intense look, bright black eyes which seemed to take in everything.

"How about that butt?" asked Lonnie.

"Okay, in a minute," the guard replied in excellent English. Lonnie nudged Ross who was still looking back toward the dock.

"This guy speaks better English than I do," he said, indicating the guard.

"I can believe that," responded Ross, but he looked at the guard with interest. "Where are we?"

The guard looked toward him momentarily and then said, "Laoag at the northern tip of Luzon."

"How come you speak English so well?" asked Lonnie. "Hell you speak English better than I do."

"I went to school for four years in Chicago. My father was a vice consul in the Japanese consulate. I was only twelve years old when we left." Then he looked more closely at Lonnie. "You look like you're starving," his look took in the entire boat. "You all look like you're starving."

"We are," said Lonnie. "Don't forget about the butt." The boat was slowing, moving in close to one of the large transports.

"Here's a pack," said the guard. "Keep them."

"Jesus Christ, thanks," said Lonnie. "If we win the war, I'll do something for you. Who do you think is going to win the war?"

The guard didn't respond. He was looking away, over the water toward the shore line.

"Come on you diplomatic bastard," said Ross. The boat had begun to empty; the men were climbing a stairway which extended from the deck of the ship. Lonnie looked down from half way up. The guard was still in his corner looking out toward the open water.

"Good luck," Lonnie shouted down and the guard waved his hand without looking up. Lonnie was on the deck, following Ross past two steam winches, waiting his turn to climb down an iron ladder into the semi-darkness of another hold. As he waited the terror came, slow eddies at first, then the crest of a great wave of fear caught him as he watched Ross disappear down.

"Hurry up, goddammit," the man behind him in line nudged him. No use waiting. He was climbing down the ladder looking up at the rungs as they increased in number against the square of light. Almost immediately his feet struck a steel floor. He was in a well-lit hold, only fifteen or twenty feet below the upper deck. Sunshine entered from numerous places where hatchboards had been removed, and an acrid odor, strangely familiar and comforting, took Lonnie back somewhere to another time he couldn't quite remember. Then it came to him.

"Horse piss!" he said aloud.

"What the hell are you talking about?" asked Ross who was waiting for him at the bottom of the ladder.

"It smells like horse piss down here," repeated Lonnie looking around.

"Well that ought to make you feel at home," said Ross. They both stood for a moment, out of the way of the men coming down the ladder, looking.

"It looks like a barn too," observed Lonnie. And it did. They were in a huge enclosure, perhaps one hundred feet by two hundred feet, as big as an aircraft hanger and almost as uncluttered except for large iron beams which jutted up in many places to support the steel deck. Above them the hatch was covered by heavy boards resting on iron girders. There was at least one hold beneath them because the same kind of boards (partially covered with a tarpaulin) made a slightly raised square platform in the center of the steel floor.

"Hell, this isn't half bad," said Lonnie, still looking around.

"At least we have plenty of light and fresh air," agreed Ross, "even if we do have to smell horse piss all the way. Where do you want to go?"

"How about that corner? It's close to the ladder. We might even get out in case the Americans hit this one too. We're above the water line this time, and nobody is going to take away those steel ladders."

They had only gone a few steps when Lonnie paused. A sound suddenly expanded from the subliminal into a thunderous frenzy of noise, airplanes moving in toward the ship at great speed. To a man, everyone in the hold cowered down waiting, but the sound passed over, lingered for a moment and was gone.

"What was that?" shouted Lonnie. "What the fuck was that?"

"Airplanes," said Ross matter of factly. "Jap airplanes, otherwise we would have heard guns firing at them."

"That figures," said Lonnie, getting up from his humped over position. "There ought to be a law against those yellow bastards buzzing ships and scaring the shit out of people."

"Very inconsiderate of them," agreed Ross pleasantly. "Come on before somebody else gets our corner."

Men were still coming down the ladders, moving out to claim small territories.

"God I'm hungry," said Lonnie, leaning back against the steel of the bulkhead.

"He must have heard you. Look at that." Ross was pointing up. More of the hatchboards had been removed from the steel girders and a large barrel with steam pouring from the top was being lowered into the hold. Two more barrels followed. Even before the third barrel reached the floor the men were lined up waiting. Those still coming down the ladders began to move at a surprisingly rapid pace.

"Hey, there's old Gentry coming down the ladder," said Lonnie, "and R. T. and Corso. Jesus Christ, he's as fat as ever. But Gentry needs a shave. How about that? That's the first time I ever saw him needing a shave."

"You're holding up the line," said Ross. "Let's get something to eat. We can socialize later."

Each man received half a canteen cup of tea, some rice and soup. Lonnie was worried because he didn't have a mess kit, but it worked out okay. When their turn came, Ross took both rations of soup and rice in his cup and mess kit while Lonnie

[153]

received the tea. They made their way back to their corner and ate. It was some meal; the tea had been sweetened, the rice was superbly cooked and the soup had meat and potatoes in it. The hunger moved back to let the fear come in.

"Maybe we're too far north for them to find us here," Lonnie said after the hold had become momentarily silent in response to an engine sound seeping in from the outside. "Or maybe the Japs have too many airplanes."

"I wouldn't count on it," replied Ross. "Do you see Gentry anywhere?"

"No, but if you'll hold our places, I'll go find him and R. T. and Corso. Maybe they would like to join us. We've got lots of room. Jesus Christ that was good soup. I feel so full I almost feel like taking a shit. How long has it been since you've taken a shit?"

"Not since we left Bilibid," said Ross.

"Me neither," said Lonnie.

"I've always said you were full of shit," said Ross grinning. "Go on and find Gentry and his crew and tell them to come on over if they want to."

"Takes one to know one," responded Lonnie. He was grinning too, scanning the hundreds of men who remarkably found hundreds of things to do. Some were sleeping, others were playing poker, a few were smoking cigarettes—Jesus Christ, thought Lonnie, I've got a whole pack of Golden Bats! He felt the bottom of his canteen holder and they were still there.

"We'll have a cigarette when I get back," he said to Ross.

"Hurry up." Ross was leaning comfortably against the bulkhead. "Man, I feel good. It's amazing what a little food will do for a guy's morale."

"Yeah, see you in a bit." Lonnie started walking around the hold about ten feet from the wall. He didn't have much trouble making his way along; there was plenty of room. Many men had gathered into small groups, talking. Occasionally someone would speak to him; warm cheery voices, vaguely familiar some of them, others unknown cyphers.

"Hey Lonnie, taken any shit from anybody lately?"

"How's the old pussy hound?"

"What's new in the worm business?"

Over near the corner where one of the iron beams jutted into the roof, he saw them. Gentry, leaning back on his elbow, was looking quizzically up at R. T. Barton who was shouting so loud Lonnie could easily hear him above the general drone of conversations and clinking mess kits.

"Those sons-of-bitches are going to bomb our asses off again, I tell you. Wait and see!"

"I imagine we will," responded Gentry easily. He grinned as he saw Lonnie moving toward them. "Look who's coming."

"I doubt if he ever has."

Lonnie caught the comment, then saw Corso stretched out flat on his back looking up at him over his big gut; the V was still there, somehow smaller, and the bulge at the groin somehow bigger.

"Well here is Chicken Licken." His little black eyes were not quite looking at Lonnie. "You got the meat, I still got the heat."

"Shit on you," said Lonnie.

Something was changing. He noticed it in his feet first, a just discernible tremor, then on the faces of the men: searching glances toward the square of blue which marked the opening in the hatchway, a quieting of conversations and the jingle-jangle, a listening. The ship was moving. As they paused, caught there between vagueness and realization, the tremors mounted into vibrations, became fused into the creaks and groans which say that a ship has come alive.

"By God, we're on our way," said R. T. quietly. "Do you think we'll make it?"

He was looking at Gentry, but Gentry was watching Lonnie remove his canteen cup from its holder. Lonnie took out the pack of Golden Bats and opened them with a flourish.

"I'm going to make it," he said as he passed out a cigarette to each of them. "Everybody deserves at least one piece of ass, and I haven't had mine yet. I'm going to live at least until I get my first piece of ass."

"And I find out too late that the secret of immortality is in remaining celibate." Gentry too was grinning now. "How about a light, Corso? Let's light up and celebrate both

Lonnie's generosity and his formula for survival. I always had a suspicion that the vulnerable point for Achilles was his prick rather than his heel. Now I know."

Corso removed a round metal container from one of the large pockets of his blue denim jacket. It made a fine popping sound as he pulled it apart. When he removed a match Lonnie saw that he still had six left, and two cigarettes. The match flared and Corso held it toward Lonnie, "See, I've still got the heat."

Lonnie didn't say anything for a moment; he sucked and saw the end of his cigarette disintegrate in a cascade of fire, saw the flame shine in Corso's eyes and felt the smoke deep in his own lungs.

"Sure you do Corso, thanks." He took another deep drag, felt a momentary burst of clarity. The square above became too bright, his hand holding the cigarette too sharply etched as he gazed down at it—somehow separate from him, floating, moving on its own.

"Where's Ross?" asked Gentry, as he took his turn at the match.

"Over there," answered Lonnie vaguely, and then guiltily as he got to his feet. "Jesus Christ, I forgot all about him. I'll go get him and bring him back."

It was more difficult walking now, stepping over men who lay everywhere, some sleeping, some just looking up toward the small clouds moving back and forth across the square of sky. The ship was heaving and falling in a medium sea.

He found Ross still leaning against the bulkhead near the ladder with his eyes closed.

"Come on, you lazy bastard," shouted Lonnie.

Ross opened his eyes and looked at him with the old strangeness, the strangeness Lonnie had seen back at the jail. The get dead look.

"Get off your ass—I found old Gentry and the other meat balls. We're going to have a cigarette together."

The paleness left Ross' face; his eyes began to act like they were looking at something rather than just away. He even grinned a little.

"Let's go up on deck to the crapper," he said, amused at the surprise on Lonnie's face, a little boy expression which lingered for just a moment, before it shifted to one of guarded suspicion.

"What are you talking about—what crapper? You mean the Japs are going to let us go up on deck? You're full of shit!" Then he noticed men going up the ladder at the other end of the bulkhead and others coming down the one near them. He also noticed that the square of blue above them was turning a little darker and felt the tightness in his stomach relax, the flare in his chest was not so bright.

"Jesus Christ!" he said. "It's getting dark and we haven't been bombed yet! By God, maybe we are going to make it. Come on, let's go take a shit—I almost feel like I could!"

Up the ladder, rung by rung, out onto the deck of the gently undulating ship. Lonnie could see land not far away, maybe a mile, a dark mass growing darker in the deepening twilight. Toward the sea he caught a glimpse of the sun, dimmed by layers of clouds until the eye could look at it; a huge red ball floating on the water. A guard, one they didn't know at all, shouted at them from his station by one of the steam winches, so they moved on.

"I hope the bastards who built this thing were good carpenters," said Ross as they sat side by side on a ten-holer enjoying the disappearing sun and crimson clouds which came in view each time the ship fell. The wooden structure of the toilet extended over the rail suspending the occupants above a stretch of white water, the beginning of the ship's wake.

Lonnie didn't say anything. He gazed unseeing at the last sliver of red sun just flickering away. Sweat beaded his forehead, his bony shoulders tense and strained in the posture of total concentration.

"Jesus Christ," he gasped, "I think I'm having a baby!"

For a moment his entire being remained fixed there, caught, immobile, and then a giving way. Looking down between his legs he saw the small dried-up ball of his achievement falling away; saw it suddenly engulfed by a vast upswelling cauldron of writhing water.

"What a flush job," he said heaving in relief. "Man that's the granddaddy of all flush jobs! Reminds me of a story about

[157]

a guy falling into a swimming pool in Texas. You ever hear that story?"

"Yes, you told it to me about five times," replied Ross. "Did you really crap or were you just being dramatic?"

"Are you kidding? A big one, man. I could even wipe my ass if I had some paper. Do you have any paper on you?"

"Oh horseshit," said Ross indulgently. "Let's go find Gentry and have that cigarette. You can brag about your big turd."

"Okay," Lonnie grinned, "you're just jealous."

It was almost dark when they went back down the ladder, the sun was gone, the land a dark jagged line. A canvas cover had been placed over the hatch opening. Four small lights, one for each corner of the hold created pools of dimness which faded gradually into the total black closing in on every side.

"Looks like the Japs don't want anybody to see this ship," observed Ross from just above Lonnie on the ladder.

"Suits me, Jesus Christ, how it suits me!" Lonnie's feet touched the steel floor of the hold. He waited there in the semi-darkness until he felt Ross beside him. "They're over there toward that corner, you just follow me."

Slowly they made their way along, stepping over people who grunted or cursed softly as they passed. They could see more clearly as their eyes adjusted to the darkness but could hardly make out the faces of the men. Once or twice Lonnie thought he saw Gentry but there was no response when he called his name. Finally they found them, directly beneath the dim light in the corner, a small cluster of bodies intermingled with but somehow separate from the rest.

"I thought you died or something," said R. T. Barton. "Hell you been gone at least an hour. Shit I smoked all my cigarette and I'm dying for another one. How about breaking out that pack again?"

"Are you okay?" Gentry asked Ross.

"Good as ever," replied Ross. Gentry's concern pleased him.

They formed a small circle, sitting with arms resting between their knees, leaning forward, backs toward the darkness and the others. Lonnie was happy for the moment; the fear had moved back into the edges and the hunger had diminished to a discontent. He saw the faces of his friends, eyes lost in dark hollows but cheekbones clear in the dim light. Even Corso seemed relaxed. He rocked slowly back and forth on his haunches humming a tune, vaguely familiar and suddenly very disturbing to Lonnie.

The hairy slob, like a big fat cat purring! Lonnie shivered, remembering when as a child he had awakened in the bunkhouse alone and in total darkness to hear a cat purring somewhere in the room. For just a moment he remembered the angle dream, could hear again, or thought he could, the keening undulating sound, and felt the terror of it.

"How about one of your bullshit stories, Gentry?" Nobody said anything for a moment and then Lonnie knew his voice had sounded strange. They were all looking at him. He was about to say something more when the voice of Father Maloney came to them from out of the darkness on the far side of the hold, clearly audible above the jumble of noises. Lonnie was relieved, both for the interruption and for the sound of the Father's voice. He glanced rapidly at Gentry who had turned his head in the direction of the sound, listening.

As Lonnie heard the Father's words a vague apprehension grew until it was almost tangible, the voice was strong and clear as usual but there was doubt rather than conviction in his words, questioning rather than affirmation.

"Oh God, mighty and all-powerful within whose view past and present, never and now are all the same reality, we thank Thee for giving us our lives for yet another day. I do not know why I live and my brother lies dead in the sand dunes or on the other ship, but I know that within Thy scrutiny these events have meaning. If within Thy vision the falling sparrow makes its mark, the agony and terror of these your children must have significance. Even now, at this very moment your glance must take us in, your love encircle us."

The Father paused and for a moment Lonnie thought the prayer had ended, but his voice came again, still clear and steady but edged with deep concern. "If these things are not so, then we are truly locked in total darkness where only matter lives, and for a moment knows itself. If these things are not so, then matter soon will know itself no longer. The small pinpoints of light which stand for suns will flicker out, and

[159]

absolutely nothing will remain! Man's love, his sacrifice, his endless struggle must have significance in the eyes of God, or when the stars go out it will be as though man had not been. It will not matter that he ever was."

Father Maloney's voice came clearer now, demanding in its intensity. It seemed to Lonnie that he was talking directly to Gentry, as if everyone else in the huge dim cavern had disappeared, except for them. Lonnie glanced at Gentry, saw the tenseness in his body, a total alertness, head held slightly sideways, eyes almost visible in the gloom as he listened to the Father's voice.

"It has been said if God is everything then man is nothing. Surely this can't be so. Surely it is only through God that man is something. If God is nothing, then man is absolutely nothing, and always was and always will be. Let us repeat the Lord's Prayer."

Lonnie heard his own voice joining with the rest. He was watching Gentry who still sat in the same hunched-over position, his head held sideways, the dim light from the small bulb far above them outlining the bony structure of his cheek. A smile flickered on Gentry's face, then he looked directly at Lonnie and grinned openly.

"Still the old psychologist, eh Lonnie? You know, I do have a story; it has to do with a case I helped win when I was working as the most junior member of good old Markham, Claybourn and Good." He paused as Corso and R. T. Barton edged in closer, suddenly cheerful. Out of the darkness, somehow aware of the diversion, others moved in around them. More came as the news spread until a series of concentric circles encompassed them with Gentry at the nucleus waiting patiently for the noise to subside.

Lonnie took out his pack of Golden Bats and handed one to each person in the inner ring.

"Light them up and pass them around," he said. "We got something to celebrate, we're living and old Gentry is going to tell one of his bullshit stories."

A ripple of laughter spread through the still-gathering crowd and grew into a roar as R. T. Barton remarked, "Damn it Gentry, you are just like some kind of fucking pied

[160]

piper—you make a few sounds and the rats start gathering. I'll bet there are some real ones out there sitting with the two-legged ones, waiting for the big story!"

Lonnie found himself laughing too, that goddamn R. T. Barton. He looked at the inner group, all grinning now; Corso with his happy bear expression, the multitude of faces beyond, dimly lit by the little light above them, faces without necks floating on skinny shoulders, row on row to the outer edges of the light, smiling faces waiting for the story.

When the noise subsided, Gentry began to speak as if there had been no pause, looking only at those in the inner circle, but his voice was loud enough to be heard by those listening at the edge.

"Anyway, I was sitting in my little cubicle, the kind new members of law firms are always given: no windows, a crummy little desk, a crummier light, and a ventilator that made too much noise, when the secretary brought in this guy. I would like to say he was ordinary, but he was much less than that. He was the ultimate in insignificance, a consummate non-entity, a person so devoid of any dignifying attribute that he achieved a kind of monumental blandness. He was, in short, a veritable walking nothing. 'Have a seat,' I said. He poured himself into my one chair and sat there across the desk from me for a full five minutes without moving. He just sat there, pudgy face, pudgy fingers, pudgy feet, pudgy mind topped off by a whining, ingratiating, pudgy voice, as it turned out. He wore an old green plaid suit which must have been a reject from a church bazaar, a tie which looked like he had just been cut down from being hung, and a blue, frayed, worn out shirt which had probably been washed only once, when it was new. From the whole mass of him, the repellent, perspirant, redolant mass of him, there emanated an odor, a stench so hideous that it ran off the scale past fetid beyond putrid. He was a literal smell salad. To put it succinctly, the total impression of this individual was somewhat like Corso during one of his better days."

At this there was a scream of laughter from the group, clapping and cries of, "Hey Corso, he's got your number. Do your dance, Corso." Corso was grinning and waving; he clasped his hands over his head, shook them and bowed, and everyone cheered again.

When the noise subsided, Gentry continued, smiling benignly at Corso.

"So I asked this guy, 'What can I do for you, Sir?' At this he comes to life, sticks part of his tie carefully inside his shirt and adjusts it so the knot stood straight out like an extension of his Adam's apple.

" 'I'm in trouble; I need a lawyer.' His pudgy hand came across the desk towards me. 'I'm Wilbur Quimby.' His hand felt like a bloated fillet of sole and I couldn't resist the temptation to wipe mine off on a piece of Kleenex which I kept in my desk for such purposes. He didn't notice but kept talking like somebody had opened up a fire hydrant.

" 'These guys arrested me, see, they came and arrested me and took me to jail, it wasn't so bad, they gave me good chow and a good bed, but they said I was a thief, and I missed the horses and old Sam—he's my dog—and then somebody came and paid some money and they let me out, but they still say I'm a thief, and they are going to put me in jail again maybe unless I get a good lawyer. Are you a good lawyer?' He looked at me suspiciously with his little froggy eyes, over his pudgy cheeks and almost caught me nodding off to sleep.

" 'The best,' I admitted, looking hopefully at the ventilator. There was a green haze in the room by now, the ventilator just kept making noises and doing nothing. 'But what did you steal, or,' I corrected myself, 'what is it they say you stole?'

" 'Sperm,' he said.

" 'Sperm?' I echoed, now not so sleepy. 'You mean sperm as in S - P - E - R - M?'

" 'That's right, sperm,' he repeated.

"I could hardly believe this guy sitting there in my chair, looking like a sincere pudgy musky toad, but honesty exuded from him so mixed in with the odor that even it seemed to smell bad. And the ventilator kept making noises and doing nothing."

"Let's have a little more relating and a little less ventilating," somebody in the back of the group complained.

"All right, shut up you, goddammit," shouted R. T. Barton.

"This is Gentry's bullshit story and if you don't want to hear it, go fuck yourself. Go ahead," he said to Gentry protectively. "There is always a shithead in the crowd."

There was a smattering of applause and general laughter as Gentry said, "Thank you, R. T., you are very kind." He took a deep drag on a cigarette which Ross handed him and continued.

"So I said to this guy with his toad frog eyes and polecat aroma, 'Why don't you tell me all about it?' and the hydrant opened again.

" 'I'm a stable boy, see?' " Now Gentry's voice took on a nasal, whining twang and his hands moved in short jerky gestures. Lonnie could almost see the little smelly, sweating bastard there in the little room with the ventilator whirring away without doing anything.

" 'I'm a stable boy. I been a stable boy for fifteen years. I been with Colonel MacLean at Balder Farms right out of Lexington. We won the Kentucky Derby three times,' the pudgy little guy sits up straight and looks proud, 'and we won the Belmont twice, and other races, all kinds of other races, the big ones. We had some of the real big horses like Wolfbane, Execution II, and Mudpaddle. We got the biggest stud farm in the state, makes maybe three million a year, just in stud fees. I work hard, keep the stalls clean, walk the horses. But I got a big job too, a real important job—the Colonel said I was the best come-catcher in Kentucky.'

"He looks straight at me with his little toady eyes and asks, 'You know what a come-catcher is?'

"I admitted that I didn't and then he really opened up. 'A come-catcher is a guy who catches come. You want to know how they do it?'

"I suddenly found I wasn't sleepy any more and hardly noticed that the ventilator wasn't doing anything.

" 'I miss being come-catcher. I miss old Wolfbane, he's the best. What they do is get a mare who's really wantin' it, see? I remember we had this little filly, Morning Star, a real looker. She comes in, pushing her butt out towards everything, kind of squattin' down, squinching her cunt. The colonel sees this and tells me to go get old Wolfbane and get the cockmit ready.

[163]

The guys put the filly in the fuckin' chute and snub her down and there she is with her cunt squinching. Old Wolfbane knows what's gonna happen; he's got a big one ready, just waitin' when they bring him in, man what a cock, big and hard. He didn't even seem to mind when they put the blindfold on him, but kept squealing like he was ready.' "

Gentry stopped and stared up towards the small light above them. Around him there was complete silence, an aura of waiting. "Anybody got a cigarette?" he asked.

Immediately there was a chorus, "Here's one!"

"For Christ's sake, give him a cigarette!"

Gentry took the cigarettes as they came toward him, six in all, held them for a moment and then passed them around. "Light them up," he said. "Let's all have a little smoke, two drags and pass them on."

A light flared and the sweet smell of tobacco smoke settled over the group and made a slight haze in the dim light.

" 'So old Wolfbane was ready,' " Gentry continued in the whining nasal voice which immediately summoned the image of the malodorous individual and the small, poorly ventilated room.

" 'And I was ready. I had the cockmit heated to just the right heat, and the grease smeared on just right. Old Wolfbane puts his nose into that filly's pussy, she squats down with her cunt all squinched out, and he mounts her real fast. But not too fast for me. I'm ready with the cockmit. I grab his cock with one hand and slip the mit on with the other, and there he is hunching away, squealing and fartin' thinking he's got it in. He gives one big hunch and I can feel his prick pulsatin' and see his balls draw up and can feel the rubber bag at the end of the cockmit gettin' hot, fillin' up.

" 'Now you know about come-catching,' the guy says looking directly at me. He crossed his legs and I could see he was trying to hide an erection," Gentry paused and smiled gently at the sounds of rattling mess kits which came when a number of his listeners shifted in position.

That son-of-a-bitch. Lonnie had to grin. That damn Gentry. Lonnie's own penis was hard and throbbing; he reached unconsciously for his LIFE WOMAN, then remem-

[164]

bered she was gone, but he saw her for a moment—legs outspread, the bulge stark and inviting.

Gentry's voice, nasal and whining, blotted out the vision. " 'Do you know how many sperm I had in that cockmit?'

"I admitted that I didn't but guessed maybe a million.

" 'Six million, six million on the average,' my smelly friend said with a supercilious smirk upon his face. 'Think of that, six million sperm, enough to make all the race horses anybody could ever want.' His voice rose, his face turned a bright red, and his hands convulsed as though holding the cockmit still hot from its exercise. 'Enough sperm to win a million races!'

" 'And you stole some of those sperm?' I said interrupting his flight into megalomania.

" 'I did not,' he said, suddenly looking deflated and hurt. 'That's what they say, but I didn't do it. I'll admit that I did think about it, all those beautiful sperm there in the freezer, three containers frozen solid. Somebody else took them, I didn't take them, I wouldn't steal the Colonel's sperm.'

"He looked at me with those toad frog eyes, so full of hurt, so full of honesty, so full of stupidity, that I believed him and to my surprise, heard my own voice saying, 'Okay, okay, I'll take your case.' "

Gentry paused again, took a drag from a cigarette which somebody immediately provided, and then continued, his voice suddenly professional.

"The trial was supposed to be held in Jackson County, Kentucky, but I got a change of venue to Louisville; the people are too sensitive about their horses in Jackson County. The court room was filled, all the important people of Kentucky were there, even the Governor. It was my first big case.

"Anyway, the prosecutor brought out his evidence, piece by piece by piece. The same day Wilbur Quimby disappeared, so did the three capsules of sperm. Later when they found Wilbur, he still had one of the capsules in the freezer section of his refrigerator (he claimed somebody had planted it on him); an assistant had noticed Wilbur in the freezer room at the farm the very same night he and the sperm had disappeared, and to top it off, a number of workers from the farm testified

that Wilbur spent most of his time talking about the sperm—
morning, noon, and night, any time anybody would listen to
him. All of the evidence seemed to be against poor old Wilbur,
but I got him off."

Gentry stopped, surveyed the crowd and then continued, a
bit of smugness, of superiority in his voice.

"You know how I got him off? I got a mistrial declared.
They were trying him for grand larceny when he should have
been tried for rustling! It clearly states in the expression of
English Law handed down from Blackstone and reinforced by
precedent after precedent, that the taking of livestock consti-
tutes rustling, a set and definite offense, not grand larceny. I
caught them completely off guard. The prosecutor tried to
plead that the sperm were not alive since they were immobile
from the cold, but I was ready. I brought in twelve micro-
scopes and put a sample of sperm under each and let the jurors
take a look for themselves. There they were, wiggling away
like crazy, definitely livestock. The judge took a look for
himself and then declared a mistrial."

Gentry stopped for a moment; there was complete silence
around him. He continued in his own voice, "It's hard to
realize that this trial took place almost fifteen years ago."

"Whatever happened to old Wilbur?" somebody asked.

"Yes, whatever happened to him?"

Gentry pursed his lips, and looked thoughtful, "Well, the
last I heard of him, about three years ago, he owned a bunch
of race horses. Big ones, like Man-of-War, Whirl-a-Way, War
Admiral, and Sea Biscuit."

For a moment there was total silence and then bedlam,
everybody began laughing like crazy.

"That goddamn Gentry."

"That son-of-a-bitch! He did it to us again!" screamed
Lonnie.

The laughter continued for a long time, ebbed away, and
then broke forth again as someone would comment on some
aspect of the story. Lonnie sat beside Ross and they both
laughed together, and Lonnie thought maybe old Gentry was
the best damn story teller that ever lived. It was good to be his
friend, to be close to him now sitting there with the dim light

showing where his hair was getting thin—but accentuating the
fine structure of his head, his well-trimmed mustache, his lips
half-smiling as he savored his small victory.

The laughter finally diminished to sporadic outbursts, then
died away completely and the ship was there again gently
heaving and falling, and the fear. For a strange eerie moment
Lonnie could see the ship as from far above, wallowing in its
own wake, running from the hunters, seeking a hiding place,
and the flare burst again in his chest.

Then from overhead came the loud staccato roar of a
machine gun and as one, every man in the hold of the ship
cowered down waiting for the blow. But no bombs fell. The
four small lights in the corners of the hold suddenly went out
leaving total darkness and a pervasive silence which grew and
pressed in around them. They waited, listening to the creaking
of the ship, to their own breathing, and the quietness
continued. It can't be airplanes, thought Lonnie, it's dark and
they couldn't find us. Maybe they saw our little lights.

He raised his head and listened but still no sounds of
engines, no sounds of anything except the creaking of the ship
and the distant rumble of the propellers. He was just
beginning to relax a little when the incredibly loud reverberating roar of machine guns came again, not just one burst but a
number intermingled into a discordant overlapping cluster of
sounds. The shouts of Japanese guards carried down into the
hold, loud and angry, unbelievably ominous, coming from
different parts of the ship. Lonnie was paralyzed by fear, his
brain doing crazy things; machine guns sound just like a string
of beads or maybe a bunch of grapes, bright round shiny "bam
bams" hooked together.

Silence again. Lonnie counted twenty heaves of the ship and
still there was silence. Suddenly the lights came on. Lonnie
raised up and saw the others looking stupidly at each other,
clearly visible in the light from the small bulb which seemed
bright now, too bright.

"What the fuck was that?" he gasped. "What the hell were
they shooting at?"

"My theory is," it was R. T. Barton, "that old Mac's boys
have taken over this ship. They shot every one of those little

lumps of shit and took over this boat. Wait and see. In about two minutes old Mac himself will appear and give us all medals for being good and brave American soldiers."

Lonnie grinned in spite of himself and almost believed he was going to see General MacArthur. One section of the hatch was being removed, the canvas cover pulled back. But it wasn't General MacArthur who appeared. It was Lieutenant Iwahara, the soft light from a flashlight playing over him, reflecting from his thick lensed glasses. He didn't say anything for a moment but just stood there blinking from the light, peering down into the hold, like somebody suffering from a bad case of fine print, as R. T. Barton described him later.

Finally he began to speak, his face contorted with anger, his gestures short and jerky.

"*Bakayaro!* Son-of-a-bitch! Somebody jump off ship, some crazy bastard jump off ship, we shoot some crazy bastard who jump off ship!"

He stopped for a moment and disappeared back from the edge of the hold; somebody had grabbed him just before he fell over. Lonnie thought it was Mr. Noda, but he couldn't be sure—looked like him, short and squatty, but they all were except for Major Imada. Lieutenant Iwahara leaned over the hold again.

"Where is that crazy Ledrosa? Ledrosa, Ledrosa, come up here! Come up here now, or I cut off your goddamn head, Ledrosa, Ledrosa!"

There was a moment of astonishment, of relaxation; a pure enjoyment of the situation and then several of the prisoners took up the cry, "Ledrosa, Ledrosa!" The cry swelled and grew, every man shouting, "Ledrosa, Ledrosa, come up here or I'll cut off your goddamn head!"

Then somebody shouted out; Lonnie was sure it was R. T. Barton, "Fee fi fo fum, I smell the blood of an Armenian!" The prisoners took up the song until the ship resounded with its cadence. Lieutenant Iwahara stared in bewilderment, but Mr. Noda was grinning a little. It was him, as Lonnie could see now when the light momentarily struck his face. Finally the song subsided and the call for Ledrosa began again. But he didn't appear. Everybody started looking for him then and

Lonnie almost expected to see a giant beanstalk grow out of the hold with old Ledrosa climbing it. But he didn't appear, nor did he ever appear again, anywhere.

Ross and Lonnie were lying side by side, their heads on their canteen holders, their naked backs cooled by the steel floor. The lights had been turned out again and quiet came gradually to the hold. The sea was heavier, pushed by a rising wind which caused the tarpaulin over the hatchway to ripple and pop. A perceptible tremor ran through the ship as it paused for a moment before dropping down, a soothing vibration most discernible just before the top of each cycle. "We're moving," thought Lonnie hopefully, "they're giving this bucket all she's got." Almost to himself, he asked aloud, "Why did old Ledrosa do it? Why did the crazy bastard do it?"

Ross didn't say anything for a long time but Lonnie could tell he was awake by his irregular breathing. Finally he spoke, "You probably answered your own question, he's crazy."

For a long time they lay in silence, Lonnie thinking about tomorrow caught again the vision of the ship from far above, zigzagging, fleeing, and then whispered, "On the other hand, maybe we're the crazy ones for not jumping. . . ."

He awoke once or twice during the night to feel the throbbing rhythm of the engine and the eerie shudder which came as the propellers came out of the water when the ship reared and tossed in a violent sea.

CHAPTER SEVEN

Someone was shouting. The Japanese were removing the hatch cover letting the sunshine down into the darkness, sunshine which moved back and forth across the floor, blinding Lonnie as he looked up. Mr. Noda was standing there like a small, squinty, baggy Napoleon, his foot braced against one of the steel girders.

"Okay you guys, okay you guys. Listen! Listen! I've got some news!"

"Tell us the news," somebody shouted up.

Others chimed in, "Lay it on us. Surprise us."

Mr. Noda grinned. "I've got some news and a very, very funny story. Do you want to hear a funny story?" he asked almost eagerly. "About Indians?"

"Sure Noda, tell us the funny story."

Mr. Noda was pleased, he was smiling in anticipation; the sun flashed off his glasses as he looked down. He paused for a moment and then explained, "This is a story about American Indians, not Indian Indians." This was greeted with a running commentary from below.

"Great, they're the best kind!"

"Some of my best friends are Indians!"

"More, more!"

"Anyway," said Mr. Noda, warming to his story, "there was this American Indian who liked to go fishing. Out in the

[170]

ocean. One day he was fishing in the ocean when he hooked something. Something really big! That really put up a fight! It was a big fight but finally the Indian won. And guess what he had caught?"

"Tell us, tell us," voices came up from below. "I can't wait. What did he catch? What did he catch?"

"He caught a beautiful mermaid," said Mr. Noda smiling now expansively. "A very, very beautiful mermaid. You would have thought that the Indian would be happy," Mr. Noda's voice became dour and sorrowful, "but he was not happy. He was very sad. The Indian looked at the beautiful mermaid for awhile and then threw her back into the water. And do you know what he said as he threw her back?"

"What the hell did the Indian say? What the hell did the Indian say?" Many voices took up the chant.

"The Indian said, 'How.' " Mr. Noda was beaming now. He couldn't control his smile; it broke out into a cackling laugh but this was rapidly replaced by a puzzled frown. There was absolute silence from the hold.

Finally, half in anger, half in appeal, he asked, "What's the matter with you guys? You got no sense of humor! The Indian said, 'HOW!' "

This was greeted by a chorus from below, "What you picking on our American Indians for?"

"Yeah, are you prejudiced against Indians?"

"Shit, I kicked the slats out of my cradle when I heard that one!"

Somebody shouted up, "Enough of this Indian horseshit. Tell us the news."

Voices chanted in unison, "Give us the news. Give us the news."

Mr. Noda was in good humor again. "I have two news. One news is bad, the other is good. The bad news is that nobody go *benjo* on deck anymore, *benjo* in buckets. Nobody go on deck anymore, some crazy bastard might jump overboard, like old Ledrosa. You understand? You understand?" he asked grinning. "Some crazy bastard might want to take a long swim."

There was a moment of silence and then somebody shouted, "How about the good news?"

[171]

Mr. Noda grinned even more widely. "The good news is that we don't have to worry any more about American planes. There was a big battle yesterday off the island of Leyte and all the American aircraft carriers were sunk, all gone, no more airplanes, no more bombs."

Another chorus from below, "That's a crock of shit!"

"Yeah, of Indian turds!" somebody else offered.

"I liked the bad news better," Lonnie shouted up, but the fear ebbed a little. "Do you think that's true?" he asked Ross, and was ashamed to hear a hopeful note in his own voice.

"More likely just the opposite," answered Ross. "I'd like to bet that if any of us survive this crazy situation, this screwed up war, we'll find that the Japs got the hell kicked out of them somewhere off Leyte."

"I'll check up on it," said Lonnie. "I'm gonna live through this goddamn mess. I'll check up on it." And then as an afterthought, hurriedly, "And so will you."

But as the days passed it began to look as if Mr. Noda had been reporting "right from the horse's ass" as R. T. Barton put it. Every day was a perfect day for bombing, cloudless with very little wind, but there were no planes. The sea calmed until the only motion was a slight rolling which let the sunlight move lazily back and forth across the floor of the hold. They received two meals a day, always the same, some brown rice, a little sugar, and a tablespoon of soybean paste. Just enough to keep starvation pushed back to the edges rather than gnawing at the center during every moment. With the tea which came at each meal, about half a cup per man, life was tolerable.

The fear ebbed as each day took them further from the terror which Lonnie knew was moving toward them from the south. Even using the latrine buckets wasn't so bad; a work detail of prisoners kept them emptied, three times a day. They were washed in salt water before being let back down into the hold. The same kind of buckets, wooden stave with metal bands, were used to let down the food and tea. R. T. Barton insisted that they got the buckets mixed up once, but Lonnie didn't think so. Old R. T. was such a bullshitter.

By noon on the fourth day the sea had calmed until there

was no discernible motion in the ship, nothing but the vibrating rhythm of the propellers. Lonnie checked it out by watching a sharp edge of sunlight against a shadow which ran along the floor; it was perfectly steady and moved inexorably as time passed, with the precision of a sundial. The edge of light had just reached the corner of the hold, casting a silvery sheen on little motes of dust which boiled and swirled when Lonnie waved his hand among them when the change occurred. No doubt about it. There was a shift in the rhythm of the ship, a slowing down. Then incredibly there were no vibrations at all, the distant rumbling of the engines had ceased. Ross nudged Lonnie who was leaning comfortably against the cool, moist bulkhead.

"We're here," he said.

"Yeah," answered Lonnie, "and we didn't get bombed. Do you think we're in Japan? Could we be in Japan?"

"We're not in Japan," said Ross, squinting up towards small tufts of clouds which now stood stationary in the sky. "Japan is twenty-five hundred miles from the Philippines, we've only been traveling for four days. We must be in Formosa, that's about the right distance, about six hundred miles. But we've made it this far, and we didn't get bombed."

He was about to continue when there was a deafening roar from the front part of the ship. Lonnie automatically humped over and put his hands over his head as did some of the others near them, but Ross didn't move.

"Boy, you're jumpy," he grinned at Lonnie. "Nobody's been killed by an anchor yet, unless it fell on them. Get your head out of the sand!"

"Shit on you," said Lonnie sheepishly.

Just after the midafternoon meal the remainder of the large boards that covered the hatch were removed exposing the entire central section of the hold to the sun. It grew hot, not a breeze anywhere now that the ship had stopped. The men crowded back beneath the permanent steel plates of the upper deck where it was shady and cool.

"Okay, you guys, you get to come up on deck now."

Lonnie was almost asleep when the voice came down; Mr. Noda's voice. He was at the edge of the hatch, resplendent as

[173]

usual in baggy pants, matching baggy light gray shirt, thick lensed glasses, and toothy grin.

"Everybody take all their belongings and come up on deck, you get to see the scenery now. We got some pretty mountains here, you come up now and see."

Lonnie and Ross were first up the ladder; they had been waiting right next to it from the moment Mr. Noda started talking, ready to go. Lonnie could hardly control his excitement; he wanted to see the water, those mountains. Up and up, steel rung by steel rung, and finally out. He stood for a moment blinking in the bright sunlight, looking at the mountains in the far distance, some of them covered with clouds, at one high peak in particular where the clouds sprayed back from the crest in a plume of dispersing mists, like a girl's hair blowing in the wind. Where the mountains diminished into foot hills as the terrain moved in towards the large harbor, houses appeared. Some of them stood alone, white little boxes, vivid against the green countryside. Others clustered in small villages, and on the west side of the harbor directly beneath the lowering sun, the houses grew larger and converged into a city with docks jutting into the water. There were ships in the harbor, lots of them, spread out in disarray, most of them at anchor, but one or two moved silently and slowly among the rest.

No sign of battle damage anywhere. Lonnie shivered remembering Manila Bay, but there wasn't one wrecked ship in sight. He also shivered from the cold, something he hadn't felt in years, a chill wind blowing in from the mountains. The men were still coming up the three ladders. Soon it got crowded on the deck and as the sun went down, it grew colder.

"I feel like a goddamn Key bird," said Lonnie.

"What's a Key bird?" asked Ross, mildly interested. He was watching long steel girders being lowered into the hold. All the men were out now.

"A Key bird is a bird which lives in the deep snow in northern Alaska," offered Lonnie grinning. "Every morning when it's about fifty below zero he crawls out of the snow, flaps his wings and says 'Key-rist, it's cold!"

"If you think it's cold now," said Ross smiling wanly at Lonnie's story, "wait until we get to Japan. They better give us some warm clothes and some blankets or we won't have to worry about getting killed by bombs or starving to death."

"You're not kiddin'?" asked Lonnie, suddenly serious.

"Not hardly," replied Ross. The cranes were lowering large hatchboards into the hold now. "It's January and Japan is a cold country. The closer we get the colder it's going to get. What do you think the Japs are doing with those iron girders and hatchboards and now those large tarpaulins?"

"Beats the sir out of me, shit," said Lonnie.

As the sun lowered to the top of one of the far mountains, the cold became almost unendurable; the wind was rising. Jesus Christ, how cold can it get? Finally the order came to move back into the hold. Lonnie could feel the warmth increasing as he climbed down. To his astonishment his feet struck a floor only a few feet from the ladder opening. The Japanese had put in a new floor about ten feet above the old one dividing the hold into two large rooms, one on top of the other. They had left a large square opening in the center of the floor, and four ladders, one on each side, led down to the lower section.

"Let's go on down," said Lonnie as he watched others already descending to the lower level. "It'll be warmer down there."

The lower section was quite comfortable and plenty of light came in through the double squares of the openings above them.

"Yes, it's warmer," said Ross, "but if we get bombed we won't have much chance of getting out."

"Why in the hell did you have to bring that up for?" complained Lonnie. "Just when I was relaxing a little. You know, you're a real wet blanket, that's what you are. As if we don't have enough trouble, starving to death, getting our asses blown off with bombs, and freezing to death, here you are scaring the shit out of me again!"

"Well take your choice," said Ross undisturbed. "We can go upstairs and freeze or stay down here and drown."

"Goddammit, there you go again," shouted Lonnie. But Ross was smiling and Lonnie soon began to grin in spite of himself.

Darkness in the lower section came rapidly. Soon nothing

could be seen except a large dim square outlined against the deeper black of the rest of the hold. But as usual with the darkness, the fear diminished. There was no sign of the four small lights; they were either out or obscured by the newly constructed upper floor. Lonnie tried to find one of the latrine buckets but gave up after stumbling over a number of reclining bodies. Then he couldn't find Ross and kept shouting his name as he stumbled around bumping into people, getting shoved away once or twice in the process.

"Looking for somebody?" a voice asked right in his left ear.

"Fuck you, you shithead. Why didn't you answer me? You been right there letting me scream my lungs out without saying a word, you shithead!"

"I like being paged. It makes me feel important."

They urinated on the floor of the hold and from the growing acrid smell, Lonnie concluded that others were doing the same thing. Just before he went to sleep, his head on his mess kit cover, he thought about the mountain, the one with the shroud of mist blown back, and of his LIFE WOMAN; but he couldn't see her very well. Then he remembered his Golden Bats, he still had four of them. "We'll smoke one in the morning."

The next pay, right after the food had been passed down and distributed, Mr. Noda came to the open hatch and announced that the sick prisoners would be moved to the upper hold.

"Let's go up," said Lonnie as he watched some of the men begin climbing the ladders in response to Mr. Noda's announcement.

"We're not sick," observed Ross, "and it's colder up there. What do you want to go up there for?"

"Hell fire, you're dense! Those sick guys will probably get extra food and maybe some blankets. Let's go!"

"Bullshit!" said Ross softly, but he followed Lonnie up one of the ladders; they moved in among the men who were congregating against the aft bulkhead where the sun was shining into the hold. Finally no one else came up the ladders. Then they saw a platform being lowered into the hold by a winch located on the deck. It disappeared into the lower section and after a while slowly came back into view, holding about fifteen men who were either dead or too sick to move much. They were carried off the platform by a detail of prisoners. The platform made four trips, and the passengers were lined up in the sunshine next to the bulkhead. A number of them were already dead. Lonnie looked fearfully into the dead faces, but didn't recognize anybody. None of his friends, just unknown dead people, already almost skeletons.

"Jesus Christ, I didn't know so many guys were sick," and with a sudden catch in his voice, "and dead! How many do you think?"

"About thirty dead," said Ross, "and about three hundred sick, if you include gold bricks like us. Let's go below, it's too depressing up here. They aren't going to get anything different from the rest of us, except more cold."

They waited for a while and then sneaked down one of the ladders. They weren't the only ones, Lonnie counted five others making the trip down. Later that day, just after the midafternoon meal Lonnie decided to make the trip again.

"I'll bet a dollar those guys have blankets by now," he announced to Ross. "I'm going to check."

But nothing had changed, he wasn't even sure the sick had been fed. The dead lay in neat rows of silent immobility. The dying gazed at the square of blue above them like they were looking for something. Urine and excrement, tinged with red, flowed in small streams along the steel plates of the floor. Lonnie was glad to get back into the lower hold.

"Pretty bad?" asked Ross.

"Yeah," responded Lonnie. Then in a low voice filled with anguish, "No goddammit, not pretty bad. Fucking miserable! I tell you it's fucking miserable!"

"Hey," exclaimed Ross, "let's light up one of those Golden Bats!"

"Why not, by God, why not?" said Lonnie, his mood suddenly changing. "Let's live a little!"

They had taken two drags each, when an American major, his gold oak leaves still on his tattered shirt, announced that everybody would be given extra food if enough rings and watches could be found to pay for it.

"I wouldn't give those Jap bastards the sweat off my balls!" said Lonnie. "What a fucking bunch of ghouls, they got us helpless in this stinking hold and now they want to rob us of what little we got left." Then looking at Ross's hand he asked plaintively, "You going to give them your ring?"

Ross looked down. The ring was heavy gold, crested with a large star sapphire. "My wife gave me this when I graduated from O.C.S.," he said quietly. "I'm going to die with it on."

"Yeah, when you're about ninety," said Lonnie quickly.

The American major came near them holding out an old blue denim cap but Ross didn't look up. Lonnie could see a number of items in the cap and observed one or two prisoners hand over something that gleamed for a moment in the dwindling light.

"Have a last drag," said Lonnie.

"Boy, those Golden Bats are great," Ross inhaled deeply. "How many you got left?"

"Two," said Lonnie. "Two and that butt, if you don't hog it all. You know," Lonnie continued, "it's funny, not long ago you couldn't light up a cigarette without everybody bothering you for butts or a drag. They don't do that any more. You notice that? They don't do it any more."

"I guess they know they wouldn't get one," said Ross, handing the butt back. Lonnie tore it carefully apart and placed the few grains of tobacco into his LIFE WOMAN pouch.

The next day they received three meals. The third meal came late in the evening, about an hour before dark, and with the extra food, the mood of the prisoners changed. There was laughter and jokes and a bit of impromptu singing. "Night and Day" was Lonnie's favorite song; when a group began to sing it, he jumped up and flapped his arms around, directing. Even Ross seemed in a better mood. When they visited Gentry, R. T. Barton, and Corso, he laughed a lot and told a dirty joke about a bum who could fart the "Star Spangled Banner." They were all laughing at the joke, a little extra because Ross had told it, when a strange rumbling sound caused everyone to look upward toward the open hatch for a few minutes. But nothing happened, except Mr. Noda.

[178]

"More good news today," Mr. Noda said. He seemed a long way up, standing there at the edge of the hatchway, grinning. "You guys in the lower part of the hold come up on deck. Lots of sunshine, see the mountains again, it's a nice day. Come on up."

Lonnie and Ross climbed hurriedly up the first ladder, past the sick and dying of the upper level, and finally through the top ladder well into the sunshine. One of the steam winches on deck was giving off a trickle of water and Lonnie actually got his canteen partly filled before he was pushed away by others eager for their turn. There was such a commotion around the winches that the Japanese finally posted guards to keep order. Lonnie took a sip of water from his canteen, it was warm and only slightly salty. He gave Ross a sip, then put the lid back on.

"We'd better save the rest," he said, screwing the lid on tight. "You can never tell what's going to happen. I didn't like the sound of that rumble we heard."

Most of the men were out of the lower section of the hold. Some didn't come up on deck at all, but remained with the sick in the upper level. Lonnie wished he and Ross had stayed down there too; he didn't like the looks of things. The prisoners who had come on deck were herded towards the rear of the ship and ordered to sit down. Lonnie and Ross were near the rail and had a clear view of the bay; although it was almost noon, a heavy mist still covered the water like a canopy. Only the upper sections of some of the ships could be seen, and in the distance vague shapes faded away into milky opaqueness. One ship was moving silently through the mist. Lonnie wasn't sure but it seemed to be coming towards them; each time he looked, the bridge which was the only part visible seemed to get bigger.

"I think company is coming," he told Ross, pointing in that direction.

"Why, is your nose itching?" Ross started to say something more but was interrupted by the shouting of the Japanese guards.

They had opened the hold in the forward section of the ship and were forcing the prisoners toward it, prodding them into

[179]

line with the usual long poles. As Lonnie moved closer to the small hatch opening his fear grew; when his turn came to descend the ladder, he looked down into total darkness and was overwhelmed by the odor of oil.

"Jesus Christ," he screamed at Ross, "they are putting us in an oil tank. Let's go back, let's go back!" He broke out of the line, receiving only a glancing blow from a long pole, and dashed toward the rear of the ship. A guard shouted at him but he didn't stop. He found one of the ladder wells, climbed down to the first level and hid among the sick lying next to the bulkhead. For a long time he expected to see a guard coming down one of the ladders, looking for him, but none of them did. He kept watching for Ross, hoping to see him climbing down. After about thirty minutes, a number of prisoners joined them, apparently the overflow from the other hold, but Ross wasn't among them. Lonnie kept looking at the ladders, hoping, a strange terror growing. He was alone.

Ross didn't come down, but somebody else did: short, squat men dressed in parts of old Japanese uniforms, complete with hobnailed boots and wrap-around cloth leggings. They moved through the prisoners without looking at them, as if they were invisible, and descended the ladders into the lower section. Almost immediately a platform loaded with large bulky sacks came down and disappeared through the square opening. It remained out of sight for a few minutes then appeared again, empty except for two of the workers, riding up. They still didn't look at the prisoners, nor did they look at them even once during the entire afternoon as the platform went up and down. Lonnie lost count of the trips it made, somewhere past sixty, but the size of the load never seemed to vary, thirty sacks full of mystery, going down into the hold beneath them on each journey.

Lonnie crawled to the edge of the square opening, looked down and saw long neat rows of fat sacks almost completely filling the bottom of the lower hold. A strangely familiar sweet odor, an odor Lonnie couldn't quite place, came up from the sacks. He remained at the edge fascinated by the loading process, the lowering of the platform on the long cable, the immediate attack on the heavy sacks by the workers. How could such little shitheads carry so much? Each sack must have weighed at least two hundred pounds. Two men would lift a sack, hold it poised for a moment until a carrier got in place, then they would throw it on his shoulders. There was rhythm in the labor, when two loaders heaved up a heavy sack there was always a broad back waiting to receive it. The work went on, load after load, layer after layer of fat sacks, and the afternoon faded into evening. They didn't miss a beat.

Once when the lower hold was almost filled, the platform, completely loaded, came swinging down in arcs so great Lonnie feared for a moment that the thing might strike him. He jumped back. The platform narrowly missed the edge of the opening but one of the sacks which protruded over its edge struck the metal and burst open, spraying its contents onto the steel deck right at Lonnie's feet. He reached down and grabbed a handful. Jesus Christ, he couldn't believe it, it was sugar. There was an immediate rush by the other prisoners; in a few seconds not a grain was left.

As suddenly as they came, the workers went away, riding the platform up, still not looking at the prisoners. A group of Japanese sailors came then and placed hatchboards over the opening to the lower hold. They worked rapidly and efficiently. Large steel beams were first, locking into slots located on the inner edge of the opening, then heavy boards fitting together tongue-in-groove, and finally over the completed structure a large tarpaulin was laid and nailed to the boards. Then the sailors too, without glancing at the prisoners, climbed on the platform and disappeared.

Almost immediately the prisoners spread out over the newly constructed floor. Lonnie made the move himself, finding a spot near the center of the broad tarpaulin. He sat down, Jesus Christ, all that sugar, tons of it, within a few feet of him. He was sure he could smell it, a heavy pungent molasses odor rising around him like a halo, reminding him of something he couldn't quite remember, try as he might, something nice from a long time ago. He couldn't think of anything but the sugar. Even when the afternoon meal came, finally about dark, he kept seeing it down there, hundreds of fat sacks of brown crystals that melted in the mouth and ran syrupy over the

[181]

tongue. He ate the rice and soybean paste, there was no soup, and gulped down his tea, but he didn't taste any of it. The memory of the sugar was there, jamming out all sensations, all other thoughts. He wasn't even lonely for Ross.

As darkness came and it grew colder in the hold Lonnie left the center of the tarpaulin but he couldn't bring himself to move back toward the bulkhead where it was warmer. He crawled to the edge of the tarpaulin and felt along, foot after foot, until he completely circumnavigated the large square and was back where he had started. No break anywhere. Not only was it nailed down, the nails had been driven through metal bands which held the edges of the tarpaulin securely in place. Finally he lay down on the tarpaulin, at the very edge where the hatchboards jutted against the steel floor of the hold. It was restful, lying there, but getting very cold. A bright star shone directly overhead, bracketed by the square of the upper hatch opening. As he watched, it seemed to move, first one direction, and then another, sometimes slow and sometimes fast. Then he didn't see it at all.

He awoke stiff from the cold, alert, listening. Something was happening. At first he heard nothing but the heavy breathing and snoring and turning of the men around him; then the sounds he thought he heard when he was asleep came again, the muffled tinkle and click of mess gear, and muted whispers. Suddenly he knew. In the total darkness he began to crawl slowly in the direction of the sounds, around sleeping individuals, occasionally over them, until the sounds were there just in front of him. He peered intently ahead but could see nothing but the vague shifting light images born in his own eyes; the darkness was total. Then almost at his elbow, somebody whispered.

"Let's wait till Bill gets back before we divide it."

The familiar pungent smell of molasses came to Lonnie, as he crouched down completely motionless, then ever so slowly he reached out and touched the sack. For a moment he remained there thinking, his hand caressing the rough material, then he withdrew as silently as he had come. When he was a few feet away he removed his canteen from its holder and took off the cup. Making slightly more noise than necessary he approached the sounds again.

[182]

"Here's my cup," he whispered, holding it out. A hand reached out and took it. He could hear crisp grating sounds as it was forced into the damp brown crystals. Then somebody shoved it into his outstretched hands, heavy with sugar. "Thanks," he whispered.

He withdrew a few feet, trembling so much he could hardly crawl, holding the canteen cup in one hand, feeling carefully along with the other. He couldn't wait any longer. He pushed his face into the heaped-up brown sugar, felt the crystals burst in his mouth, stream into his stomach, rampage through his arteries, nurtured his screaming cells. He couldn't stop, mouthful after mouthful, until the canteen cup was empty. Somehow it didn't help, he was hungrier than ever and still shaking. He approached the sounds again, outstretched cup in his hand.

"I'm back," he whispered.

"Sure you are, you motherfucker," somebody said. Something heavy and flexible struck him across the forehead with such force that he fell to the tarpaulin, stunned.

"Get out of here, you thieving son-of-a-bitch," the same voice whispered. "If you try that again, we'll kill you! Next time it won't be a canteen belt, it'll be a knife!"

Lonnie didn't say anything, he lay where he had fallen, listening to canteen cups grate against the packed sugar in the sack. Carefully, then, he felt into his pouch for a little piece of amber glass he had found that morning on the deck.

"Never can tell when you might need something like this," he had told Ross as he picked it up from near one of the huge mooring rings next to the outer rail.

"Sure," Ross had grinned. "A guy can never tell when he might need a piece of broken beer bottle."

Slowly Lonnie extended his hand, holding the broken glass, until he found the sack. Carefully he sawed away, slowly and methodically until eventually a hole was opened and the sugar came out streaming over his fingers. First he filled his LIFE WOMAN pouch, then the canteen holder, and finally his canteen cup again. When it was done, he moved away, backing slowly, feeling with his feet until the sounds couldn't be heard any more. No one had noticed him.

[183]

He stopped, hesitated for a moment, unmindful of the complaints of somebody he had just crawled over, then moved back until he could hear the sounds again. "Fuck you, you sons-of-bitches! I got your fucking sugar anyway!" he shouted.

He crawled away quickly, stopping a number of times to listen for pursuit, but he couldn't hear anything. He could feel it getting warmer as he moved beneath the upper deck toward the bulkhead. Finally he was there with the cool steel against his back, filled with exhilaration, convinced now that he could make it through the trip. He thought about Ross for a moment, hoping that he was okay over there in that damn oil tank. Wish he had some of this sugar. He ate some more of it, taking small pinches from the heaped-up canteen cup, letting each bit melt slowly in his mouth.

"What you got there?" somebody near him asked. "What are you eating?"

"Nothing," Lonnie responded to the darkness. "Not a fucking thing." He lay down and tried to think of his LIFE WOMAN but she was far away, a vague image there on the ice. Probing around with his finger he found a large lump of sugar almost at the bottom of the canteen cup. He put it in his mouth and gently sucked it. Just before he went to sleep he thought, "I better wake up early or some thieving bastard will steal my sugar."

He did wake early, just as the square was beginning to cast a faint light even back under the steel deck. He checked his sugar and it was still intact, beside him. Soon others wakened and saw that Lonnie had accomplished the impossible, had somehow realized their own dreams.

"Where'd you get the sugar?"

"How'd you do it, Boy?"

"How about a little of that sugar?"

"I'll trade you some," said Lonnie. He immediately began making commercial transactions. For five tablespoons of sugar, heaped-up, he obtained a mess kit complete with fork. For three tablespoons, leveled off, he was able to buy futures on whatever food would be issued at the next meal other than tea and rice, for eight tablespoons, heaped-up, he obtained futures on two issues of rice, and for six tablespoons also heaped-up, two rations of tea.

[184]

He was just making the last deal with some skinny bastard with bony buttocks and sunken eyes who immediately ate the sugar in slavering gulps when a silence settled over the hold. Sharp and clear in the sudden hush the sound of guns could be heard, heavy and resonant; large weapons, first a sharp metallic report, then some seconds afterwards a dull boom somewhat like thunder. Even as they listened the sounds faded and the panic went away. Normal noise levels had just returned again when the food buckets appeared overhead. Lonnie was ready with his new mess kit. After he received his rice and tea and to his unabashed joy, a little soup, he began making his rounds collecting. The individuals with whom he had made the rice deals paid up without difficulty, they seemed too sick to care about much anyway, but the tea people couldn't be found. The soup people gave him the most trouble. Two out of three contended that the deal was null and void. They maintained that they had traded the soybean paste which usually accompanied each meal, not soup.

"You dirty, crooked lying bastard," Lonnie shouted at the last one who offered up this logic. "We made a deal, goddammit and you know it!"

"Get out of here, you skinny little creep, or I'll kick the shit out of you!"

"Well, for Christ sake, if you want to get nasty about it," sniffed Lonnie and went away.

But he did collect the third issue of soup; the fellow grumbled, but gave it up. Lonnie's mess kit was completely filled. He looked down at it, brimming with rice, in the center a pool of rich soup; not just any soup, there was meat and potatoes in it.

"Jesus Christ, a feast, a goddamn feast!"

He finally found an open space just big enough for him on the outer edge of the tarpaulin. Directly above him two rows of heavy hatch boards reduced the sky to a narrow rectangle of blue, touched here and there with high flying, almost transparent, clouds.

He sat down and was just in the process of digging into the resplendent meal with his new fork, when a knowledge came to him. The interior of the hold with its hundreds of men, sitting, standing, talking, eating, surged by in a series of stark images. The sky above with its wisps of clouds became too blue. He was caught, frozen in a milli-second nightmare as he felt the sound. One that he knew in his bones, in his chest, in his guts: almost hypersonic, a high-whining shriek he had heard before when he lay on a field in Mindanao and watched the bombers drop their burdens and saw the bombs fall down, ever so slowly, singing as they came.

He watched his legs move slowly under him, saw his right arm, the hand still holding the brimming mess kit, straighten out as his left searched for the floor to help his legs along. Those near him were stricken by the terror in the sound he made and saw imprinted on his face. He had only taken four steps when the bombs struck. There was a series of blinding light flashes, of sounds too loud to be significant to the human ear, sounds heard by every part of him.

He fell to the floor, just where the tarpaulin reached the steel plates, others as frantic as himself falling over him, covering him with their bodies, protecting him from the hatchboards which came down with smacking sounds among the individuals who lay stunned under the opening. Only one hatchboard struck him; a glancing blow in the back before it fell and teeter-tottered across the body of a man who lay across his head and shoulders. Slowly he disentangled himself, pushed off the unresisting bodies of the ones who shielded him. Almost absently he saw the gaping chest, the pink lungs and still pulsating heart of one of them, who had lain as armor across his head and shoulders, who now lay quietly on his back, his life exposed, the mists of dryness growing in his eyes.

Lonnie stood up and tried to look around but blood flowed into his eyes and he couldn't see. "I'm dying now," he thought. "I'm like that guy with his guts tore out, I probably got it in the head. That's it, my brain is hurt so I can't feel the pain." He kept standing there, waiting for darkness to take the place of fear. But it didn't come, he didn't even fall down!

"Well I'll be goddamned!" he gasped aloud as he wiped the blood out of his eyes and looked fearfully over his body. Small pieces of shrapnel had struck him in both arms and in the left knee; minute slivers of steel which disappeared into the flesh but caused no bleeding. On his left thigh there was a larger wound, a small volcano in his flesh, oozing blood and containing small threads. The wound on his head which had caused the blood flow in his eyes was nothing, a small cut in the scalp just above the hairline. Lonnie couldn't believe it, he was still alive and didn't even seem to be hurt very much, except maybe for that funny round wound in his thigh.

He looked around the hold then with casual interest. Most of the men were standing, crowded against the sides of the ship beneath the steel plating of the upper deck. Many of them had managed to retain their food during the explosions and were now busily eating, stopping every now and then to glance at the havoc under the hatchway. Lonnie looked for his mess kit but it was gone, either picked up by someone or hidden under the fallen hatchboards or beneath the bodies which lay intermingled with them. He picked his way among them, careful not to look into any of the faces, searching for something which might be useful; but to his astonishment every article had already been appropriated by someone. He saw others bent on the same mission as himself, moving slowly among the dead and dying, occasionally lifting a hatchboard or rolling over a body to get a better look.

One of the searchers was having trouble removing a ring from the finger of a severed hand which lay inoffensively on one of the hatchboards. Lonnie had thought about taking it himself; it was a fine ring, heavy gold with a bright red ruby and writing, "West Point, Class of '36" clearly visible, but he couldn't bring himself to lift the hand.

"What are you doing, you goddamn ghoul?"

But the man paid no attention; he just kept working the ring, trying to get it off. Lonnie started looking for rings then, but couldn't find any. Finally he saw a canteen cup, half hidden, under a fallen hatchboard. He hastily picked it up and fastened it to his web belt. As he did so he felt his LIFE WOMAN pouch and his canteen holder and was gratified to find that both were still filled with sugar. "Shit, I'm not so bad off," he thought, looking over the scores of dead beneath the hatchway. "I'm still alive and I've got something to eat."

He looked to see if the bombs had caused a breach into the lower hold where all the sugar lay, but there was none; the tarpaulin hadn't even been torn. He wondered idly how the individuals who had struck him with the belt had gotten to the sugar. He also wondered where the bombs had struck, there was no sign of damage anywhere. None of the hatchboards were splintered, they had just fallen down. He looked at all sides of the ship but could see no holes, yet the shrapnel must have gotten in some way; there were scores of wounded men. It was as confusing as hell. Finally he decided that one or more bombs must have struck the superstructure above the hold, or perhaps had hit the bridge and had showered metal pieces down to ricochet around the metal sides. "That's probably it," he mused, "that would explain the light flashes and the heavy concussion."

He looked at his wounds again, the large one in his thigh was still oozing but the others had ceased bleeding altogether. He felt strangely exhilarated, and except for the after effects of the heavy blow on his back by the hatchboard, he could get around well and there was no pain. He sat down in an open space, under the section of the hold covered by the steel deck and ate a handful of sugar, licking his fingers, savoring the brown crystals. He was thirsty and was on the verge of trying to trade sugar for something to drink when he saw the dull glint of silver beneath one of the bodies under the hatchway. He got up, slightly bent over by the heavy bruise on his back, and walked in that direction, once again stepping over the dead and dying, careful not to glance into the faces. Almost completely hidden under the right shoulder of one of the bodies he found it, a canteen almost three-fourths full of tea; he couldn't believe his good luck. He took two large mouthfuls from the canteen and attached it by the chain to his web belt. He felt even better now and hardly noticed the pain in his back as he made his way back to the open space beneath the steel deck.

The day moved into afternoon, Lonnie watched the sun trace its arc upon the tarpaulin, saw it cast a sheen of brightness over the havoc under the hatchway, a mélange of overlapping images of fallen hatchboards and bodies intertwined; a study of light and shadows, red blotches, the subdued effect of varied shades of pink, all starkly etched on the large canvas. Toward evening the sun searched out the far corners of the hold leaving the tabloid under the hatchway silent and peaceful, veiled by shadows. Above deck no sound could be heard, no voice. "Maybe the Japs are all dead," thought Lonnie, and he grinned at the thought. "Maybe the bastards are dead everywhere in the world. Maybe everybody is dead but us." He looked around the hold, hoping to see someone he knew but all the faces were unfamiliar. He thought about Ross and wondered what had happened in the other hold, of Gentry and Corso and R. T. Barton, and where they were. "Maybe out there among the hatchboards, or maybe in the other hold."

Just before dark an American officer, the one with the bright gold oak leaves, stood among the fallen hatchboards and dead bodies, where he could be seen. Lonnie couldn't help admiring him, the son-of-a-bitch, him and his shiny oak leaves, standing there like it meant something to be an officer in the army of the United States of America. Bullshit. But he listened.

"Well, there's no doubt about it now," the Major said in a voice edged with a note of pride. "The Japs are really on the run or our boys wouldn't be able to bomb this far north. Hell, this is Formosa and those were high-flying land based planes that hit us. This war can't last long now. Within a month or two we will all be back home eating steak and drinking good beer. All we have to do is act like American soldiers, and we can take it. Goddammit, we can take it. Okay, now let's get off our asses and get this mess down here cleaned up. Shit, this is something you'll be proud to tell your grandkids about. I know you can take it, I've been watching you, you are as brave as hell, and some of you are going to get the silver star and the purple heart, and advancements in rank. Now let's get out there and get this goddamn mess cleaned up. Pile all the hatchboards over there in that far corner, take the clothes off the dead and pile the bodies next to the hatchboards. All the wounded should be placed against the inner bulkhead where it's warmest at night. All extra clothes should be given to them. Okay, now goddammit, let's act like American soldiers and get in there and get this mess cleaned up!"

[189]

Lonnie was amazed to see how rapidly it all happened. Suddenly there were hundreds of men in action; moving the hatchboards, undressing the dead, stacking the bodies, gently moving the wounded. Within fifteen minutes, except for the red splotches on the tarpaulin, the signs of destruction were entirely cleared away. Just before it became dark in the hold, Lonnie moved in among the wounded next to the bulkhead. It was fairly crowded but he finally found an open space between two individuals who had turned away from each other. He lay down on the steel floor, thankful for the warmth near the bulkhead; the bombs had opened the hatch completely and it was getting cold in the hold.

Lonnie was about to doze off when he noticed something right there in front of his eyes not three feet away. He raised up on his elbow to get a good look and in spite of the dwindling light, could clearly see them, THE SHOES! Still resplendent with much polishing, a rich brown which caught the dim light and reflected it into Lonnie's eyes. The owner of the shoes, the young Captain with the bright bars and the new uniform, lay humped over as if in terrible pain. No sign of blood, maybe one of the hatchboards hit him. The bars were still bright, they gleamed in the dim light, but the uniform was caked with dirt. Lonnie lay back down again, comforted by the close presence of the shoes. As he dozed off he could see their brown luster, the solidity and tangibility of the thick soles.

During the night something woke him, a gentle tugging at his canteen belt. He lay there in the total darkness without moving and it came again, a hand was reaching into his canteen holder, taking out the sugar, slowly and carefully.

"Get out of here you thieving son-of-a-bitch," Lonnie screamed into the darkness, and the hand withdrew.

He thought he heard somebody crawling away but wasn't sure and then was asleep again, dreaming. He seemed suspended in a grey slow motion world, filled with the familiar angles, wedges of jagged steel within an endless plane of transparent liquid through which he moved spasmodically, ever so slowly. He heard the eerie whirring, keening sound again coming from everywhere, and felt the fear of it. Then over the entire scene a giant presence came gradually into being, a wall of pressure somewhere behind him, turning and turning as a world might turn. Less fearful to see than to remain in darkness he looked backwards and saw a hand, giant in all dimensions, impelled by nameless energies, swinging in strange rotation. On the middle finger of the hand, a massive ring of gold. As it turned, rays from the ruby in its crest fanned out in all directions to tint the total scene with overlapping duplicates in red. Then from the edge he heard, or at least it seemed he did, the sound of singing armies. "Fuck 'em all, fuck 'em all." Faintly at first but growing stronger, blending with the whirring sound.

Then somebody was shaking him and he awoke to stare fearfully into a face he didn't know. He sat up grabbing his canteen holder.

"What the hell do you want?" he gasped, almost unable to speak.

The face grinned, "Nothing, you must have been having one hell of a dream. You were screaming, 'Mother! Mother!' at the top of your goddamn voice!"

"You're shitting me," said Lonnie, suddenly relieved. "But thanks for waking me up anyway."

It was light in the hold; the sun was up, some of the winch standards on the topside were bathed in sunlight. He figured the angles and moved over where the sunlight should first enter the hold. It was difficult for him to walk, his back hurt each time he moved, and the leg with the large wound was beginning to swell; a curious transparent liquid was seeping from the opening. "Some son-of-a-bitch has got some sulfa, I've got to get me some, I've got to get some sulfa or this goddamn leg is going to drop off." He finally found an open space on the edge of the tarpaulin and sat down, shivering slightly from the cold. When the sun's first rays touched the bottom of the hold, they found him still sitting there beside the great iron girder, asleep with his arms wrapped around his knees. As he grew warm in the sun he slowly relaxed until he was coiled around the girder, holding on to it with both arms. Even after the sun had moved across the floor of the hold to leave him lost in shadows he continued to sleep, hour after hour, until the day was nearly over.

Finally just at sundown he awoke to hear the strangely

welcome voice of Mr. Noda making an announcement. He stood, as usual, peering myopically down, holding on to one of the hatch cover supports. He wasn't grinning as usual, though. There was a strained, almost hysterical quality in his voice, high-pitched and pleading.

"Okay you guys, somebody has been taking sugar out of the hold. Somebody cut the tarpaulin and took out some sugar. The person who took the sugar better say so right now or you, none of you," he said with emphasis, "will get anything to eat today. You have ten minutes to come forward and confess, or none of you will get anything to eat today. I will be back in ten minutes and the guilty person better confess." He disappeared from view. Lonnie expected to hear angry comments, but none of the prisoners said anything. They just remained where they were, occasionally looking up toward the opening, disinterested, unconcerned.

Soon Mr. Noda was back. "Okay you guys, your ten minutes is up. The guilty guy had better come forward now." He waited looking expectantly into different sections of the hold but nothing happened. Finally one of the prisoners came forward, dirty and unshaven. He moved slowly from beneath the steel platform of the upper deck. He seemed familiar, and as Lonnie watched he was suddenly overwhelmed with sadness and remorse—it was Gentry. The light was in his eyes as he looked up, but everybody heard what he had to say.

"Hey Noda, you've got to be kidding. We've got a hundred dead men down here, three hundred more are wounded and all of us are starving to death. Do you really think you can keep these men from eating sugar if they can get their hands on it?" Then his voice, magnified by the steel plates of the ship's sides, resonated and grew in volume; overlapping echoes, strangely metallic, apocalyptic. "Why don't you be merciful, you bastards, and kill us now? You people are not even human; you could give us water, yet you let us die of dehydration; you could give us food but you let us starve; you could give us medicine and bandages to bind our wounds; you could give us clothes and blankets to keep us from the cold; you don't even let us remove the dead. Look over there in the corner, Noda, the pile is getting higher every hour. And you

[192]

ask us to be concerned about a bag of sugar. You try to blackmail us with a promise of even more misery if you don't get your confession."

He paused for a moment, still squinting in the bright light, looking up towards Mr. Noda who stood stricken, immobile, his hands held out as if in silent plea.

"You can treat us this way now, you people," Gentry's resonant voice continued, "but remember this." His voice rose and everybody in the hold was thrilled by the sound of it. "They are coming,—they are coming by the millions,—and they are going to have ships like you've never seen before and planes, and tanks, and bombs. They're going to push you people back until there's nowhere left. Nowhere! Nowhere!"

Gentry stopped, looking up, not towards Mr. Noda but towards a section of the hatch which Lonnie couldn't see. A strange silence extended over the hold, an apprehension, a waiting. Mr. Noda wasn't looking down any more but across the opening and even before Lonnie crept over to the edge of the tarpaulin and looked up, he knew that Major Imada was standing there. Other prisoners were moving quietly out from under the steel deck onto the tarpaulin, carefully, respectfully, every now and then glancing furtively upwards.

Major Imada stood with his right hand resting easily on one of the iron uprights, a brooding, ominous, alien presence, not looking down, not looking anywhere. He stood as if completely alone, gazing absently towards the setting sun which lingered for a few moments on the crest of the far mountain, casting a brightness about him. Then he began to speak, still not looking down, quietly and slowly, yet his voice carried into the hold so everyone could hear him.

"These are bad times but there are worse to come." He paused and looked more intently at the setting sun. "The barbarians are coming from the south and you are right, they are coming by the millions." He paused again now gazing down into the hold, his black eyes showing starkly in his pale face. He seemed to be looking directly at Gentry, who still peered upwards, totally absorbed, completely attentive. "You American soldier, the one who spoke like a brave man, you are right. It is the year of the barbarian. Down through history

[193]

barbarians have been good at one thing, good at killing. It is the year of the barbarian, they are coming and a terrible plague rests upon my country. A land civilized for thousands of years before your land was even known." He spoke slowly, carefully, still staring down into the hold. "When your ancestors were still wandering from place to place like animals, like savage beasts through the forests of Europe, my people walked in learning and respect. Now there is no hope for us. You cry because you are cold and hungry and because you die. But your children are not dying,—your country is not dying." He paused, his hand upon his sword, upon his face both anger and contempt.

"No, I was wrong, barbarians are good at two things, they are good at killing and they are good at crying. Japanese do not cry. If your people come in a thousand ships, in airplanes by the thousands, if they kill our children, destroy our cities, violate our land, we will not cry. We will fight them on the oceans and in the air, we will fight them on our sacred land. Though your people come and kill and kill, as impersonally as sharks, as pitiless as the sun, we will not cry!" He paused again, the last rays of the sun touched the ornaments upon his sword and sent multicolored light sequins dancing through the darkness of the hold.

"It is the year of the barbarian, but do not take comfort. Two thousand miles of dangerous water waits for us. I do not think that any of us will live until this voyage ends. But whatever happens, we will play this game. You as the cowards which you are and I as the soldier which I am. Nothing you can do can change it, nothing I can do can change it." He paused again, looking down, not angry now and then spoke almost softly. "Perhaps I am wrong. Perhaps you are not cowards. Perhaps you will not cry. Maybe you are soldiers. When more bad times come, I give you something to think about. It is the Japanese soldier's creed, something to say, to believe in when death time comes." He spoke loud and clear, his voice vibrant, without trace of accent, "And so now I die, but I shall live to fight again!"

A silence extended so long Lonnie thought Major Imada was not standing up there any more. But then almost too quietly to hear, Lonnie caught his last words, "So says the soldier." The prisoners remained under the open hatch, occasionally looking up, admiration and confusion fixed upon a face here and there. On others, bewilderment. Lonnie kept hoping the Major would say something else but he had disappeared into the deepening twilight. But Mr. Noda was still there, a vague blob at the edge of the opening.

"Okay, you guys, I am still waiting for the person who took the sugar out of the hold to confess. You must confess. If you will confess right now, you will all receive food in the morning, food and tea." There was a long silence and then someone out of the darkness of the hold, Lonnie could have sworn it was R. T. Barton, began to mutter.

"Fuck you, you crummy little shithead. The barbarians are going to get you. When those bastards get through with you there won't be anything left but some buck teeth and a little broken glass!" This statement was greeted with a roar of laughter from the hold.

As soon as the laughter had diminished just a little, somebody else said, "Naw, those barbarians are good guys. They'll get you a job, Noda, in a zoo, substituting for an ape on his night out!" Another roar of laughter.

"I've got a better idea," shouted Lonnie, hardly able to control his laughter, "you can sell your picture, Noda. The barbarians can put it in toilets to gag ass holes!" Another roar of laughter which fell away, flared up sporadically, and then finally died to leave a big hole in the night.

"Okay, you wise guys," to Lonnie's astonishment Mr. Noda was giggling as he spoke, "you are a real bunch of unfunny guys, picking on a real nice guy like me. But let's get back to business. I still want the person who took that sugar to confess. If you will confess right now, you will get some extra food. If you will confess right now you will get an extra ration every day until the trip is over."

Lonnie was on the verge of confessing when four people beat him to it. Mr. Noda took down their names, squinting at a piece of paper which was almost invisible in the darkness. Just before he turned away to disappear from the opening, he cleared his throat and said softly, "I'm afraid I have some bad news for you." There was something in his voice, a note of sadness, of regret, which caught the attention of the men and quieted them. "The people in the other hold were not so lucky as you, most of them were either killed or wounded. Some bombs hit the water near the ship and blew big holes above the water line; the shrapnel killed many of your friends, the concussion from the bombs killed many more. But," and now his voice took on a happier tone, "some of them are still alive, a few of them are not even hurt at all. Tomorrow the ones who can walk will come back into this hold, so you may see some of your friends again. And tomorrow you will receive some food, some good brown rice and some tea. I must say goodnight now."

No one answered him, not even a curse or insult; they were all thinking about the men in the other hold. Lonnie crept back to his spot near the bulkhead. In spite of the darkness he could see the shoes glinting vaguely and the shape of the young Captain dimly outlined, still humped over. He sat staring at the shoes, Jesus Christ it must feel good to have shoes on your feet. He lay with his head propped up on his canteen, eating the sugar from his LIFE WOMAN pouch. He didn't drink any of the tea in his canteen, there were only four or five swallows left. "I'll save it for Ross. He'll be coming tomorrow." But he didn't really believe it. He knew Ross had been killed and even now lay dead in the other hold, probably in a large stack, like the dead ones over there against the far bulkhead, except bigger. He would really have something to tell Ross's wife, he would tell her how brave he had been when he took the raft to the drowning men after the bombing of the first ship, what a good man he had been, and all that shit.

He lay there savoring the smell of brown sugar that came from his LIFE WOMAN sack trying to remember what it reminded him of thinking he would find Gentry and R. T. Barton and Corso, and join them in the morning. Maybe they wouldn't want him. He gazed toward the square of the hatch opening and could barely see the dim trapezoidal image, made of starlight. Tears rolled down his cheeks but he didn't try to stop them or brush them away. He let them well into his eyes until a blink would break them loose and send them flowing down. It felt good to cry a little, it was the least he could do for Ross, and anyway his leg was hurting him some, it was swelling more. He thought about an old joke about a guy with an oriental disease, how after three days his prick dropped off. No problem. He grinned a little just before he went to sleep.

Three days passed. Twice each day buckets of rice and tea were lowered into the hold and twice each day the latrine buckets were emptied by a work detail. Each morning Lonnie looked hopefully toward the ladders, expecting to see the men from the other hold coming down, but nothing happened, no one appeared. "That goddamn Noda, that lying bastard! They are probably all dead now. One great big pile of bodies without a wiggle anywhere, bigger even than the one over by the bulkhead." Lonnie couldn't help looking over there occasionally, noticing how the pile kept growing, probably two hundred guys there now. Even from where he was, clear across the hold, he thought he could smell them or maybe it was him stinking. His leg looked real funny, the strange transparent plus still running from it, and around the edges of the hole a yellowish white rind covered the wound, reaching deep into his leg.

On the morning of the fourth day the dead were removed from the hold. Three different ropes were let down, run by a single winch on the upper deck. The guys of the burial detail just tied each of the ropes to a leg, and up they would go, three at a time, swinging together. Lonnie couldn't help watching. They reminded him of chickens hung together in the milkhouse back home just after they had been scalded and picked and gutted, waiting for Sunday dinner.

Suddenly out of the impersonal mobile of overlapping, gyrating, rotating limbs, the picture loomed into focus. Upside down, one leg hanging loose, jogging up and down as the tensions of the rope shifted. Rutledge! Rutledge! The great laugh rang out and boomed and fused into an image of overlaps, of legs and arms, and fluid rushing from mouth and nose, of his own mortality lurking there just at the edges.

Lonnie didn't look anymore but turned to examine THE SHOES which still retained their glow even under a coat of

[197]

dust. "That guy isn't taking care of those shoes right. They should be kept dusted off, at least that." He kept hearing the screeching of the winch, in the background of his concentration on the shoes. Then he listened more carefully, a voice was mingled in with the sound of the winch, jumbled and almost inaudible it rose and fell even as the ropes came and went, down empty and away with burden, Father Maloney's voice. Lonnie tried to hear what he was saying, but couldn't understand a word. Must be Latin, some kind of Catholic bullshit, but he was glad Father Maloney was there giving the guys a send-off, little enough.

"Hey look up there." Through a haze of sleep Lonnie came slowly into the reality of clicking mess gear, the hum of conversations and pain. His leg throbbed with each pulse beat and his back hurt when he moved. He looked at the middle ladder, and felt a surge of hope; three Japanese medical corpsmen were climbing down into the hold. They were covered from head to foot with long white gowns, and wore gauze masks over their faces. Each carried a little black bag, "probably full of just what I need," Lonnie watched them climbing down. One had trouble getting down the ladder, the trailing end of his robe kept getting caught under his foot. "Hope he doesn't drop that bag." Lonnie waited among the seriously wounded but the corpsmen didn't even look in that direction. They set up their equipment on a little collapsible table in the middle of the tarpaulin, directly beneath the open hatch, and proceeded to treat anybody who could make it to their station.

"Jesus Christ, they're not even going to treat these guys," thought Lonnie. "As far as they're concerned, these bastards are already dead." He found that he could walk very well then. His leg hurt and his back ached like a tooth ready for pulling, but he made his way to the end of the line and waited his turn. It took a long time, inching along, chatting with the other guys. One of them gave him a drag on a cigarette which made him feel dizzy. The sun edged down into the hold, it felt good on his bare shoulders.

Finally he was standing before the white robed figure, holding out his wounded thigh, looking hopefully at eyes

[198]

which appraised him through narrow slits in a gauze mask. The eyes looked at Lonnie's leg for a moment, a voice said something in Japanese, and another white robed figure took out a bottle, Lonnie guessed it was gentian violet, and filled the wound with purple liquid. Then he went on down the line where another "member of the Jap KKK" as R. T. Barton later called them, put a compress on his wound.

"Jesus Christ, thanks man," said Lonnie when deft fingers had finished placing a pad upon his thigh and securing it into place by wrapping it again and again with a narrow strip of bandage.

"I hope it gets better," responded the white figure in excellent English. "It's not so bad. You will be okay."

When Lonnie returned to his place among the wounded next to the bulkhead, he felt strangely happy; those goddamn Japs were really good guys, some of them. They did care about the prisoners. Or maybe the Americans were getting close and the Japs were getting scared the barbarians were going to get them. Lonnie grinned, thinking about it.

As suddenly as they had come, the Japanese went away, awkwardly climbing the ladders in their flowing robes, rung by rung. Lonnie tried to guess which one had put the compress on his leg, the one with the nice voice and deep concern, but they all looked alike, with their long white doctor robes, black bags and hobnailed boots clicking on the rungs as they took each careful upward step.

Lonnie was still looking at the ladders, when he saw them, the men from the other hold. From where he lay, looking across the entire hold, they seemed to be strong enough, coming down the three ladders, one after another, three long lines. It couldn't be, but there he was coming into view on the third ladder, the one on the far right, Ross, moving slowly, using only one hand on each rung, holding his left hand close to his body. Lonnie began to shout.

"Hey Ross, you son-of-a-bitch, you're supposed to be dead. Hey Ross! Ross!" And soon he was standing over him, looking down, a peculiar look of relief and happiness on his face.

"Jesus Christ, you have a big mouth. I could hear you hollering from the top of the ladder. I thought somebody was killing you and here you are as skinny and sickly-looking as ever." Then more quietly, "Are you okay?" He appraised the compress on Lonnie's leg. "I lost some fingers, just two, and got it in the left shoulder."

"Shit, I'm okay, just a bang in the leg but I got it all fixed now. What happened over there?"

Ross surveyed the hold as he took a seat beside Lonnie. "It was lots worse than this. We don't know for sure, but about three bombs must have hit the water close to the ship, right next to our hold. They knocked all the hatchboards down, the heavy steel support beams fell down too. It was sudden, no warning, one big long roar, then it was over, with big holes in the side of the ship, and practically everybody dead or wounded." He paused for a moment looking down at his left hand which was heavily wrapped with long strips of bandage. "About three hundred died, most of the rest of us were wounded, about a hundred maybe. The shrapnel came in through the holes in the ship and sprayed around inside. It was just a big tank, with thousands of slivers of steel screaming around inside."

Ross shivered and looked at Lonnie. "It was a mess, they left us down there with those dead guys for days, for five days I think." He stopped then, and brightened perceptibly. "Guess what I got? Two cigarettes; some Jap, one of the medical men, was handing them out when we came up out of that tank. Let's light one up."

"I had some tea and some sugar I was saving for you," said Lonnie. Then a little guiltily, "But I drank it and ate it all, three or four days ago."

"Let's wait until we eat before we smoke our cigarette," said Ross, looking toward the center of the tarpaulin where the first buckets were already being removed from the ropes. "Let's get in line!"

After the standing, the inching forward, the waiting and minutes stretched to hours, they finally received some rice, soup, and tea. They had plenty of containers; Ross still had his mess kit and had managed to pick up an extra canteen cup. Lonnie felt dizzy waiting and his leg hurt him; he released the bandages a little and the pain eased. He didn't say anything about it, but he felt Ross' concerned look as he untied the knot.

"How's your hand?" he asked Ross. "And your shoulder?"

"About the same as your leg, I guess. Just keep thinking about that cigarette we're going to smoke."

"The last time we had soup like this, I didn't get to eat it," Lonnie observed, his mouth full. "I'm going to eat this fast in case those bombers take another notion to ruin one of my meals."

"It was inconsiderate of them," agreed Ross. "I didn't get to eat that meal either, the buckets were just coming down when the bombs struck and everything including the food detail was blown into the water."

But no bombers came this time. After eating Ross managed to get a light from a guy smoking near them; they sat back leaning on their elbows taking turns on the cigarette. With each drag, the terror and pain of their situation diminished, a calmness came, a kind of sleepiness.

"Having a good cigarette is the best thing in the world," observed Lonnie. "It must be."

"Pussy is better," said Ross.

"You're kidding," said Lonnie, looking at him suddenly. "How could it be?"

"It's better," repeated Ross. "It just is. Which is better, fried chicken or spinach?"

"Fried chicken, naturally, you shithead!"

"Well pussy is as much better than cigarettes as fried chicken is than spinach."

"Shit on you," said Lonnie, grinning. "I wouldn't know about all that stuff." Then he laughed out loud. "I've never eaten any fried chicken."

Ross laughed too. They lay there taking it easy smoking the cigarette, feeling comfortable, not lonely. The sun shone directly into the hold creating a warm bright square on the tarpaulin reflecting both light and warmth even back beneath the steel plating of the deck, making it nice for them.

"How many do you think are left now?" asked Lonnie suddenly. Ross didn't respond for a moment. He was thinking, counting.

"About half," he said finally.

"You mean about eight hundred?" asked Lonnie. "Jesus Christ, that's a lot of guys to die." Then he added quietly, "Old Rutledge didn't make it. I saw them pull him up." There was a long silence. "Did you know that it was me and him that ate Major Imada's cat?"

Ross didn't say anything. He sat looking at the dirty bandage which wrapped his left hand, a strange expression on his face.

"Damn it, I said I saw them pull Rutledge up. Didn't you hear me? I said I saw them pull Rutledge up!" Then at the top of his voice, "What's the matter with you? Don't you give a shit?" He stopped, puzzled and suddenly afraid. Ross was looking at him now, but somehow not seeing him; a vagueness in his eyes, a searching inward. "Don't you give a shit?" repeated Lonnie, his voice low, almost a whisper.

"You know it's funny," said Ross finally. "I know I should be sad for Rutledge. But I'm not; I'm not even sad for myself any more." He paused, looking at the dirty bandage again which Lonnie noticed was wet from a dark serum, "Nor afraid for myself any more. I know I'm not going to make it but it doesn't matter now. It's funny but you called it like it is. I really don't give a shit. Too many guys have died, too much has happened, too much more is going to happen. It just doesn't seem worth it." And then looking slowly over his own body, "There just doesn't seem enough of me left to be worth making it."

"You dirty son-of-a-bitch," said Lonnie, trying to steady his voice, "you dirty selfish bastard. What about me? What about me, Goddammit! You just want to leave me here alone!" For a moment Lonnie saw it all, a long slow trip of dying, all alone, or maybe a quick death in icy water, still alone. He began to whimper, small catches of breath in his throat, but to his amazement he couldn't shed any tears. It seemed he was watching somebody else be sad. He stopped making any sounds at all then and they both sat for a long time just staring out, not saying anything.

Finally Ross spoke, calmly, matter-of-factly, "Anyway it's warm and comfortable here."

[202]

"Yes," responded Lonnie. "Everything is okay right now."

"Well what more do you want?" asked Ross half smiling. "That's all there is, the right now."

"That's a crock of shit," observed Lonnie, now quite interested. "There's yesterday and there's tomorrow too. Not just today, not just right now. I'm not worried about yesterday but tomorrow scares the shit out of me. Tomorrow we may get our asses bombed off again, tomorrow we may be deader than a bunch of dead fish."

Ross was looking at him indulgently, but Lonnie continued. "Goddammit, I know what you're talking about, you and your fucking college education. That the only time we live in is the present minute, the right now. Hell, I know that but I also have enough brains to know that the right now that may be coming in a minute or in an hour or a week may be the last one, the one where we go bye-bye, goddammit. You and your fucking college education. . . ."

CHAPTER EIGHT

They heard that voice again, Mr. Noda's. "Okay you guys, we are going to get on another ship. If you can walk okay come on up the ladders." He was standing with a foot on the one iron girder which had remained in place during the bombing, looking as nondescript as always, squinting down into the relative darkness of the hold. "If you can't walk so good stay where you are. A platform will come and pick you up, and carry you away, just like," and here he paused laughing at his own little joke, "just like Alice in Wonderland."

Even before he finished talking men were gathering under the ladders, waiting their turn, forming lines which kept getting longer as more and more individuals picked up their bits of gear and fell in at the end. Ross and Lonnie waited watching the lines grow then slowly Ross stood up, fastened his mess gear to his web belt with his good hand, put his canteen in its holder.

"Let's go," he said, looking down at Lonnie who still leaned comfortably against the bulkhead, warmed by the sun.

"You go ahead," said Lonnie. "I've got to get used to getting along without you, you and your Get Dead Wish, so I'd just as soon get started now."

"You're kidding," said Ross, suddenly stricken.

"I wish I was," said Lonnie, looking away. "I'm going to stay with the wounded and ride away to the happy hunting

[204]

ground when the big platform comes. You go ahead, I'll be okay." He wasn't looking at Ross. "I'll be okay," he repeated in a small voice.

Ross stood for a long moment, looking down, pursing his lips. Finally he turned and walked toward the end of the long line waiting in front of the first ladder, and became fused into the crowd there. "Just another pair of skinny legs," thought Lonnie as he caught sight of him when the line moved, his blond hair glinting in the sun, his eyes dark hollows.

Lonnie didn't move from his place against the bulkhead. He sat listening to the clicking of mess gear, the rasping of bare feet on the steel rungs of the ladder. The sun moved across the hold and left him alone in the shadows. Finally he heard the screeching of a winch and saw the platform descending, fifteen feet square with cables tied to each corner, coming straight down, swinging a little. As it came to rest on the floor of the hold the cables became lax as the weight drained from them.

"Good-bye again," Lonnie looked around the hold for the last time. "Good-bye to all the horse piss and the bullshit and yesterday and right now. Hello tomorrow." He smiled a little as he crawled on the platform, "up, up, and away just like old Superman. Alice in Wonderland, shit! Everybody but that little shithead knows she didn't go up, she went down, down, man, down into a hole in the ground."

Others were crowding onto the platform, sick ones who suddenly found they could walk, some who could only crawl and one loud bastard who kept screaming for help until somebody finally reached out and gave him a hand. Lonnie kept watching the loose cables, waiting for the stretch to come. It finally did and they moved up, out of the hold into a January afternoon, still bright with sun. And suddenly there they were, the mountains; the tall one had lost its plume of hair, but it stood proud with the sun riding its left shoulder and the shadows of clouds drifting casually along the foothills, blobs of grey against the green grass and low lying shrub. As the platform swung over the side, he saw the bay, still filled with ships, some lying at odd angles but most looking smug and ordinary, undisturbed by wind or wave, just lying around with their anchor cables hanging loose. He had had the notion

[205]

that there would be another ship tied beside them, waiting, but no ship was waiting, just a small boat at the foot of the stairway, the same stairway he had climbed up (Jesus Christ, it seems like a year ago) ten days before. As he looked around the bay he tried to guess which ship would be their new home but there were too many of them, maybe a hundred.

The platform descended with squeaks and grinds until it hovered just above the water so close to the small boat that everbody, even the sick bastard with the loud mouth, crawled in without so much as a skinned elbow, just like getting out of bed. Lonnie found a place in the front of the boat near the one guard who was leaning into the angle of the prow with a bored look on his face and a rifle which seemed long and skinny and ineffectual. Only one other Japanese was in the boat; a short fat one in a faded navy uniform who kept fiddling with an old single cylinder engine which seemed just on the edge of dying but kept banging away, once every now and then. Lonnie asked for butts on a cigarette the guard was smoking. The guard took a long drag and flipped the butt, a real long one, overboard without as much as a look in Lonnie's direction.

"The dirty Jap son-of-a-bitch, he'll get his one of these days." Lonnie looked up to see the platform coming down with a bunch of bare feet and skinny legs dangling over the edge, swing back and forth right over them. "Hope none of those bastards fall off; no way to dodge if they did, hell of a way to die, smashed by some bony bastard." But nothing happened, the platform stopped, swung near the boat for a moment before hands reached out and steadied it. Not a breath of wind anywhere, water in the bay as smooth as glass, like a mirror. On the far side of the ship, towards the high mountain where the sun was just disappearing, a little notch already gone, Lonnie saw a double sun, one raging on the mountain, the other almost as bright, flaring in the water. The beat of the boat's motor increased, the side of the ship moved slowly past, like the world moving; in a moment he was looking back toward the stern, squat and broad, hunched down in the water with the anchor chain hanging loose out of a hole near the deck on the left side, like a misguided ass hole in action. He grinned, old R. T. Barton would appreciate that one.

[206]

He glanced over the side and marveled how the prow of the boat sliced through the water without a sound, smooth as silk, snicker snack, urged on by the two-banger. Suddenly he saw the old John Deere back home, back on the Cimarron, pulling a huge scoop filled with mud, lugs biting deep, flywheel spinning like crazy, bang, bang.

The green faded, he looked back where the sun had just slipped down behind the mountain, and saw the track of their small boat fanning out behind them; a multiple of angles, one within the other, expanding and growing. Within the angles, a bursting kaleidoscope of shifting color patterns, purple, yellow, gold, a thousand shades of pink and red from blood to pale, shimmering on the water, brought to animation by their passage, a liquid mobile. Dirty bilge oil, pollution on the march, the blood of dead ships rusting on the bottom, bubbling up the stuff.

Towards the front he saw a shape slowly growing larger than the rest, a dark rusting iron hulk, a freighter, smaller than the last one. "But large enough," thought Lonnie, "with all the guys dead, probably not more than eight or nine hundred left now."

The cadence of the motor lessened as the boat moved in beneath the rusty side, another stairway extended down almost to the water. The sailor at the tiller of their small boat took it in stern first, backing slowly until it came to rest against the ship, the stairway right there handy. A Jap corporal, a new one, waited on the deck, looking down, leaning on the stair rail fiddling with his sword. The prisoners started up, a few helping others who were having trouble; but most of them climbed a lot better than they should have considering they were supposed to be sick or wounded. Lonnie waited his turn falling in at the rear of the line as the boat emptied. He glanced again at the guard who still leaned into the V of the prow but decided against asking him for a cigarette. Mean looking son-of-a-bitch.

He was on the verge of climbing the stairway when he saw a man lying in the bottom of the boat, his eyes half open, not looking at anything. Lonnie went back; Jesus Christ, it was Mason, a guy from his outfit. The little shithead who was always giving him trouble. The son-of-a-bitch who told the

[207]

Captain on him when he went for a swim with Me-ling and her brother, the one who turned out to be queer and kept offering to satisfy the "carnal needs" of his body. The damn Captain had put him on K.P. for a whole week for that one, and him the First Sergeant of the outfit. That goddamn Mason. Lonnie reached down and shook him but he didn't move, just settled down snug and comfortable, looking just like he used to right after he let one rip at the mess table and then sat there smirking, trying to control a snicker. Lonnie looked closer, his eyes were glazed. He was deader than a door nail. He saw something else, a string around Mason's neck, like something was attached, maybe a bag with something in it, or a ring. Shit, he didn't need it any more. Lonnie starting pulling on the cord and saw something large and bulky snaking up Mason's belly. But he didn't see anything else. Something hit him, a hobnailed boot, right between the eyes, knocking him down into the bottom of the boat. Stunned, he looked up to see the Japanese guard, the mean looking one, standing over him.

"You goddamn thief, you steal from dead man, maybe I shoot you, you goddamn thief!" The voice came from a far distance, but clear, echoing with a strange metallic resonance.

Then Lonnie heard another voice, plaintive, begging, his own. "Shit, I was trying to help him, I wasn't trying to steal nothing, I was trying to help him. I was trying to get his stuff to send to his mother, I was trying to get his picture to send to his mother."

The long skinny rifle was pointed right at him, its hole looking small and ridiculous, too little to hurt anybody. "Shit," thought Lonnie, "the bolt isn't even drawn back. He isn't going to shoot me." He heard his own voice again.

"I was just trying to get his stuff to send to his mother, when the war's over."

The gun wavered and dropped.

"To his mother," Lonnie repeated, but the guard wasn't looking at him. He was looking up toward the Japanese corporal, who wasn't leaning against the rail any more, he was coming down the stairs, screaming at the top of his voice, not at Lonnie but at the guard. Lonnie got to his feet then, moving fast. He didn't even notice his sore leg. He met the corporal halfway up the stairs and hardly felt the whack he got with the broadside of the corporal's sword. Suddenly he was on deck, looking down a short stairway into another hold. He didn't hesitate long, the Japanese corporal was coming back up the stairway, shouting at him now. He moved down, step by step, feeling a strange wetness on his leg. The wound had burst open and was flowing freely, not blood, but a whitish yellow serum which smelled like hell. He could almost feel the tension draining from his leg. By the time he got to the bottom of the short stairway, it had quit hurting completely. He could hardly believe it. Nothing like almost getting shot for curing an ailment. He grinned, thinking about it.

"You hear a funny joke?" somebody asked him right at his left ear. "Jesus Christ, you stink!"

"I didn't get my morning bath," said Lonnie, still grinning.

"You're assigned to Bay Thirteen, way down there on the right side, near the bulkhead. Can you see?"

"About as good as you can smell," said Lonnie pleased with himself. "How come I got lucky?"

"Gentry asked for you, he's down there."

Lonnie could see the speaker plainly now in the semi-darkness, one of the officers, the Major who had brought order into the hold right after the bombing. Suddenly he was interested.

"Why are you doing this?"

"What do you mean?" the Major asked absently, looking down at Lonnie's leg which had almost stopped flowing.

"Why in the hell are you standing here directing traffic, using up all your energy; what's in it for you?"

"Not a damn thing," said the Major. "Get moving before that Jap corporal gets you."

Lonnie moved then, picking his way down a narrow aisle. They were in the very top section of the hold, right beneath the deck. There was a raised section directly below the completely covered hatchway, just like on the other ship, nailed down, tarpaulin and all. Maybe there's sugar down there. He could see well enough now. Small bulbs dangled haphazardly throughout the hold creating a yellow twilight in the large enclosure.

[209]

The small aisle in which he was walking separated this raised section from the bays which stretched down the length of the hold, on each side. There were other bays against the bulkhead, but Lonnie noticed sunlight towards the front, some kind of opening that way onto a lower deck. All of the bays were filled, about forty men per bay, twenty above and twenty below. Many of the men were laying back taking it easy; a few were asleep. He even saw one poker game in progress, a pantomine of concentration under one of the small bulbs: half naked, skinny skeletons staring at little pieces of dirty cardboard as if their lives depended on them, they were playing for the next meal.

The tarpaulin over the raised section in the center was completely covered with individuals, they were everywhere, a seeming random distribution. But Lonnie noticed a pattern in the crowding, a perceptible ordering into small clusters of three or four men each. They sat facing one another in small irregular circles; small self-contained social units achieving aloofness and aloneness in the multitude, their backs turned against the rest of the world. Lonnie suddenly felt left out of things, as if he didn't belong anywhere. He moved a little faster now, on toward the two stacks of bays, one jutting out from the bulkhead, the other from the side of the ship. At last he was there looking hopefully, almost fearfully into the semi-darkness first into the top bay, then into the lower where the darkness to his unaccustomed eyes was almost complete.

"Well if there isn't Chicken Lickin'," a voice said out of the darkness. And suddenly everything was okay.

"Yeah, come into my den, said the spider to the fly," voices encircled him with warmth.

"Yeah, come on back."

"We're all here now."

The loneliness went away, he was standing there grinning, peering beneath where faces floated, buoyed up by darkness. Here and there a cigarette glowed and gave clarity to features. Gentry's, and to his relief, the pale profile of Ross flared into view.

"Well quit standing there with your teeth hanging out." It was R. T. Barton. "Come on under."

Lonnie crawled beneath the bay, moving back on his hands and knees. The steel floor was covered with litter, as if it hadn't been swept for a long time and a vague odor of human sweat and urine added a strange comfort. It was like crawling into a den, reeking of animals, of their processes.

"Smells like a goddamn boar's nest back here," Lonnie observed. "How many of you bastards are under here?"

"Nineteen good and true American fighting men," R. T. responded, "and now you. Shit, we are going to have a time. We got it made now. Old Gentry with his bullshit stories. Corso for fun and games. Ross for his sensible analysis, me for brilliant discourse and you as avid listener."

"Yeah, how about that?" said Lonnie, grinning. That goddamn R. T. Barton. He could see better now. They were in a space about fifteen by twenty feet going back to the metal side of the ship on one side and the steel bulkhead on the other. The ceiling was about four feet above them; Lonnie could hear people overhead and occasionally see movement through small cracks in the wood. In the center of the bay a square opening jutted up from the floor, covered by a wooden door, hasped and locked. Lonnie moved to the door and tried the lock; it was massive, made of fine steel. No way in there. Then he saw something more, much more! THE SHOES! They gleamed in the dim light which came in through a crack where the wooden structure of the upper bay failed to mesh with the steel side of the ship. He saw the young Captain then, a dark immobile shadow against the ship's side. He lay there without moving. Maybe he's dead. If he's dead, he won't need those shoes any more. "I'm going to get those shoes," Lonnie said half aloud. He looked quickly around fearing somebody might have heard him.

"What in the hell are you doing, sittin' there blinking like an owl, talking to yourself. Come join the group!" R. T. Barton moved over to make room and Lonnie crawled into the circle of humped over people.

"I was just adjusting my eyes," said Lonnie. "Can't see a damn thing under here. You think there's sugar down there?" He motioned toward the locked door leading down into the lower hold.

"Same old Lonnie, concerned with fundamentals," laughed Gentry. To Lonnie's astonishment, he was clean-shaven, leaning back in characteristic fashion against one of the wooden supports, his sharp features and well trimmed mustache now easily distinguishable.

"Not really," said Corso. "He's just concerned about his belly, not about what's really fundamental." Corso sat swaying back and forth on his still-fat buttocks, his legs spread wide apart, the dark mass of his pubic hair somehow more vivid though nearly hidden in the shadows. Lonnie noticed that the V wasn't so large and that the ponderous belly was saggy, hanging loose like an old condom he had once found with a round vibrating bulb at the bottom. Jesus Christ, what a repulsive bastard!

Lonnie sat down beside Ross who had moved over to make room for him, naturally, just like always.

"How's the leg?" Ross asked, his eyes showing concern even in the dim light.

"Shit, it's okay now," replied Lonnie, adjusting himself among the pieces of rubble; the hard metal hurt his rear end. "Damn it, my ass bones are about to punch clear through the skin. Damn steel plates. I'm fine now. I almost got the shit kicked out of me by that Jap guard in the boat. Scared me so bad I ran clear up the stairway and broke open my leg, let go like somebody had pulled the plug, like Niagara. Stinks some though. Are you okay?"

"Sure I'm okay," said Ross.

"Sure he's great," observed R. T. Barton. "Fingers blown off, a big hole in his shoulder, starving to death, sure he's fine. We're all fine. Just a happy bunch of bastards on a little ocean cruise."

Lonnie wasn't listening, he was happy, strangely content there with the others, with Gentry, and Ross, and R. T. and even old Corso, the goddamn queer with his cruddy crotch and sagging gut. He looked away and saw the shoes glint dully as the young Captain moved a little. He wasn't dead after all. The other guys in the bay were lying around on the hard metal looking out, eyes shining, faces white, reflecting the little light coming in under the bay. Some of them were lying on grass mats and one guy had a blanket, a new gray one. He sat leaning against the bulkhead wrapped up like an old Navaho Indian Lonnie had seen once during a trip he had made to Taos with his father. Jesus Christ, a million years ago. He could hear the voices of the other men, of his friends in the circle, droning on as from a great distance, could see their faces shining in the dim light, their lips moving, their hands moving; they were alive and he was, in spite of the hunger and his stinking leg and all the other shit. "Well, that's something."

They didn't get anything to eat that night. Lonnie kept waiting for a sign, a slight increase in activity, some change in tempo which might indicate that food was on the way but nothing happened. As the hours passed the conversations became sporadic and died altogether. Gradually the men began to separate into small groups; Gentry and R. T. Barton found a place in the far corner where the side of the ship met the bulkhead and Corso moved in near them, close but somehow separate, a huge dark shadow hunkering down there right in front of the young Captain with the shoes. "He's after those shoes too," thought Lonnie, "the greedy bastard!"

Lonnie and Ross lay down side by side near the square opening into the lower hold, the one with the wooden door and the massive lock. It was cold and the metal floor hurt Lonnie's hip but he didn't mind, Ross was right there next to him. He felt a vague hurting in his chest and stomach, even his legs. Hunger. It seemed he could smell sugar somewhere. He put his nose against the crack where the wooden door meshed into the metal casing.

"There's sugar down there," he whispered. Ross didn't say anything but he moved closer until Lonnie could feel his warmth.

Sometime during the night he awoke, cold and uncomfortable, his leg throbbing a little and knew that for a long time he had been hearing, even in his sleep, the distant rumble of propellers. Now that he was half awake he could feel the almost imperceptible sway of the ship as it moved in gentle swells of the open sea. He raised his head and looked across the bay at the other men, small clusters of humanity lumped

[213]

together for warmth; R. T. Barton and Gentry vaguely outlined against the dark of the ship's side, a tangle of arms and legs, snuggled against the warm bulk of Corso. "Like a bunch of lovers," thought Lonnie. He couldn't help grinning. "They'll shit their pants in the morning when they wake up and find themselves laying there eyeball to eyeball, bad breath to bad breath. I'll bet old Corso's a warm bastard. And me with nothing but this cold bag of bones." He snuggled up to Ross then and was grateful to feel his warm back against his chest, was relieved to feel the regular machinery of his breathing.

The rattle of mess kits woke him, stiff with cold, his arm still around Ross who was readjusting his canteen holder under his head trying to get some more sleep. The rattling rose in volume and suddenly Lonnie was on his feet searching for his own gear.

"Come on you shitheads, we're going to eat!" He crawled out from under the bay and saw food barrels with great gouts of steam still rising from them being lowered into the hold. "By God, goodies are coming," he said to Ross who joined him now at the edge of the tier. They heard the Major's voice, the same one who had directed Lonnie back to the bay. He was standing in the middle of the raised area under the covered hatchway. But Lonnie wasn't listening. He was looking around the hold, stricken with surprise, he stooped hurriedly and looked under the tier. The Captain with the shoes was still there, Lonnie could see him stirring, clear back there against the ship's side, trying to raise himself on his elbow.

"Look at that," said Ross. "Jesus Christ, do you see that?"

"I see it," said Lonnie. "Deader than door nails, nakeder than jaybirds."

They heard the Major saying then, "Nobody eats until the burial detail takes care of these dead guys. If you want to work on the burial detail you will get some extra food."

"What do you think?" asked Ross. "Do you think we could do it?"

"Are you crazy?" shouted Lonnie. "I can hardly walk around and you've only got one good arm and you want to go around picking up naked dead bastards." Then in a calmer voice, "Where did their clothes go, who got their clothes?" He stopped, Ross was looking at him with his indulgent look. "You mean to say somebody stole them, last night somebody stole them? What a fuckin' bunch of ghouls!"

"I don't imagine they needed them any more," said Ross mildly.

All of the men, at least those who could walk, were out from under the tier now, lined up waiting.

"Anybody dead under there?" Lonnie asked Gentry as he came out from under.

"Nobody but me," said R. T. Barton. "And maybe Corso, he smells like it."

Corso pushed in close to Lonnie, and by God, he did smell dead. They waited and watched the steam rise from the barrels, watched the burial detail move around the hold, looking carefully.

"No trouble finding them," observed R. T. Barton. "They stand out like dandruff on a black cat."

The men on the burial detail worked systematically, two men to a body, one by the hands and one by the heels, some of them were so stiff that they didn't even bend much. Certainly weren't hard to carry, couldn't have averaged over seventy-five or eighty pounds. Lonnie didn't look at their faces, probably couldn't recognize anybody anyway but he didn't want to take the chance. Pretty soon the details with their burdens were going up the stairway, "up, up, and away," thought Lonnie, "over the side and then the long slide down through the green water, getting darker as they go down; and that's it."

Well maybe not, maybe there is something else. Father Maloney stood by the stairway, waving his hands a little bit and saying a prayer as each detail with its burden passed him. Lonnie felt better, maybe there was something else, but shit that didn't matter now. That would take care of itself when the time came. That's the important stuff, right there with the steam rising from it. But he couldn't keep from watching Father Maloney making his motions there by the stairway. A light shone down and made his face bright as he turned his head to look at somebody going up the long trail. He seemed

close to Lonnie then, his face floating above the guys who had
crowded around the steaming barrels, holding their mess kits,
waiting. Then it was all over. The men from the burial detail,
or as R. T. Barton called them, the chumming detail,
returned.

"What's that?" Lonnie asked Ross later, looking up from his
rice and soybean paste. "What the shit's chumming?"

"Chumming for shark! For Christ sake, don't you know
what chumming is?"

"Well I sure as hell ain't chumming with you, you
shithead," said Lonnie grinning, proud of his reply.

Ross didn't say anything, he was absently pursuing rice
grains around the groove in his mess kit. But Lonnie could see
that crazy look in his eyes, the get dead look.

"We've got to get the food detail next time," he whispered
to Ross. "That goddamn chaplain cheated us."

"How do you know that?" asked Ross absently.

"I saw the son-of-a-bitch," answered Lonnie. "When he
divided up that mess kit of rice he packed down one end,
harder than hell, and he fluffed up the other end. Guess where
we got our rice from?"

Ross didn't say anything for a moment. "It won't matter
much anyway," he finally said. "If they don't feed us more
than this, six men to a level mess kit of rice and a little soybean
paste and tea, we won't live long."

"Fuck you, you son-of-a-bitch, there you go again. Goddammit, we're going to live if I have to steal every ring, every
watch, all the stupid clothes off every one of those dead
bastards."

"We may have to, if we're going to live," said Ross. "I
sometimes think they are trying to kill us in a way that nobody
can blame them, even if they lose the war, just so they won't
have to feed us."

"They'll lose the war," said Lonnie glancing over his
shoulder. He had seen something gleam, a small flash out on
the tarpaulin where the sun cast a square of moving comfort
down through a rectangular hole in the hatchway.

"In the morning, about three or four o'clock, you know
when everybody's asleep, you and me, we're going on an

[216]

expedition. We're going to look for rings and watches and clothes, and anything else we can find. Shit, those dead guys can't use them. Somebody is going to get them, I've already seen some guys smoking Japanese cigarettes. We can trade what we find for cigarettes and water, maybe even some medicine." He looked down at his leg which was beginning to swell again. "If I don't get some medicine this damn leg is going to drop off."

Ross didn't say anything. He was looking at Lonnie's leg and then at his hand, still covered with dirty bandages. He sat leaning against the raised section of the hold next to the heavy steel lock, his arms around his knees.

"Look what I found," said Lonnie. He was holding something toward Ross, something which shone feebly in the dim light, a paper clip.

"Well, I'll be damned," said Ross, suddenly interested, "where in the hell did you find that?"

"I found it, that's what matters," said Lonnie. "Do you want to try it first? I don't know anything about locks."

"I don't know anything about locks either," said Ross but he moved to the square door, a dim outline in the shadows, but the lock was visible, shiny. There was eagerness in his movements.

"You forgot the paper clip," said Lonnie holding it out. Ross took it and fiddled with it for a while, bending it straight first, then putting a small elbow at the end. He picked the lock up in his left hand and inserted the paper clip. Lonnie settled back against the wooden bay support watching Ross work, hoping. But nothing happened. Just the small grating sounds of the paper clip.

The young Captain with the shoes was still lying there against the bulkhead. Must be asleep, he wasn't moving. Over in their corner, Gentry, R. T. Barton and Corso sat leaning against the steel side of the ship, looking out occasionally. Beneath him the continuing rumble of the propellers set up a rhythmic cadence which rose and fell, moved into sound and out again as one listened or didn't.

"Hell fire," said Ross finally, with a note of exasperation in his voice, "I can't make heads or tails of this lock. It isn't like any lock I ever saw."

"It probably has a left hand thread," said Lonnie, "like everything else the Japs make."

"Sure," said Ross, "probably does. Why don't you try it for a while? You seem to have a built-in left hand thread." Lonnie took the paper clip and started working, trying to cause some movement within the mechanism of the lock, prying it this way and that way.

"If I had a pig's prick I could get this thing open," he said to himself, aloud.

"What's a pig's prick got to do with anything?" asked Ross, casually interested.

"A pig's prick is a corskscrew, that's what," replied Lonnie, looking up. "Didn't you know that?"

"You're full of shit," Ross was grinning a little. "You're getting worse than old R. T. for bullshit."

"Well fuck you, goddammit, you don't know everything, you and your college education. Pigs do have corkscrew pricks, I've seen them lots of times. And if I had one," Lonnie was grinning too now, "I could open this fucking lock."

"In a pig's asshole," responded Ross, now in good humor. "Why don't you use your own prick? It's about the right size."

"Shit on you," said Lonnie.

He kept working at the lock, but nothing happened. It remained solid and unrelenting in his grasp. Finally he too gave it up, and placed the paper clip carefully in his LIFE WOMAN pouch, then joined Ross who was stretched out amid the rubble on the steel floor.

"I heard someplace," Lonnie confided, "that you could put a monkey at a typewriter and if he kept typing for a billion billion years, he'd write a book or something, something from Shakespeare maybe. If we keep picking at that lock we're bound to get it. If we just keep picking at the lock, it'll give one of these days."

"Or one of these months," answered Ross sleepily.

"Well we got lots of time; we got nothing else but time," said Lonnie. He settled down, put his canteen, still fixed in its holder, under his head. His left leg was hurting some, but he didn't seem hungry. That was funny, he didn't seem hungry. He thought about it for a while. He hadn't eaten much, just that little bit of rice they got from the fluffed up end of the mess kit, where that son-of-a-bitch had cheated them. He got mad thinking about it, and decided to get on the food detail, if he got a chance. I'll show them how to press down rice, those sons-of-bitches! He placed his head down against the steel floor, his ear flat to the metal. He could hear the monotonous rhythm of the engines, the vibrations of power spinning the propellers, the creaking of timbers giving punctuation to the rise and fall of the ship.

"Must be moving into a heavier sea. The creaks are getting stronger. Yeah, the old bucket is really moving up and down. Jesus Christ, I wonder why nobody's been seasick, not one puker in the bunch during this whole trip. Shit nobody's got anything to puke. Not many farts in one bean. Gotta get on that food detail." The creaks faded.

The next thing he knew Ross was shaking him, whispering, "We're going to eat again in a little bit. Let's get in front, maybe we can get on the food detail."

Without answering, Lonnie got on his hands and knees, and both of them eased toward the outer edge of the bay. They waited there in the half light for a few moments, then heard the almost imperceptible sounds of change, slight increases in tempo which always suggested that something was about to happen. Soon they saw the mess detail going up the stairway, and in a few moments steaming barrels of rice and tea were lowered into the hold. When the call came for a mess detail from each bay there was a general rush of interested volunteers but Lonnie and Ross were first.

"The early birds are going to get the worm," said R. T. Barton as he saw them already in line.

"I'd like to get a worm," said Corso, looking at Lonnie.

"Fuck you," Lonnie muttered watching Gentry crawl casually from beneath the tier, clean shaven as usual.

The call came and Lonnie and Ross, carrying four mess kits and four canteen cups, moved toward the center of the tarpaulin where a line was already forming. Lonnie could smell the rice from halfway across and his hunger came in a rush, sharp almost like pain. His legs began to tremble and for a moment he had trouble making them walk along. As he glanced down he saw that his wound had opened up again, that a small trickle of yellow pus was flowing down his shin bone, over his foot and between two of his toes. What the hell, he couldn't bother with that now. He was holding out the two mess kits.

"Pack it down man, pack it down," he said as the guy on the mess detail filled an oval salmon can and scraped it level with a flat stick. And the guy did reach down and put in a little extra. "Jesus Christ, thanks man." It was good brown rice, not that white stuff without vitamins, without vitamin B-1. Now for the tea, two full cups, rich and pungent, and a little bean paste, just like a mushy brown turd, right on top of the rice. Lonnie looked towards the bay as he followed Ross back, the small of the hot tea heavy in his nostrils. He saw the faces waiting, the eyes observing. Jesus Christ! He turned away for a moment, lifted one of the canteen cups and took a large gulp of tea. Nobody saw; nobody saw. But they did. There was a sudden shout, some son-of-a-bitch saw!

"I saw you, you thieving bastard, I saw you drink some of that tea. When you get over here, I'm going to beat your goddamn brains out, you dirty thief!"

"I didn't take any tea," said Lonnie. "It just looked like I did. Shit I didn't take any tea. I wouldn't take any tea. Ask Ross here, he knows I didn't take any tea. Did you see me take any tea?"

"I didn't see you take any tea," answered Ross.

They were back, the men gathering around to receive their portions, the incident seemed forgotten. Lonnie couldn't even figure out who had done all the screaming. Maybe that cunthead Chaplain, the one who had cheated them.

All eyes were on Lonnie as he divided the rice. Four men to a mess kit. He pressed it down carefully, then made three tentative cuts across it with a mess kit knife.

"Cut her straight," said R. T. Barton. "Cut her right down the middle, that's the way. How in the hell do we expect to get an expert job out of old Lonnie here?" R. T. looked around the group. "He's never had any experience cutting, he admitted it himself."

"I've done about as much cutting as you have licking," said Lonnie spooning out the rice.

"If you steal any more tea I'll give you a good licking," said Corso looking coyly around the group.

"Go suck yourself," said Lonnie. The men came by one by one as he spooned out the rice. He was damned happy about it, he had managed to compress the rice more at one end than the other in all four mess kits. He was careful that Gentry, R. T. Barton, and Corso got their portions from the compacted ends, and that the one with the hardest packing was left for him and Ross. Ross passed out the tea and Lonnie felt less guilty when he saw Ross nudge their portions just a little. Shit, who could blame him. Lonnie did feel bad about the young Captain, the one with the shoes, getting his portion from the fluffed up side, and thought the shoes might be available soon. Then he felt so guilty he stopped thinking about the Captain and the shoes completely for a little while.

After they had eaten, damned if Corso didn't pull out a cigarette he had kept hidden some place, maybe in the folds of his belly. They were certainly loose enough now that he had lost weight. Could probably hide a pack of rats in there, Lonnie grinned thinking about Corso and his creases. Hell, you could hardly see the V now, he was so thin. Another month or two, and he'd look almost decent.

Corso had just lit the cigarette, and Lonnie was waiting not too patiently for his drag when they heard a voice coming in from the edge of the bay, Father Maloney's voice. Suddenly they were stricken into a strange paralysis, like guilty little children caught doing something bad. In unison everyone glanced at Gentry who remained unmoving, looking towards the sound of Father Maloney's voice, a tenseness in his face. Then he smiled. Lonnie was happy to see the warm expression in his eyes, to see the light shining from his fine white teeth. Jesus Christ, he was a handsome bastard.

"We've been holding a drag for you, Father," said Gentry. "Lonnie was just saying that he didn't care for his, so this means that you get two drags." Everybody in the circle laughed, Lonnie laughed harder than anyone.

"He's just making trouble again, Father, you know how he is."

There was a momentary strain but it was immediately washed away by R. T. Barton.

[221]

"Come on under, Father. You can see we've all gotten together again. Birds of a feather, and all that sort of shit. Come on under, and say a few words for our salvation. We've been listening to old Gentry here for an entire week, and I don't feel one step closer to Heaven."

"Maybe that's a good thing," the Father said as he crawled beneath the bay. Lonnie moved over to make room for him, and Corso drew back a little bit. Suddenly everything was natural, as if nothing had happened, as if there had been no argument. With the circle of sympathetic eyes upon him, Father Maloney took the cigarette, drew deeply until the small light flared red against the wood of the upper bay. He passed the butt on to Lonnie whose hands were shaking. He could hardly wait to feel the warm smoke deep in his lungs, to feel the faint tremors of the nicotine bloom into a joy which made hunger and thirst unimportant for a moment.

"How does it look to you, Father, how are our chances now?" Gentry looked intently at Father Maloney, his expression soft and gentle. The antagonism was gone as far as he was concerned, forgotten.

Father Maloney smiled in response, pleased with the questions, but more pleased with the warmth of their expression. "I think our chances are better now," he said looking at the different members in the group. "We're three days out of Formosa, and nothing's happened. We're moving deeper into waters which surely must be controlled by the Japanese Navy and the Japanese Air Force. We've been moving further and further from immediate danger. I don't think we have to worry about the bombs any more. Perhaps some submarines. Our major concerns are the oldest ones, starvation, disease, and of course the cold. Have you noticed," he looked up around the circle again, his eyes somehow touching everyone who watched him, making them more secure, "how it gets a little colder every day, how even now you can feel a draft from somewhere? Cold, penetrating cold." Lonnie felt the cold on his back and against his legs and shivered a little in spite of himself. "But still I think," the Father continued, "some of us will make it. I am praying every day that all of us will make it." He looked shy, almost timid, as his eyes sought Gentry's. A silence extended so long Lonnie couldn't stand it. Suddenly he spoke, much more loudly than was necessary.

"What does all this shit mean, anyway, Father? Do you think it makes any difference to Jesus that all those guys died last night? That all those guys were thrown naked into the sea? Do you think it really matters?"

The Father examined his fingers, and didn't look directly at Lonnie. "If it doesn't mean something to Him, then nothing does, anywhere."

"Jesus Christ, we're getting morbid," said R. T. Barton. "But I am curious about something. How in the hell did it all begin? This little old ball of wax, that great big flaming sun, and all those pebbles that keep swinging around and around."

"Yeah," said Ross, "and all those suns, maybe a billion billion suns, extending out, on out there forever. How did it all begin?"

"Well I'll give you my view," the Father smiled, glancing at Gentry. "It has always been from looking into the distant sky on a clear night, not so much with my eyes but with my imagination that I have seen both the most evident proof of God's existence and the rationale for that existence. At some indeterminate time, in some incomprehensible way, for some unfathomable reason God created all of that multiplicity and even as He created, He projected into it, its significance, its meaning. How did it all begin, you ask. God began it. I realize that for some, and I can easily understand why; that for some," here he looked directly at Gentry for a moment with a warm smile on his face, "this is no answer at all; that it merely pushed the problem back a step. But for me it is the answer, because for me, God is more than an abstraction, more than a label to cover up our ignorance. I believe that God is a personal presence in our every waking moment. When I say God created all of our reality, it is as meaningful to me as saying that Corso fashioned that cigarette we were just smoking."

"Hell fire, he didn't fashion it," said R. T. Barton. "He picked it up from some reluctant Jap by trading some of that garbage he carries around in his ball sack."

"I can believe that," laughed the Father.

[223]

Lonnie surprised himself by asking Gentry the same question, "How do you think it all began, Gent?"

Gentry looked startled for a moment, then after glancing at the Father, grinned and said, "Well personally, I believe in the Yo-Yo theory."

"What in the hell is the Yo-Yo theory?" said Corso. "What the hell do Yo-Yos have to do with that?" But suddenly, even he seemed interested and raised up slightly on his elbow. Lonnie could see how his belly sagged now, how his ribs showed through the skin just like everybody else. Lonnie felt a pang of sadness for Corso, for all of them.

"Yeah, what the hell do Yo-Yos have to do with the scheme of things?" asked R. T. Barton.

Gentry cleared his throat and settled back, smiling. And all of them felt caught by the old charm, by the realization that a story was about to happen.

"Well, according to an erudite gentleman I met one evening in the Harvard Club, an astronomer who had been sipping martinis for a couple of days. But his brain seemed clear enough, about normal for a Princeton man, he was a visitor at the Club. Anyway he maintained that the best evidence available suggests that about twelve billion years ago, all of the matter in the universe, from all the galaxies everywhere, was gathered up into one great big ball."

"Some ball," said Ross.

"Yeah, a lot of ball or bull," said R. T. Barton.

"Even more in there than in old Corso's ball sack," said Lonnie, looking at Corso who was grinning. All of the tension was gone; they sat for a moment in silence, in the warmth of the occasion.

Finally Ross said, "Get back to the big ball, Gent."

Gentry cleared his throat and continued, "Anyway, everything was there in the big ball. All of reality compacted, compressed, growing denser and denser, growing more potential, growing more pregnant, growing more unstable until at some precise, cosmic moment, the entire mess exploded, and all matter, all of everything, began to rush away from the explosion. And it has been rushing away from that point ever since, ever since some twelve billion years ago."

There was a long silence, all of them lost in thought.

"What a crock of shit," said R. T. Barton finally. "And how in the hell does a Yo-Yo get into the picture? Do you mean to say that all the stars and everything we see, and all the suns they talk about, started out from one big blob, and that everything is really exploding out, expanding out?"

"That's exactly what I mean," said Gentry smiling. "As for the Yo-Yo; according to the theory, in about five billion more years the force of gravity emanating from all these particles of matter will slowly but inexorably stop the outward movement, and finally bring it to a halt. For a moment, perhaps for a billion years, everything in all reality will be completely static. Then the backward rush will start; slowly at first then ever more rapidly the contraction, the implosion, the movement inwards will occur, until at some moment, perhaps twenty billion years from now, all of reality will be contained again in the same big ball."

"Is that really true?" said Lonnie. "Do people really believe that?"

"Yes, they do," answered Gentry. "Some of the wisest and most learned men of our day believe that."

"You mean that's all there is, just this moving in and moving out, this moving out and moving in? That's all there is?"

"According to this view," said Gentry, looking gently around the group, "that's all there is."

"Well I think it's a crock of shit!" said Corso. "I like Father Maloney's explanation a hell of a lot better than that scientific bullshit. Whoever wanted to play with a fucking Yo-Yo anyway? Shitty things with the string always getting fucked up."

"I agree," said R. T. Barton. "Tops are better, or jacks. Did you ever try playing jacks?" he asked, grinning at Corso. "Jacks are fun."

Corso didn't respond. His small eyes, black in the dim light, moved from face to face. There was tension in the group now, an anxiety that hung tangibly over the circle, an apprehension that grew as the silence continued.

"That's enough of that shit," said Lonnie. "Tell us one of

your bullshit stories, Gentry. We got enough trouble without all this bullshit about the beginning of the ending of things. That's not really important anyway. Who really gives a shit about what happened twelve billion years ago or what will happen twenty billion years from now? And does it really matter who started the whole damn thing? We're right here on this ship, we're alive now, and I'd like to hear a story. Tell us one of your bullshit stories, Gent."

"Yes," said R. T. Barton. "I like your bullshit better than your ball shit. Tell us about one of your famous law cases. You know, like the one you told us about that poor little pudgy bastard who stole all those sperm and became a millionaire. Tell us about one of those law cases."

Gentry settled back, assumed the retrospective look which Lonnie loved, his right hand stroking his small mustache. Immediately, as if some strange magnetism emanated from Gentry, others in the bay began to move in, forming an outer circle. Soon even some of those quartered on the tarpaulin beneath the covered hatch edged in towards the bay.

"Well actually this is not a story having to do with one of my law cases," said Gentry, "it is much more profound than that. It reaches into the depths of human hope, human accomplishment, and I suppose, human failure. But it is a true story. Somehow I don't think the situation here is right for one of my more elaborate tales. So let me just tell you this small true story, about a young woman who lived and died in a little town not far from Indianapolis, right in the heart of the Midwest.

"Her name was Melody Blain. A pretty name but an ugly girl; she had an angular unattractive body, and a similar face. She seemed to be all knees and elbows. On the few occasions (three to be exact) when she went swimming in public, those near her were astonished to observe how clearly her backbone, her ribs and her shoulder blades protruded; indeed she seemed to be a symphony of odd angles, covered by taut skin. But if she was angular in body, she was warm in temperament. She was round with love; filled with the desire to be loved and to give love.

"As a child, she rescued every stray cat, every stray dog that

[226]

came off the highway to their small farm home. 'Damn it, Melody,' her father used to say, 'it's hard enough for me to make a living for you and your mother and your two worthless brothers without you bringing in every stray dog and cat.' But she persisted, and her father, somehow responsive to the profound yearning in this young girl, was content to berate her every now and then. The population of stray animals on their small farm grew apace, and Melody grew older. When other girls her age started dating, she waited hopefully for some young boy to ask her to go to the small drugstore where the other kids congregated for a coke, or to the small theater, The Varsity, to see a movie. But none ever did. She grew older, fourteen, sixteen; she graduated from high school at seventeen, valedictorian of her class. She was the top student of the twenty-five who graduated that year, from the small newly consolidated country school.

"Her father, although a poor man, somehow found the money to send her to the state college, and even as had been the case in high school, straight A's marked her record. But no young man came calling. She walked in angular isolation through the campus, through the years. On graduation day, she once again dignified her name and justified her father's sacrifice; she graduated with highest honors in library science and almost immediately a number of schools and universities offered her a job."

"Jesus Christ, small wonder," said R. T. Barton. "The school that hired her wouldn't have to worry about her getting married and leaving. Sleeping with a woman like that would be like bedding down with a bunch of clothes hangers in a gunny sack. Probably get a splinter in my tongue."

"Shut up, goddammit," said Corso. He was sitting up straight for him, looking intense, his small black eyes very bright.

"Yeah, shut up, R. T.," said Lonnie. "Get on with the damn story, Gentry."

Even the Father seemed deeply involved, impatient with the delay.

"Anyway," continued Gentry, "she took a job at the same state university from which she had just graduated, as assistant

[227]

librarian. There were eight assistant librarians, and she was the most junior of them all. But soon she displayed such a grasp of the intricacies, not only of the Dewey Decimal System but of the Library of Congress System which was at that time just being put into effect, that within three years she became assistant to the head librarian and was put completely in charge of the complex transformation.

"Years passed, but the warmth, the desire, the need for emotional realization did not pass, did not diminish. She worked diligently at her desk, her skinny shoulders bent over the typewriter, her glasses pushed down on her long nose. She always seemed totally absorbed, completely interested. But if one were to have observed her carefully when some young man, lean of hip, broad of shoulder, flat of belly, stopped at the check out counter, they might have seen her eyes following him. Following him with a warmth, a longing, and a loneliness that can only be born of isolation, of always hoping and never knowing.

"On her thirtieth birthday, the librarians gave a party for her with her own special cake. After cake and tea some wine was passed around, sparkling red wine, sweet to the tongue. It was during the wine pouring that Melody first saw John G., a young man just hired by the university who worked in the periodical section of the library, down in the basement. He had black hair and black eyes, an Italian name, and the body of a Greek god. He poured the wine. When Melody, holding out her cup looked up and saw his eyes fixed upon her own, her hand shook so she had to set the cup down. She complained immediately of being ill and after a few hurried excuses left the party accompanied by many sympathetic and worried glances. Thereafter Melody would wait for John G., his name was John Gordino, just to see him when he came to work in the morning. As the time approached for his entrance she would busy herself at her desk; but always just as he turned to descend the steps to the periodical room, she would glance up, observe the breadth of his shoulders, the lithe slimness of his hips, the way he held his head, the locks falling low on his neck, black and glistening, like a grackle's wing.

"It was about this time that Brenda May came to work at

[228]

the library; new at the reservation desk. She embodied within her ample frame as much of roundness as poor Melody did of angularity. Brenda May was not beautiful, she wasn't even pretty, but no man could pass the reservation desk without casting an appraising and then a longing look in her direction. She was blue eyed, with an open cow-like expression, a warm dumpling body which invited, almost demanded violation. When John G. came into the library early one Friday morning and glanced at the reservation desk, he saw her and she saw him. There was immediate and total mutuality; a synchrony of involvement that put them both atremble and started within the heart of Melody, who observed their millisecond eyeball interaction, a downward spin towards doom. The knot in her chest twisted into a total suffering. The agony of a small but desperate hope, a pitiful but totally necessary flame, snuffed out.

"So," here Gentry stopped to adjust his rear end on the steel of the ship's floor. "Jesus Christ," he said, "what a place for comfort. What I couldn't do for a feather pillow for my poor derriere."

"To hell with your derriere, whatever that is," said Lonnie. "Let's get back to Melody."

"Let's get back to Brenda May," said R. T. Barton. "She's a girl after my own heart, that Brenda May."

"Does she remind you of that paper doll of yours?" asked Ross. "You know, the one you're always singing about?"

"More like the one he's always talking about eating," said Corso.

"Come on, cut it out you guys," said Lonnie. "Gent, get back to the story."

"So the relationship between John G. and Brenda May budded and then blossomed. Brenda May was a totally giving, totally loving, generous person, and John G. was a taker. And he often took her. Indeed, after a few weeks, they established a small apartment, one that everybody knew about and everybody talked about. But not a soul condemned it. It was a rare person, whether male or female who didn't at those odd drifting moments that come to everyone on certain days, see themselves in the role of one of these two lucky people. And

Melody too; sometimes late at night when checking the alignment of the books she would absently pick a volume from its place among its fellows, and stand there turning through its pages seeing herself caught up in the embrace of this warm, this magnificent Italian with the nose and eyes of a hawk, the body of a Greek god and hair like a grackle's wing.

"Well everyone expected marriage for Brenda May and John G. and even Melody was resigned to that sad day; she had already picked out the wedding present she would give, an expensive set of 'his' and 'her' toothbrushes with gold plated handles. She felt strangely happy when she thought of John G. using her toothbrush to clean his fine white teeth, felt warmed that his fine lips would caress the present that she gave. But time passed, and no wedding announcement came. The small apartment became a permanent establishment. In the evenings Brenda May cooked fine Italian meals for John G. and then, as Melody often contemplated, moved through the heaven of a total night with him. This occurred day after day, month after month, year after year.

"At first Brenda May seemed somewhat dismayed by the failure of the relationship to come to full fruition. At first. But as time passed she became completely accepting and then somewhat vocal about the whole thing. When she became Melody's assistant (Melody picked her from seven other candidates) she would speak about her relationship with John G. with remarkable candor, in embarrassing detail. She would tell about the meals she cooked, and on occasion gave little tidbits about the delicious intimacies of the relationship. Once she even admitted to Melody that she actually didn't care now whether they ever got married. 'Why buy the bull when meat's so cheap?' she said.

" 'I'm not really sure that's the way the saying goes,' murmured Melody, but she understood. As the months passed, Brenda May began to confide more of the intimate details of her relationship with John G. And Melody listened, avidly, eagerly. Many times she had to keep her hands hidden because they trembled so.

" 'Yes, he comes in, eats all the spaghetti that I cook, all the meat sauce, drinks about a quart of white wine, and then you know what, Melody? He wants to go to bed. I guess I shouldn't tell you this, Melody, but he likes to have me naked when we sleep together. I can always tell when he's about ready. I can see the small bulge in the front of his trousers begin to grow. He gets restless then; so I hurry with the dishes. Then I go take my clothes off in the bathroom, and when I'm naked I go into the bedroom and get in between those new blue sheets, you know the ones you gave me for my birthday. Pretty soon I hear him coming through the doorway. I don't even look sometimes. I can hear his shoes falling, one after the other, beside the bed, hear the jangle of his change as he takes his trousers off, and then, do you know what Melody? He always pulls the covers down and kisses both my breasts right on the tips, and then he sucks each one just a little. Isn't that crazy, Melody? You know what, Melody? Sometimes when I work late, like on Thursday nights when I don't get home until ten, I go in the back door and take my clothes off first thing and wait for him there in the darkness and pretty soon in he comes. The first thing he always does is pull down the covers, and then he kisses both my breasts, and then, oh Melody, oh, you wouldn't believe it.'

"But Melody believed it. And hating herself more each time she did it, she encouraged Brenda May in her rampant tales. Brenda May sensing the depth of Melody's appreciation, the uniqueness of her involvement, embellished the stories. Then one day, it happened. A call came for Brenda May over Melody's phone. Brenda May's father had died suddenly, in a distant town, an automobile accident, a strange voice said. Melody summoned Brenda May from her little office and shed tears with her, as she sobbingly recounted the sad news of her father's passing.

" 'I must go home, now,' said Brenda May, 'poor Mama.'

" 'Why go ahead, go right on home. Pack your things and go,' said Melody.

" 'Will you call John and tell him?' asked Brenda May, sobbing gently. 'It's his afternoon off and he's gone to Indianapolis. He won't be back until late this evening. Would you call him and tell him?'

" 'Why certainly I will, you know I will,' said Melody. 'Go home and pack, your mother needs you now.'

"Brenda May went to the apartment and packed. And she

took the first bus south to Evansville. It was Thursday night. Melody worked patiently, steadily at her desk, a great confusion in her face, a trembling in her arms and legs. When nine o'clock came she closed the library early. The students were all gone. Then in the darkness she began to walk towards Brenda May's little apartment, at first with hesitation, but as she moved a firmness came, a resolution. She went to the back door. It was unlocked as she knew it would be. John G. was not back yet. She went then to the bedroom."

"Jesus Christ, this is the goddamnedest story you've ever told," said R. T. Barton. "As fucked up and hungry as I am, my prick is as hard as a rock!"

"Yeah, this story's really something isn't it?" Lonnie was looking proudly at Gentry.

Even Father Maloney seemed totally involved in the story. He looked gently from one face to the next and then shyly down at his hands. They all waited, looking at Gentry who readjusted himself on the hard steel plates, leaning back on his elbow. The circle of listeners moved in a little closer. Lonnie could see a number of individuals congregated now at the outer edges of the bay waiting patiently.

"Get on with it, goddammit," said R. T., a note of exasperation in his voice. "Leave it to old Gentry to savor the essence of a moment. What a fucking egomaniac you are, Gentry! Get on with your story. Back to Melody."

There was a general chorus then, chiming in from the outer edges. "Back to Melody."

"And so Melody went through the bedroom door into the pitch blackness, felt her way across the floor, and finally touched the bed. She stopped then and listened; she could hear nothing but the dripping of a faucet somewhere in the small apartment. Or perhaps it was the beating of her heart, the cadence was so fast. She hesitated but only for a moment, then off came her dress over her head; off came her shoes one by one; off with the white slip, crisp and clean, now the brassiere. As she felt this small inhibiting contraption fall away, she also felt a sudden surge, a strange fullness in her breasts. She couldn't help but touch them, and indeed they did seem larger; the tips stood out, hard and rubbery beneath

[232]

her fingers. A strange thrill shot through them, shot down her stomach, down her belly; small bolts of nervous lightning, striking again and again into the warmth between her legs. Off with the panties now. She was stark naked! For a moment she stood there in the darkness, her head held sideways, listening, longing. Under the covers now; feel how the cool sheets caress the body, touch the warm limbs, thrill the taut breasts, cling to the longing hips.

"There was little waiting. Just as the stage was set, the actor ready, the curtain came down. As in a dream she heard the footsteps coming up the walk, heard the front door open, felt the tenseness loom throughout the house, a sensuous, tiger, presence. The refrigerator door made a loud metallic sound as it opened; the wine bottle clicked against the table. Small sounds of chewing. An audible burp resonated through the small apartment. Still she waited, drugged by total terror, consumed by complete desire.

" 'He's coming now,' she thought. And indeed he was. Through the bedroom door, through the darkness to the side of the bed. He sat down and the entire bed moved in that direction. His hand reached out and touched Melody, found her breasts uncovered, waiting. His fingers tweeked each one just for a moment, and Melody almost died there in the darkness. The shoes dropped to the floor, then the trousers with the jangle of the coins, now the soft cottony sounds of shirt and underwear almost inaudible in the room. She could smell him then, not the clean antiseptic smell of French cologne but the pervasive, perspiring, virile odor of animal. The smell of maleness, a lion reek. He knelt beside the bed, kissed each of her trembling breasts, sucked each one just a little. Then with a deft motion, the covers were laid back and Melody felt his hot fingers seek the warmth and moisture of her sex. Greater joy in anticipation than in realization? 'Oh how false that is,' thought Melody. 'Oh for the realization now.' And the realization came. For a moment his hard body poised above her own, then the penetration, hard, thrusting, irresistible, moving deeper into warmth. Joy, sweet joy, beginning with a stroke of pain, but the rhythm, growing as she felt each contact of his thighs against her own, mounting as

[233]

she felt each deeper penetration. Her body moving on its own, undulating, searching for itself. From a small pool into wild rapids, a great froth of waterfalls, of shifting circling lights.

"As suddenly as it began, the machinery of sex was over. John G. turned his back toward Melody and in a few moments the sounds of his breathing slowed, increased in depth. Just as the little wisps of snores were expanding into the snorts of heavy sleep, Melody stole from the bed. Quickly on with the underwear, quickly on with the clean white slip, the prim dress and the solid shoes. Quietly, now, out of the house bearing her joy, bearing her fulfillment, bearing her burden."

Gentry stopped then and looked around the group. There was absolute silence. Eyes sought his own in admiration and astonishment. Finally Father Maloney spoke.

"That was a truly fine story, Gentry. That was one of the gentlest stories I have ever heard, and it makes me realize what I always knew even when I was being overwhelmed by a total lack of Christian empathy, that you are truly one of the finest Christians of us all."

It was Gentry's turn to look astonished. He sat for a moment considering what the Father had said, glancing occasionally at the Father, at the others in the circle. Then he said gently, "But the story isn't over yet."

"What do you mean the story isn't over yet?" demanded Corso. "Sure the story's over! What more could there be?"

"Hell-fire," said R. T. Barton, "if Gentry says the story isn't over, then the story isn't over, it's his story isn't it, dammit!"

"Well then finish the story," said Lonnie. "What the hell are we waiting around here for, finish the story if there's more to it."

"I'm not sure you'll want to hear the end of it," said Gentry.

"Oh, come on, quit being a goddamned prima donna," said R. T. Barton, "finish the fucking story."

There was a general chorus from the listeners that ringed the little group. "Finish the story!"

"Give him a cigarette," somebody said. "Who's got a cigarette?"

Much to Lonnie's astonishment, three cigarettes found their way from the outer edges. They were delivered hand over hand until Gentry had all three still unlighted in his hand.

"Hell, let's light them up," he said. A match from somewhere flared magically in the semi-darkness and the soft warm smell of tobacco smoke filtered out to where Lonnie could enjoy it.

"Pass 'em around, Gent. Light them up and pass 'em around."

And Gentry did. Lonnie waited until his turn came, and felt again the warm passage, the alien involvement, "kinda like Melody gettin' screwed," he thought. "Gee if pussy's better than cigarettes, it must really be great." He heard Gentry's voice continuing.

"So Melody moving like a wraith through the night found her way home. Later she recalled nothing of that walk, nor did she remember entering her own apartment. All night long she lay sleepless in her bed, staring toward the ceiling, feeling again and again the warmth of realization, the fulfillment of being feminine, the all pervading spasm. The next day, much to the astonishment of everyone at the library, Melody didn't come to work. It was the first time she had missed in ten years. And indeed, she didn't come to work for three days. When she finally appeared in her small office those near her observed that she was strangely altered. There seemed to be a softening in the angularity, a deeper warmth in the brown eyes, a lassitude in her movements.

"As the days passed into weeks, and into months, the transformation in Melody quickened, the angles of her body became muted, the tenseness in her features drained away; the compulsive strident demands she sometimes imposed upon her inferiors ceased altogether. But the greatest transformation was in her body. Where angles had been, soft curves developed; the sallowness of her face was changed to bloom. Even the long nose seemed to soften and melt back into her face, to achieve an integration that was almost beautiful. Brenda May kept remarking on these changes.

" 'My goodness, Melody, what's happened to you? You know, you're getting beautiful, what's happened to you?'

"It wasn't long until everyone knew what had happened to Melody. Her growing roundness made it obvious. But how it happened and with whom was quite another matter. Immaculate conception was one of the most common theories voiced.

[235]

Melody herself overheard a conversation in which one of the assistant librarians, an ugly fellow with a pock-marked face, remarked, 'I think it's the second coming. Yes, the second coming is at hand.'

"Melody just smiled warmly in his direction. Once she caught John G.'s head turned in her direction just before he descended the stairs to the periodical room, his eyes strangely fixed upon her, and she had smiled at him for just a moment before she continued happily with her work. In her every action, in her every look, Melody displayed such contentment that the entire library staff and many of the students and professors participated with gentle empathy in her fulfillment. No harsh words were ever spoken about her and in her presence there was genuine concern expressed by everyone.

" 'Why don't you take the day off?' the head librarian said on a number of occasions.

" 'Let me do that work for you,' said Brenda May often.

" 'Don't carry that heavy stack of books,' said students who just happened to be passing by her in the library.

"As the roundness of her body grew, the gentleness of Melody's disposition grew apace, until everyone sought her presence, and found excuses to linger for a moment by her desk or to involve her in a gentle conversation.

"Then something happened. For a few weeks there appeared to be no change in Melody's body, no increase in roundness. She just seemed to hang there, suspended on a strange plateau of pregnancy. Then almost unnoticed at first the roundness seemed to be diminishing. Those who knew her thought they saw the angles begin to reappear. Yes, it was true, the roundness was diminishing, receding. And even as the signs of her pregnancy receded, a strange fear grew in the eyes of all who knew her. A strange questioning fear which spread slowly through the library and out on the campus. Everyone was talking about Melody, small clusters of conversations, in muted voices. Melody saw the eyes that sought her out and turned away, intent upon her own terror.

"Just as suddenly as the roundness came, the roundness went away. Slowly at first and then rapidly accelerating, the roundness diminished and the angles came again. The nose

[236]

again jutted sharply from the face, the bloom died from the cheeks, the sallowness came again. The shoulder blades protruded once more from the poor back."

Gentry paused for a moment, took a last drag from a cigarette, and handed it on to Lonnie. But Lonnie didn't take it, he just sat there staring at Gentry. There was absolute silence among the group. No one spoke, no one moved. Finally Corso said in a small half-strangled voice.

"You son-of-a-bitch, what did you do that to her for? You really are a son-of-a-bitch!"

No one else said anything. They just sat there, staring at Gentry. Gentry returned the look, gazing intently into the accusing eyes. Finally, with a lingering glance at Father Maloney, he continued.

"One morning in December, just before Christmas recess, Melody didn't come to work. They found her later in her small apartment, an empty bottle by her bed. She looked like she was sleeping. She lay there with the bed clothes arranged neatly about her, her head resting gently on the pillow. And that's the way the story ends."

Gentry looked around the group, but no one spoke. Finally R. T. Barton muttered, "That's the cruddiest story I ever heard. What the hell do you want to tell a cruddy story like that for? Jesus Christ, we're miserable enough here without having to cry for some poor dumb girl."

And to Lonnie's astonishment, he saw that R. T. actually was sniffling, a tear rolled down his cheek and glistened for a moment.

"I agree," said Father Maloney, thoughtfully. "I agree with Corso and R. T. You didn't need to make it come out that way. We need a happy story, not one with gloom and terror at this time. Why did you make it come out that way, Gentry?" Father Maloney glanced directly at Gentry now, and there was a demanding, half-angry note in his voice.

Others in the group joined in the question. "What the hell do you want to make it come out that way for? What's the matter with you?"

Lonnie heard his own voice added to the chorus, "What a crap story. What did you want to do that to her for?"

Gentry didn't say anything for a moment, and then quietly, so quietly that those in the outer circle could hardly hear him. "I didn't make it come out that way! I told you, it's a true story. I simply told it the way it was. In life there aren't any vouchers for happiness. There aren't any guarantees of fulfillment. Indeed, there is just the opposite. If you follow any life for just a while you inevitably find tragedy. Melody's story is much more real, much more true than most of the antics humans indulge in to hide from themselves the true nature of their dilemma. I told you Melody's story here at this time—at this unhappy time because even here, with death around and in us everywhere, I still believe that we as human beings will find more dignity in accepting our real condition, as bitter as it may be, than by making it palatable with some distorting panacea. If we must die, and surely we all must, then let us die as human beings with the cold reality of what we are before our eyes. I for one would rather die miserably in the truth than live nobly in a lie."

Now Lonnie heard his own voice, sharp and angry. "You are a real bastard, Gentry. I think you told that damned story just to fuck us up good. Or just to make a great big deal out of your damned Yo-Yo theory. Jesus Christ, if that's all there is to life, if that's all there is to reality, then why go to all the trouble?" There was a break in his voice. "As far as I'm concerned, I'm done with all of you bastards and your mumbling and your mouthing. All the talk in the world isn't going to make any difference anyway, it's what you do, not what you talk. I think you're crazy, God damn it! I think maybe Father Maloney is crazier than you are. You know, you're just alike. You both have your ways of hiding from life. Well fuck you both. I'm going to go open that lock!"

He got up then and moved to the door where the lock still shone, brighter now, polished by hands, working fingers. He took the paper clip from its resting place in his LIFE WOMAN sack and inserted it in the lock. Slowly he worked it back and forth, up and down, not looking toward the others in the bay who now were silently dispersing. He noticed that the lock was strangely wet and feared for a moment he had cut himself, but finally realized that it was wet with his own tears.

[238]

"I better watch it, damn it," he thought. "Might get salt water in the mechanism, and then we'd never get the damn thing open." He wiped his nose on the back of his hand and continued in his work. After a long time he looked up to see Ross in the shadows there beside him, calmly watching him, a warm look of appreciation and affection on his face.

"I agree with you, Lonnie," he finally said. "There is more truth in what you do than in what the rest of them, regardless of their education, regardless of how much time they spend in thinking—there is more truth in what you do, than in what they say. Come on, give me a turn at the lock."

Suddenly, Lonnie felt a lot better, as if a darkness had been pulled away. He moved aside and handed the paper clip to Ross. "You know what we're going to do tonight?" he said as he watched Ross insert the paper clip. "We're gonna make a little trip. You know all those dead bastards we saw this morning? Well, there's gonna be a lot more tonight. They're not gonna need their rings any more, they're not gonna need their clothes any more, hell, they're not even gonna need their shoes any more." He looked toward the bulkhead where the young Captain still lay, a vague lump in the shadows.

"Suits me," said Ross. "It's getting colder all the time. If we're gonna make it, we're gonna need some more clothes."

"By God, we're gonna make it!" said Lonnie, suddenly pleased with Ross. "I like the way you're talkin' now, man we're gonna make it!"

They took turns at the lock, prying, turning, twisting the bent paper clip. But nothing happened. The lock remained, massive, impregnable, in their hands. At last they gave it up, Lonnie returned the paper clip to his LIFE WOMAN sack.

"We'll work on it again tomorrow," he said.

"And the next day, if need be," said Ross.

They lay down together then, on the hard metal, their heads on their canteen holders. It was cold. Lonnie moved over, until he felt Ross's body.

"Yeah, come on, snuggle up," said Ross. "If we're gonna make it, we gotta try to keep warm."

"I'll wake us up," said Lonnie just before they went to sleep.

But he didn't. Out of a fog he felt a strange rhythm and realized that Ross was shaking him.

"We'd better go now, if we're going to go," he heard Ross whisper.

"We're gonna go," replied Lonnie. He raised up, stiff from cold, his leg so sore he could hardly move it but he followed Ross from beneath the bay, and stood blinking in the almost total darkness. Except for dim lights strategically located above latrine buckets, darkness obscured everything. There were sounds though, the sounds of sleeping men, soft snores, the rasping of flesh on bare metal, as bodies turned seeking less discomfort. A few conversations here and there, out of the dark.

"I'll go one way and you go the other," said Ross. Lonnie could hardly see him although he was right next to him.

"Okay," said Lonnie. "We'll meet back here at the bay. Good hunting!"

"Yeah, good hunting," whispered Ross, and disappeared. Lonnie could hear him moving slowly, stealthily down the small corridor which separated the raised section of the canvas covered hatchway from the tiers which formed the bays. Lonnie eased along feeling his way, stepping over sleeping men, gently touching hands and faces, feeling to see if they were cold. Only a few feet down the aisle he stumbled over a body lying in his path. He felt the arm and then the face, suddenly his excitement grew. It was cold. Rapidly he felt over the entire body and found to his satisfaction that it was clothed in a full length pair of trousers and a long sleeved shirt. He began to work then, unbuttoning the shirt and the trousers, unbuckling the web belt. The pants didn't give him too much trouble, he just started pulling. The body slid a little, but almost immediately the trousers came loose and pulled smoothly over the rapidly stiffening legs.

The shirt was trouble. He raised the body to a sitting position, tried to hold it with his left hand while removing the shirt over the arms with his right. But he couldn't hold on. The body kept slipping from his grasp and falling back causing the legs to rise and get in his way. Finally he was able to raise the body by pulling it by the hair and at last released the shirt from one of the arms. He let the body slump back then and had no trouble getting the shirt off the rest of the way. He stood there in the darkness for a moment, holding his two prizes, thinking about them. Then he put on the shirt and almost immediately felt the warmth of the cloth against his skin. He started to put on the trousers but realized at once that they were wet, "probably with pus or piss," he thought. He considered discarding them, but changed his mind and rolled them up into a tight ball before continuing his way down the aisle, feeling as he went. Occasionally, as he felt the faces, someone would waken and once an individual struck out at him cursing.

"Get outa here, you fucking ghoul!"

He slunk on down the aisle, still intent on the search, unmindful of the insults, disregarding the difficulty of climbing over reclining figures. He was almost halfway around the hold when he almost fell over another body, also lying in the aisle. The darkness in that section was total. He put his hand on the bare chest and could discern no movement, the hands and face were cold. But the body was clothed only in a pair of Filipino shorts. He considered removing them but found they had been soiled, so he gave it up and moved on, feeling his way, moving carefully. When he was about halfway around the hold, he passed someone in the darkness, thought maybe it was Ross, but wasn't sure, so he didn't say anything. At last, almost fainting with fatigue, he found himself back at the bay. Ross was there already, waiting for him. He could hardly wait to tell him about his success.

"Man, I got a good shirt and some pants," he said. "The pants will be great when they dry out. I got the shirt on. How did you do?"

"Not so damn loud," whispered Ross. "I got a shirt and a ring."

"You got a ring? Jesus Christ," said Lonnie, "you got a ring? Man we can trade that for water, maybe. Maybe even for some cigarettes. You really got a ring? Let me feel it."

He felt Ross's hand on his arm and reached out and there it was, solid and heavy. A West Point ring, he knew. He had seen lots of them.

"Hell fire," he whispered, "we oughta get two or three canteens of water for that!"

[241]

They returned beneath the bay, snuggled down, content with their night's work. Lonnie kept thinking about the ring and about the water, or maybe the cigarettes, they were going to get for it.

"Shitfire," he whispered to Ross just before he went to sleep, for the second time that night, "we are going to make it! Both of us, man."

"Sure we are," responded Ross.

They both slept late the next morning and missed out on the food detail. They stood helplessly by as others divided the rice and gave them their small portion from the fluffed-up side of the mess kit.

"The dirty sons-of-bitches," said Lonnie, as they were mixing the spoonful of soybean paste in among the succulent brown grains. "The dirty sons-of-bitches. We gotta keep getting in on that food detail. They're a goddamned bunch of cheaters. You saw how that bastard fluffed up the rice on the end we got ours from."

"I saw it," agreed Ross. "Just like we did when we were dividing the rice."

Lonnie didn't respond for a moment. He kept munching his rice, looking at Ross, taking an occasional sip of tea from his canteen cup.

"The trouble with you, Ross, is that you're too goddamned honest. I sometimes wonder how anybody can be as honest as you are."

"Well, I'm not quite perfect," said Ross mildly. "I sure wish we had some water to wash out these mess kits. They haven't been washed now for weeks."

"How in the hell can you talk about water for mess kits when we're starving to death?" asked Lonnie. "Hell, I could drink two canteens of water right now, if I had it!" Then in a lower voice said, "Where's the ring? Still got the ring?"

Ross felt at the bottom of his canteen holder, appeared satisfied, "I still got it."

"When are we gonna trade it off? Do you want me to try? I'll take it down there if you want me to."

"No, I found it, I'll trade it," replied Ross. "You stay here and watch the mess gear. I'll be back in a little while." He

[242]

started crawling out from beneath the bay, holding his canteen carefully in his hand.

"Here, take my canteen too," said Lonnie, "you might get lots of water."

Ross took it and disappeared from beneath the tier. Lonnie relaxed against the steel support which held up the upper level of the bay. He could see Gentry and Corso and R. T. Barton over against the bulkhead. Gentry looked his way once, but Lonnie didn't look back. "What a bastard, and Father Maloney's just like him. They just care about what they believe in." He looked over toward the side of the ship and saw the young Captain, still lying there, THE SHOES visible. He went to the lock then and started working on it, moving the paper clip up and down, around and around. "Complicated goddamned thing!" He thought he heard a click and pulled hard on it, but it remained as massive and impenetrable as before.

"Where in the hell is Ross? He should have been back a long time ago. He's out there fucking around someplace. Probably drinking up all that water. Oh no, he's too honest for that." Then he saw him, stooping down, coming into the bay. He still had the canteens, but they jangled loosely. There wasn't any water in them. He crawled back and sat down beside Lonnie without saying anything. He just sat there, looking peculiar.

"Well what the hell happened? Where in the hell is the water?"

Ross seemed shy, almost afraid. "I didn't get any water, damn it. I didn't get any water. I went back there. There was a Jap guard on duty all right. I offered him the ring. I offered him the ring to trade, but he started jumping up and down, acting like a crazy man, like he was going to shoot me! I didn't know what to do, so I started back and then I met this guy who had been watching. He said he knew where to trade the ring, to get some water and some cigarettes. So I let him, I let him, I let him have the ring!"

"You son-of-a-bitch!" said Lonnie in a low voice. "You son-of-a-bitch! You mean to say you were stupid enough to trust some bastard with that ring? Don't tell me any more. I know what happened. He disappeared, didn't he? You never saw him again, did you?"

Ross didn't answer, he just sat there leaning against the steel support. Finally, he said, "I waited for him, I waited for him a long time."

"Goddammit," said Lonnie. "You really are a trusting, honest bastard. You should have known better than to trust anything with anybody in this fucking place. You know how many honest men there are left down here? You know how many? ONE, you! You want to know what happens to honest men down here? They die, God damn it, they die!"

Lonnie lay down then, put his head on his canteen, his hands found his LIFE WOMAN pouch. For a moment, just for a fleeting moment, he could see her. He lay back with his eyes closed, tears running down his cheeks. He didn't wipe them away. He just lay there thinking about the water that they didn't get and the cigarettes and his LIFE WOMAN. He drifted off to sleep, he didn't know for how long.

When he woke up, Ross was still sitting as he had been, leaning against the steel support. Lonnie got up and moved over beside him.

"How many guys died last night? How many do you think?" He looked at Ross carefully, his eyes were deeply sunken, dark hollows; his face gaunt and ashen. "What the hell are you sitting there feeling sorry for yourself for?" Lonnie said. "Shit, who gives a damn about a fucking ring anyway? Shitfire, there are lots of rings out there. Must have been fifty or sixty guys kicked the bucket last night, and there'll be more tonight. We'll find more rings, don't you worry about it. Hell, we got some clothes. You know what, I was pretty warm last night, I feel pretty warm right now. Hey, you know those pants I found? I bet they're dry now. How would you like to put 'em on?"

Lonnie reached up and found the pants where he had placed them on one of the girders beneath the upper floor. And sure enough, they were dry. "Hell man, here, put these on. You'll be warm then."

Ross didn't say anything. He just looked at Lonnie for a moment, then he took the pants, lay back on the steel floor, and put them on over his Filipino shorts.

"My God, Lonnie, you are a survivor. These do feel warm. Let's go to work at that lock."

Lonnie gave him the paper clip and watched him work. The lock held in the hand with the missing fingers, the paper clip in the other. The gentle rasping and clicking sounds went on and on. Lonnie took a turn at the lock, and Ross took another turn when Lonnie got tired. But nothing happened.

CHAPTER NINE

Five days passed and nothing happened. They made three more midnight searches, but found no more rings. Somebody else had always been there just before. They did find more clothes, a pair of Filipino shorts and two shirts. Twice they were able to get on the food detail and Lonnie became expert at packing down and fluffing up the rice. Each morning there was a long procession of naked dead men up the stairway, over into the sea. And always at the stairway Lonnie could see Father Maloney making his crazy motions over the dead and sometimes, maybe when the wind was right, could hear his voice jumbled and incomprehensible in the far distance. The incessant rumble of the engines, the vibration of the propellers, and the creaking sway of the ship remained in the background, became such a constant that Lonnie didn't even notice them unless he listened. One thing was not constant. The cold grew as the days passed.

Lonnie was glad they were in Bay Thirteen, clear in the back next to the bulkhead; it was the warmest place on the ship. Up toward the front where the Japanese guards stayed, the wind whipped in through the opening. The men who had been quartered there moved back, leaving the front section of the hold almost deserted. The Japanese guards who still lived in a small shack on the deck in front of the opening wore long overcoats now.

"How many of us do you think are left now?" Lonnie asked Ross one evening after they had finished their small issue of rice and tea. "We started out with sixteen hundred and nineteen men, how many do you think are left now?"

"Maybe six hundred," said Ross, thoughtfully, "not more."

"What's killing them? What are they all dying from? Gee, we wake up and every morning there are fifty or sixty dead. What in the hell are they all dying from?"

Ross gave him an appraising look. "Well, it's not hard to figure. There are lots of reasons, like wounds, like starvation, like cold, and now many of them have dysentery. Haven't you noticed how some guys keep running to the latrine buckets? I've noticed something else," continued Ross, "a guy does pretty good as long as he makes the latrine bucket, but if he ever fails to make it and craps in his pants, he's had it."

"Yeah, I've noticed that too," said Lonnie. "Do you have the shits?"

"Are you kiddin'?" said Ross. "I haven't taken a crap in a month. What about you?"

"Not since I did my biggy on the deck of the other ship. Remember?"

"How could I forget," said Ross, smiling a little.

"Jesus Christ, look at that," Lonnie said suddenly. "It's old R. T. Barton. What the hell is he doing over there?"

They both looked toward the bulkhead, and there almost hidden in the shadow they saw R. T. Barton. He was making strange motions. Lonnie looked closer and saw that he was licking the steel of the bulkhead.

"Jesus Christ," said Lonnie, "look at that poor bastard. He's trying to get the moisture off the steel of the bulkhead. Hell, he must be crazy. Jesus Christ, old R. T. has gone crazy."

Lonnie crawled toward the bulkhead and shouted, "Hey R. T. quit that, dammit, you're going to wear your tongue out. Shit, you're not gonna get any water out of that iron. Keep your tongue for eating pussy. Stop it goddammit."

But R. T. Barton didn't stop. He didn't even act as if he heard. He just kept licking the bulkhead. That night when all the lights were out except those above the latrine buckets, they

[247]

could hear R. T. shouting, he kept moving around, calling for someone. At first he shouted for Colonel Watson, then he began screaming for Major Morgan, the medical officer, kept demanding some medicine.

"Hey Morgan," he kept screaming, "I've got the shits, man; I'm dying, man. I know you got a bunch of pills, someplace, I gotta have some pills. Give me some sulfanilamide!"

Old R. T. kept moving around in the darkness. Once he approached Lonnie and Ross. Lonnie could smell him as he went by. He had crapped his pants. Then he moved over to the far side of the hold. Lonnie could still hear him, not so loud now. He was calling for his mother. His voice stopped moving around. Every now and then, once every couple of minutes, they would hear him out there in the dark, calling for his mother. Then they didn't hear him any more.

The next morning Lonnie crawled out from beneath the bay, stood for a few minutes watching the burial detail pick up the ones who had died during the night. He looked for R. T. Barton, but he didn't see him.

"Guess maybe I missed him," he thought. The long line up the stairway had been in process for some time before he came out from under the tier. He did see Father Maloney though, still stationed by the stairway, making his strange motions over the dead bodies as they moved up, out and over. Jesus Christ! Lonnie turned and went back into the bay, suddenly lonesome. Ross was working at the lock, but making no progress. Lonnie sat beside him for a moment looking around the bay. Gentry and Corso were still there in the far corner. They had found a grass mat and some extra clothes.

The young Captain with the shoes was still there. Wonder how he takes a piss? He can't walk. Lonnie looked close and made sure the shoes were okay. They were. He heard his name being called by somebody in the next bay, one of the guys from his outfit. Old Bessel, the fat one from Oklahoma, part Indian. He was the son-of-a-bitch who had reported him to Captain Kinsey, the company commander, when he stayed out all night playing poker with the guys in the Fifth Air Base group, the night he won two hundred dollars. But it didn't matter. The Captain didn't give a shit anyway.

[248]

Lonnie crawled over. Bessel wasn't fat now, he was just a bunch of bones, lying hunched over, all curled up like he was hurt bad someplace.

"What do you want?" Lonnie asked. "What's the matter with you anyway?"

"I got hit by one of those hatchboards on the other ship, right in the back," answered Bessel. "I could walk for a while, then I could crawl around for a while, but now I can't move, I think I've had it. I need some help. I need some water."

"Hell, man, I haven't got any water," said Lonnie. "There isn't any water, there isn't any water any place."

"Yeah, I know," replied Bessel, "but I got something to trade here. I got something to trade, but I can't walk. I can't go out there where the Japs are, so I need somebody I can trust to do the trading for me."

"Well shitfire, Bessel, you know damn well you can trust me. Hell I'm your First Sergeant, man."

"Yeah, I know," said Bessel, he had a small crooked smile on his face. "You sure are."

"What ya got?" asked Lonnie.

"I'll show you if you promise to trade it for me and to bring the stuff back. I'll give you part of it. I'll give you a third of what you get."

"Okay, okay. Sure, I'll do it. Sounds good to me. What ya got?"

Bessel pulled his canteen out of its holder and reached inside. Lonnie couldn't believe it. He saw the dull gleam of gold, the long chain, THE WATCH. Colonel Nelson's watch.

"Where in the hell did you get that?" asked Lonnie. "How in the hell did you get a hold of that?"

"I got it when I was still able to walk around," said Bessel. "Anyway, what difference does it make? I got it. Will you trade it, and bring the stuff back you get?"

"Sure I will," said Lonnie. "Give me the watch. I'll go up there right now and trade it off. Man, we ought to get some water, and some cigarettes for that."

"See if you can get some pills too," said Bessel, "I'm getting the shits. Man, I don't think I'm gonna last very long, unless I get some pills." He handed the watch to Lonnie, and Lonnie

took it and put it carefully in his LIFE WOMAN sack. It felt
solid there, next to his skin and the tautness of the string gave
testament to the weight of it.

"I'll be back as soon as I can, Bessel, okay?" Lonnie moved
back to Bay Thirteen where Ross was still fiddling with the
lock.

"I bet you'll never guess what I got around my neck," he
said to Ross in a low voice. "Man, you'll never guess in a
million years what I got."

"How about Colonel Nelson's watch?" answered Ross
noncommittally.

Lonnie stopped, stricken. "Well how in the hell did you
know that? How in the hell could you know that?"

"Well for Christ sake, everybody could hear you over there.
You got a big mouth, you know. I'll bet the Japs on the other
side of the ship are getting ready to make the big deal right
now. You've already advertised enough."

"Fuck you," said Lonnie cheerfully. "I'm going up there
now. And when I come back, we're gonna have some water
and some cigarettes. Give me your canteen. Dammit, I'd
better go back there and get Bessel's canteen. Maybe I can get
three canteens full of water and some cigarettes."

"Why don't you try for a blanket?" said Ross. "Or maybe
one of those grass mats like Gentry and Corso found some
place."

Lonnie left then, moving back through Bay Fourteen,
picking up Bessel's canteen. He crawled out from beneath the
wooden tier and moved slowly down the aisle which separated
the bays from the up-raised canvas covered section. He was
surprised to see how few men were left; not more than fifteen
or twenty remained on the broad canvas, the front section of
the hold was almost entirely deserted, and even towards the
rear there were empty areas everywhere.

"Jesus Christ, if we don't hurry, there won't be anybody left
when we get where we're going." He looked for familiar faces
as he went along, but saw no one he knew, and no one greeted
him. He was amazed to see how many grass mats had been
found. One group of three individuals had three mats, laying
on one and using the other two for cover. Looked pretty snug
in there.

[250]

He came to the alley which separated the front bays from those along the side of the ship. Ahead he could see the wooden bars which separated the prisoners' hold from the guards' section. Two guards were stationed there. One he had never seen before or at least didn't remember, and by God, the other one was the same son-of-a-bitch who had caught him and Ross sitting by the wall after curfew way back there in Bilibid, a thousand years ago. Lonnie took his LIFE WOMAN pouch from around his neck and removed the watch. He held it by the chain and let it dangle through the bars.

"Hey, Meatball, *Mizu, Mizu. Golden Bats.*"

"Okay, okay." The guard walked over, looked at the watch for a moment, then without warning, struck Lonnie a glancing blow on the head with his fist, *"Bakayrd,* son-of-a-bitch, you steal watch!"

Lonnie retreated rapidly down the aisle as fast as he could and finally paused, leaning against the wooden support of one of the bays, trembling. "That son-of-a-bitch, that dirty yellow son-of-a-bitch!" He heard a voice then at his elbow.

"Old Meatball got ya, huh? Well for Christ sake, you should have known better than to try to trade anything with him. He's the only honest Jap in the South Pacific. What ya got to trade?"

Lonnie was relieved to see his friend, Opdahl, a Navy Corpsman, a guy he hadn't seen for weeks, standing there; looking damned healthy too.

"What in the hell you been eating, Opdahl? You look fatter than a pig!"

"I do okay," said Opdahl. "I know how to trade with the Japs. You want me to trade what you got?"

"Can you really do it?" said Lonnie.

"You better believe it, sure I can do it."

"You don't mind if I go with you while you do it, do you?" asked Lonnie. "We just had some bad luck, trading. You don't mind if I go with you and watch, do you?"

"Not a bit," said Opdahl. "What ya got?"

"You won't believe it," said Lonnie. He removed the watch from his LIFE WOMAN pouch where he had placed it during his retreat. Opdahl seemed duly impressed. He stared at it, lifted it by the chain.

"Well, I'll be damned," he said. "How about that? Let's go make the big deal. What do you want? What do you want to get?"

"Well," said Lonnie, "we'd like three canteens of water, as many cigarettes as we can get, and maybe a grass mat. Does that sound reasonable?"

"Sounds good to me," said Opdahl. They moved together around the central bay area and down the aisle on the opposite side of the ship. Finally they came to the bars that separated the two sections of the hold. The other guard was stationed there.

"This is the guy you should have been dealing with in the first place," Opdahl confided. "Psst," he said. Finally the guard saw him and moved over. Opdahl showed him the watch, but suddenly he began to scream at them and to make menacing gestures with his rifle.

"Get out, goddamned thieves! Get out!"

They did, moving rapidly back down the narrow alley.

"Well, I'll be damned," said Opdahl. "Every fucking one of those Japs must have taken a bunch of honesty pills. I can't understand it. I made a deal with the same damned Jap yesterday!"

"What are we gonna do?" asked Lonnie.

"Beats me," said Opdahl. "I guess you better try it again when the guards change. Maybe the next ones won't be so damned honest."

"Well, give me back the watch," said Lonnie. "I'll try when the guard changes."

Opdahl returned the watch then, and to Lonnie's shock and astonishment, the chain was missing.

"Where's the chain?" he asked. "What did you do with the chain?"

"Shit, there wasn't any chain on the watch when you gave it to me," said Opdahl. "What do you mean, chain?"

"Goddammit, there was a chain on there. You son-of-a-bitch, you stole the chain," said Lonnie. "Give me back the chain!"

"Look you skinny fucking creep, there wasn't any chain on that watch when you gave it to me," replied Opdahl. "If you say another word, I'll beat the shit out of you."

"You know goddamned well there was a chain," said Lonnie. "I'm going to . . . ."

He was suddenly overwhelmed by a series of sharp blows that sent him reeling back against the wooden structure of the outer bays.

"You skinny son-of-a-bitch, you lying bastard, there wasn't any chain on that watch."

"Okay, okay," said Lonnie. "There wasn't any chain, you're right. I guess I was wrong. I guess I was just thinking there was a chain on the watch. You're right, okay."

"Okay. If you tell anybody else about this, I'll kill you, you son-of-a-bitch. If you tell anybody a bunch of lies about me stealing that chain, I'll kill you. You understand me?"

"Shit, I already told you," said Lonnie, "there wasn't any chain. I guess I'm just getting all screwed up because I'm so damned sick. Hell, there wasn't any chain."

"You better believe it," said Opdahl. "Now get the hell out of here!"

Lonnie walked away, staggering a little. A small trickle of blood ran down his forehead. He felt his face; the cheek was swelling a bit, but other than that, not much damage. He walked slower as he got near the bay, stopped for a moment next to Bay Fourteen, then saw Ross waiting for him, looking worried.

"What the hell happened to you? Good God, what happened to you?" asked Ross, a note of concern in his voice. "Who in the hell has been beating on you?"

"It doesn't matter," said Lonnie. He was crying a little now. "Some big son-of-a-bitch pushed me down and stole the chain off the watch. Then one of those cunthead Japs hit me. But I've still got the watch. I still got it, right here!"

"Well, for Christ sake," said Ross, the concern still in his voice. "Come on under and rest a while. It looks like you've really been through it. I'll go over and tell Bessel what happened."

"He'll probably think I stole the chain," said Lonnie. "You know I wouldn't steal that chain, don't you?"

"Sure I know that," said Ross. "Give me the watch and I'll give it back to Bessel. He'll understand okay."

"Hell, no, I'm not going to give him back the watch. I'm going to trade it. Just as soon as the guard changes, I'm going to trade the watch. Tell him that the guards on now wouldn't trade, but as soon as the guards change, I'm going to go and trade the watch. You tell him that, okay?"

Ross hesitated for a moment, and then said, "Okay." He crawled off towards Bay Fourteen.

"That fucking Opdahl," sniffed Lonnie. "That son-of-a-bitch, and I thought he was my friend. Hell, I said it myself, I even said to Ross, you can't trust anyone around this asshole place. You oughta have better sense than to trust anyone with anything in this asshole place. Shit, I don't even trust myself." He grinned a little then wiped a tear away. "Fuck it," he said. "I'm still gonna trade off that watch, and we're still gonna have some water and some cigarettes, and maybe a grass mat."

Ross returned just as the mid-morning meal was being lowered into the hold. Lonnie jumped up quickly with his mess kit and got out in front of the bay. He was the first one there.

"Hurry up," he shouted at Ross. "Hurry up! Man, we're on the food detail this morning, hurry up." Ross joined him and they waited as others crowded in around them.

"What's the count this morning?" asked Lonnie. "How many we got in our bay? Still alive."

"Eight," said Gentry.

"Eight? You mean out of forty people we got just eight left?" asked Lonnie.

"Eight is the number."

"I'll tell them we got fifteen. Hell, nobody knows the difference. So damned many people have died, nobody's kept track. I'll say we got fifteen."

"Why not say twenty?" growled Corso.

"No, I think fifteen is just about right," said Gentry.

"I hate to lie about it," said Ross. "Do we have to lie about it?"

"Goddammit, you don't have to lie about it," said Lonnie. "I'll lie about it. You do the eating, I'll do the lying!"

The call then came for the food details, and Lonnie and Ross moved toward the center of the up-raised section. They received rations for fifteen men, two mess kits filled to the brim with rice and two canteen cups filled with steaming tea. There was a particularly large blob of soybean paste.

"Jesus Christ," said Lonnie as they moved back toward the bay, "we're doing okay. Look at all that. Man, we're going to have a real feast today. Shit, this ain't bad!"

Others in the bay agreed. Each man had more to eat than at any meal since they had gotten on the third ship.

"Jesus Christ, I feel almost full," said Lonnie, "but I'm thirsty. You'd think those yellow bastards would give us enough water to drink. That little dab of tea they give us every day isn't enough for one good piss. And that soybean paste just makes you thirstier. Saltier than hell. Think the guards have changed?"

"Probably," replied Ross. "It's been a couple of hours now since you had your unhappy encounter with the big guy who threw you down on the floor and took the chain. One thing bothers me," continued Ross, "why didn't he take the watch too? He threw you down, why didn't he take the watch? Why did he just take the chain?"

Lonnie paused, stricken for a moment. "I had hold of the watch, that's why I've still got it. I had a good hold on the watch and he grabbed the chain and pulled it loose, goddammit. What's the matter with you, goddammit, don't you believe me?"

"Sure I do," said Ross. "I was just wondering."

"Give me those canteens," said Lonnie abruptly. "I'm gonna go trade that damn watch."

He made his way back down the aisle feeling the cold increase as he went along. He kept a sharp lookout for Opdahl, and when he thought he saw him, moved to the opposite side of the hold. Finally he was there looking through the wooden bars; the guards had been changed. They saw him standing there and both of them came over immediately. Lonnie stood away a few feet from the bars and showed them the watch.

"*Mizu, Mizu,*" he said pointing to the three canteens. *Golden Bats*, cigaretos, Golden Bats."

One of the guards took the three canteens and entered the small hut. He returned in a moment and Lonnie could see from the way the canteens swung on their chains that they were full.

"You got grass mat?" asked Lonnie.

But the guards didn't seem to understand, he hesitated for a moment and one of them removed two packs of Japanese cigarettes from his belt container, and handed these with the three canteens through the bars. Lonnie gave him the watch.

"Jesus Christ, it was easier than falling off of a log." He moved away from the bars a few paces, unscrewed the top from one of the canteens and took four or five heavy pulls. "God, that was good, good fresh water, none of that lousy crummy tasting tea." He was putting the top back on the canteen when someone touched him on the shoulder, some skinny bastard who looked like he was about to fall over.

"Hey, gimme a drink of that, would you? Man, I'm dyin'. I got the shits and I'm dyin'. I gotta have a drink of water!"

"Hell, man, I can't give you this water. It ain't my water. I was just trading for somebody else. It ain't my water, I can't give you any."

"What were you drinkin' it for then? I saw you drinkin' it. If you don't give me some, I'm gonna go tell! I'm gonna go tell!"

"Get the hell out of here," said Lonnie. He moved rapidly down the aisle, diagonally across the up-raised section, and within a few moments found himself back at the bay.

"Here's a canteen of water for you," he told Ross. "Jesus Christ, I did pretty good. I got two packs of *Golden Bats* and three canteens of water. I didn't get a grass mat though. They didn't understand me or something."

"You better take the cigarettes and water to Bessel, hadn't you? It was his watch."

"I'll take him some water and some cigarettes," said Lonnie. "Hell, he just stole the watch, I did all the work. Didn't I get the shit beat out of me? Hell, I figure we deserve a lot more of these cigarettes and a lot more of this water than he does. But I'll give him some cigarettes and some water."

He crawled beneath the bay and through the divider into Bay Fourteen. Bessel was waiting for him, lying there, humped over in the same position.

"Goddammit, it's about time you showed up," he said as he saw Lonnie. "What did you get for the watch?"

"I got two canteens of water and two packs of cigarettes," answered Lonnie. "You get a pack of cigarettes and a canteen of water."

"Fuck you, I oughta get more than that," said Bessel. "It was my watch."

"Well that's all you get. I had a hell of a time making that deal. Some bastard tried to steal the watch and I got hit in the head. Look at that," he pointed to the small gash, which by now was hardly perceptible.

"Well give me the canteen of water, give me the water and the cigarettes and get the hell outa here."

Lonnie handed him the canteen from which he had already taken the swigs and one of the packs of cigarettes. Immediately Bessel took the lid off the canteen and drank its entire contents.

"You oughta go easy," said Lonnie. "You're gonna kill yourself drinking all that water at one time, you crazy bastard. You better take it easy, man."

Bessel didn't say anything. He looked peculiar for a moment, then vomited the water up.

"Jesus Christ," said Lonnie. "I'll see you later."

During the afternoon, Lonnie traded off five cigarettes for a grass mat. That evening they received extra rations of food and tea. They weren't on the food detail, but Corso was and he reported fifteen people in the bay. That night he and Ross were almost warm. They lay on half the mat and curled the other half over them. Just before they went to sleep, they took a sip of water out of one of the canteens and shared a cigarette.

"Hell, this isn't half bad," said Lonnie. "I'm almost warm. And you know what? My leg doesn't even hurt much. How're your fingers and your shoulder?"

"I'd practically forgotten all about them," answered Ross, in the darkness. "They don't hurt at all."

The next morning Lonnie noticed a number of the men in Bay Fourteen smoking cigarettes. And then saw that Bessel was missing.

"Old Bessel went on the long trip," he announced to Ross.

"I know," said Ross. "I saw the burial detail drag him out while you were still snoozing in the grass mat."

"Well, he had a cigarette and a drink of water before he went," said Lonnie, cheerfully. "That's not so bad."

That morning, one of the officers from the mess detail came by and took a head count. Only seven men were left in Bay Thirteen. One more had died during the night, so their rations were restricted accordingly. Lonnie and Ross were on the mess detail and received only two mess kits of rice shaved off and one canteen cup of tea.

"They're starving us again," said Lonnie. "You notice how fat those bastards on the food detail are? That son-of-a-bitch who came by and took the count must have weighed a hundred and thirty pounds. I'll bet those bastards take all the food they want and give us what's left over."

"What would you do if you were on the food detail?" asked Ross.

"Fuck you," said Lonnie. He paused then, looking back toward the metal side of the ship. "How that guy keeps living . . . . ." he said quietly.

"Who do you mean?" asked Ross.

"That guy with the shoes back there. He can hardly move. Must be freezing to death, but he just keeps on living. You think maybe it's because he's got warm feet?"

CHAPTER TEN

It grew colder in the hold as each day passed; and with each day the food ration diminished, and so did the number of men. Lonnie and Ross spent most of the time huddled under their grass mat. They had lots of company. Lonnie felt them crawling all over his body. It seemed as if his head was a moving crust of matted hair. He tried to pick them off, but gave it up finally. He could see them glistening among the hairs on the nap of Ross's neck.

"Must be a million of those bastards, honest," Lonnie confided. "Where did they all come from?"

"Where do lice usually come from?" said Ross. "From lice eggs. And from the looks of your head, you're a real louse hatchery."

"Thanks," said Lonnie. "Wish we could find another grass mat." He looked out across the bay. There were only six people left. Over against the bulkhead he could see the pile of mats which represented Corso and Gentry. The young Captain with the shoes still lay there against the steel side of the ship. "Tough bastard."

He noticed then that someone new had moved into the bay, someone strangely familiar. It was hard to recognize anybody in the semi-darkness, he looked closer and realized to his astonishment that it was Father Maloney. The Father sat alone, leaning back against one of the steel supports. His face was ashen and his eyes sunk so far back in his head they looked like pools of darkness. His hair was matted, his beard scraggly and dirty, he was so thin he didn't look much like Father Maloney any more.

"Are you okay, Father Maloney?" Lonnie asked, half-shouting.

But the Father didn't move. He sat staring out towards the light area under the hatch. But he was saying something.

"What did you say, Father?" Lonnie asked again. "What did you say?" He listened, and heard the Father's voice, barely audible above the low rumble of the propellers, but he couldn't understand a word.

"Hey Ross! Hey, something's the matter with Father Maloney. Look at him sitting over there, he's acting real funny. He's saying something, but I can't understand it. Hey Gentry! Hey Corso, come over here," Lonnie shouted now at the top of his voice. "Come over here, come here. Something's the matter with Father Maloney!"

"There's nothing anybody can do," said Ross. He had crawled over and sat looking at the Father who still leaned against the support, looking out towards the lighted area. Gentry and Corso crawled over and they all sat watching the Father.

"Can't he hear us?" asked Lonnie. "Can't you hear us, Father Maloney?"

"He just hears his own voice," answered Gentry.

"Do you know what he's saying?"

"Listen, listen."

They heard the Father's voice then, suddenly clear, against the ship's noises. "I must confess to Thee, Almighty God, to You, Father. I have sinned in thought, word and deed, through my fault, through my fault, through my most grevious fault. May Almighty God have mercy on me, forgive me my sins, and bring me life everlasting."

The Father stopped speaking then, for a moment. He looked around the small group that had gathered near him, but gave no sign of recognition; it seemed as if his eyes were seeing something far away.

"My God," said Lonnie, "he's dyin'! Let's do something. Go

[260]

get some water. Go get some of that water we got, Ross. He needs some water."

Ross moved away and returned soon with a canteen. He hesitated for a moment and then passed the canteen on to Lonnie. Lonnie took off the cap and held the canteen out to the Father. To his surprise the Father reached out and grasped it firmly in his hand. He poured a bit of the water into his left hand and returned the canteen to Lonnie. With his right hand, he touched the water, then placed his fingers upon his eyes, on his ears, on his nostrils, on his mouth, on his hands, and finally on his feet. He looked again toward the lighted section beneath the hatchway and in the silence, his voice seemed strong and clear.

"May the Lord forgive me by this holy anointing and by His most loving mercy, the sins that I have committed with my sight, with my ears, with my nostrils, with my mouth, with my hands, and with my feet. And most of all, Dear Lord, forgive me for the sins which I have committed with my mind."

The Father stopped speaking again and looked around the small group for the second time. This time he was there with them, a small smile upon his face.

"It was good for you to come and visit me at this time; Lonnie, thank you for the water. And Corso, I always knew you were a much more sacred person than others knew. And Ross, what a fine and noble man you are. Look after Lonnie. Perhaps I should say to Lonnie, look after Ross. And then there's my dear friend, Gentry." His eyes met Gentry's in the half-light. "Perhaps you have heard a message I simply could never hear."

The Father stopped then as he swayed away from the steel support. He caught himself though and lay gently down upon the steel deck. For a long time he didn't say anything. His head was still turned, his eyes looking directly at Gentry. Finally, almost so low those near him could hardly hear his words, "So good-bye, dear friend, . . . you have won your wager."

They waited for a long time, but the Father didn't say anything more and made no movement.

"Jesus Christ, he's dead!" said Lonnie.

"Yes, he's dead," agreed Ross. They both looked at Gentry, who sat with a peculiar questioning look upon his face, staring at the reclining form of the Father. Finally he looked up at them.

"Yes, that's all there is," he said. He started crawling toward the bulkhead without looking back. Corso waited a few moments, and then followed him.

Just then, one of the men from the morning burial detail stuck his head down beneath the bay and shouted.

"Got anybody under there? Anybody dead under there?"

"Yeah, there's one under here," replied Lonnie. "Over there, next to the support. Hey, you know," he said to Ross, "somebody ought to be out there to say a prayer for Father Maloney as he goes up the stairs. He's been saying prayers for all those people, and now he's going up, there's nobody to say a prayer for him. Do you think we ought to get out there and say a prayer for him as he goes up?"

"Go ahead," said Ross. "I don't feel like it. I don't feel like doing anything right now."

Lonnie crawled out, walked across the up-raised section and finally reached the stairway. The procession was already underway, naked bodies, one man holding the hands, another holding the feet, going up the stairway. But one body was not naked. Lonnie saw the two men bringing him, walking carefully, and to his astonishment the Father's face seemed tranquil, relaxed, at peace. As they moved past him, Lonnie looked closely at the Father.

"Hey, Father Maloney," he said, "no use my saying a prayer for you, you don't need one." With that, he turned back, walked across the tarpaulin towards the bay.

He found Ross coiled up in the grass mat, not looking at anything in particular, just staring out.

"What the hell are you doing in there, just laying around? We got three cigarettes left, let's have one. Let's smoke a cigarette. Let's smoke a cigarette for Father Maloney."

Ross didn't do anything for a moment, then he pushed back the flap of the grass mat and sat up.

"Okay," he said, "let's smoke a cigarette. When a man like the Father dies, something big should happen, like suns colliding, but we at least can do something. We can smoke a cigarette."

Lonnie finally found a light, somebody was smoking in the next bay. On the way back, he was stopped three times by people wanting drags. He didn't speak to them, he didn't even look at them, he just kept crawling. Finally he was back with Ross, under the grass mat. They remained there, side by side, half covered, partly protected from the cold breeze coming in from the front section, taking turns taking drags. Lonnie felt his legs become numb, felt himself spin away, as if the whole thing was just a dream, the ship on the sea, the people in the ship, Father Maloney, Corso, Gentry, and R. T. Barton licking the bulkhead and crying for his mother. All just a dream.

"Jesus Christ, this couldn't be happening. This sort of thing could never happen to anybody, it just couldn't be happening." Not to him, the kid from Clayton, New Mexico, the kid who spent most of his life riding a horse around, or shooting rabbits, or swimming in the Cimmarron. Jesus Christ, it just couldn't be happening. Things like this crazy fucked up situation didn't happen to anybody, let alone to a kid from the Cimmarron!

"Just a goddamn dream," he said aloud.

"No, it's not a dream," responded Ross, with perfect understanding. "It's a nightmare, and a crummy nasty one at that."

"Well it sure as hell is a cold and hungry one," agreed Lonnie. "Jesus Christ, do you think it's gonna get any colder? It's so damn cold now, I can hardly stand getting out from under this grass mat. How in the hell do you think those guys take it out there. And that Captain laying over there against the side of the ship. How in the hell does he keep living? It's damn near freezing down here. How can anybody keep living, laying out there on that steel deck?"

"Most of them don't keep living," replied Ross. "That's why we've been having the long parade every morning. If you're hungry and thirsty and freezing to death, it's hard to keep living."

"And wounded," added Lonnie, and moved his left leg a.

little, just to check. He found it was much sorer than yesterday. It seemed to be getting worse now. He thought he could smell it, it had a strange green pus oozing from it.

"Yes, and wounded," agreed Ross.

"Jesus Christ, we sure are feeling sorry for ourselves," said Lonnie. "To hell with this shit. I'm gonna go work on that lock."

"Go ahead," said Ross. "I'm gonna stay here under the grass mat."

Lonnie didn't work very long. His hands soon got stiff from the cold, and the lock itself was almost too cold to touch.

"Shit," he said as he crawled in beside Ross. "We're never gonna get into that damn lower hold. That goddamn lock is as strong as the Rock of Gibraltar. It would take a stick of dynamite to open that son-of-a-bitch. We're never gonna get down into that lower hold."

"Well, there's probably nothing down there anyway," said Ross.

"What are you talkin' about, goddammit, there's sugar down there," said Lonnie. "You know damn well there's sugar down there. I know there is, I can smell it."

Ross didn't answer. Lonnie snuggled up to him then and was grateful for his warmth. He lay there for a long time feeling his own scalp move. He tried hitting his head with his knuckles and thought he heard minute popping sounds as the lice exploded. Jesus Christ!

Then he thought about a place in New Mexico; a place he used to visit when he was a little kid. In the early spring just when the days were getting a bit longer he liked to ride his horse up the canyon to a little rincón which faced the morning sun. He had found the place by accident one day, when a strong cold wind was blowing in from the north, once when he was out beating the brush for stray cattle. He had been so damned cold he could hardly sit up there; coldest place on earth, on a god-damn horse, when a north wind's blowing, coming in off the Baldies. He had ridden down into this small rincón and suddenly there was no wind, and the sun shone down and glanced off the white rocks, and by God, it was as warm as toast. First time he found it, he had spent two hours laying around, lapping up the sun while his crazy brother was out freezing to death, looking for those fucking cattle, and screaming for him at the top of his voice. He could see the rincón again, see the white rocks tinged with red streaks, could almost feel the warmth of the sun. He could see the ledge where he used to lie down, lonely but secure, could feel again the warmth of the white rocks against his body, could see again a pool of black water like a shining mirror there in a hole in the rocks, a large indention made by a dinosaur millions of years ago, his brother said, but Lonnie didn't believe him. But the water was there, bright and clear, and he could see again how he used to get off his horse and lie down with his belly on the warm white rocks and take a drink. And he could feel again how the water ran cool down his throat. Man that was really something, down in that rincón.

He heard somebody moving past and peeked out from beneath the grass mat. It was Corso. He was crawling with a rapid intensity, which suggested something important was taking place.

"What's cooking, Corso?" Lonnie asked as he crawled past.

"Man, I got the shits," growled Corso. "I got 'em real bad. This is the fifth time since this morning. You got any water?" There was a whining note in Corso's voice. He paused, just for a moment to look at Lonnie and then moved rapidly away, without waiting for a reply.

"I ain't got any water," Lonnie shouted after him. "I had some, but I drank it all up."

All during the afternoon, Corso continued his pilgrimage to the latrine bucket, and at each passage, he seemed to be diminishing in size. His huge belly was almost entirely gone now. It looked like an empty sack as he crawled along, hanging loose, folded in upon itself. There was no V now. As a matter of fact Corso's pants hung on him and Lonnie could see his shoulder blades sharp and clear beneath his denim jacket.

"I'll give you five hundred dollars for a canteen of water," he said to Lonnie, on his way back from one of the trips. Ross was awake now and he looked out to see who was there beside them.

"We don't have any water, Corso. We don't have a bit of water."

"Well you had some when the Father died, this morning. I

[265]

saw a canteen almost full this morning. What did you do with that?"

"We drank it up," said Lonnie. "Hell man, you know money isn't any good here. What can you do with money?"

Corso didn't answer. He was sitting back on his haunches, gaunt and haggard, a look of terror in his eyes. Lonnie could barely look at him.

"I know you got some water, goddammit!" Corso rumbled. "I'll give you a thousand dollars for a canteen of water." Suddenly his body seemed racked by an inner turmoil. He started up rapidly and struck his head on one of the rafters which supported the roof of the bay. He fell back then, onto the steel deck and lay there for a few moments, stunned. Lonnie could see that he had crapped his pants. "I know you got some water, you sons-a-bitches," Corso finally said. "I know you got some water, and you won't give me any." He crawled away towards the bulkhead where Lonnie could see the humped up outline of grass mats where Genty lay.

Gentry didn't let Corso back under the mats.

"Can hardly blame him," Lonnie commented to Ross. "Bad enough to sleep with him when he's okay. Who could stand him after he's shit his pants? Jesus Christ! Wonder what he's got in that ball sack? Wonder what he's got left in that ball sack?"

"You know, the poor bastard's dying," said Ross gently. "Do you think we should have given him some water?"

"Hell fire," replied Lonnie, "everybody's dying. If we give him what little water we got, we'll be dying next. Do you think that bastard would give us any water?"

Ross didn't say anything for a moment. Then he asked, "What's he doing?"

Lonnie peeked out again. "He's sitting over there next to Gentry, rocking back and forth. I guess old Gentry won't let him under the mat with him. Not that I can blame him."

Corso started wandering around the hold. Once he stopped and tried to crawl under the grass mat with Lonnie and Ross, but Lonnie told him to go away. "Go back to Gentry, damn it Corso, he's your sleeping buddy, not us. Hell these mats aren't big enough for two people, let alone for three. Anyway, you

[266]

shit your pants. You know damn well nbody's gonna let you underneath after you shit your pants."

Corso didn't say anything, he just crawled away. He didn't show up at the bay for the afternoon meal. Lonnie thought he saw him on the opposite side of the hold, crawling up and down the aisle.

But the next morning, he was back in the bay, lying next to the support where Father Maloney had died. He didn't have a stitch of clothes on. The ball sack was missing. He lay without moving, his body bluish white, strangely glistening beneath the black hair. He was lying on his back with his arms outstretched, his eyes open, like he was seeing something up towards the ceiling of the bay. Lonnie examined him carefully and was surprised to see how handsome he was, how his hair fell down to frame his face, a good strong face covered with a fine dark beard. He didn't look like Corso, somehow. "More like a picture I saw some place," thought Lonnie. "Jesus Christ, yes, in Sunday School, hanging there above old lady Eddy's desk."

"Have a good trip," Lonnie shouted out from beneath the mat when the burial detail came and dragged Corso from beneath the bay.

"What a hell of a thing to say," said Ross. "The poor bastard's dead, and you act like he's just going for a little walk."

"What else is there to say?" asked Lonnie.

Ross didn't reply.

The mid-morning meal came and went; they ate their few spoons of rice and drank their bit of tea. Lonnie wasn't as hungry now, but he was much thirstier.

"That damn soybean paste, that's what does it," he muttered to Ross. "You know, I sometimes think those yellow bastards are trying to kill us all just so they won't have to take care of us when we get to Japan. They don't give us enough to eat, or enough to drink, and they do give us that damn salty soybean paste. No wonder all those bastards are dying out there."

"If it weren't for the bit of protein in that soybean paste," said Ross, "more of us would die. But you would think the

[267]

Japanese could afford to give us a little more food and water. We can't be getting over five hundred calories a day. In this cold, nobody can live on that."

He was interrupted by a strange voice coming in under the bay, Mr. Noda's voice.

"Hey, you guys, under there. You guys okay? Pretty cold, huh? You guys okay?"

"Sure, we're great, Noda," said Lonnie. "What are you doing down in this hell hole? Why aren't you up there having a cup of tea? With Major Imada? What are you doing down here with us skeletons?"

"I just came down here to see everybody," said Mr. Noda. Lonnie could see him clearly now, squatting down, peering beneath the bay. He looked thin, even for Mr. Noda, and his clothes hung on him like he was some kind of little oriental scarecrow.

"We don't have much to eat either," said Mr. Noda. "We lost our food on the ship, on the first ship. Not much to eat here. I'm losing my beautiful figure. See?" He took up his belt to show how loose it was, and by God, he was skinny. "See, I'm not so pretty as I was," said Mr. Noda.

"Great," said Lonnie. "Hey Noda, when are we getting in? When are we getting to Japan? Jesus, we can't last much longer, we're dying of starvation down here, we can't last much longer. When are we getting to Japan?"

"Pretty soon now, pretty soon now," said Mr. Noda. He stooped down and crawled beneath the bay. To Lonnie's surprise he went directly to the massive lock which guarded the lower hold. He inserted a key, there was an audible metallic click and Lonnie saw the lock spring open. Mr. Noda undid the hasp, raised the door, and disappeared from view. In a little while he reappeared, carrying a sack partially filled with some substance.

"What ya got there, Noda?" asked Lonnie. "What's in that sack? Sweets?"

"What is sweet?" said Mr. Noda. He lowered the door into place, put on the lock and snapped it shut. He began to crawl away on his hands and knees, carefully holding the partially filled sack above the metal floor. Just as he was about to move from beneath the bay, he stopped and looked around him. Lonnie followed his eyes and saw them take in the men, some huddled together for warmth, some lying in the open without protection, others beneath grass mats. Mr. Noda made a small hissing sound with his teeth.

"Pretty bad for you guys down here," he said. "Pretty cold, pretty hungry. Pretty bad for you guys." He turned then and looked directly at Lonnie and Ross, who had both raised up on their elbows and were watching him from beneath their grass mat.

"Yeah, it's pretty bad," said Lonnie. "We're all dying. We're all starving."

Mr. Noda sat on his haunches, staring at them for a long moment, then he said something in Japanese, barely audible, almost a whisper. He crawled back to the door into the lower hold, inserted the key and the metallic click sounded sharp and clear in the silence. Lonnie thought he was going to raise the door again but he didn't. He crawled immediately from beneath the bay. Lonnie could see him walking across the raised section of the hatch, across the tarpaulin, his half filled sack thrown across his shoulder.

"How's it going, Noda?" Lonnie heard somebody shout.

"My name isn't Noda," came the quick reply. "Just call me Santa Claus."

"Hey Ross, you know what happened?" said Lonnie. "You know what happened? That little creep, that little son-of-a-bitch left the door unlocked! That crazy little Jap bastard left the door unlocked! He must have. I heard the lock click. Let's see what's down there."

"You go look," said Ross. "I'll stay here and guard our grass mat. And just in case there is something down there, take our canteen cups with you."

"Shit, man, there's something down there," said Lonnie. "I know what's down there, there's ten thousand tons of sugar down there, that's what. Give me your cup."

Slowly Lonnie approached the door, saw the massive lock gleam brightly there in the half-light. He reached for it then, his hands shaking. To his horror he saw that the lock was closed. "Goddammit, I was wrong," he thought. "That little

[269]

bastard didn't leave it unlocked." But when he took the lock in his hand and pulled, it suddenly sprang open. He couldn't believe it. It was open. He unhooked it then, lifted the hasp and slowly raised the door. When it was open even just a crack, the heavy succulent odor of brown sugar filled his nostrils, and he felt the sudden rush of saliva in his mouth. He raised the door completely and lay it back exposing a square hole, with nothing but darkness below. He stared down but couldn't see a thing, nothing but total black.

"That damn Noda went down, I'm going down." He shouted across to Ross. "I'm going down." He put his legs over the casing, knew a moment of wild terror as he felt himself slipping over and down. "Jesus Christ, I'm so damned weak, I'll never get out if there's nothing below, nothing but a great big hole down to the bottom of the ship."

But his feet struck something solid almost immediately. He stood there for a moment, then let himself down to a sitting position. The molasses odor of brown sugar was overwhelming, and wherever he put his hands he felt huge sacks, taut with their contents. "My God, we got enough sugar to last us a million years!"

He found the string on one of the sacks, carefully untied it until he finally could reach in. He buried his hand deep into the moist sugar and brought it forth full. He filled his mouth and knew again the exploding sweetness of the dissolving crystals. They crunched between his teeth like sand before changing into a warm syrup, which ran almost unbidden down his throat. He kept eating the sugar until the taste of it changed and he didn't want any more. "Christ, I must have eaten a half a gallon of that damn stuff. I better not eat any more. Too much of that stuff can kill you."

He filled the canteen cups and stood up, head and shoulders above the up-raised border of the door. He could see out toward the lighted area beneath the hatchway, and hear Ross's voice then.

"What the hell have you been doing down there? I've been hollering for you for the last ten minutes. Why didn't you answer me? What in the hell have you been doing down there?" There was a deep note of anxiety in Ross's voice.

[270]

"I've been having a banquet," answered Lonnie. "I've been eating the best meal of my life down here. Have I got news for you! There's enough sugar down here to last us a million years. Man, we're not gonna be hungry again. We got enough sugar to feed every man on this ship ten times over. Man, we're not gonna be hungry again! Hell, we're gonna make it, by the time we get to Japan, we're gonna be as fat as a bunch of hogs."

"Quit shouting," said Ross, "and bring me up some." He was sitting up now, still partially covered with the grass mat, but there was an eagerness in his movements, an intense note in his voice. "Bring me up some, don't just stand there with your head and shoulders sticking out!"

"Come over here and get it," said Lonnie. He placed the two canteen cups, each brimming with sugar, on the steel floor and climbed slowly out through the door. He hesitated for a moment looking around him and then shouted at the top of his voice. "Hey you guys, come and get it! Come and get some sugar! Hey, you guys, the door is open, the lock is unlocked, come and get it. Hey Gentry, get out from under them grass mats, come and get it." He paused and noted a slow stirring in the nearby bays.

Slowly they came. First, singly and then in small groups, carrying canteen cups and mess kits. Lonnie moved up and out of the way, and announced to everybody who passed.

"You know what happened? You know how you've been picking on that little Jap bastard? Well, I got news for you. He left that door open so we could get that sugar. Old Noda, he's a pretty good guy. You remember that when you're eating that sugar. Old Noda left that door open."

Within an hour every man in the hold had some sugar. Lonnie crawled over where the young Captain with THE SHOES still lay against the steel side of the ship.

"Give me your canteen cup," he said, "and I'll get you some sugar."

"Hey, thanks," the Captain sat up, leaned over on his right shoulder. "Hey thanks a lot."

Lonnie took the Captain's cup to the edge of the square opening, and shouted down, "Hey fill this for me, would you?

[271]

It's for a guy who can't walk." A hand came up and took it, and in a moment there it was again, filled to the brim.

"Hey thanks," said the Captain, as Lonnie handed it to him.

"Don't thank me, thank old Noda," said Lonnie. "He's the guy that left the lock open."

Lonnie noticed something peculiar then. The Captain was dressed in a warm, American issue field jacket.

"Where in the hell did you get that jacket?" Lonnie asked almost in awe. "Where did you get a jacket like that?"

"I've had it with me from the beginning. If it wasn't for this jacket, I'd have frozen to death a long time ago."

"Yeah, that's for sure," said Lonnie. He returned to the grass mat and found that Ross had eaten an entire canteen cup of sugar.

"I didn't know anything could taste so good," Ross seemed in excellent spirits now. "How much of that stuff is really down there?"

"Oh, about ten thousand tons," said Lonnie. "Enough to last us for a while. Hey," he said suddenly, "did you see old Gentry today?"

"I haven't seen anybody," said Ross. "At least not until recently. I been lying here under the mat. Didn't he come over to get some sugar?"

"I didn't see him," said Lonnie. "Maybe I'd better go check." He crawled toward the corner, stopping for a moment to make way for the line of men moving in and out of the opening into the sugar hold. He could see a pile of mats next to the bulkhead and finally reached it after cracking his head against one of the cross supports.

"Jesus Christ, it's dark back there," he said. "Hey Gentry! Hey Gentry! Did you get some sugar?" But there was no answer. Finally Lonnie reached out and shook the pile of mats. He could see the outline of someone beneath the covering.

"Hey Gentry, wake up, dammit, you're missing all the sugar." There was a stirring then; he was relieved to see Gentry's head appear, vaguely outlined against the darkness of the bulkhead.

"Come get some sugar, Gent," said Lonnie again, squinting to see better. "What the hell are you doing, hibernating? Old Noda left the lock open. Everybody's got sugar now. Hell, we're all gonna make it. We got plenty to eat now."

"I'm not gonna make it," said Gentry softly. "Since Father Maloney died, I've known that I wouldn't make it. I can't stand up now. I can't even crawl. All I can do is raise my head. I couldn't even make the latrine bucket. I was real thirsty for a while, terribly thirsty for a while, but now I'm not thirsty any more. You know what's happening, Lonnie? I'm dying now."

"You're full of shit," said Lonnie, incredulously. "You're full of shit! You can't die, hell you're not the dying kind, Gent." Lonnie moved closer. He could see Gentry's face more clearly now; it was covered with a dark stubble. His cheeks were streaked with dirt and his hair looked like dirty straw. He didn't seem like Gentry at all. Lonnie looked away. Jesus Christ, he didn't look like Gentry at all.

"Don't you want some sugar?" he asked finally. "Christ, there's a million tons of sugar over there, just waiting. I'll go get you some sugar."

"I couldn't eat anything," said Gentry, "but you can stay here with me for a little while. I want you to stay here with me."

"Okay, I'll stay with you. Hey, do you want some water? I got a little water here in my canteen. How about some water?"

To Lonnie's surprise Gentry suddenly sat up, his head and shoulders sticking out from the grass mats. Jesus Christ, he looked lousy, dirty as hell and that crummy beard.

"I can sure use some water," Gentry said finally. "Pour it in here." He was holding out his mess kit.

"Why not just drink it from my canteen?" said Lonnie. "Hell you'll get it dirty in that mess kit and probably spill some of it."

But Gentry was still holding out the mess kit so Lonnie poured some of his water in it, not much, just two gurgles.

Gentry didn't drink the water. To Lonnie's astonishment he began patting it all over his face. Then he fiddled around under his grass mats for a while and pulled out a mess kit knife and started shaving. Patting water on his face and shaving, just by feeling. But he was doing a lousy job. Even in the dim light Lonnie could see he was missing big patches, really botching it up.

When he was done he turned to Lonnie. "How do I look?"

He looked like hell actually, face still streaked with dirt, straggles of beard, sunken eyes and skin as yellow as old Iwahara's teeth. He had cut himself a little on his right cheek and the blood was still dripping down. Jesus Christ!

"You look great," said Lonnie. "How about some sugar now?"

Gentry put the knife away and rearranged himself in his grass mats. "No, I don't want any sugar, but I do have a story to tell. Why don't you go out and tell the guys that I've got a story to tell, a good one, one they'll remember."

"Hellfire, Gent, I don't know, it's colder than hell out here, and there ain't many guys left. I don't think anybody will want to hear a story now."

But Gentry was still looking at him, like he expected him to do something, and anyway he was freezing his ass off just sitting there.

"I'll go tell them, Gent, just hold on. They'll all be here in a minute."

Lonnie crawled back to Ross. His head was sticking out of the grass mats and he was madder than hell.

"I've been worried about you, dammit. What the hell you been doing? I thought maybe you were dead out there."

"No such luck," said Lonnie. "Hey come on, old Gentry's got a good bullshit story he wants to tell us. You go on over and I'll tell the other guys. He's over there in the corner."

Ross didn't say anything. He just pulled his head back under the grass mats.

"Come on, goddammit!" shouted Lonnie. "Old Gentry needs us to tell a story to."

Ross mumbled something from under the mats but didn't move.

"Well fuck you!" said Lonnie finally. He crawled to the edge of the next bay and started shouting.

"Hey, come on you guys. Old Gentry's got a story for us.

Come on! Come on! Old Gentry's got a bullshit story for us."

Lonnie waited for a few moments, but there was no response, not a sound; nothing but the creaking of the timbers of the ship and the low rumble of the propellers. Finally he crawled back towards the corner, feeling cold and sad. Sad for old Gentry. It was hard to see again and damned if he didn't hit his head on the same cross beam. Goddamn! Ahead he saw the pile of grass mats with something sticking out, Gentry's head. Lonnie felt crummy.

"They ain't coming, Gent. There aren't many out there, anyway. Not many left and they don't give a shit about anything but staying under their damn grass mats. But hey, Gent, I'll listen to your story. I'd like to hear it. Shit, I'd rather listen to one of your bullshit stories than anything!"

To Lonnie's surprise Gentry's voice sounded strong and steady and he could see his eyes now, looking at him.

"There isn't going to be any story, Lonnie. Too late for that now. I know that I'm dying and that it won't be long, but thanks to you at least I got a shave. But I'm dying."

Suddenly Lonnie was interested. "Do you think you're gonna pray, Gent? I heard that when guys start to die, all their religion comes back. Maybe you're a good Catholic, after all? Do you think you'll do some praying Gent?"

To his surprise, he saw a small smile appear on Gentry's face and suddenly the old Gentry was there again, the same guy he knew, his eyes strangely bright as he looked at Lonnie there in the half-dark.

"I have done my living without it, and I think I can do my death without it," he said finally. "But you stay here and watch. I feel it coming now." His voice was lower. Lonnie had to lean closer to hear him.

"How's it feel?" Lonnie asked.

"It doesn't feel anything," whispered Gentry. "I just don't feel my legs any more. But I can still see you. I can still see your face floating there. There isn't any pain."

Lonnie saw his eyes move towards the lighted section. And for a moment he looked strangely like Father Maloney, just before he died.

"You know what?" asked Gentry, his voice a little stronger.

[275]

"The most amazing thing about dying, is that at that time, at this time, you don't care anything about living." He looked at Lonnie then and said, "Do something for me, will you?"

"Sure I'll do it, Gent. What do you want me to do? Sure, I'll do it," Lonnie said loudly. "What do you want?"

There was a long silence and Lonnie thought he was already gone.

"Tell them I didn't pray," said Gentry. And although Lonnie waited there in the darkness shivering in the cold, Gentry didn't say anything more. Lonnie shook him once, but he didn't move.

"I'll tell them you didn't pray," Lonnie said as he pulled one of the grass mats away from the pile. "You won't need this any more, Gent, so I'm taking it. But I'll tell them that you didn't pray."

"What did Gentry have to say?" Ross asked when Lonnie finally got back to their place. "You been gone a long time. I was beginning to get worried about you, it's cold out there."

"Yeah, I know," said Lonnie. "Look what I got. Gentry gave it to me."

"Gentry gave it to you?" asked Ross. "Why would he give you one of his grass mats?"

There was a long silence.

"He doesn't need it any more," said Lonnie. "He's dead. And you know what? He didn't pray. Old Gentry didn't pray."

Ross didn't say anything. He just kept looking at the grass mat.

"It's awfully cold," he said finally. "Let's fix these mats. Maybe we can get warm for a change." So they rearranged the mats, and then snuggled down side-by-side like two grubs in a cocoon. They were almost completely covered, except for a small peep hole through which Lonnie could see the line of men moving back and forth from the opening into the lower hold. And they were almost actually warm.

"Do you think there's anything after this?" Lonnie asked.

"After what?" replied Ross.

"After this damn stinking life we're living, that's what. Do you think maybe Father Maloney's still around some place?

Do you think there might be something to that notion about golden streets and pearly gates and people flying around with wings?"

"Who knows," said Ross.

"Anyway, if there is," said Lonnie, "I'll bet old Gentry will be there. That would really be a big joke, wouldn't it, if old Gentry woke up and found himself flying around among all those damn angels? Yeah, that would really be a big joke, wouldn't it? Old Gentry would shit his pants, wouldn't he?"

"Sure," said Ross. "Some surprise for everybody."

"You know why I think old Gentry would be up there if there is a place like that?"

Ross didn't answer, so Lonnie continued, "I tell you why he'd be up there. Because, if there's something to it, Father Maloney must have a real in with those people and he'd say a few words for old Gentry. Hell-fire, I think he liked Gentry better than any of us, you know. Kind of funny, isn't it?"

"Go to sleep," said Ross. "I'm warm for a change and would like to get some sleep and you keep talking."

"Fuck you," said Lonnie. He lay beside Ross, warm and almost comfortable in the grass mats, trying to think about his LIFE WOMAN, but she kept floating away. He could catch her for just a moment, but then she wouldn't be there. She kept floating away and nothing would be left but funny orange doughnuts.

He thought about home, about the square house, built of red rock and adobe, back there on the Cimmarron, and about Eula Gaye Quiggly. He could see her full lips and funny hazel colored eyes, with specks of light floating in them, just as clearly as if she had been standing right beside him. That Eula Gaye, she was something else. He was thirteen years old when she came to stay, she and her no-good father and her mother who had the broadest hips he ever saw. They came driving in one day, in an old Model-T Ford that kept missing and backfiring until it finally died just as it got up to the front gate. His father had taken one look at Eula Gaye's mother and hired her old man to help work in the fields.

That Eula Gaye was really something. She had a slender body, but not too slender, just beginning to spread out into

hips and small firm breasts. Real beauties. Lonnie had seen
them once when he stumbled in accidently while she was
taking a bath in the big wash tub by the stove in the kitchen.
She was all covered with soap and her body gleamed silvery
gold in the lamp light. Her breasts were just like his dreams
said they would be, sagging down a little, but firm; the nipples
standing out, brown, slightly tinged with red. He had remained there paralyzed, unable to move as she turned and
looked directly at him.

"Get out of here, you little creep!"

He had taken one last look just before he left, saw the flare
of her hips and the warm hair between her legs. Jesus Christ,
that Eula Gaye was something! She had the finest breath he'd
ever smelled, particularly right after she'd just had a big glass
of Ovaltine. He used to say, "Hey Eula Gaye, how'd you like
some Ovaltine?" And she'd always answer.

"I'll drink it, if you'll make it."

Then he'd go get the Ovaltine box and two glasses of milk.
He was a real expert, mixing in the Ovaltine carefully with
the spoon, stirring it in until the milk made a fine chocolaty
swirl. He loved to see the faraway look in Eula Gaye's eyes as
she downed the whole glass in one long gulp. He'd get real
close to her then so when she turned his way, he could smell
her breath. Man, that was something!

She had a way of walking with her breasts thrown out and
her hips tucked in. Lonnie loved to think about her hips, and
the full roundness of her bottom. Man, there was that time
when he and Eula Gaye and his sister Edna and his brother
Sam were all in the back of the pick-up, the new one his father
had bought just before he'd died, and left his mother with
about a hundred payments to make. They were going over a
rough road holding onto the cab one behind the other. He was
right behind Eula Gaye who was leaning forward holding on
to the top of the cab. He looked down and saw her round
bottom right there in front of him. As the pick-up jiggled up
and down, he moved in against her. He knew she could feel it.
She didn't seem to mind for a few moments, and let him. He
could still feel the roundness of her against his hips. Boy, she
was really something! He used to think about her at night, and

how nice it would be if his horse would fall while she was near, and she would come running over and put his head on her lap. Once she had even said, "You know, Lonnie, I like you better than any other boy that's younger than me."

And then there was the time on the way to Clayton when they were all packed in together in the back seat of that 1935 Ford which could run so fast in second gear, she let him hold her hand. He remembered how his hand had moved close to hers, had touched her hand for just a moment and how she had reached out and took his fingers in her own. He had sat there overwhelmed, afraid to move a muscle with his heart beating ninety miles an hour. But it didn't last long. They made a turn in the road and the moon shone through the car window, almost as bright as day. He looked down and saw that his brother Sam had his hand up between her legs. "The son-of-a-bitch, he was always ruining everything." But Lonnie had forgiven her. They both took piano lessons and practiced a lot together and got so they could do a fine duet. One evening they had a concert. The whole family was there, Eula Gaye's father and mother, Sam, Edna, Lonnie's Daddy and Mama, the whole works. He and Eula Gaye did the "Red River Valley," and were just starting in on "There's an Old Spinning Wheel in the Parlor," when to Lonnie's horror and disbelief Eula Gaye let a thunderous fart that was barely hidden by the bass to which she had just given heavy emphasis. That was bad enough, but Lonnie had to stand there playing treble while the smell of it rose around him. Nothing was quite the same after that, he didn't enjoy smelling her breath any more. As a matter of fact he couldn't think about her at all without remembering that fart. And even now there in the hold of the ship the very thought of it caused her image to fade and his erection to dwindle.

"Fuck it," he said to himself. He was warm, and except for the lice which kept crawling along his scalp and across his back, quite comfortable. He could feel Ross's slow steady breathing, and hear the distant rumble of the propellers. The ship had a perceptible pitch and sway. Lonnie listened to the creaking of the timbers and enjoyed the sudden empty vacuous feeling which comes when a ship drops down just

[279]

before it reaches another swell. He went to sleep, then, soothed by the warmth of Ross's back against him, lulled by the monotonous rhythm of the slowly undulating ship.

Sometime during the night he awoke. Suddenly alert. Something had changed. Something was missing. He lay there in the darkness, his mind racing. The ship still vibrated in its usual fashion and the sway and creak were still there. Then with a growing horror, he knew what it was. Ross wasn't breathing any more. He held his own breath and waited, tried to pick up some movement of Ross's body against his own. But there was none. In his terror, he grasped Ross by the arm and shook him.

"Wake up! Wake up!" he said. "Wake up, goddammit! What's the matter with you. Hell-fire, it's warm and we've got sugar to eat, don't leave me here! Don't go away, don't leave me here. Wake up!" But there was no response. Lonnie finally lay back, listening to the tempo of his own heart diminish and become steady and slow again. Finally he got up, hardly able to see in the darkness and removed the grass mats from Ross's body. Using his feet for better leverage, he rolled Ross away from him down towards the outer edge of the bay. He returned to the grass mats, rearranged them, and covered himself.

He lay staring out into the darkness. "Jesus Christ, there's nobody alive now in this damn bay but me, and that Captain over there with the shoes. We're all that's left, just me and the Captain." He thought once about getting up and taking Ross's clothes, and Ross's ring. He could sure use them. It kept getting colder. But he didn't do it. He lay staring out for a long time and then lulled by the warmth of the grass mats and by the continuing sway of the ship, he went to sleep.

He didn't wake up until he heard somebody shouting, it seemed right in his ear.

"Hey, Bay Thirteen, what's the matter with you? We been serving chow out here for fifteen minutes. Hey, Bay Thirteen, get your mess gear up here and get your chow!"

Lonnie grabbed his mess gear and crawled out from under the grass mats. Jesus Christ, it was cold.

"I'm coming," he shouted, as he crawled from beneath the bay. He looked carefully then and saw that Ross was gone.

The burial detail had already made its rounds. "Good-bye, old Ross," he thought, "you were right all along. You didn't make it. But I'll go see your wife, I'll tell her about how you saved those poor bastards on that crazy raft you made. I'll tell her all about it."

"Are you Bay Thirteen?" the checking officer asked him as he approached the steaming barrels.

"Yeah, I'm Bay Thirteen," replied Lonnie.

"How many men you got under there?"

"Only five left," said Lonnie, "just five of us."

"That's a crock of shit," said a familiar voice. "I was just over there and checked, there's just two under there. This guy and another guy." It was the same Major, him and his fucking oak leaves. The son-of-a-bitch seemed to be everywhere.

"How many you got under there?" the mess officer asked him again.

"Well, maybe I miscounted," said Lonnie. "I don't know how many there is under there, I thought there were five. Okay, say two, that's okay."

He was given half a canteen cup of tea and a small salmon can of rice.

"Be damned sure you split that with the other guy under there," the Major said as he walked away.

"What the hell do you think I am, some kind of goddamned thief? Sure I'll split it with him." And Lonnie did, very carefully, this time. He divided up the tea and gave half to the Captain and then separated the rice into two piles and gave the Captain his choice, but he wouldn't make it.

"Either one will do," he said, raising up on his elbow. "Either one, it really doesn't matter much."

"Hey," said Lonnie, "we're the only two guys left alive in this bay. You want to join up? I got two grass mats. It'd be warmer with two of us together. Want to join up?"

The young Captain didn't respond for a moment and then finally, peering closely at Lonnie, he said, "There's not much use joining up with me. I don't think I'm going to last very long. I was cold for a long time, but I'm not cold any more. There's not much use joining up with me. I don't really want that rice. You eat it."

[281]

"Okay," said Lonnie, "see you later." He crawled back to his mats then, and huddled beneath them, eating his rice and drinking the hot tea. Jesus Christ, it tasted good, that hot tea. He lay down then, covered by the mats, looking out towards the lighted section beneath the hatch. The food buckets were being raised now on their ropes, and the latrine detail had just started picking up the latrine buckets and were moving them toward the center of the tarpaulin.

Absently, Lonnie saw them swing up and away, thought about Rutledge and about how he had taken the big ride, the big swinging swaying ride. Then he noticed something. Men were moving up and down the stairway. By God, it was true! Every now and then somebody would go up and then, after a while, he'd see the same person come back down. What the hell was going on? Lonnie got out from under the mats, crawled from beneath the bay and stood up; sure enough, men were moving up and down the stairway. He walked across the up-raised section noting as he passed how empty the hold was now. "Jesus Christ, there can't be more than four hundred men down here." The entire front part of the hold was empty. Not a man. Towards the rear certain bays were crowded, people pulling back from the cold. "It's funny they don't come back to Bay Thirteen, I could sure use some company back there. That damned Captain isn't much company."

Halfway across the tarpaulin he ran into the Major with the oak leaves. Jesus Christ, he looked healthy, almost fat.

"How come those guys are going up and down the stairs?" Lonnie asked. "You mean to say the Japs are letting people go up and down the stairs?"

"That's right," said the Major, glancing toward the stairway. "Since this morning. You can go to the latrine on the upper deck, if you want to. But I wouldn't advise it," he said looking closely at Lonnie. "The wind is colder than hell up there. Hell, you wouldn't last five minutes up there in that wind."

"I'm going up anyway," said Lonnie. "I want to see what the world's like out there."

"Help yourself," said the Major.

Lonnie started up the stairs, moving carefully as he went.

[282]

His left leg hurt him some, but he didn't even look at it. "What the hell." As he approached the top of the stairs, he felt the cold wind whistling down around him, but he continued to move upward, and at last was on the deck. It was just as he had remembered it, cruddy little bridge, steam winches, everything. He looked down into the section where the Japanese guards stayed and saw two of them walking around aimlessly, carrying their rifles like sticks. They had on long overcoats and kept moving, "probably to keep from freezing to death." The door of their small hut was open and he could see somebody brewing tea or maybe cooking something over a *hibachi*. He walked to the guard rail and looked down at the water and then away into the distance. To his surprise he saw rocky points sticking up everywhere; nearby they rose sharp and clear out of the sea but further away they were lost in the mists. A lot of birds were flying around, big white ones and some little gray ones.

On one of the rocky points which jutted up not more than a hundred feet from the ship, Lonnie saw a white bird sitting, leaning into the wind to keep its perch. Around the rocky point, the waves of the sea moved silently, back and forth, up and down, like liquid lead. Suddenly he was stricken by the loneliness of it all, the emptiness of it, the coldness of it, and thought about Ross down there somewhere in that molten sea, lying among the cold rocks, moving back and forth as the water moved. "Jesus Christ!" He looked again at the bird, still leaning into the cold wind, struggling to hold its perch on that rocky point. Hanging on.

He walked to the other side of the ship, the same kind of rocks jutted up there also. The fog seemed deeper on that side, more forbidding. In the distance the rocks became by degrees indistinguishable from the surrounding fog. "One thing for sure, no airplane is going to find us in this crap. But I sure hope those Japs know where they're going. One miscue and we're goners."

He turned to go back, chilled to the bone, his feet and hands numb with the cold. Just as he was about to descend the stairway, he looked up and saw Major Imada, standing on the bridge not thirty feet away; his hand was resting on his sword.

He was looking out toward the open sea. Just as Lonnie looked up, Major Imada glanced down at him. Lonnie stood there transfixed for a moment, overwhelmed with the presence, the immediacy of the other man. Suddenly he stood straighter, and while still looking up directly into the eyes of the Major, he saluted. He remained there, half embarrassed, not knowing what else to do, holding the salute. The Major on his part, removed his hand from the handle of his sword, stood more erect, a look of astonishment, almost of shock, on his usually impassive face. For a long moment they remained thus, then almost imperceptibly, the Major nodded his head and turned away.

Lonnie went down the stairway then, slowly and carefully. It was so cold he could hardly feel the metal of the steps against his bare feet, and his hands felt like pieces of ice beneath his armpits where he had placed them. But he felt strangely content, almost happy. "That damned Jap Major is really somebody."

But his contentment didn't last very long. When he got back to the bay, he found that his grass mats were missing. He couldn't believe it. "Those thieving sons-of-bitches!" He crawled back to the young Captain.

"Goddammit," he said. "Somebody stole my grass mats! Did you see anybody steal my grass mats?"

"Yes, I did," said the Captain, raising himself up on his elbow. "Yes, I saw someone take them, and I shouted at them, but it didn't matter. They just took them anyway." He paused for a moment, then said, "You'd just as well forget it, you'll never get them back, even if you found out who took them, you'd never get them back."

"Jesus Christ," said Lonnie, "I'm freezing to death, and those sons-of-bitches took my grass mats." He crawled to the door that led down into the sugar hold and let himself over. It was warmer down there. "Anybody down here?" he shouted. But there was no answer. "Jesus Christ, it's not so bad down here. It's almost warm. You'd think people would be staying down here." He moved back away from the opening into the total darkness and sat down on one of the sacks of sugar. He looked up and could barely make out the lighter square of the

[284]

open door. "Some son-of-a-bitch might shut that door and lock it. Man, some way to go, me and a million tons of sugar." He untied one of the sacks and began to remove the sugar, handful after handful. Every now and then he would take a mouthful and suck it till it disappeared. Finally, the sack was empty enough for him to turn it upside-down and release the remainder of its contents. He kept working and within an hour had emptied three sacks. He lay down then and covered himself with the sacking material. He felt almost warm. "Hell, I'll just stay down here. No use going back up there where it's so damn cold, I'll just stay down here."

He lay there, half-dozing, listening; the creaking of the ship and the rumbling of the propellers seemed much louder, with his head pressed against the filled sack beneath him. Every now and then, somebody would come down into the hold. He could hear them scrabbling around, hear their hands making gritty sounds as they dug into the brown crystals. Then they would go away.

Something woke him, something strange and different. He listened, but could hear nothing but the heavy thuds of his own heart, the creaking of the ship and the propellers. But the cadence of the engines had increased. He knew it. He suddenly felt the ship lean heavily, making a sharp turn. Then he heard the sound again, the one that had awakened him. A heavy explosion. "Jesus Christ, how can it be? In this fog, among these rocks, here, right next to Japan, those bastards are going to get us! Those sons-of-bitches are gonna get us!"

A series of explosions came now. He could hear them clearly, one after the other, in the distance. Then he heard strange metallic cracks, sharp snapping sounds against the metal side of the ship. "Jesus Christ," Lonnie said aloud, "I'm getting out of this goddamned place!" He grabbed his sugar sacks and started searching for the square opening. At first he couldn't find it, and for a long moment suffered the terror of being imprisoned, entombed there. But finally he saw it, a faint square of lighter darkness against the total black. In a frenzy, he crawled up and out, holding his sugar sacks clutched in his left hand.

For a moment he squatted beside the opening, almost

blinded by the sudden light. The explosions came again, one after the other, dull, slow, methodical, and again he heard the snapping reverberations of the concussion striking the side of the ship. "Submarines! Those goddamned Americans are gonna kill us with submarines. Those sons-a-bitches!"

He put his head under the sugar sacks waiting for the torpedoes to strike, and thought about the icy water, the leaden waves, the deep cold, and listened to his heart, thudding away there in his chest. And then for some reason he wasn't afraid any more. He looked around, and to his astonishment saw that no one seemed afraid. Wherever he looked, he saw men huddled down in grass mats, some were in sugar sacks like him, others simply clumped together for warmth. There was hardly any movement. Nobody was waiting at the stairway to get out, nobody was doing anything. Lonnie listened for a long time for another explosion, but none came. The ship continued to lean heavily every now and then as it zigzagged through the water, but there were no more explosions. He lay down and covered himself with the sugar sacks. "Damn near as warm as a blanket. Shit, except for the smell of them, and for their stickiness, they're not half bad."

When the mid-afternoon meal came, everyone received extra food. The ration of rice was almost double, and Lonnie had a half-canteen cup of tea, all to himself. That night, he slept well, almost warm in his sugar sacks.

Strange sounds woke him. Lonnie wasn't sure what they were or where they were coming from. He lay in his sugar sacks, listening, trying to figure them out. Finally he located them, they were coming from directly above him, someone was up there messing around in the upper bay. "Jesus Christ, what are they doing up there? Nobody's been up there for days. It's colder then hell up there!"

The sounds continued. Someone was crawling around stopping every now and then, staying quiet for a few moments then he would hear the sounds again. Lonnie had almost forgotten about them when he was suddenly covered by a warm viscous liquid that came draining down through the cracks in the floor above. He couldn't believe it at first, but finally the strange putrid smell of it convinced him. His head was covered with it, and it ran down his face and neck.

"You dirty son-of-a-bitch," he started screaming at the top of his voice. "You dirty bastard! You shit all over me. You filthy son-of-a-bitch!" He crawled from beneath his sugar sacks which were partially drenched and staggered out, half crawling, half running to the edge of the tier. There was somebody up there, he could see him plainly, lying against the steel support, just above his own position. He was dressed in a small Filipino jacket, that was all, no trousers. Lonnie could see the outline of the pelvic bones and the loose skin where buttocks once had been. A bloody diarrhea ran from him, pooled out on the floor, and seeped down through the cracks. "You dirty son-of-a-bitch," Lonnie said under his breath, "you dirty bastard. You're dying and I'm glad!"

Lonnie felt the cold then, the wetness of his head and face and shirt increased it. He stood for a moment, leaning against the wooden structure of the tier. Then he began to cry, softly, so no one could hear him. "What in hell am I going to do? That son-of-a-bitch. I can't wash, I got this shit all over me, it's in my hair, it's all over me. It's all over my sacks. What the hell am I gonna do?"

He didn't remain outside very long; the cold was too much, too bitter. He crawled beneath the tier again and squatted down beside his sugar sacks. "Fuck it," he finally said half aloud, and crawled beneath them. They were wet in places, and the bloody putrid odor pervaded them, but it wasn't as cold there. "What's the use?" he thought. "Shit, dying's better than this. It must be. What's so wonderful about this life, anyway? Starving, freezing to death, goddamned wounds, dirt and lice, and now I'm covered with shit. Shit, this is no life. Hell, I'll probably die anyway. That son-of-a-bitch! Those fucking Japs!" He settled down beneath the sacks, and when the call came for the mid-morning meal, he didn't get up.

He could see himself, inside a large glass bubble, lying on a mattress, and he was bright and clean, and warm. It was comfortable on the mattress, it was just like a featherbed his Granny made and sent to them on Christmas, when he was only eight years old. Jesus Christ, that was some featherbed! On cold nights he and his brother used to snuggle down and feel the feathers puff up around them. Warm, comfortable. He was floating above the ship in his glass bubble, in the bright sunlight, looking down at a lot of ships, the entire Japanese Navy strung out there on the water; he could see the strange rocks sticking up all around and the birds flying. And by God there it was, that same bird, as clear as day, sitting on that rock, struggling into the wind. Sure was warm in the bubble, lying with the feather mattress all puffed up around him. He could hear music playing, coming from the old Victrola in the big room, back in the old square house. He loved to wind it up, put on a record and let it go. The music seemed to come from a long way off, but there it was, easy to make out, "A long, long way to Tipperary." He liked that song, his mother used to sing it to him when he was a real little kid. It faded, and be damned if he couldn't hear old R. T. Barton singing, as clear as could be, "I'm gonna buy me a paper doll I can call my own." But that couldn't be, old R. T. Barton was dead. Shit, that couldn't be, he could hear his voice. He looked down and saw the Japanese Navy again, strung out, wide across a clear bright ocean. The fog had lifted and the rocks had disappeared.

"I'll get them, by God, I'll get them all." He turned the dials in front of him, just like old Buck Rogers, saw two bright blue flames moving almost parallel, slowly coming to a point, converging. And when they did a great explosion moved along the water, and ship after ship simply flew apart. Soon all the ships were gone, every fucking one of them. Nothing was left but the boiling of the water, the final agony and turmoil of their disappearance. Then he heard his Mama calling, "Orlando Ray, Orlando Ray," faint at first but getting louder. "I hope Daddy doesn't hear her call me that. I better go in or she'll keep screaming her head off until he hears her."

"I'm coming now," he said and was just about to set the controls, when he heard a voice from somewhere, loud and strong and clear. "Goddamn that little Jap, anyway." It was Mr. Noda's voice.

"How are you guys down there? Listen. I've got good news today, I've got good news. In two days, we get to Japan. We're almost there. Just two more days and we get to Moji. So you guys cheer up. You guys don't be sad. You be happy now."

Lonnie stuck his head out from under the sugar sacks so he

could hear better. "That little son-of-a-bitch, he couldn't be lying. We're gonna make it. By God, we're gonna make it yet!"

"In two days our trip will be over," he heard Mr. Noda's voice, even clearer now. "When we get to Japan, you will be given new clothes, good warm Japanese uniforms. You will be given good food. You will be given Red Cross packages with butter and meat and Lucky Strike cigarettes. So let's have no more dying down there. You guys want to live. You want to smoke those Lucky Strike cigarettes. Okay? Okay?"

When the call for the mid-afternoon meal came Lonnie was waiting. "I'll get our chow," he shouted across to the young Captain. "I'll bring it back. Did you get something to eat this morning?" There was no response, but he thought he saw a slight movement over there. "He's still living."

He waited near the steaming barrels until his bay number was called. Someone was speaking to him.

"You know, I've seen dirty filthy people. We're all dirty filthy people. But I swear to God, you're the worst I've ever seen. And you smell the worst. What in the world have you got on you?"

"Sweet shit," said Lonnie. He was grinning.

"It doesn't smell sweet," said the Major. "Get your chow and get out of here."

He was given a full mess kit of rice, a full canteen cup of tea, and a large blob of soybean paste.

"Don't forget to share it with that guy back there," the Major reminded him.

"Sure, sure," said Lonnie. "I'll share it with him. Do you think we're really gonna make it in day after tomorrow?"

"Sounds like it," answered the Major. "Now get outa here. You smell too sweet for me."

Lonnie returned to the bay and crawled back to the young Captain. "Hey, we got big chow," he said. "Wake up man, let's eat."

The Captain didn't respond at first. Finally he raised his head and looked at Lonnie. "I can't eat anything. But could you help me with a little of that tea? I could sure use a little of that tea."

Lonnie poured some of the still steaming liquid into the Captain's canteen cup and helped him raise his head. He drank four or five swallows.

"Thanks," he said. "That was sure good. You eat the rice. I couldn't eat a bit of it."

"Thanks," said Lonnie. "But I'll save some tea for you. When you want some tea, you just holler, and I'll bring it over. Okay?"

"Yes, I'll do that," said the Captain.

Lonnie crawled back to his place by the sugar sacks and ate the entire mess kit of rice. It tasted damned good. And all of a sudden, he felt good. "By God, I am going to make it," he said aloud. "I'm gonna make it."

He snuggled down in his sugar sacks. They weren't wet any more, a little hard and crusty in some places, but not wet. "Hell, they don't even smell bad now, but maybe I just can't smell anything." He went to sleep, but he slept fitfully.

Towards morning something woke him. He listened in the darkness. For a few moments, he didn't hear anything. Then it came again, peculiar scraping noises and the sounds of breathing, heavy panting as if someone was working hard. Lonnie knew what was happening. He got out from under his sugar sacks and began to crawl toward the side of the ship. He stopped every now and then to listen. He was sure now. Somebody was trying to get the young Captain's clothes. Somebody was trying to get THE SHOES. "The son-of-a-bitch!" He crawled back more rapidly, into the total darkness. Almost there, directly in front of him, he could hear clearly and distinctly the sounds made by the worker. Suddenly, Lonnie screamed.

"Get away from that guy, you son-of-a-bitch! Get away from him!" He didn't say any more. A sudden kick sent him sprawling backwards, head over heels. For a moment he lay on the steel deck, stunned, feeling the biting cold of the metal seep through his clothes. "Goddammit, those are my shoes." Quietly he got up and moved at an angle until he reached the side of the ship, then carefully, silently he followed the steel plates down, feeling as he went along. Finally his outstretched hand touched a shoe. Quickly he began to unlace it, feeling the body move as his fellow worker struggled to get the coat.

He pulled, and the first shoe came off. He placed it behind him, against the ship's side and started working on the other. It was tied with a hard knot, a damn granny knot. In his desperation and in the darkness, he couldn't untie it, it wouldn't come loose. He tried to break the string, but it wouldn't break. Finally he bent down and began to gnaw the string with his teeth. Those big teeth of his were good for something; he could feel with his tongue that the string was half chewed through. He pulled then, with all his might and the string gave away with a soft thunk. In a few seconds, the shoe was unlaced, and he had it in his hand. Silently he backed away, retrieving the other shoe as he went. As he crawled back to his sugar sacks, he could smell the good leather, could feel it soft and pliable in his fingers. He couldn't get to sleep for a long time. He kept thinking about HIS SHOES, kept enjoying the smell and the feel of the leather. Finally he dozed off, snuggled up against his shoes, holding them in his arms.

When he awoke the next morning the shoes were still in his arms, solid and comforting. He carefully rearranged the broken string and tried on the first shoe. It was a perfect fit. "By God, how about that." He looked down at his foot, at the warm rich leather that encased it. He put on the other shoe then, laced them both, and crowned his achievement with a bow knot. Jesus Christ, they were beautiful!

Something was happening in the hold outside the bay, a change in tempo, an increase in the activity of the men. Conversations could be heard. People were moving about the hold, visiting, exchanging news, asking about people. Just before the mid-morning meal was lowered into the hold, a careful count was taken of the men left in each bay. "How many you got left in Bay Thirteen?" the Major asked Lonnie as he waited in line to get his food.

"Nobody but me," replied Lonnie cheerfully. "They all took the big trip. There's nobody left but me."

"Well, I'll be damned," said the Major. "You don't look the type."

"What do you mean by that?" asked Lonnie. "I don't look what type?"

"Forget it," said the Major. "Get your chow."

There was a large ration of food again. Lonnie received half a mess kit of rice, some soup that had pumpkin and potatoes in it, and half a canteen cup of hot tea. He returned to the bay and ate the rice and soup immediately. He sipped the tea slowly, enjoying it, letting the cup warm his cold hands.

He thought he heard a voice then, one he knew, so he crawled from beneath the tier and looked up. Major Imada was standing there, looking down through the opening in the hatchway. Lieutenant Iwahara was standing near him and over on the far side of the opening, Mr. Noda peered down, squinting as usual.

"Our long journey is almost over," said Major Imada in his perfect English. "Many of your comrades are not here. They died along the way. They are scattered through the ocean for two thousand miles. But you are here, four hundred and twenty-seven men are here. Some of you are cowards, some of you are brave men. But that doesn't matter now. You are here. When we reach Japan, you will be sent to different prison camps. If you are sick, you will be sent to a hospital. If you are well and can work, you will be sent to the coal mines. In the days to come, my country will be put to a great test, and you will do what you are told to help us survive that test. But have no fear, we will survive. We have been tested many times, and we have survived. In a great dark hour of our history, when doom seemed to rest upon us, the mighty Kamikaze, The Divine Wind, saved our land. This I know, again the Kamikaze will come. And the barbarians will be pushed away from our Sacred Land. Tomorrow you will be given warm clothes and sent to the different prison camps. You will not see me again. I will not see you again."

He turned away from the hold. Lonnie saw him give one last glance downward, then he disappeared, and the other Japanese followed him.

All during that day, the tempo in the hold increased. Voices were louder. People were moving back and forth. Lonnie thought he heard laughter. Twice during the afternoon, right after they had eaten, people came by to ask about some man who had been quartered in Bay Thirteen.

"Nobody here but me," Lonnie answered each time. "They

[292]

all went down the long road. Nobody under here but me. They're all gone."

He could hardly sleep that night. He lay wrapped in his sugar sacks, holding his shoes in his arms, the strings tied around his wrists to keep them from being pulled away. Every now and then he would put his face into one of the shoes just to smell the leather, until he went to sleep.

Slowly it came seeping in, something weird, almost unbelievable, there was no motion in the ship. The propellers had stopped.

Lonnie lay there in the dark, savoring the silence. Thinking, "I did make it. We're here. We're on land again. I made it!"

He was reawakened in the early morning by the Japanese guards shouting. *"Kisho, kisho."* Men were already gathering their belongings, making ready to move out.

"By God, we're going. We're really going." He crawled from beneath the bay, saw the line of men forming, noticed that it was much warmer, the heavy draft of cold air was no longer coming down through the hold, thought about it for a moment then threw the sugar sacks as far as he could, back beneath the tier. "The Japs might beat my brains out if they caught me with them." He took his place in line then; slowly it inched along, down the narrow aisle, past the bays in the front section of the hold, and finally into the open area where the Japanese guards had been stationed. The wooden bars separating the two parts of the hold had been removed. Two guards were there, one making marks on a tablet, the other distributing uniforms from a huge pile which covered a good portion of the steel deck.

When Lonnie's turn came, the guard took one look and threw him a pair of heavy baggy Japanese trousers and a thick uniform coat. "By God, they looked warm." Lonnie could hardly wait to put them on. "Jesus Christ, it was damn near another perfect fit!" They were baggy, all right, and hung on him like he was a coat hanger, but they were long enough. He fell back in line, and found himself moving along the steel deck toward the stairway which led out of the hold, onto the upper wooden deck, where the steam winches were already being put into operation. "To get the sugar," thought Lonnie.

"All that sugar." He could see out now. They were in a large bay. All around them other ships were tied up to piers or moving in and out of a narrow inlet; huge warehouses lined the waterfront, row on row. In the distance Lonnie could see other large buildings, some maybe four stories tall. On the pier directly beneath the ship, he saw Japanese workers dressed in quilted uniforms loading trucks with heavy sacks, probably sugar. Occasionally one of them would look up toward the prisoners who now crowded the railing of the ship. They were squat, square men, with sallow faces and black eyes, impassive expressions. They didn't pause for long.

The line of prisoners moved down the deck slower than hell, like always. Ahead Lonnie saw a ventilator, one that looked like the horn on an old Victrola, with a bunch of guys clustered in front of it. He inched forward, feeling the biting cold even through his new clothing, until he was finally in front of the ventilator with the air pulsing around him. Hot, fetid air from the bowels of the ship. It was like standing in the breath of a hot fart. Lonnie grinned. Old R. T. Barton would have appreciated that one. The son-of-a-bitch, the poor bastard wearing out his tongue on that bulkhead. Lonnie suddenly stopped, stricken. Jesus Christ, all of them were gone, Ross, Gentry, Father Maloney, Corso, and R. T. Barton. All of them gone but him. He felt sadder than hell for a moment, and lonely, and looked at the men standing in line close to him. Not a familiar face in the bunch. Jesus Christ, why him? Why Orlando Ray, still living, and all the rest of them deader than door nails, down there floating around in the water. Maybe he was being saved for something big. Something really important that God wanted done, like Father Maloney might say.

He lost his place in front of the ventilator as the line moved along and the cold came again, fresh and clean like ice water, like the water poor old Ross was floating in.

He saw another ventilator ahead, just like the first one and soon could pick up the odor from it, but it was different. Suddenly as he walked along, the warmth enveloped him like a sweet breath, and he knew what it was, the smell of brown sugar and then by God he knew what it had reminded him of

[294]

all along, OVALTINE. "That goddamn Eula Gaye!" She was something, really something!

It was his turn now at the gangplank and that same American Major, the one with the bright gold oak leaves was standing there writing in a funny-looking green book. The Major was looking at him, pencil poised.

"What's your name, goddammit? You're holding up the line!"

"Orlando Ray Wilson," Lonnie shouted at the top of his voice. "And I made it goddammit, and you know what I'm going to do as soon as I get home? I'm going to screw Eula Gaye Quigly, that's what I'm going to do!"

"You couldn't screw a limp soda cracker," the Major said mildly, smiling a little. "Get your ass down the gangplank, you're holding up the line."

"Fuck you," said Lonnie.

He started moving down, still thinking about Eula Gaye. He reached into his LIFE WOMAN sack, took out a lump of brown sugar and started sucking on it. When he stepped off the gangplank onto the cement dock he glanced back at the ship, for just a moment. Then he turned and moved in the direction of a group of prisoners already lining up. As he walked toward the formation he stood straight, his shoulders back; he was proud of his uniform and his shoes.